PENGUIN BOOKS

BOOTS BENEATH HER BED

Taylor Esposito is a romance novelist from deep in the heart of Texas. She was born and raised in San Antonio but has lived in Austin for the past twelve years. She enjoys writing love stories with delicious angst, sizzling tension and tall, handsome, taciturn men. When she's not writing, she can be found walking her chocolate Lab, Ruby, cooking or drinking dirty martinis with her friends.

BOOTS
BENEATH HER BED

Taylor Esposito

PENGUIN BOOKS

PENGUIN BOOKS

UK | USA | Canada | Ireland | Australia
India | New Zealand | South Africa

Penguin Books is part of the Penguin Random House group of companies
whose addresses can be found at global.penguinrandomhouse.com

Penguin Random House UK,
One Embassy Gardens, 8 Viaduct Gardens, London SW11 7BW

penguin.co.uk

First published in the United States of America by Berkley,
an imprint of Penguin Random House LLC 2026
First published in Great Britain by Penguin Books 2026
001

Copyright © Taylor Esposito, 2026

The moral right of the author has been asserted

Penguin Random House values and supports copyright.
Copyright fuels creativity, encourages diverse voices, promotes freedom
of expression and supports a vibrant culture. Thank you for purchasing
an authorized edition of this book and for respecting intellectual property
laws by not reproducing, scanning or distributing any part of it by any
means without permission. You are supporting authors and enabling
Penguin Random House to continue to publish books for everyone.
No part of this book may be used or reproduced in any manner for the
purpose of training artificial intelligence technologies or systems. In accordance
with Article 4(3) of the DSM Directive 2019/790, Penguin Random House
expressly reserves this work from the text and data mining exception

Book design by Kathleen Soriano-Taylor
Printed and bound in Great Britain by Clays Ltd, Elcograf S.p.A.

The authorized representative in the EEA is Penguin Random House Ireland,
Morrison Chambers, 32 Nassau Street, Dublin D02 YH68

A CIP catalogue record for this book is available from the British Library

ISBN: 978–1–405–99088–2

Penguin Random House is committed to a sustainable future
for our business, our readers and our planet. This book is made from
Forest Stewardship Council® certified paper.

To my mom—my first reader, my first phone call, my first (and always biggest) fan

CHAPTER 1

There's been a knife tucked underneath Grace Underwood's pillow since she was sixteen years old. The bone handle is the first thing she reaches for when her internal alarm clock goes off at 3:45 A.M., signaling the start of another day. With the lightest touch, she traces the familiar rivets, the guard, the heel, and the blood groove the same way she does every morning. Each ridge and scratch and stain on its surface is imprinted permanently in her brain, so she doesn't need to lift the pillow to look at it. The cool, unsheathed steel against the warmth of her fingertips is enough.

Mechanically, her body starts to move. It knows exactly what to do and where to go, even in the pitch dark. This early in the morning, the sky is still black and full of stars. There's no respite from the darkness save for the dim, milky light of the moon.

On go the well-worn denim jeans. The dusty, ancient Red Wings are tugged onto sore, calloused feet with a grunt, and shoulder-length chestnut hair is thrown into a messy ponytail. A dollop of grocery store sunscreen from the communal bottle is rubbed onto her sun-kissed, freckled face, then her neck, and behind her ears. Grace brushes her teeth at the ancient sink and rinses her mouth with water directly from the faucet. One look at herself in the mirror reveals puffy, dehydrated cheeks and lips, and a muddiness in her dark brown eyes from endless nights of fitful sleep. On her way out the door, she grabs her Longhorns hat from its place on the rack—it was burnt orange at some point in the past but has faded into more of a school bus yellow—and yanks her ponytail through the hole. She's ready.

The mares are easy to make out even in the dark. A few are grouped up near the hay bales, heads bowed like they're swapping juicy gossip. Off on her own, staring out into the blue-black sky is Vesta the palomino, who, when she spots Grace approaching the paddock, ambles over, whickering her morning greeting. Grace smiles, hoisting herself up until her bottom is resting against the top rung of the enclosure. "Someone's in a good mood this morning."

For a few precious minutes, they stay in that spot together, Grace relishing the silence and solace of the ranch before the day truly begins, and Vesta still and steady at her side. A majestic, golden sentry.

Leaning down, Grace presses her forehead to Vesta's muzzle and sighs. "Is today gonna be a good day? What do you think?"

Vesta lets out a comforting, almost resigned little nicker in response. A sound that tells a truth of which they are both intimately aware: Good days are few and far between at Braxton Ranch.

"Yeah, I know," Grace replies, stroking Vesta's muzzle with the tip of her nose. "Maybe we can get out to the trail this afternoon." She knows in her heart that it's wishful thinking at best. She'll be lucky if she sees Vesta again at all today, or any of the horses for that matter. Grace's currently being punished by way of keeping her from the stables; she's been exiled to the fields because she was five minutes late to the barn last week and then went on to fail at saddle-breaking a stubborn colt.

Strikes one and two, her uncle, Bellamy Whitlock, had growled.

She's talking to Vesta still, recounting the way she nearly slipped and fell into a pile of manure the day before, when the telltale cadence of boots scraping heavily against dirt sounds behind her. A pit instantly forms in her stomach, and with a quick glance over her shoulder, Grace confirms her suspicion that it's Bellamy, now standing still as a statue across the pasture, glaring at her. She looks away, taking a deep breath through her nostrils, trying to mentally prepare for whatever bullshit he's planning to spew today.

When his gravelly voice cuts through the peacefulness of the morning, it's as grating as nails dragging along a chalkboard, and as fury inducing as a blaring alarm clock right in her ear. "You forget about breakfast?" he asks loudly.

Without even looking back at him, she can picture him vividly—that terrible posture causing him to hunch over a tin cup of steaming coffee, what's left of his scraggly brown hair hanging limply under his black felt Stetson. The sound of phlegm rattling along a tobacco-coated throat echoes through the air—and then with an aggressive hawk that sounds almost painful, a loogie hits the dirt with a wet, hard *whump*.

When he's apparently cleared his sinuses enough to speak, he continues. "You got more important things to do than kiss on that horse. Get to the kitchen."

Hopping down from the rung, Grace mutters under her breath. "I wasn't kissing her."

"You sure as hell wasn't workin', neither," Bellamy argues.

He has an irritatingly sharp ear, one of the only well-functioning components of his decaying form. He slips a cigarette between his lips and lifts his chin in her direction as she walks around the enclosure to where he stands. "Tell me something, Gracie."

Grace looks anywhere but his eyes as she comes to a stop, folding her arms over her chest. "What's that?" she asks flatly.

Slowly, Bellamy plods over to her, the slight limp in his gait making him look much older than his sixty years. How someone so unappealing to look at shared blood with her mother, Grace will never understand.

Another rattle of spit and grime in his throat precedes his next words, loud and thick enough to turn her stomach. "Why should I keep payin' you when all the other hands start earlier and work harder than you do? You think 'cause you're my kin that I won't throw you out into the woods?"

This gets Grace's attention. She glances up, anger rising to the occasion before any other emotion. Every bone in her body wants to argue with him, to punch him in his two front teeth for considering what he gives her to be *payment*. He houses her, feeds her, and lets her work with the horses when she's not fixing every bolt and pulling every weed and cleaning piles of shit across every acre of Braxton. To him, that's payment enough for keeping her around. For *letting* her stay. She opens her mouth to speak, the ire bubbling up in her throat, when he smiles, and the gleam of a silver molar sparkles in the moonlight.

He tuts, "Ah, ah, ah," and shakes his head. "Don't start with all of those empty threats now. You remember what happened the last time you tried to quit, don't you?"

Grace's nostrils flare, the blood beneath her skin starting to boil. Like a rushing flood, she remembers a series of doors slammed in her face at every business in town, calls from pay phones left unanswered and unreturned, service refused at diners she'd frequented for more than a decade. She remembers the hunger, the restlessness, the feeling of being watched. She remembers the startling clarity of how far Bellamy's reach stretched, how strong the choke hold was that he held on the towns surrounding the ranch. Like some sort of redneck gang, he and his lackeys posed too big of a threat for anyone to risk harboring her. When her meager savings had run out and even a last-ditch effort at hitchhiking failed, she remembers crawling back to Braxton with her tail between her legs. Defeated. Broken. Utterly trapped.

"If I'm such a shit employee, why keep me around?" she asks, impatience and irritation making her bold. "Why continue to put up with me, day after day, year after year?"

Bellamy chuckles, and it's a low, unsettling sound. "You know the answer to that question," he replies, then takes a long drag from his cigarette. "That debt of yours hasn't been repaid. And every time you screw up and cost me a sale, every time you give me lip, every time you think you're hot shit enough to make it on the outside, your interest rate goes up." He's closer now, the toes of his overly shiny ostrich boots creeping into her field of vision.

"Get on now," he barks. "Get to the kitchen. And don't burn my goddamn bacon like you did yesterday."

Grace stands still for a moment, edging on too long. Bellamy's eyes sparkle with malice, practically daring her to argue.

But after nine years of this, she knows better. She swallows a retort along with her pride, and it's like vinegar sliding painfully down her throat. With that, she nods and walks past him without another word.

As instructed, Grace makes her way to the east end of the ranch, where a haphazardly renovated barn now acts as the chow hall and their pseudo visitors center—not that they get many visitors; Grace chalks it up to Bellamy's poor salesmanship and their less-than-stellar Yelp rating. It's been four years since she made her way into the kitchen one dark, cold morning before the rest of the hands, and Maryann, the ranch cook, nurse, and begrudging cleaning lady, beckoned her in, demanding she cut cold butter into flour for biscuits. Her usual help, a seedy, wandering-eyed guy named Jeff, had called out sick with the flu. Grace had stepped in to help without complaint, and found the task to be rather soothing, especially when it later resulted in soft, pillowy biscuits she'd slathered in sausage gravy. It became an unspoken agreement between her and Maryann after that. Jeff eventually left Braxton for good, and ever since, Grace has helped with the little tasks while Maryann handles the larger, more complicated ones, and together, they put out semi-decent meals three times a day.

She finds Maryann wiping sweat from her brow with a kitchen towel, standing over a cast-iron skillet where two pork chops sit, bubbling in a shallow pool of oil. Her silver hair flows in a long braid down her back, kept out of her face by a red bandana secured at her hairline. Somewhat of a collector of odds and ends when it comes to clothing, she looks like the human embodiment of a patchwork quilt. A wildly different bright, clashing pattern for her shirt, skirt, and socks.

"Mornin'," Grace says as she walks directly over to the aprons hanging near the deep freezer.

Maryann uses the hand not holding a pair of metal tongs to wave in her direction without turning around. "Pork chops and eggs," she shouts, starting the process of carefully flipping the chops in the pan. "All scrambled. I don't have it in me this mornin' to take custom orders."

Grace nods, happy for the simplicity. "You got it."

When the food is done, Maryann starts pulling the serving platters down from the high shelves that line the kitchen walls, and Grace refills the sugar canisters and the powdered creamers for coffee.

"What's the verdict today?" Maryann asks as she spoons ladles full of bouncy, pale yellow eggs onto a platter. "Think you'll get back to King Breezy?"

Grace bites the inside of her cheek, watching a small mountain of sugar make its way to the top of the glass canister. She thinks about the stubborn colt who'd given her a run for her money earlier in the week, further soiling her name with her uncle. She doesn't hate King Breezy for not cooperating—he's smart and mean like his daddy, and she can't fault him for that—but he certainly isn't her favorite horse of the bunch right now. "Probably not. Too much other stuff to do."

"Gonna be hard to break a horse you don't spend any time with." Maryann sighs. "Seems like a waste of all Hal's teachings for that man to have you shovelin' shit and toilin' away in the fields." She rarely refers to Bellamy by his name—he's always some variation of *that man*, *that fool*, or *that rotten old bastard*.

Unlike Hal Hendricks, Braxton's late horse trainer who took Grace under his wing when she was still a teenager. Maryann lovingly, frequently, and correctly recalls his name.

"Preachin' to the choir," Grace says.

Maryann clicks her teeth. "You're young and spry, and far too smart to be at his beck and call. Hal would hate to see you still kickin' around this place, wastin' that talent."

"He'd hate to see you still here, too," Grace volleys back. Maryann has no retort for this except a slight quirk of her brow. With a rueful smile, Grace starts to take the full platters and sets them on the plastic folding table they use as a makeshift buffet. "It's a job," she says over her shoulder, "and Bellamy's my family."

Maryann barks a laugh. "Oh, honey. That sounds less true every time you say it."

Grace says nothing, and Maryann doesn't poke her any further, knowing from experience that it's a futile effort. She shuts the kitchen window that looks out into the dining room and gives Grace a nod that signals her to ring the mealtime bell. As that familiar chime echoes through this place she calls home, Grace wonders when blood ties and a shoddy roof over her head will no longer be enough.

At the table, Grace and the other hands all shovel bites of eggs and pork chops and jelly-slathered toast into their mouths as though they haven't eaten in days. They drink orange juice and coffee out of foam cups, and they talk shit. All the hands ever, *ever* do is talk shit.

Grace is minding her own business like she always does, chewing the meat off a pork chop for so long her jaw has started to ache, when Trey, a seasoned hand who loves to rag on her, leans forward from his place a few seats down. He pins her with an amused look that sets Grace immediately on the defensive. "What?" she barks through a half-full mouth.

Trey shakes his head. "She wasn't listenin'. She never is."

"'Course she wasn't," says Pritchet, the oldest of the group. He points his fork in her direction, pursing his lips. "She don't like to get down in the mud with us pigs."

Grace grumbles, looking back down at her plate. "Y'all are never talking about anything interesting anyway. Why should I try to keep up with your conversation?"

Trey huffs out a humorless laugh. "Well, sunflower," he begins, and out of the corner of her eye, she can see a maniacal grin spread slowly onto his face. "I think what we were discussing is *quite* interesting. You see, we were talkin' about girls and bulls. You ever ridden a bull, Gracie?"

Without looking up, Grace shakes her head. She tosses the gnawed bone from her pork chop down amid the scraps of toast on her plate. "Can't say I have."

Trey hums, and his fingertips begin to drum a quick beat on the table. "But you know what they say, right? About girls and bulls?"

"No," Grace replies, picking up her chin to face him and whatever disgusting remark he's going to make head-on. Eyes forward. "What do they say, Trey?"

Snickers and snorts sound across the table. Forrest, the resident crybaby, smirks and eggs Trey on with an elbow to his side.

Trey's voice is low and menacing. "If a girl can ride a bull," he says, sweeping his hand in her direction, "she can ride a cock."

A cacophony of whooping and hooting erupts, and Grace watches all their faces as they laugh and nod and chime in with their own chauvinistic remarks. She tilts her head and stares at Trey with all the disgust in the world as she bites back, "I've seen the kind of equipment you're working with, Trey." Her eyebrow kinks as her eyes travel down his form. "Comparing that pinkie dick of yours to a bull may be the most delusional thing I've ever heard."

The jeers and snorts and hums of laughter all end abruptly, like a radio switch being flipped off. The silence that cuts through the dining room in place of the racket is somehow even louder. A dark look blooms over Trey's face as he stares at Grace, and she maintains eye contact with him, watching as his azure irises turn to ice. She tries to dig into them, to unearth something resembling humanity, but no matter how hard she looks, she finds absolutely nothing behind that cold, unforgiving blue. It's written all over his features—she's crossed a line.

The rest of the hands eventually return to their general unsavory conversation, but Trey's glare doesn't falter. As soon as her plate is clean, she rises and walks toward the giant plastic trash can near the front door.

"Bye, Gracie," he calls in a chilling, singsongy voice. "We'll see you later."

Grace doesn't turn around. She clenches her fists, takes a deep breath, and walks out. The sound of their raucous laughter follows her all the way back to the bunkhouse.

The rest of the day looks just like any other. Grace manages to unload a trailer full of hay, feed the slew of exotic animals Bellamy likes to collect and neglect, and mend a large gap in the southeast fence before any cattle can wander off. With how boiling hot it is, it's nothing short of a miracle that she's able to do it all before dinner, and by the time she lies down in her bunk that evening after an ice-cold shower, her eyelids are drooping.

Hours later, when her eyes shoot open, it isn't the internal alarm that wakes her. It's Bellamy, shaking her shoulder so hard she nearly bites her tongue. She sees his eyes first—wide and wild, blazing with a kind of anger she's seen only a few times during her tenure at Braxton. When he speaks, his voice is low, unlike his usual barking croaks. "Don't say a goddamn word," he seethes. "Get out of bed, put on some clothes, and meet me at the southeast fence."

It takes almost twenty minutes, but she makes it to where Bellamy's posted up with a giant flashlight pointing down to the dry brush beneath his boots. Once she's made her way over to him, he lifts the flashlight and points it toward the fence she mended this afternoon. Or, at least, she thought she mended it. But the gap, the one she closed through sweat and painful pricks of barbed wire into her thumbs, is still there. And it's three times wider than it was before.

What's worse—beyond it, probably half a mile outside, is Brick, the longhorn that set Bellamy back a hefty sum of money at auction last year, and indubitably his most prized possession across the entirety of the ranch.

Now completely off his property, roaming free.

"You wanna explain to me why in the ever-loving *fuck* my longhorn is outside the property line right now, Grace? Or why there's still a gap as wide as my truck in this fence when you were supposed to fix it this afternoon?" His voice is still chillingly soft, the timbre deep and unsettling.

Grace's eyes dart from Brick to Bellamy and back again, then to the fence, where the barbed wire she'd strung together so carefully now lies useless on the ground. "I did fix it. I swear, I did. I made sure—"

"If he'd gotten any farther than that," Bellamy seethes, cutting her off and pointing in the direction of the animal, "I'd put my pistol in your mouth right now."

Too stubborn and stupid to look away, Grace raises her chin. "You know I don't make mistakes like this. It's Trey. I pissed him off at breakfast, and he's trying to sabotage—"

"I don't wanna hear it. Bring him in," he says, nodding toward Brick. "And fix this goddamn fence. Don't come back until you do."

Grace's eyes scan the immediate area. Not a pair of pliers or gloves in sight. "I need tools. It's barbed wire."

Bellamy shrugs. "Shoulda thought about that when you were half-assin' it the first time." He drops the flashlight onto the ground and turns away from her, and without another word, pulls himself up into the truck and drives off.

It takes three and a half hours, and by the time Grace is done, her palms are so tarnished from the barbed wire that her handprints will be forever altered. A trail of bloody droplets follows her all the way back to the main house, where Bellamy sits on his front porch in a rocking chair with a cup of coffee.

"It's done," she rasps, sliding down a wooden post, unsteady from the lightheadedness. Her eyes screw shut, and she begins to lift her hands above her head. "I need—I need stitches."

"Go see Maryann," he orders. "Now. You're bleedin' all over my porch."

Slowly, with a substantial amount of effort and blinding pain, Grace stands. She trudges across the porch, wincing at the soreness in her muscles and the sharp throbbing in her hands.

"One more thing," Bellamy calls out.

Grace turns her body halfway, her neck craning to look at him. There's something else now in his hand besides the newspaper—something she doesn't make out right away. But as she takes a couple of steps closer, her stomach drops.

Because hanging limply in his hand is Vesta's bridle.

The breath in Grace's lungs rushes out of her all at once, and she has to reach out to the siding of the house to keep herself upright. A dozen questions collide in her head, all half-formed and indecipherable. She can barely think in full sentences, but she manages a croaked "You— Did you— If you hurt her—" as tears begin welling in her eyes.

Bellamy scoffs, tossing the bridle in her direction before turning back to the newspaper. "Pritchet took her into town while you were gone. Got twenty-five hundred for her. Idiot overpaid, you ask me."

The words hit Grace's ears, cavalier and final, and her knees wobble, threatening to give out from under her. The world tilts on its axis in an excruciating, permanent way.

Her horse. Her Vesta. Her beautiful girl with those sparkling, ageless eyes and that heart of pure gold. The best friend she's ever had, sold to the first person willing to take her off Pritchet's hands. Tears begin to fall down Grace's cheeks as her thoughts snowball, wondering in a flurry of panic if Vesta will be happy wherever she is, cared for and loved the way she deserves. It's *that*—the vision of Vesta being bred over and over again without proper care, being fed the cheapest and worst quality of hay, never being brushed or petted or kissed, that sends Grace over an edge she's been toeing for the past nine years of her life.

She swallows down a sob and looks at Bellamy through puffy, bloodshot eyes. Her nostrils flare as the words leave her lips. "You fucking bastard."

The motion of his rocking in the chair stills. His eyes drift upward, away from the newspaper, before he slowly turns his head to look at her. He blinks, then asks, "Come again?"

"You heard me," Grace growls, stomping toward him, ignoring all the pain that vibrates through her body, fighting the unsteadiness. "You're a fucking bastard. You're cruel, and stupid, and disgusting, and evil. I'm ashamed to share any blood with you. Almost ten years of my goddamn life, I've been your obedient dog, and you've never shown me even a fragment of kindness." She's still crying, but the tears are no longer made of sadness. They're angry. Vengeful. She closes in on Bellamy, who leans back in his chair, alarmed. Her voice is lower and quieter as she says, "Hell was invented for people like you. So, when you finally do the world a favor and fucking die, we can all rest easy knowing you're rotting down there. Forever."

Bellamy's lip curls. "You ungrateful bitch—"

Grace grabs the arms of the rocking chair with her bloodied hands, ignoring the searing pain, and shoves. As hard as she can. The chair wobbles for a split second before crashing to the ground, sending Bellamy tumbling.

He's grunting and cursing under his breath, struggling to stand and spewing threats at her as he does, but Grace isn't listening. She stands over him, watching as he tries and fails to lift himself up, and for the first time in a long, long time, she is not afraid of him, or afraid of what he might do.

"I'm leaving. I hope this place burns to the ground. I wish to God that I could be the one to light the match."

Bellamy looks up at her, and his face devolves from panic, pain, and embarrassment into something far more chilling. A sinister, knowing smile spreads onto his lips, slowly, deliberately. He laughs then—a wheezing, terrible sound. Gooseflesh breaks out over Grace's bloody skin, but she ignores that blaring alarm in her gut and turns on her heel to walk away. She won't let him scare her into submission ever again.

His raspy voice hits her ears when she's nearly off the porch. "You think there's anywhere you can go that I won't find you?"

Grace pauses, gritting her teeth. The threats are always severe. This is nothing new, and she knows from experience that there may be nothing out there for her. She knows Bellamy can—will—blacklist her name throughout the entire state of Texas if she leaves. But that fear of the outside—of slammed doors and hunger pains and concrete benches doubling as beds—isn't scarier than the hard, inescapable truth that waits for her if she relents. Because if she stays, she'll die here. Whether by his hand or her own.

"I'll always find you, Grace," Bellamy promises loudly. "You can bet on that." He laughs again, throaty and thick. "I'll find you, and then I'll tell the whole world what you did."

Even with every fiber in her body telling her to stop, to turn around and apologize lest he make good on his promise, Grace doesn't give in.

She keeps walking.

CHAPTER 2

Three Months Later

The bell above the door of Murphy's General Store dings as Shaky Rick Gentry plods in. Standing behind the counter with a lukewarm cup of coffee and a years-old issue of *People* magazine, Grace doesn't even have to look up to know it's Shaky. The shuffling of his shoes against the tile floor and the alcohol-soaked air that permanently clings to him is enough for her to know it's almost five in the afternoon, and he's here for his daily re-up of malt liquor. Grace goes back to idly flipping pages full of celebrity horoscopes and trendy summer shoes.

The bell dings again a few seconds later, and this time, Grace looks up to see a woman on her cell phone, walking quickly toward the back of the store. It's hard to say who it is, but by the neat, slim-fitting clothes and the shiny brown hair, she doesn't appear to be a local. No one in Minetta dresses like that. In fact, no one who lives within ten miles of Treesaw County dresses like that. Maybe she's from McBrayer or passing through from

Austin or San Antonio. She'll forget about this place as soon as she crosses over the train tracks on Main Street.

Grace takes a long pull of her coffee, now verging on cold, and turns back to her magazine. She's in the middle of looking at a picture of Ben Affleck hauling a trash bag into a dumpster when she hears the telltale shuffle of Shaky's shoes.

"Hey, Grace," he says in a soft voice. In his hands are two bottles of Olde English 800 that he slowly sets atop the counter.

Grace smiles as she rings him up. "How you doin', Shaky?"

"Still breathin', somehow." He shrugs as he digs into the pockets of his ill-fitting jeans. "Keep tryin' to die, but God don't agree with that plan, I guess." He pulls out a couple of crumpled dollar bills and some linty nickels and dimes but then seems to reach the bottom of the well.

The little monitor above the register shows the total is $10.06, about seven dollars more than Shaky has to offer. Their eyes meet, and Grace's heart squeezes. "Murphy said if the till is short again, he's gonna start docking my pay and put in cameras. I wish I could help you, I really do—"

"Please, Grace," Shaky pleads, gripping the counter with his bony fingers. "I can't . . . I can't sleep. I just want to sleep, but my head, my body, it . . ." He seems to be barely holding himself upright, like the counter is the only thing anchoring him.

Grace sighs, looking out into the store, then back to him, to the way his brows have pulled together and his eyes have started to shine with tears. "If it were up to me, you know I'd give 'em to you, no questions asked. But I need this job."

Shaky's head falls forward, and she hears him sniffle. It breaks her heart; if she had the extra cash to float him, or if she could count on Murphy not counting the till down to the last penny, she'd make it happen. But as it is, they're both coming up short.

A crisp, brand-new fifty-dollar bill slides into Grace's view, pushed by delicate fingers bearing silver and turquoise rings. The shiny red polish atop the long, perfectly manicured nails gleams under the overhead lighting. The scent of beer and stale sweat wafting off of Shaky swirls with an unfamiliar, luxurious blend of deep vanilla, crisp tobacco, and mint. Grace glances up and is met with a pair of brown eyes and a smile that crinkles them at the corners. "Allow me," the woman says, nudging her head in Shaky's direction.

Shaky turns to her in disbelief. "That's awful kind of you, ma'am. Are you sure?"

The woman nods and places a manicured hand on Shaky's shoulder. "It wasn't too long ago that I was desperate for a good night's sleep, too." There's something behind the look in her eyes—a knowing, an understanding shared between the two of them in mere seconds. "I hope you find it. And if you can't, there's a place in McBrayer that can help. For free. All you'll need is the bus fare to get there."

"Thank you," Shaky says, nodding. "Thank you very much."

Grace, watching the entire interaction in a sort of awe, only spurs into movement when the woman looks back to her, her eyes drifting to the bottles on the counter.

"Sorry," Grace blurts out, then reaches quickly for the brown bags beneath the register. She hands the bottles to Shaky once they're wrapped up, and he leaves her alone with the glamorous, mysterious benefactor.

Now that she has a moment to actually assess, she sees two

large bottles of water tucked under one of the woman's arms, and a bag of sunflower seeds bigger than Grace's head in the other. The woman has an enigmatic, all-knowing kind of smirk on her lips as she sets the items on the counter. "Grace, right?"

Grace nods as she starts to ring everything up. "Yes, ma'am."

"I'll take a pack of Virginia Slims and a Lucky 7s scratch-off, too, if you wouldn't mind."

"Of course." Spinning around, Grace grabs the pack of cigarettes and then pulls on the spool of Lucky 7s and rips off a ticket. It seems odd—considering the obvious wealth this woman has—for her to be buying cheap scratch-offs, but Grace doesn't comment on it. She sets the ticket on the counter, then rings up the cigarettes and hands those over, too.

"Those look like they were painful," the woman says, and Grace looks up to see her staring at Grace's upturned palm where the pack of cigarettes sits. Beneath the cellophane-wrapped box is the collection of scars she tries—and fails, evidently—not to put on display.

"Yes, ma'am" is all Grace says, before promptly going back to her task of bagging up the water bottles and sunflower seeds.

A beat of quiet passes while she takes the fifty-dollar bill and counts the change, but as she reaches to hand over the coins and cash, she notices the woman is staring right at her. She reaches for the change, softly gripping Grace's hand as she does. With a little smile folded into ruby-red lips, she asks, "You used to be a horse trainer over at Braxton Ranch. Is that right?"

Something akin to panic starts to bubble up in Grace's stomach. Heat blooms on her cheeks under the woman's attention. For a moment, she's sure she misheard her. Swallowing a lump in her throat, Grace asks, "Beg your pardon?"

"I have an old friend. We used to be very close—attached at the hip, really—but we don't get to see each other much anymore. Anyway, I talked to her recently, and she told me all about this real talented horse trainer who was scraping by working at a general store in Minetta. Said she was only working there because she'd walked away from Braxton Ranch and couldn't land another ranching job."

"Your—your *friend*," Grace stammers, knuckles going white as she grips the counter.

The woman nods. "Dear friend. Maryann Hartford."

Grace blinks, not fully processing the information. "Maryann?"

Another quick nod. The woman looks at the nails of her left hand, first by curling them inward, then stretching her palm and spreading her fingers out. The diamond bedecking her ring finger is so large and sparkling that it creates fragmented, dancing light patterns over the walls. "I told Maryann I'd just lost one of my trainers—idiot decided to move to Montana because he was *finally fed up with the heat*." She uses air quotes with her fingers as she says it, rolling her eyes. "And Maryann told me she knew of just the person who could fill the spot."

The words start to intertwine in Grace's brain like a tangle of barbed wire. She can't imagine how she must look right now, and trying to make sense of it only confuses her more, so finally she blurts out the question she should've asked right out of the gate. "Forgive me, ma'am," Grace says breathily, holding out her hands. "But would you mind telling me who you are?"

The woman lets out a soft chuckle. How a chuckle can sound elegant, Grace isn't sure, but the woman manages it. "I was wondering when you'd ask." She sticks out a hand in Grace's direction. "I'm Renata Caldwell. I own Halcyon Ranch."

That night, in the parking lot of the studio apartment she lives in on the edge of town, Grace calls Maryann from a prepaid cell phone. "C'mon, c'mon," Grace mutters as she paces back and forth, cursing the woman for only having a landline.

Maryann picks up on the fifth ring, simply shouting, *"What?"*

The familiar annoyance in her tone sends a pang of homesickness shooting through Grace's gut. With a little smile, she says, "It's Grace."

"Oh," Maryann sighs. "Hi, honey. Been a while."

They exchange quick pleasantries before Grace reveals the true reason for the phone call. "I met Renata Caldwell today."

"Well, that woman works quickly, I'll tell you what. Didn't waste a single second findin' you in that Podunk town. She offer you that job?"

Grace chuckles in disbelief. "She offered me a *shot* at the job, but only because you talked me up more than you should've, I'm sure. What'd you even say to her?"

"I told her the truth! You're the finest horse trainer in the state, and she just so happens to have a job opening for a horse trainer. Don't question my judgment."

Grace looks up at the sky, rubbing her thumb and index fingers across her brow. "I wasn't planning on going back to training. Or ranching, for that matter." A beat of silence hangs between them, and Grace wonders for a second if Maryann's hung up. The only indication that she hasn't is the sudden click of her teeth. Grace frowns. "Maryann?"

"Oh, I'm sorry," the older woman says, "I was just sittin' here wondering if you're stupid or just plain dumb."

Grace's mouth falls open in indignation. "That's—"

"Listen to me. You spent almost a decade of your life in this hellhole until you mustered up the courage to walk away, and I'm so proud of you for that, Grace." Unexpected tears start welling in Grace's eyes at her words—she fights them off by gritting her teeth and exhaling deeply through her nostrils. "But if you stay away, if you leave behind the thing you love the most because you're scared, or hurting, or *stubborn*, well . . ."

The neon sign above her head detailing the name of the rundown complex blinks in an uneven flicker, a death rattle of light. Grace's voice is shaky as she asks, "Well, what?"

"You'd be lettin' that rotten bastard win. Is that really something you want to do?"

Grace sighs, crouching down onto a curb and setting her forehead between her knees. She doesn't respond right away, but she doesn't have to. They both know the answer to that question, even if only one of them is brave enough to say it out loud.

Restless, Grace lies in bed, trying and failing to balance the tip of her knife on her index finger. She catches it each time it topples over, letting out long, dramatic trills through her lips whenever her eyes dance over to the upturned milk crate she's using as a nightstand. Renata's card sits on top of a couple of dusty books, staring at her. Grace sets the knife down atop her stomach and reaches for the card, impressed by the weight of it. It feels and looks expensive—the looping letters of Renata's name are perfectly placed and embossed. Her phone number is bordered in gold.

The sound of a drip near the tiny bathroom interrupts her

examination, and Grace's eyes flit upward. The ceiling is patched with water stains; it wouldn't be surprising for chunks of drywall to start tumbling down at any moment. Above her, moldy ceiling, and below her, a ratty carpet, in the kind of condition that screams it's seen things she can't even begin to imagine. And to top it off, her absolute favorite part of living here is sharing an extremely thin wall with Hutch Lawson, the circumstances of which seem to get worse with every passing night. The man's hand must be as soft as a baby's bottom at this point. Grace looks at her watch and sighs, knowing he's probably settling down with his brick of a laptop and bottle of Vaseline right about now.

Like clockwork, she hears the telltale sound of a belt and jeans being unbuckled. Tossing the card onto the milk crate and grabbing a pillow from the other side of the bed, Grace covers her face and ears with it, pushing as hard as she can to drown out the inevitable wet slapping sound that is soon to follow.

It doesn't help. Hutch gets carried away, and when he does, he's unconscionably loud.

With an annoyed grunt, Grace slams the pillow back onto the bed and sits up. She doesn't think twice when she grabs the card and her cell phone and leaves the apartment, making sure to slam the door extra loudly behind her so Hutch knows he's disturbed her evening *again*.

There are two options here: stay or go. As she paces back and forth in the parking lot for the second time that night, she weighs them carefully. She looks up at the stars, wishing she knew anything about constellations and what wisdom they might hold.

But then, from behind the door of the neighboring duplex, she hears Hutch yodel in ecstasy, and her decision is made.

She fishes her phone out of her pocket, dials the number on the card, and Renata Caldwell answers on the second ring.

A fraying bright orange duffel bag with a sticky zipper is packed to the gills with all of Grace's belongings. She doesn't dwell on how sad it is that everything important in the world to her can fit in a ratty old gym bag—traveling light means it isn't hard for her to be ready to go in thirty-six hours. Three hard, booming knocks sound at her apartment door around 6 A.M., and she jolts slightly from her place at the edge of her unmade bed.

With the bag slung over her shoulder, she opens the door and finds a man who takes up most of the doorway with his imposing figure; if he weren't hunched over with his elbow leaning against the doorframe, he'd knock his black cattleman hat off his head just by walking through.

"Hey," Grace says softly, offering a hesitant half smile. "Good mornin'."

Renata had mentioned she'd be unable to fetch Grace from Minetta herself but she'd be sending the ranch's foreman, and "not to worry about" any sort of unfriendliness, because "grumpy is sort of his default setting."

His voice is raspy and thick with sleep when he says, simply, "Are you Grace Underwood?"

"Yeah," Grace says, and then follows quickly with: "Are you the foreman?"

The man lets out a little huff. "Among other things," he says. "Let's go." He jerks his chin in the direction of her bag, beckoning with his hand for her to give it to him. She does, and then watches him toss it into the bed of a pristine, gigantic F-350 as though it's stuffed with feathers.

Some trucks this size have the little step stool to assist the vertically challenged, but this one doesn't. Grace opens the passenger-side door and is sort of silently amping herself to jump up when a hulking figure appears at her side. He looks younger in the dark, less severe under the softness of dawn, and there's a slightly amused shine to his eyes that has her cheeks starting to pink. She looks down to find his hand held out for her, and the fact that it looks proportionate in size to this behemoth of a truck he drives around, well—

"I can do it," she argues, brow knitting together.

"I'm not gonna let you break your neck before we even get out of the parking lot," he counters, his hand stretching farther in her direction. "C'mon. Up you go."

She holds his stare, challenging him. When he doesn't relent, she sighs and grabs on, unwilling to admit to herself or him that it's much easier to climb while using him as leverage. He holds on until she's fully in, and when she looks back at him standing with his arm outstretched, their gazes lock for a brief moment. Grace nods her thanks to him with a small smile, one he returns not with his mouth but with his eyes. They're dark, much like the rest of him, but they're soft, somehow. Almost sparkling.

The truck smells clean and leathery, like it just rolled off the lot. The seat squeaks as she slides into it, and she's suddenly very aware of the permanent film of dirt that clings to her jeans no matter how many times she washes them. The burly chauffeur slides into the driver's seat without much effort, his long limbs lending to a swift, graceful movement. As he gets himself situated, Grace takes a moment to survey him. Before, she'd been so caught off guard by the sheer size of him—easily six foot three, maybe taller, and built like a damn linebacker—that she hadn't noticed much else. Now, she sees the black waves that stick out under his hat, the freckles and moles dotted across his cheeks and neck, and the way his jaw never seems to settle. It works and works, and she wonders whether it's a tic. Or—more plausibly—something he does when he's annoyed.

He starts the truck, then places a hand on the back of her headrest as he reverses out of the parking lot and onto the empty road that will lead them out of town. Filling up silence with empty conversation has never been a compulsion of hers, but something about this man—the stern look on his face contrasting with the ease of his hands as he drives the truck, the way his black button-down hangs on his body like it was created specifically for him—she can't help herself.

"So, you're the foreman," she repeats, then awkwardly clears her throat when he doesn't acknowledge her. "Renata didn't give me your name."

His lips twitch. A subtle movement she would've missed had she not been staring directly at him. Grace blinks, waiting for him to say something. *Anything*. He glances at her quickly, then looks back at the road and says, "Crew. Crew Caldwell."

Grace's mouth drops open. *Wait*. "Caldwell, like—"

"Like Renata Caldwell is my mother."

"Oh," Grace says, a bit dumbstruck. She'd considered going to the library to google the Caldwells and Halcyon Ranch the day before, but decided any research would only make her more nervous. She's regretting that decision with every bone in her body right now. "I didn't realize."

He looks at her again, more appraising this time. "Where're you coming from?"

Leaning back a bit farther into her seat, Grace clasps her hands together in her lap, gripping her fingers a little too hard. "Braxton Ranch, out near Hopeland."

Crew's brows pull together, and whatever semblance of a smile he'd worn moments ago starts to sour. "Braxton Ranch, as in Bellamy Whitlock's Braxton Ranch?"

Looking away, Grace looks out into the endless, open road ahead. "Did your mother not tell you how she found me?"

"I didn't ask," he admits. A beat of quiet, and then, "But I'm askin' now."

Grace's lips press into a line, and she starts to wring her hands together, tugging at the scarred skin on her palms. In a quieter voice, she says, "Bellamy's my uncle."

Silence hangs between them for a long moment. Grace wishes the radio was on—a droning AM station would be better than this tense, unrelenting silence. Eventually, he asks, "He do that to you?"

She looks up and notices him staring at her hands, which are unfortunately illuminated in the dim blue light of the truck cab. The keloid scars are thick, pink, and obvious to anyone with eyes. She immediately turns her hands over, pressing them into her jeans.

"Not directly," she says, digging her stubby nails into the denim.

"Well, it all makes sense now," Crew muses.

Grace prickles a little. "What makes sense?"

With a slight lift of his shoulder, he says, "You're not the first lost soul Renata Caldwell has tried to save. I've made this drive plenty of times."

"From Minetta?"

"Minetta, Swift, Bellhaven, Ingram—hell, I've gone as far as Waco before. All the places your kind like to wander."

Grace pins him with a look, but his eyes remain on the road. "My *kind*?"

"Y'know," he says, reaching over her to fiddle with the glove box. She pushes back into her seat, trying to maintain as much distance between them as possible as he pulls it open and grabs hold of a bag of sunflower seeds. He hauls the bag out and then holds the open end up to his mouth. With a handful of seeds muffling his voice, he says, "The runnin' kind."

It irks her, how he thinks he's pegged her so well—how she must be a dime a dozen in his eyes, and how this trial is starting to sound more like a charity project. A pity party for the mistreated cowgirl. She considers telling him to stick it where the sun doesn't shine, because she didn't *run* from Bellamy Whitlock. She walked away with bloody hands and her chin high. She fought tooth and nail to get far away from Hopeland, almost dying in the process. She rewrote her own history, erasing the Whitlock name from the narrative. Crew must sense some inkling of the tension vibrating under her skin, because before she can throw back her own snide assessment of *him*, he reaches across the center console and offers her the open bag. Grace looks at it, looks at him, then reaches in and grabs a handful of seeds.

At some point, he, too, must tire of the silence, because he flips on the radio and hits the scan button until he finds an old Waylon Jennings song he seems to be okay with. Grace watches him do this, and two things occur to her: One, he may be the only person on planet Earth who still listens to the radio, and two, he has the music taste of a sixty-year-old man. Every few minutes, he rolls the window down and spits out shells, only to quickly refill with another shake of the bag into his mouth. Grace follows suit, happy to have something to do besides stew in her own melancholy.

Around the four-hour mark, she has cottonmouth from the salty seeds and her legs are aching to stretch. She looks around and behind them, seeing nothing but vast, verdant hills and endless blue sky. Sitting back in her seat, she looks over to Crew. "How long till we get to the ranch?"

He smirks as he turns a seed over between his teeth. "You're already here."

CHAPTER 3

Through taciturn statements and grunted affirmatives, Grace learns Halcyon Ranch is just south of two hundred thousand acres. It's nearly a third of the size of Rhode Island. It has its own *zip code*.

"What was it like," Grace asks, her body angled almost entirely toward the passenger window, "growing up here?"

Crew doesn't answer right away, doesn't huff out a humorless laugh like he has in response to some of her other questions. Grace sneaks a glance at him over her shoulder, and he looks pensive. After another beat of silence, he seems to remember himself as he grumbles, "Lotta shit shovelin' and lawn mowin'."

Grace refrains from rolling her eyes. "Really?"

"Thought you'd worked on a ranch before," he says, side-eyeing her.

"This ranch, compared to Braxton . . ." Grace shakes her head. "I've never seen anything like this before."

He grunts and starts to tap his thumb against the steering wheel in rhythm with the George Strait song now playing on the radio. "You get used to it."

She gives him one last glance before turning back to the window, still in awe of the way the hills seem to go on forever. No, she thinks—she isn't sure she ever could.

Eventually, a structure on the horizon line comes into view. A log cabin at its heart, but in reality, it's something straight out of one of those fancy architecture magazines. Tall roofs, artful dormers, lined with cobblestone and dark, lush wood siding. All coming together to make a storybook mansion, the biggest and nicest house Grace has ever seen with her own eyes.

"Wow," she blurts out when they turn onto the quarter-mile-long driveway.

Gravel crunches under the truck's giant tires almost comically, as if it ever stood a chance against the steel-strong rubber.

"Don't get too excited," Crew says. He jerks his chin toward a different house in the distance, one decidedly less magnificent than the one ahead. "You get the job, that's where you'll be living."

It's a barn—whether it was actually ever used as one before is unclear—with stark-white shiplap, black eaves, and a giant *H* on the side. Crew doesn't—can't—understand how even this barn-turned-bunkhouse would possibly be the nicest place Grace has ever lived. She hasn't even seen the inside of it, but she knows it's far and away better than the bunkhouse at Braxton, which was basically a tiny sauna that stunk constantly of mildew and stale armpit. The digs here look spacious and new, built in this century. Probably even air-conditioned, and she'd be willing to bet the mattresses don't feel like they're stuffed with hay.

"Looks all right to me," Grace counters quietly.

A grid of large, well-maintained paddocks spans the area between the bunkhouse and the stables, and it's obvious already that Halcyon takes better care of its horses than Braxton could ever hope to. They probably grow their alfalfa from the finest soil and have an equine vet on retainer.

They pull up to the house and park next to two trucks identical to Crew's, all bearing the same flourishing *H* as the bunkhouse on their driver-side doors. It's strange to be thrust so quickly into a place where money is clearly not a concern, where everything in sight drips of wealth and prosperity. The awe of it must be all over Grace's face, because when Crew shuts off the truck and makes to get out, he does a double take after he looks at her. Leaning in to rest his arm on the center console, he says, "It's just a house."

Grace barks a laugh, peeling her eyes from the house to gape at him. "I wouldn't call it a house. It's a freaking ski lodge."

His lips twitch. "You ever been to a ski lodge?"

Her mouth snaps shut, and her eyes narrow. "No, but I've seen one on TV."

Crew nods toward the passenger door. "C'mon," he says, reaching for his hat where it lies on the back seat. He pops it on, then opens his own door and steps out. "Lunch'll be ready soon."

Somehow, the interior of the house is even more gorgeous than the exterior. It shouldn't surprise Grace—Renata Caldwell is a woman of impeccable taste, and though Grace knows next to nothing about interior design and styling, it's evident that great care and thoughtfulness has gone into every inch of the home. There's such refinement to it, an ease and sophistication that doesn't scream old money but whispers it elegantly, a comforting caress across your cheek instead of a slap. The cherrywood floors squeak with every step Grace takes through the foyer, which leads into a sitting room complete with dark brown leather couches covered in plush, soft-looking pillows.

Taking in the art on the walls, the shelves lined with hundreds of books and gilded trinkets, Grace notices a shelf dedicated to framed pictures, all varying in sizes and shapes. She takes a few steps closer to get a better look, seeing first that there are three large frames with three similar-looking portraits—school pictures. The one on the far left looks a lot like Crew, though he had yet to build the muscle that would eventually complement his too-tall frame. In the photo, he looks like he's all limbs, and the smirk on his mouth is far less serious than anything she's seen on the man she's encountered today. But it's the eyes that give him away, signaling that it's definitely him—as dark and discerning as they are now, and far deeper than any belonging to a teenager. Next to Crew's photo is one of a girl, and it's uncanny how much she looks like Renata. Though her teeth are covered in braces and there are stubborn sprinkles of acne on her cheeks, Grace knows immediately, in the same undeniable way she recognized Crew, that the girl is Renata's daughter and Crew's sister. And the last of the three—another boy, the youngest and most carefree of them all. He's smiling wide, showing off a gap where a canine baby tooth used to be, and his eyes are alight with joy and mischief. Grace smiles, wondering how long it must've taken him to sit still for the photograph.

Though it's not visible from where she stands, the kitchen can't be far off, because a delicious, savory smell hits Grace's nose and a pang of hunger throbs in her belly. She's been so caught up in the magic of the house that she hasn't noticed Crew leaning against the threshold, hands in his pockets. Watching her. A flare of self-consciousness sparks under his scrutiny, and Grace folds her arms over her chest as she says, "Nice place you've got here."

Crew lifts a shoulder—a gesture Grace is beginning to notice he is wont to do. "It's not mine. I live up the hill."

It's a different version of *I'm not rich; my parents are rich*—such a typical response from someone with generational wealth that she almost has to laugh.

"Right," Grace says, nodding. "I'm sure it's a real fixer-upper."

His eyes narrow slightly, and he appears to be gearing up for a retort when he's cut off by the click of heels against the wood floor.

Renata Caldwell bursts into the room seconds later, her entire face lighting up in a sparkling grin as soon as she sees Grace. "Grace, ah—honey, I'm so glad you made it," she exclaims melodically, walking directly into Grace's immediate space and wrapping her up in a hug that is surprisingly firm for such a petite woman. It lasts about five seconds longer than Grace expects it to, and when the woman finally pulls back, she's still grinning from ear to ear. "My son didn't give you any trouble, did he? He's a real curmudgeon, but we love him for it." She doesn't look at him when she asks this; Grace looks over his mother's shoulder to see Crew ruefully shaking his head.

"Not at all," Grace replies, returning Renata's smile with a small, reserved one of her own. "I appreciated the ride. I didn't think you'd bring me out so quickly."

Renata nods, then takes a step back. "I hope it's all right. We have a stud who needs some serious work."

"Of course, ma'am," Grace says. "I appreciate the opportunity."

"You hungry, honey? Ronnie cooked up some enchiladas, rice and beans, and sopapillas. But if you're not a Tex-Mex person, she can make you whatever you like."

The little upturn of Grace's lips, that conservative smile she keeps on for the sake of politeness, evolves into a real, full-blown grin. It's been three months of eating cheeseburgers and tacos out of greasy paper bags; the thought of a homemade meal has her practically salivating. "That sounds wonderful. Thank you."

Renata waves a hand, encouraging Grace to follow. She leads her into a dining room, bright with natural light from the floor-to-ceiling windows and anchored by an enormous table that's really just a giant slab of what looks like unfinished mahogany, deeply red and rustic with industrial bolts scattered about the middle.

Two seats at the table are already occupied—an older gentleman at the head, dressed smartly in an expertly starched pearl-snap shirt, and a younger, scruffier man to his left, two seats down. They're leaning in to talk to each other, not yet noticing the new people in the room, and Grace recognizes similarities in the way they both smile—wryly, slowly, like they're hard-earned and always brief. It reminds her of someone . . .

She turns around then, catching Crew's eyes as he makes his way toward the table, lingering behind them by a few steps. The puzzle pieces fall into place, and Grace looks back to the table, now understanding this must be his father, and this appears to be the grown-up version of the other boy from the photographs—the younger brother, surely. They all look too much alike to be anything but immediate family.

The two finally look up and spot Grace, Renata, and Crew now standing at the edge of the table. They stand, the younger man jumping to his feet, while Crew's father takes a little longer and grunts quietly as he lifts himself out of his chair.

"Boys, this is Grace," Renata says, walking to what must be her seat at the left hand. "Grace, this is my husband, Clint." She places a hand on Clint's shoulder, then gestures to the other man. "And my youngest, Cooper."

Grace smiles, making a point to lock eyes with both of them for a brief second and nodding. "So nice to meet you both," Grace says, then does a quick scan across the room. "You have a lovely home. I appreciate you welcoming me into it."

"Aren't you sweet," Renata says, squeezing Clint's shoulder. "Isn't she sweet?"

He gives his wife a lovingly amused glance before turning back to Grace with a quick nod. "It's a pleasure to have you, Grace. Have a seat, now. Ronnie's just about done with lunch."

Grace nods, walking up to the seat at Clint's right and pulling out the chair. She doesn't notice until he's stepped into her space that Crew is right behind her. She has to crane her neck to look up at him as he stares downward, eyebrow kinked.

"That's my seat."

From across the table, Cooper barks out a laugh. "As if you ever eat in here."

Crew doesn't look at his little brother as he says through hard-lined lips, "Well, I'm eatin' in here now, aren't I?" He points to the vacant place setting a seat down. "You can sit there."

The more time she spends in his presence, the more Grace is beginning to understand this man is a walking contradiction. Accommodating but also impatient, like he was on the drive, and now, boldfaced rude but also polite, evidenced by the way he pulls out the chair next to his and gestures for her to sit in it. When she does, he even goes out of his way to tuck her into the table. She feels something akin to whiplash with how quickly he seems to switch between hot and cold.

Once everyone is seated, a quiet settles—not uncomfortable, but appraising. Grace can feel them all looking at her, even if they aren't doing so with their eyes. The thought makes her gaze drift down to her jeans, insecurity rearing its ugly head as she looks at the stubborn coffee stain on her left thigh and the ever-expanding hole above her right knee. She's generally pretty diligent about showering—even when she lived at Braxton and only had hot water once or twice a week—but compared to the cozy, clean scent that seems to pump through the air vents of this home, she can't help but wonder if, even after three months away, she still reeks of manure.

The panic settling under her skin is interrupted by the sound of two French doors swinging open. An apron-clad woman holding a giant platter emerges, smiling warmly at everyone as she walks toward the middle of the table. Behind her, two men come out holding more ornate-looking vats, and they all begin to set them down gently on the runner that spans the long table. Grace sits up a little straighter and observes a tray of enchiladas topped with bubbly melted cheese, beans, and rice bespeckled with little bits of tomato and onion. The plate of sopapillas, fried tortillas dusted in cinnamon sugar and covered in honey, sits toward the end nearest to Clint, and the warm, sweet scent rolling off them has Grace almost licking her lips in anticipation.

"Thanks, Ronnie," Clint rasps, a white porcelain coffee cup at his lips. His eyes scan the plate and the steam emanating from the various dishes. "Smells good."

Ronnie, who can't be a millimeter over five feet tall, looks more like a kindergarten teacher than a chef. Her curly hair is tied in an artfully messy bun atop her head, and bright, colorful flowers are scattered over every inch of her apron. She returns to the doors that lead to the kitchen, claps her hands together, and looks around the room with the same smile on her lips. Her journey comes to a halt as her eyes land on Crew, lingering for a brief second before moving to Grace. "As I live and breathe," she says, placing a hand at her hip. "Is this what it takes for you to come to lunch, Crew Lee? A pretty girlfriend to sit next to?"

Grace's eyes widen, and beside her, Crew chokes on a sip of water. Renata lets out a barking laugh from across the table.

"Rons, you know Crew doesn't date," Cooper says. "He'd actually have to talk to a woman to do that."

Crew's head swings, and he shoots Cooper a look that says a thousand words, a classic older-brother scowl that has Cooper raising his hands in mock surrender with an equally classic cheeky, little-brother smirk.

"This is Grace," Renata says. "She's here to see if she might be a good fit to replace Gary."

Ronnie nods, then smiles at Grace. "My apologies, honey," she says, shrugging. "Thought I might be witnessin' a miracle."

"All right," Crew huffs out, setting his hands on the table and folding his lips into a line. He's staring straight ahead at the food as he says tightly, "Thank you for the meal, Veronika. I'm sure it'll be delicious, as always."

Ronnie gives him an affectionate eye roll and says, "Y'all, enjoy. Holler if you need anything," before leaving the dining room.

Hands begin to reach inward to grab the platters, spoon food onto plates, and then pass to the right, almost like clockwork. They don't even look at the dishes as they're passed, as though this is a practiced, expected motion they've grown used to after hundreds of meals eaten together. Grace is impressed by the fluidity and ease of it all, but part of her can't help but feel a tinge of sadness. To know one another so well they don't have to wonder what someone's next move may be—she's never known that kind of intimacy. With family, or otherwise.

Cooper passes her the enchiladas, and Grace nods her thanks as she accepts. On and on the carousel of food moves until she's gotten a little bit of everything. When the first bite of the freshly made enchiladas and delectably savory refried beans hits her tongue, tears almost sprout in her eyes. It's already the best meal she's ever eaten. No contest. A goblet—likely made of the finest glass south of the Mason-Dixon Line—filled with ice water sits before her, and as Grace reaches for it, Renata's voice cuts through the low hum of dining and the clink of utensils striking plates. "So, Grace—I understand you worked at Braxton with Maryann and trained horses, but that's about the extent of my knowledge. How long were you there?"

The morsel of food in Grace's mouth suddenly tastes slightly sour at the thought. She swallows it, dabs her mouth with the cloth napkin from her lap, and says, "A little over nine years, ma'am."

"Sweetheart, I know you were raised in Texas, and from what I can see, probably don't have a disrespectful bone in your body," Renata says, then holds out a hand. "But please stop callin' me *ma'am*. Renata's just fine. You're making me feel like a senior citizen."

"If the orthopedic shoe fits," Cooper says under his breath.

Renata doesn't look at him but snaps a finger in his direction and responds, "Bite your tongue, Cooper Matthew." Clint uses his coffee cup to hide his smile, and a quiet snort sounds from where Crew sits.

"Anyway," Renata continues. "Nine years. My word, that's quite a long time for someone so— Actually, I don't think I ever asked: How old are you?"

Grace lops a piece of enchilada off with the side of her fork and says, "Twenty-five, ma'a—" She stops herself just in time, snapping her mouth closed before the word is spoken in full. "I'm twenty-five."

"Twenty-five," Renata parrots, then looks at Grace curiously for too long a moment. Grace knows she's connecting the dots, doing the mental math and figuring out in real time that Grace was a child when she started working at Braxton. "So, you were, what? Sixteen, when—"

"Honey," Clint interrupts, gently covering his wife's hand with his own. "Let's not give her the third degree while she's eating her lunch."

Renata and Clint share a look, and an unspoken conversation happens between them in the span of seconds. Renata gives him a soft, quick nod and turns back to Grace. "I'm sorry, Grace. You'll learn soon enough that I'm notoriously nosy."

"Nothing to apologize for," Grace counters, but doesn't supply anything else. She glances at Clint, overwhelmed with gratitude that he rescued her from that line of questioning. She smiles, and he gives her a wink before returning to his meal.

"Surprised you're still here," Crew grumbles from where he sits, and Grace looks over to see him eyeing his brother across the table. "Is *showing up for work* not a requirement at your job?"

Cooper's fork stops on the way to his mouth, and he flashes Crew a wide, sardonic grin before taking the bite. Muffled by the food he's still chewing, he replies, "I'm on sabbatical."

Crew huffs. "Didn't know they let interns take sabbaticals."

"There's a lot you don't know about corporate America, brother. It's a brave new world out there. Just wait until you learn about internet stipends and on-site masseuses."

"Cooper," Clint cuts in. His stare isn't unkind, but it isn't soft, either. He seems to be the type of father who offers little quarter to his children, because there's a glint, a sharpness in his eyes that has Cooper sitting up straighter in his chair.

"I didn't find it especially fair that I was getting coffee and picking up dry cleaning for executives when I was promised actual finance experience, so I quit. I've decided to take my long-awaited gap year."

Crew stares at his brother through narrowed eyes. "Isn't a gap year something you do before you graduate?" he asks, sitting back in his chair. "When you do that after you've already gotten a degree, I think it's just called *being unemployed*."

"All right," Renata says. She looks at Grace, and a smile—one that Grace is noticing now looks practiced, routine, maybe a little bit disingenuous—spreads widely on her lips.

"First, let's remember we have company." Then, her gaze becomes pointed as it zeroes in on Crew. "Second, don't make your brother feel bad for wanting to be home. All I *ever* want is for my children to be under the same roof with me—" she says, then seems to stop herself from finishing the thought, her mouth closing abruptly.

Clint glances sidelong at her as he sips his coffee.

Renata recovers quickly, taking a deep breath before adding,

"He can stay as long as he likes. Forever, if I have any say in it." She reaches over and pats Cooper's cheek, and he ducks bashfully, gently waving her hand away. "And you're going to help him reintegrate," she tells Crew. "Let him bond with the hands. Give him things to do around here."

At this directive, Crew actually smiles, but it's more of a smirk. "Happily," he tells his mother, and then offers his brother a wink, one that seems to gleefully promise to give him many, *many* things to do around the ranch. And for the first time since the meal began, Cooper looks wholly unsettled.

They continue eating without engaging again; Renata and Clint share a quiet conversation, Cooper scrolls on his phone, and Crew eats silently but heartily, helping himself to seconds and then thirds. Grace's plate is empty faster than she would've hoped, and she stares longingly at the remaining food, particularly the sticky-sweet tortilla triangles that have gone mostly untouched. Despite knowing with some level of certainty that Renata would encourage her to eat as much as she'd like, it still feels wrong to reach for more. To take without having anything to give in return. Maybe she'll prove herself and help them, paying them back for this meal and then some, but there's also a chance that she'll fail miserably and be back in Minetta by the end of the week, proving instead to be a waste of gas money and groceries. Not willing to gamble with that possibility, Grace places her hands in her lap. She's had more than enough. As she stares down at the empty plate streaked with remnants of enchilada sauce and leftover grains of rice, something comes into her field of vision that she doesn't expect.

A helping of the sopapillas. A big one, too.

Grace looks up as Crew sets it down on her plate and then quickly sucks off the sweet glaze remaining on his thumb and forefinger. He doesn't look at her as he turns back to his own food, but quietly, only loud enough for her to hear, he says, "Eat."

After lunch, everyone scatters. Crew and Cooper kiss their mother on the cheek before they go, and Grace watches with amusement as Crew grabs his kid brother by the scruff and shoves him out of the house. They don't get more than a few steps outside before Crew is barreled over, trying to dodge Cooper's fists aimed at his abdomen. Renata watches them go with a loving, knowing expression—a mother used to seeing her children pick on each other. Grace wonders about the picture of the girl sitting between Crew and Cooper on the shelf—the sister, the middle child, the only one who doesn't have a reserved seat at the table. She wonders where she fits in, if she fits in at all, but thinks better of asking. The Caldwells seem to be a forthcoming, confrontational bunch, willing to not only acknowledge but also shine a glaring spotlight on *all* elephants in the room. There's bound to be a reason why the topic didn't come up.

"Grab your stuff. I'll show you to the bunkhouse," Renata says, interrupting Grace's theorizing, then nods in the direction in which Crew and Cooper ran off. "The hands are all out working, but you'll meet everybody at dinner."

"Great." Grace shoulders her duffel bag and follows Renata to the barn she'd seen on the drive in. The closer they get, the more nervous she becomes. Compared to her last bunkhouse, it's a mansion. A five-star resort. The paint looks like it was recoated recently—crisp white with black accents and not a streak or smudge in sight. The grassy pathway leading to the front door feels soft under Grace's boots, as if it, too, is more refined.

Renata pushes open the barn door with some difficulty, sliding it to the right until it latches into place. The scent of aftershave, coffee, and a cowboy musk that is inescapable no matter how nice the living quarters may be hits Grace's nose, and her eyes go wide.

Maybe it isn't as artfully decorated or chic as the main house, but it's something to behold on its own. While there are bunk beds, they aren't the ancient, rickety twin things from Braxton. They're full beds—on bottom and top—held up by strong, sturdy-looking wood panels and ladders.

A blast of cold air is enough to have her grinning as she walks in, scanning the high ceiling and the crisscrossing wooden beams above. Where Braxton's ranch hands treated the bunkhouse floor like their own personal hamper, the hands here all seem to have their own designated bins. There's a shoe rack toward the back of the room sitting atop a jute rug, and an array of boots and shower shoes are stacked neatly across the six shelves.

As Grace takes all of it in, she tries to keep her mouth snapped shut, for fear of letting her jaw hang in childlike awe. But she fails miserably as soon as the pool table and foosball table come into view, both in perfect condition. And behind them, a kitchen with stainless steel appliances and a dining table that looks big enough for an entire football team.

Renata stands behind Grace as she moves through the bunkhouse slowly, appreciating every square inch. She comes upon a bed that looks vacant, a bottom bunk with a soft-looking quilt and pillow sitting at the edge of the mattress. She turns to see Renata smiling with her arms folded over her chest. The woman nods, then says, "That'll be yours while you're with us."

With a slight pit forming in her stomach, Grace clocks the very specific way she phrases that statement. This ranch, this family, this bunkhouse, every last bit of it, could be very temporary.

"Settle in, change, do whatever you've gotta do, and then I'll walk you over to the stables."

Grace nods, setting her bag atop the mattress. Renata turns to leave, and the words bubble up in Grace's throat and out of her mouth before she can stop them. "Renata," she calls, feeling slightly wrong and weird using just her first name.

Renata turns, eyebrows lifting upward.

"Thank you for this. For everything."

With a knowing smile, the owner of Halcyon Ranch says, "Don't thank me yet, Grace. You haven't met the horse."

CHAPTER 4

"Long story short—an old rodeo girlfriend of mine called me and told me her husband was going to blow a gasket because she'd bought the horse at an auction, but the investment proved to be a bad one when he wouldn't let anyone get within five feet of him," Renata explains, walking shoulder to shoulder with Grace toward the stables. "I used my powers of persuasion and told the husband we'd work on him, and promised that when we were through, they'd be able to sell him for double what they paid. I thought it'd be a quick turnaround, but then we actually got the horse."

She sucks on her teeth, tilting her head, and adds, "Then Gary decided to quit."

Grace glances over at her. "I thought he left because the heat got to him."

Renata grimaces slightly, then gives Grace a faux-innocent smile. "I may have fibbed a little bit about that." She must recognize the look of confusion swirling with fear forming on Grace's face, because she adds quickly, "Look, Gary was stubborn as shit. Ask anyone here. The horse is wild as wild comes, but nothing an experienced, patient trainer can't manage."

"How long did he work on him before he left?"

A pause, pregnant and lingering. Grace practically knows the answer before Renata can even spit it out. "About a day."

Grace's brows pull together. Her steps slow, nearly coming to a stop as she holds up her hands. "Hold on now. What exactly am I walking into?"

Renata sighs, unsurprised by Grace's reaction. "I'm tellin' you, Grace, it was the straw that broke the camel's back. We let Gary get too comfortable. He was used to doing things his way and refused to try new methods. He took things too fast, and the horse put him in his place. There may have been a little bit of a kick involved, but he was fine. No permanent damage."

Grace's eyes widen. "Renata . . ."

"C'mon," the woman urges, grabbing on to Grace's arm to encourage her to keep walking. "Don't let Gary's stupidity scare you away. You make up your own mind. If you meet him and want to hightail it out of here, I'll put you in our nicest truck and send you home with a Tupperware full of enchiladas."

It's all Grace can do to continue to keep step with this determined woman who doesn't seem to understand what it's like to not get her way. Grace wonders how the conversation between her and Gary must've gone, wonders just how stubborn he must've been, because there doesn't seem to be a single problem in the universe Renata Caldwell can't finesse her way out of.

The horse comes into view as they approach the metal ring. He's a young tobiano—maybe five or six—with a sorrel base and big, irregular white patches. Grace clocks a few things about him apart from his appearance right away: He's had little to no interaction with humans, likely has been touched seldom if ever. He's afraid, evidenced by the way he doesn't seem to want to stop moving his feet, and he's lively. Fast as all get-out.

A man with long gray hair and a well-worn straw Stetson stands in the ring with him, smartly keeping a wide berth as the animal runs back and forth, back and forth, with no discernible destination—anything to protect himself from the danger he feels is imminent every time the man gets closer.

"Pretty, isn't he?" Renata asks.

Grace nods, then jerks her chin in the direction of the man. "Who's that?"

Renata leans her forearms onto the metal bars and smiles. "Forty. He's been with us since my daddy was still running things. Not much of a horse trainer, as you can see, but one hell of a hand and a great cook. You'll get to see for yourself later at supper."

Still observing, clocking the way the horse refuses to even look in Forty's direction, Grace prods, "So, he's just risking his life for the fun of it?"

Renata chuckles. "He's been more successful than Gary. The horse wasn't scared of him; he just plain disliked him. Saw something we didn't, I suppose."

Grace doesn't doubt that—in her experience, horses don't even have to interact with a person to understand their makeup. They can immediately sense the goodness—or the malice—in someone's soul.

Renata waves to Forty, and he walks with a bowlegged gait over to them, ruefully shaking his head. The woman smiles and nods in Grace's direction. "Forty, this is Grace. She's a trainer, here to see if she's gonna take Gary's job."

Forty tips his hat and puts out a hand, one that Grace squeezes and notices is covered in the kind of leathery calluses forged over years of hard labor. "Pleasure to meet you, Grace."

"Likewise."

"Ever tame a wild horse before?" he asks, an eyebrow raised.

"Yes, sir."

"Well, then," Forty says, nodding. He reaches over to the opening of the enclosure and pops up the lock. Holding it open for her, he smiles. "Let's see what you've got."

There is one objective and one objective *only* for Grace's first time meeting this horse: *Do not become an enemy*. It's simple but not easy, and her success in this endeavor will be a good indication of whether she's cut out for this. Whether they are a good match. As important as it is for him to be exposed to humans to relieve some of that fear of the unknown, she knows taking it slow is the only way they're going to make any substantial progress. And since Renata has yet to give her an official deadline, she doesn't think it's necessary to rush it. Instead, she starts with something easy.

Hal taught her the method when she was a teenager and still a little afraid of wild horses and their unbound power. "It's a dance," he'd said, walking confidently toward a horse until it relented and made eye contact with him. Then, he'd turned his back and walked the other direction, the horse visibly relaxing in his wake. "A catch and release."

Grace echoes that now, her feet moving in those same confident steps. This particular horse is definitely more stubborn than she'd hoped, unwilling to give her even a slight side-eye as she approaches. He keeps running away, fast and strategic in his efforts to put as much space between them as possible. "All right now," she says softly, planting her boots farther into the dirt. Her strides are slow and purposeful, cutting him off at the pass with a careful mix of authority, patience, and gentleness. "C'mon."

Straight-on eye contact—a feat that usually takes her about fifteen minutes to accomplish—takes nearly two hours. And even then, it's fleeting. She has to repeat the exercise more than a dozen times before he relents and gives her any sort of quarter, finally standing still for nearly thirty seconds. And then he's off again, pounding his hooves into the dirt with so much force that the earth seems to shake beneath them.

Eventually, they figure out their own dance. It's not fluid or comfortable yet—more clunky and apprehensive than anything else—but it's something. Near the end of the session, Grace has managed to establish an extremely tentative level of trust, so much so that she can even get him to start running in the direction she determines instead of in his previously unpredictable zigzags. The last thing she does is bring out a training flag, which she uses with varying levels of success to direct him, and also get him used to objects moving closer and closer into his personal space.

By the time the dinner bell rings and Grace has corralled him safely into the stables, she thinks she might actually have a shot at this.

Alone and riding somewhat of a high from a challenging but rewarding first session, Grace walks back to the bunkhouse. She's smiling to herself when a familiar sound hits her, turning her stomach and causing her heart to thud a little harder: cacophonous laughter and shouting echoes from within the walls of the bunkhouse. The howling of wolves preparing for slaughter. Halcyon's bunkhouse and ranch hands may be unknown to her, but at the same time, she knows their kind like the back of her hand—the obnoxiousness of large groups of men, the unspoken danger that lingers between the lines of their jovial conversation. There's a cruel type of camaraderie that links them all, a shared belief that their opinions are law, that their desires are paramount. At Braxton, anytime she entered a space in which they were congregating, the air would shift. Their eyes would snap to her, scanning up and down her body with leering, predatory grins etched onto their lips. A litany of comments would inevitably follow, some made directly, others among one another, as if she weren't standing directly in front of them. Grace had learned very early on in her tenure there that the only way to get through it was to tune it out—to not give them the satisfaction of reacting.

Which is exactly what she intends to do as she walks through the barn door of Halcyon's bunkhouse. Her hackles are already up, ready to protect her from familiar foes. Her fists involuntarily clench at her sides as she takes in the scene, noticing a great deal of things very quickly. First, and perhaps most notably, there's little fanfare when she enters the room. The Halcyon hands are scattered about the space doing various things—a couple are tucked into their bunks with earbuds in, one is attempting to polish a pair of boots that appear to be permanently scuffed, and three stand in the expansive kitchen, backs turned as they focus on dinner-related tasks, completely unaware of her presence. In fact, not a single person even acknowledges her existence, which is strange and wonderful and confusing all at once.

Grace stands near the doorway, somewhat awkwardly shifting on her heels, until Forty turns and spots her. He's in the middle of barking orders at the hands helping him when his eyes light up and a smile erupts across his face.

"There she is," he exclaims, wiping his hands on his jeans as he walks over to her.

Once at her side, he turns to face everyone and clears his throat. "Listen up, kids," he calls out, and a wave of attention spreads across the room, all eyes shifting to them. To her.

Grace's cheeks start to warm.

"This is Grace. She's working with the stud Renata snagged off that Real Housewife of Dallas. Once she breaks him, she'll officially be the new Gary. I expect y'all to be kind and hospitable, and don't ask her too many questions." He points at one of the hands with that comment, a shorter man with a dirty-blond faux-hawk who looks a little offended but puts his hands up in compliance anyway. "Grace, this is everyone. I'm not gonna tell you all their names, because you won't remember them. Hell, I don't even remember them half the time."

A few of them greet her from where they are, a couple even flash genuine, welcoming smiles, and Grace returns them, waving.

And then everyone simply . . . goes back to what they were doing. Like Grace is just a person, someone working at the ranch like they are, and not some shiny new toy to bat around and examine. She lets out a long, shaky breath and feels a thick, heavy tension rush out of her, her shoulders slumping in unexpected relief. Forty offers her a kind smile before turning on his heel and walking back to the stove to tend to a large, steaming stockpot.

Grace figures it's as good a time as any to make up her bed, but before she can venture across the room, a warm, high-pitched, decidedly female voice cuts through the low murmur of the bunkhouse and stops her.

"Hi, Grace."

Grace turns to find a petite, smiling woman has appeared at

her side. The top of her head reaches Grace's chin, so she has to crane her head downward slightly to meet her eyes. She looks about Grace's age, and just as bronzed and freckled from hours spent in the sun. Her blond hair is curly and long, nearly down to her tailbone.

She holds out a hand, and with a crooked but confident grin, says, "I'm June."

Grace returns the handshake and her own tentative smile—the confidence and lack of shyness isn't her expertise. "Hi. Nice to meet you."

Behind them, a cowbell sounds. It's loud, too loud for the size of this room, but no one seems surprised. In fact, they all become animated instantly, leaving their posts in waves to find seats at the giant dining room table.

"Bell means food's ready, as I'm sure you guessed," June says, looking back to the kitchen ruefully.

With a slight shake of her head, she adds, "Hope you like slop, Grace. That's all you're gonna get in this kitchen. And the occasional flapjack."

"I can hear you, ma'am," Forty grumbles, not turning to look at them.

"Turn around and I'll say it to your face, Forty," she counters, then rolls her eyes mirthfully as she turns back to Grace. "How'd it go with the horse today?"

Grace looks around the room, noticing the way ears seem to be perking up as she prepares to answer. It seems they all would like to know how it's going with the stud. "Not bad," Grace says, shoving her hands into her pockets to stop herself from wringing them under the mass scrutiny. "I only spent a couple of hours with him, but we made some good progress."

June purses her lips. "Well," she says, giving Grace a surveying look that feels more . . . antagonistic than her friendly greeting would've suggested. Then she adds, "Aren't you just the prettiest horse whisperer there ever was?" and Grace knows, sadly, instantly—this is one to keep an eye on.

"Leave her alone, Junie," a man with red hair cuts in, walking up to the two women. He stands between them and gives June a stern, brotherly-type look, then his gaze flits to Grace. "Don't mind her. She's just mad because she and Gary were . . . entangled," he says with a suggestive bounce of his rusty eyebrows. June's lips tighten, and then, without ceremony, she elbows the man directly in his stomach, which makes him grunt as he hunches over. She then, promptly and wordlessly, leaves them both to find a seat at the table.

Grace decides not to be offended by the sudden hostility, even if it had been hidden behind a seemingly welcoming, bubbly smile. It's not a new thing—women being combative with other women on a ranch, especially among fellow hands. In Grace's experience, there's a competitive, territorial energy that rarely gives way to any type of sisterhood, despite the commonality of sharing space with a bunch of sweaty oafs.

"I'm Raymond," the redhead says, slightly raspy. Still hunched over, he reaches out with a limp hand. "Great to meet you, Grace."

Grace chuckles. "You too, Raymond."

"C'mon," he says, nodding toward the table. He slowly returns to a fully vertical position and beckons her with a wave. "Let's eat."

Once dinner is ready and everyone is seated around the table, it's almost impossible to parse out the overlapping conversations.

Some are lighthearted, others seem to be verging on actual arguments. But, strangely, there's no tension. No anger. And most of all, there doesn't seem to be any concern with the fact that not one but two women are sitting among them. Too often at Braxton, Grace felt like a captive animal on display with drooling, hungry men poking and prodding at her cage. Here, she's left alone to eat her food, which does look like slop but tastes like heaven. Potato soup of some kind, with thick morsels of bacon and gooey cheese and sprinkled with green onion. She enjoys each spoonful, for once, not feeling the need to rush through her meal and get out of the spotlight.

The engagement she does experience is friendly and curious. They ask about her past without prodding too much; they seem genuinely interested in getting to know her at whatever speed she's comfortable. It's an odd, pleasant conversation she is not accustomed to in the slightest, but she tells them about her favorite music (country), food (steak), and movie (*Forrest Gump*).

She learns about them, too—all nine of the hands, except for June, who doesn't seem especially keen on offering up any information about herself. Raymond is from Tennessee; he loves to rope and competes in the local rodeo. Harrison, a Texas native, is an aspiring poet whose smile is interspersed with silver-capped teeth. There are two ex-convicts, Bryan and Michael, who did brief stints for possession charges and found a home at Halcyon after being released, when they had nowhere else in the world to go. Caleb, Alec, and Pierce all love to drink and often make it a competition among one another amid games of Hold'em and blackjack. And then there's Forty, the unspoken dad of the group, whose face lights up when she tells him she likes to cook and would love to help him in the kitchen. "Well, good," he says, pointing his spoon in her direction. "I'm gonna hold you to that, because these idiots can't tell an onion from a goddamn apple."

A raucous protest sounds around the table from the affronted cowboys, and Grace can't help but laugh. It's different, a little strange, even, to feel any sort of joy among fellow ranch hands, but she lets herself feel it anyway. If she only gets a few days of this loud, loving, patchwork family, she's going to sop up as much of it as she can. She eats her delicious soup, listens to their stories, and for the first time in a long time, the smile on her face isn't forced.

At breakfast the next morning, while he stands beside her and dries the dishes she washes, Grace learns that Michael "Mikey" Chapman—the owner of the faux-hawk—is an open book. He's more than happy to gab away about his time in lockup and all of his strange experiences inside.

"I'll have to teach you how to make my special ramen sometime," he tells her as he wipes down an old, heavily seasoned sheet pan. "You like Flamin' Hot Cheetos, right?"

Grace tilts her head, considering. "Sure, they're okay."

Mikey gasps. "Okay? The greatest snack God ever invented is just okay?"

Scraping bits of egg off a skillet, Grace says, "Didn't Frito-Lay invent Flamin' Hot Cheetos?"

"That's heresy, ma'am," he says, eyeing her with a humorous scowl.

They work through the pile of dishes, laughter and gentle ribbing continuing until another presence makes itself known in the kitchen. It's odd—though the person doesn't make any noise, Grace can still feel the energy shift around them. With a quick glance over her shoulder, her suspicion is confirmed.

Crew Caldwell. Looking just as pleasant as he had the previous morning.

He stands at the counter, pouring coffee into a giant thermos, and he doesn't look up or acknowledge them, even when he's done. He simply stands there, sipping his coffee, frowning.

From what she's gathered so far—which isn't much, just what she could pick up around the dinner table and then the subsequent fire they all sat around, cradling Solo cups of Jack Daniel's—Crew is unforgiving and tough on the ranch hands. But he doesn't seem to work in a loud, spurious way like Bellamy does. His authority is quieter, more intense, and more intimidating than Bellamy could ever hope to be.

When he notices Crew standing behind them, Mikey's laughter quiets down until there's no sound in the kitchen except the running faucet. He flashes a smile at Crew and, in a somewhat endearing attempt to include him in the conversation, offers, "You like spicy, right, boss? What do you think about Flamin' Hot Cheetos?"

Silence stretches, and Grace nearly turns around to see if he's actually just left without responding when his rumbling voice hits her ears.

"I think Cheetos are something you can talk about on your own time," he says, words raspy and rough.

The sound makes Grace wonder if he actually sleeps; she'd spotted him earlier that morning, jogging on the paved road that loops around all of the housing structures on Halcyon. She'd seen him sitting out on his porch the previous night, too, when she'd remained outside after the fire died down to stare at the moon and listen to the blaring symphony of crickets and cicadas. He'd been accompanied by a dog, who sat faithfully at his feet. She figures that if he does sleep, he must not do it very well, considering how perpetually grumpy he seems to be—a theory that's supported even further when he adds, "You got all the equipment ready for that burn yet?"

"I was just finishing up here, I'm gonna go get it all—"

"Because it seems to me like you thought flirtin' with the new girl is a better way to spend your morning."

Mikey sets the sheet pan on the counter. "'Course not," he says, shaking his head. "I was just leavin'." He gives Grace a sympathetic look, a silent apology for abandoning his task.

"Hm," Crew murmurs as Mikey passes them, quickly speeding out of the kitchen, then hopping on one foot through the door as he hastily yanks on his boot.

Left alone and no longer comfortable with her back to him, Grace shuts off the sink and turns, leaning against the counter. "Good morning," she tries, mustering her best, most professional smile.

"Sure is," Crew says dryly, then takes a sip of coffee, surveying her over the lid with his piercing brown eyes. "You had enough yet?"

Grace tilts her head. Her hair falls over her shoulder as she does, not yet tucked away into her regular ponytail. Crew's eyes follow the motion, tracing from her neck to her shoulder and then back up again. "What kind of question is that?" Grace asks.

He shrugs, a small, halfhearted motion. "An honest one. That horse is a stubborn bastard. He doesn't want to be broken."

Grace huffs out a humorless laugh. "Does anyone?"

For a moment, he simply stares at her, pinning her with a look that feels exposing, like he's silently stripping away one of her protective layers without even trying. "All I'm saying is, it's okay if you decide this job isn't for you. Not a lot of people can handle a horse like that."

"Your mother doesn't share that opinion, and she's the one who brought me here," Grace says, folding her arms over her chest. "She thinks I can get through to him."

"My mother is an unfailing optimist."

Grace considers him for a moment. Then, because she's irritated that he's doubting her without even knowing her, and without having seen the progress she's already made, she frowns and asks, "You seem to know a lot about horse training. Why haven't you tried with him?"

Crew chuckles, wholly unfazed by her boldness. "I don't have time to rescue any more lost causes, I'm afraid."

The dig stings. Taken aback by his rudeness, Grace pushes off the counter and steps toward him. "What's your problem with me?"

His gaze travels downward slightly until their eyes are locked again. "Why, exactly, would I have a problem with you?"

Grace's eyebrows shoot up. "No clue, but you seem to have a hell of a bone to pick, which is odd considering we just met. Or is this"—she looks him up and down—"your natural state? Do you just default to dickhead?"

Crew's eyes narrow, and a game of chicken begins between them, both silently daring each other to look away and neither willing to relent. He takes a step inward, chin dipping down even farther; he's fully towering over her now. No doubt used to using his behemothness to his advantage. He hums, then asks,

"Is that any way to speak to someone who might be your boss one day?"

With her chin held high, Grace volleys back, "So, now I have a shot at sticking around? Thought I was a lost cause. Thought I shouldn't quit my day job."

His jaw works restlessly back and forth. "Guess time will tell."

Her eyes harden. "I guess it will."

A cheeky little smirk folds onto his lips, and Grace feels a primal urge to slap it off of his face. He walks away without another word, whistling as he goes.

By lunchtime, Grace has roped the stud, and she's also quietly started to refer to him as Waylon, because some *bastard* whistling "Good Ol' Boys" this morning got the song stuck in her head and it just . . . happened. Roping Waylon is not an easy feat—he resists it intensely at first, but she continues to patiently utilize the pressure-release method that's worked well enough so far. When he finally gives in and stops yanking away from her, she gives him a break, letting him get used to the sensation of the rope against his body.

Through a few more rounds of this—she pulls, he yanks, he stops, she releases—she manages to get him to follow her lead for a few steps. And then, toward the end of the session, like some kind of miracle, his hind legs join his careful, tentative walk.

In the paddock adjacent to Waylon's, they've brought in a Quarter Horse gelding named Duke. Duke is meant to set an example for Waylon, to help him understand how to behave. He was handpicked by Crew because he's the calmest of the herd and nearly the oldest. Grace finds that she agrees he is calm, but Duke is also ornery. He is generally displeased about his new babysitting gig, and he shows that to her with sidelong glances, litanies of grunts and sighs, and by taking carrots from her hand with a little too much force. When she tells Forty as much, he chuckles and says something to the effect of *You know what they say about animals taking after their owners*, which is how Grace learns that Duke has been Crew's horse since he was a teenager.

With a little time before lunch, Grace decides to leave Waylon under Duke's unenthusiastic supervision and heads to the main house to update Renata on her progress. She doesn't know exactly what the threshold is for her to secure the position—saddle-breaking, if she had to guess—but the fact that Waylon was willing to follow her lead even for a moment is a good sign he'll continue to progress. It won't be an overnight affair, but if she continues to work with him and build trust, she should have him ready to ride within the next week or two. Whether she's been allotted that kind of time for this trial, she isn't sure. They never really discussed that part.

She comes up near the back of the house, which faces the stables and the bunkhouse. There's a wraparound porch that's complete with multiple rocking chairs and outdoor couches with lush pillows, and wind chimes that hang from the eaves and echo a soothing, quiet song.

But the peace of the chimes is interrupted when the sound of voices begins to cut through the windswept music. Grace's steps slow; her first instinct is to turn around—whatever conversation is going on sounds intense, and she doesn't want to eavesdrop. But then she hears something that sounds suspiciously like her name, and she can't help but move a little bit closer. Once she's within earshot, she recognizes both of the voices almost immediately.

"Has she done something to make you think we can't trust her?" Renata asks. Her voice is calm, her tone mild.

Crew's voice, on the other hand, is not. "She's from Braxton." He's firm, exacting, and verging on loud. "Nothing good comes out of that place."

Grace's heart sinks in her chest. Hearing the words that are constantly playing on a loop in her mind, spoken aloud and with such conviction—

Renata maintains her calm; her words are slowly enunciated, with the kind of patience only a mother can manage. "That's quite a judgment for someone you barely know."

"You don't know her, either!" he shouts. "It's not like she had a résumé with a list of references. You chose to ignore the inbox full of actual applications from actual professionals for someone who shares blood with Bellamy Whitlock. Please, enlighten me on the logic behind that decision."

Grace's head hangs as she continues to listen. With every word out of his mouth, Crew breaks her down, dismantling all the confidence she'd built up that morning with Waylon.

Renata sighs. "I don't need to explain myself to you, Crew, especially if you're gonna raise your voice at me. But I'll have you know, she actually *did* have a reference—someone I happen to know and trust."

A long, silent pause passes between them. "I'm sorry," Crew finally says, softer but still slightly on edge. "But even if she breaks that horse tomorrow, I don't want you promising her a place in my bunkhouse. That's my call to make."

"Fine," Renata says, sounding tired. "You want to be irrational about this? You want to make snap judgments about her based on her family, something that is completely out of her control? You want to take this opportunity away from her, when she's so clearly excellent at what she does? Fine. Make the call, son. But it'll be on *you* to find someone else. Someone better than she is."

"Fine. Like I said, there's a full inbox of applicants."

"Great."

"Good."

Loud, thumping steps follow the clipped declaration—Crew's heavy boots stomping down the porch stairs, if Grace had to guess. Angry, defeated tears begin to well up in her eyes as she processes what she just heard, and her first instinct is to drop everything and run for the hills. She's already felt like an impostor, like she's taking advantage of their hospitality by eating their food and enjoying their air-conditioned facilities without having secured the job. And if the foreman of the ranch—and the heir to the Halcyon throne, no less—already has his mind made up about her, well. That doesn't seem like a battle she's going to win. She can't change who her family is. Grace turns around, kicking dust with her boots as she rushes back to the bunkhouse, painfully gritting her teeth to keep the tears in her eyes at bay. She immediately starts strategizing—the walk to get to the Halcyon property line will be brutal; it'd probably be smart to see if she can find a spare canteen, and maybe some of that deer jerky Forty's been insisting that she try. If she can make it off the property, she can get to the main road into town, and then hitchhike until some gracious soul takes pity on her, all alone and boiling in the Texas heat. It's as good a plan as any—once she makes it to town, she'll figure out the rest from there.

So caught up in her own thoughts, it doesn't even occur to her as she bursts through the bunkhouse door that it's lunchtime. The dining room space is bustling with noise, and the stench of sweat and dirt mixes with the lemony, sweet scent of hot tea and grilled cheese sandwiches. Forty has one perfectly golden one atop his spatula at the stove, which he proceeds to flip over his shoulder, sending it soaring through the air. With only a tiny bit of assistance from Raymond, the sandwich lands with a *thunk* on his paper plate.

"Still got it, old man," Raymond says before devouring almost half of it in one bite.

Grace stands somewhat dumbfounded in the doorway, her mission halted by the unexpected company. And then they all notice her, and she learns quickly that the greeting she received the previous night wasn't a onetime thing. She isn't quite yet old hat, so they all light up with smiles and beckoning hands, urging her to join them.

Reluctantly, she does, sitting next to Mikey and nearly moaning when the first bite of grilled cheese hits her tongue. The group talks loudly around her, engaging with her here and there, but she can't offer much besides a closed-lip smile—Crew's words are still stuck in her head, in the pit of her stomach, in the bubble in her throat. It feels like if she tried to actually talk, all that would escape her lips would be a rasping sob.

And then someone says something to her and pulls her out of her panicked spiral. "Saw you out there with the horse this morning." It's Pierce, sitting across from her and looking impressed. "You seem to really know what you're doing."

"That right?" Caleb asks, mouth half-full of Doritos.

"Oh yeah," Pierce says, leaning back in his chair and nodding adamantly. "That thing damn near kicked me to death when I tried to wrangle it. Grace got him roped on the second day. Bet she'll saddle-break him before the week's out."

"Well, hell, girl," Forty chimes in. "I figured you were good, but I didn't realize you're a goddamn magician."

The onslaught of compliments is so unexpected, so different from anything she's ever known. It's an odd sensation, feeling like the center of attention and not wanting to shy away from it. There's no disingenuousness in the way they're speaking—it's as though every statement, every commendation is simply an inarguable truth. And as they continue to sing her praises and rebuild the shattered remnants of her confidence without even knowing they're doing it, Grace makes a decision.

She likes it here. She likes these people. She's even starting to like Waylon.

With her belly full and her cheeks warm with delight, she decides she isn't going to run, and she definitely isn't going to let some snide, spoiled cowboy prince ruin this for her. This little taste of family. This strangely wonderful sense of belonging.

CHAPTER 5

Breaking Waylon turns into a mission after that. Instead of waking with the rest of the hands, Grace is up an hour earlier, quietly slipping into her work clothes and boots and leaving the bunkhouse in the smallest hours of the morning. She tells herself it's good to work with Waylon longer and harder on a daily basis; the more human interaction he has, the more comfortable he'll be when it's finally time to ride him.

They stick with the lead rope for three full days. As determined as Grace is, she also isn't stupid enough to try to push Waylon into something he's not ready for. He's a moody, grumpy thing—some hours he's cooperative, walking nearly the entire pen at her back with ease. Others, he's resistant, blowing air through his nose like an errant toddler and refusing to even look at her.

"You can be pissy all you want," she tells him one afternoon, with sweat beading at her brow and a belly full of pulled pork and coleslaw. "But you're gonna let me halter you tomorrow. Not only are you gonna let me"—she yanks gently on the lead rope as Waylon pulls in the opposite direction, but not with much force—"you're gonna be a gentleman about it. And if you *are*, well, I think some of that mighty fine alfalfa over there has got your name on it."

Grace has always had a sense about horses. More than any other animal she's ever encountered, they seem to have a higher level of understanding of humans and language. There's an indecipherable common ground forged between a horse and its trusted companion, one that breaks through the wall of species-specific communication. This theory is further supported by the way Waylon's eyes seem to twinkle with delight at even the *mention* of alfalfa. She wonders about Duke—who watches her training Waylon with an expression that can only be described as scrutinizing—and Crew, and whether the two have any common ground apart from being perpetually grumpy.

Forty, though confident in her horse-training abilities, is skeptical of her kitchen skills. At first, when she reminds him of her offer to help with meals, he only passes off the task of chopping vegetables for a stir-fry. And even then, as she chops carrots into coins and broccoli into florets, Grace can feel him occasionally monitoring her progress over her shoulder. When she volunteers to make the sauce, he's even more hesitant, but once he tastes the tangy, sweet and salty concoction she pulls together, he eases up.

Four days have passed since Grace's torrid eavesdropping incident, and she's hardly even laid eyes on Crew. She thinks he must spend the majority of his time out in the fields supervising controlled burns, or dealing with the cattle, or maybe lying in a coffin somewhere to avoid sunlight. Whatever the case may be, their paths, thankfully, haven't crossed.

Which is why it's so strange when he just *appears* at the stables on the morning of Grace's fifth day at the ranch. Nearly a full week since she arrived. Must be some sort of test, she assumes—perhaps her time has finally come to a close and it's now or never that she proves she should be permanently put on the payroll.

She's in the pen with Waylon, using a lunge whip to slowly caress his back. It's an exercise she conducts daily, incrementally extending the time by a few minutes in each consecutive session. She needs to get him ready to be saddled and handled, and she's quite proud of how tolerant he's become of the sensation.

And Crew's just . . . standing there. Leaning up against Duke's paddock, a cup of coffee in his ginormous hand, staring at her. Eventually, Grace can't take it anymore. She can't be expected to continue her session like this, with his eyes tracking her every move.

"Need something?" she asks, adjusting her ball cap so she can stare at him fully without the impediment of the brim.

He surveys her silently for a prolonged moment. She's on the verge of repeating herself, though she's almost certain he heard her, when he jerks his chin in Waylon's direction. "When are you planning on haltering him?"

The way he asks—it's less of a question and more of an accusation. Like the progress she's made so far is irrelevant, like Waylon isn't leagues better than he was before she got here. It doesn't sit well.

Grace pauses her task and lets Waylon have a much-deserved break. She tosses the whip toward the edge of the enclosure, then walks a few steps closer to Crew. "I guess I should've probably clarified before this moment," she begins, diplomatic as she can possibly manage. "Am I on a deadline here?"

Crew huffs through his nose and takes a sip of coffee, as flippant as ever. "Well," he replies after a teeth-gritting swallow. He must like his coffee as black and bitter as his damn heart. "If you don't think you can do it, we'll need to start looking for someone else, won't we?"

"I can do it," Grace bites out.

He stares at her with that stupid, indecipherable expression and an equally stupid sparkle in his brown eyes, and curtly replies, "Mm-hm."

Patience running ever so thin, Grace sighs. "If you're so sure he's ready, why don't you get out there and halter him?"

The bastard has the audacity to *smile* at that. Alarmingly, and against her will, a thought surfaces in her brain—it's the first time she's seen him smile with his teeth. Teeth that are imperfect and slightly coffee stained but somehow endearing despite the shit-eating grin they make up now. They seem to be the only part of him still reminiscent of his boyhood, because the rest of him—as much as it pains her to admit it—is all man. Judgmental, impatient, hulking man.

Frustrated and eager to get back to business, Grace turns away from him. Over her shoulder she spits, "I'm getting him used to things touching his muzzle and neck with that first." She points toward the lunge, abandoned in the dirt.

"I'll leave you to it," Crew says.

A few seconds pass, and Grace can hear his footsteps begin to recede. But then, because he doesn't seem to understand how to leave well enough alone, he adds, "But time's ticking."

That evening, with only a half hour or so before she needs to head into the kitchen to help with dinner, Grace decides it's as good a time as any to give it a shot. At the very least, she can get Waylon acquainted with the sight of the halter, the feel of it on his muzzle, the rope on his back. He's in good spirits even after a long day of work; he walked all the way around the pen with her multiple times without complaint. It seems only logical that they should move on to the next step in his training.

It absolutely has nothing to do with that skeptical stare Crew gave her earlier in the day, or the way he seems to be convinced that she isn't worthy of *his* ranch.

But Grace is good at this. She understands this, the art of it, the push and pull of getting an animal as powerful as this one to trust. Which is why, when the halter goes on without incident, she feels a rush of self-satisfaction. A validation that even someone as mean-spirited as Crew Caldwell can't take away from her.

Of course, that slightly ballooning ego deflates entirely about twenty minutes into the attempt, when Waylon uses his body to disagree with Grace in an extremely abrupt and painful manner. She *has* him haltered, which is half the battle, but getting him to accept it is another story entirely. She tries to pull him gently in one direction, not tugging so hard that he associates the halter with force and aggression, but he doesn't care. He yanks with full force backward, and she goes flying.

It isn't like she hasn't been sent to the dirt by a horse before. That part isn't the issue. The issue is that the pull is hard enough that it dislocates her shoulder—not entirely, but enough to have her nearly scream out in pain as soon as she hits the ground. By some miracle, she keeps it in, not wanting to scare him any more than she already has. She lies on the ground for a good five minutes, breathing through the pain. The message has been received loud and clear: Waylon would not like to be pushed any further.

With tears beading at the corners of her eyes, Grace wrangles him into the stables, collapses onto a bench in the barn, and tries and fails to move her right arm. After a few ragged breaths, she psychs herself up enough to slowly trudge back to the bunkhouse, where she'd very much like to swallow about six Advil and pass out.

The other hands are concerned when she walks in—the state of her must be something quite alarming if their faces are any indication—but she waves them off, telling them she just got the wind knocked out of her and needs to sleep it off. They seem wary, watching her as she struggles to lie in her bunk, grimacing and hissing the entire way down. Forty comes by at some point, but Grace's vision is blurry enough that she can hardly make out the salt-and-pepper beard and the concerned eyes. She tells him she's fine, just exhausted. When she apologizes for not helping with dinner, he tells her she doesn't need to do anything but sleep.

She tries to do just that, but it's fitful at best. She keeps leaning on her arm and being awoken by a shooting pain that radiates through her entire body. She pushes herself up against the wall, lying flat and still like she's in a coffin, hoping the barrier will keep her from moving in her sleep. She's right there—*just* on the verge of falling into a blissful oblivion—when a deep, unfortunately familiar voice interrupts her almost-slumber.

"Wake up, Grace."

Grace doesn't know who says the words. Frankly, she doesn't

care. Her eyelids make a feeble attempt to open but only flutter, too heavy to do anything else.

"'M sleepin'," she mumbles, letting her drooping eyelids fall shut once again.

"Grace," the voice repeats, tone firm enough to tell her it isn't going to let up.

Grace frowns, coming back to full consciousness regretfully fast. Slowly, she forces her eyes to blink open, and then, for a fraction of a moment, she doesn't know where she is.

What happens next feels like it's in slow motion. Still half-asleep, she reaches beneath her pillow with her good arm, somehow possessing the wherewithal to leave the injured one alone, and grabs on to the hilt of her knife. Her grip is ironlike as she yanks it from its hiding place and swings it toward the strange, deep, stern voice. Only when the tip of it is pressed into a tanned, stubble-covered neck does she fully come to, remembering herself and her surroundings.

Grace gasps, letting the knife fall from her hand and onto the bed with a quiet *thump*. She glances frantically around the bunkhouse, humiliation tempered only slightly by the fact that no one else seems to have witnessed such an outburst.

Crew is unmoved and weirdly calm, considering she had every intention of slicing clean through his jugular only seconds ago. His eyebrow is kinked, and he looks more . . . annoyed than anything else. Like she poses about as much danger as a Chihuahua.

"You oughta be careful with that thing," he says quietly, evenly. "Could hurt yourself."

Irritation flares in her belly right alongside the embarrassment. She lets herself lie back down, hoping he'll take the hint and leave. When he doesn't, she turns her head and maintains eye contact with him for a brief moment to utter, "Go away."

"No." He doesn't move. Doesn't look away from her. "You're hurt."

"So?"

"So, I'm going to help you."

She nearly laughs. "That's rich."

"Sit up."

"Go away."

"Grace," he says, and the second she feels his hand touch her arm, she can't help it. It's an old reflex, born out of necessity and anger and, presently, irritation.

"*Don't* touch me," Grace growls. Her voice cuts through the pleasant murmurs from the dining room, and all their conversations begin to quiet.

Crew's hands fly upward as he backs away, completely removing himself from her personal space. Maybe he'd been a little less unmoved by a knife at this throat than she thought. He assesses her calmly for a moment before turning to look at the dinner table. Grace keeps her stare trained straight ahead so she doesn't see exactly who he's looking to, but whoever it is, they seem to be able to read a silent command in Crew's expression. Within seconds, there are sounds of the ranch hands grabbing their plates and silverware and shuffling out through the swinging door; it closes softly behind them, and then Crew and Grace are completely alone in the bunkhouse.

A long beat passes and then his eyes soften—just a touch. "I'm trying to help you."

Through gritted teeth, Grace spits back, "Why? Isn't this what you wanted?"

His brow pulls together. "What I wanted?"

"If I'm hurt and can't keep training, you'll have your reason to kick me off the ranch. Isn't that what you want? I'm no good, untrustworthy, a bad seed. Sharing blood with Bellamy Whitlock means I'm not worthy of Halcyon. Right?"

The recognition, the remembrance washes over his face slowly. He sets both hands on his thighs and looks away from her. For a moment, Grace is sure he's about to reprimand her for eavesdropping, especially when his jaw moves in that way it does when he's frustrated or growing impatient. But then he says, "I didn't know you were listening," and his voice is raspy and sounds suspiciously close to regretful.

Grace swallows, grimacing at the dry, sandpapery feeling of her mouth. "Would you have said something else if you did?"

His lips twitch, and though she can see only one side of his mouth, the corner of it pulls up just slightly. He says nothing, which is answer enough. Grace shakes her head, sitting up fully in her bunk and grimacing as she pushes herself back against the slats until she's completely upright and there's a wide berth between them. A tense silence settles over the room until she finally clears her throat and says, "I'm nothing like him." Crew looks at her. In this light, his eyes are deceptively soft. Open. Thoughtful. There are flecks of green amid the amber and chocolate in his irises. He hardly blinks as his eyes hold hers. His lack of response is unnerving, and, growing more irritated with every passing second, Grace adds, "You don't know me."

He nods. "You're right."

"You don't *want* to know me."

At that, Crew's nostrils flare. "Knowing and trusting don't always go hand in hand. My first priority is and always will be the safety of this ranch and all the people on it."

"And you think I'm a threat to that?"

"I'm not saying you are, but like you said: I don't know you."

"Ask me something, then."

He tilts his head, a flash of amusement crossing his face. "What?"

Grace nearly shrugs but manages to stop herself before she lands in a world of hurt from moving her shoulder. Instead, she raises her brows questioningly. "You don't know me because you haven't tried to know me. Ask me something."

He seems to consider her challenge for a moment, and then briefly looks like he isn't going to give in, but then he scoots backward and settles himself on the opposite side of her bunk. He releases a long breath through his nostrils and then asks, "Where were you before Braxton?"

Grace is already starting to regret this little game she's introduced, but it *was* her idea. "I lived with my parents until I was sixteen" is all she gives him.

Crew waits for her to continue, and when she doesn't, he says, "And?"

"And what?"

"What happened when you were sixteen?"

There's a thing that always happens when Grace thinks about that night. Akin to someone leafing through a scrapbook, pictures with varying degrees of gore and terror begin to take shape and start shoving themselves to the forefront of her brain. She can hardly even see Crew anymore, because her vision is too clouded by a red so dark it's almost purple, viscous and rolling down the faded wallpaper in fat, slow drips. It coats the rusty blade of the kitchen knife sitting atop a peeling vinyl floor.

"Grace?"

She comes back slowly and then all at once. The word falls out of her mouth before she has a chance to even process what just happened in her head. "What?"

Crew's eyebrows tug together. "Are you okay?"

Grace clears her throat, glancing around the room quickly, assessing where she is. Halcyon. Bunkhouse. Bed. Safe. She nods, then turns back to him. "I left home when I was sixteen. My parents couldn't care for me anymore," she says.

It's not a lie, but it also isn't the whole truth. Besides her uncle, she's never given *anyone* the whole truth.

Seemingly satisfied with this, and possibly—shockingly—emotionally intelligent enough to know not to poke that soft spot any further, Crew nods slowly. In a strategic pivot, he asks, "Why'd you stay at Braxton as long as you did?"

And there it is. The question she knew he'd ask, and the one question she can't answer. She reaches for the palatable, civilized answer that has gotten her through other probing conversations similar to this one. "I wasn't good in school. Dropped out when I was a sophomore. Hal—Braxton's horse trainer at the time—took me under his wing. I was shit at math and English and science, but horses . . . I understood horses. I never looked back after that. I did leave once, but he—" Grace stops herself. She blinks, looking away from Crew, and shakes her head. A quick release of an onslaught of painful memories. "My uncle has power in that part of Texas. I couldn't go anywhere without people knowing exactly who I was, knowing exactly what was coming for them if they showed me any sort of kindness. I ran out of money eventually, so I went back."

Crew listens quietly, intently. When she's finished speaking, his eyes dart back and forth between hers—almost as if they're seeing her for the first time. It's oddly endearing when he responds not with sympathy or apologies, but with "He's a piece of shit."

Grace barks out a laugh. "Understatement of the century."

A half smile forms on Crew's lips. His eyes, sparkling slightly in the warm light of the bunkhouse, carry more of the joy of his smile than his mouth does. "Look," he says, tapping his thumb against his jeans. "I don't think you're a bad seed."

She huffs. "But you still don't trust me."

"It doesn't matter. Not really," he counters, but there's no malice in his voice. He's almost gentle about it, like he's trying to—comfort her? A preposterous, pain-induced assumption. "The fact is, you've done well with the horse. Better than any of these idiots could do. Better than I could do."

The honesty catches her off guard and makes her heart squeeze a little in her chest. She gives him a quick but sincere smile. "Thanks."

"But you're not gonna be able to keep at it if I don't fix that shoulder," he says plainly, all soft comfort gone. "Now, may I?"

She can almost *feel* the pain that's waiting for her if she agrees to this, but he's right. Irritatingly so. If she doesn't regain full mobility, she can't get in the pen with Waylon. The quicker it gets reset, the quicker she can recover and get back to work—so she concedes. "Fine."

Crew nods, then jerks his chin toward the pillow at her side.

Standing up from the bed, he commands, "Lay down. On your stomach."

A flush of heat blooms in her cheeks. "What?"

That familiar, amused look flashes in his eyes again. "The best way to fix a subluxation is to stretch the arm until it pops back into place. It shouldn't take long." He stands before her bunk and folds his arms over his chest. "Unless you're difficult."

They stare each other down. Grace wants to argue, wants to tell him she'd rather let the arm fall off entirely before putting herself in such a vulnerable position, but there's something nagging at her to cooperate. A flare of intuition that is urging her to trust him. She finally gives in, positioning herself slowly, as he instructed, hissing a little when she moves her arm to lie flat against her body.

"Let it hang off the bed."

Grace's eyes flicker up to his. When she doesn't immediately obey, he tilts his head, evening out their eye contact.

"Can't stretch it if it's glued to your side like that."

Once again, she complies, slowly and painfully, until her fingertips graze the wood floor beneath her bed. Though she should've expected it, it's still surprising when Crew lowers himself to his knees and sidles up next to her—so close that she can feel the warmth emanating from his body. She's never given much thought to how he might smell this close up, just sort of assumed it'd be some combination of *outside* mixed with man, but it's something else entirely. A lingering cologne, spicy like a cigar but with a hint of clean, fresh linen. There is definitely some of that outside smell, but it isn't unpleasant or excessive. It mixes perfectly into a strangely entrancing blend that has her almost leaning closer, if only to understand it better.

He breaks her out of this ridiculous train of thought when he reaches for her upper arm, taking it carefully into his hands. They're large enough that they dwarf her bicep entirely, but somehow, they're gentle, too. He starts slow, introducing a small amount of movement, rocking it back and forth. The pain throbs, and though she wants to keep her eyes open to be able to anticipate what he's going to do next—she can't. They squeeze shut, and she tries to fall into the blackness, into some lovely, beautiful other place where her arm doesn't feel like it's about to unhinge itself from her body.

Crew picks up the pace gradually. He works the limb like he's been trained to do this, and it's growing more tolerable by the second—but then he slowly tries to pull her arm upward and Grace lets out a grunt, eyes opening wide as her vision swims.

"Easy," he says, keeping her arm elevated but still. "You're okay. Keep breathing."

She grits her teeth and nods. His thumb caresses soft circles into the skin of her forearm, and she lets out a shaky breath at the sensation.

It gets a hell of a lot worse before it gets better, but eventually, he gets her close to a full range of motion. It doesn't feel *good* or normal, but it's something.

"You should wear a brace for a couple of days," Crew advises, leaning back on his haunches as Grace shifts into a seated position on the bed.

Her throat is muddy from the exertion, so her response is raspy. "A what?"

Crew huffs through his nose. That little half smile he seems so fond of returns to his lips. "A brace. We've got one around here somewhere."

"I can't halter a horse with a brace on."

"You also can't halter a horse if you cause permanent damage to your shoulder. It needs to heal properly first. In a brace."

Grace's stomach sinks. If Crew thinks she's out of commission, there's a chance he could walk out of here and tell Renata they need to bring in someone else. Someone less fragile. She looks away from him, mentally preparing to argue her case—she doesn't *need* a brace, even if it is the smart thing to do. Permanent damage isn't a sure thing. She can be cautious and use her left arm, it'll just take some getting used to.

Crew—continuing to surprise her with his emotional intuition—seems to sense her panic. He cuts into her spiral with a simple, direct "You're not gonna get kicked off the ranch for hurting your shoulder."

She looks at him. There's an earnestness to his words that makes her want to believe him, but that's not what convinces her. It's his eyes, the deep pools of darkness that convey every word he can't bring himself to say.

I'm not going to do that to you, they seem to whisper.

Then he's standing, and, as quickly as he appeared, he's gone.

Grace sleeps like a rock after that, only waking up when the sounds of chirping birds outside her window signal that daylight has come. She rubs the sleep out of her eyes and sits up, the pain in her shoulder reduced to a dull throb. She kicks something at the foot of her bed, and when she narrows her eyes to get a better look, she smiles, realizing what it is.

Brand-new. Unopened.

A brace.

CHAPTER 6

The end of Grace's first week at the ranch comes around quickly, and she learns on Friday morning that everyone's planning on going into town after dinner that evening.

"Second Saturday of every month, we get the morning off," Forty explains, ladling pancake batter onto a butter-soaked griddle. "So, on the second Friday, we do what cowboys do best." He pauses, and Grace glances curiously over at him, pulling her attention from the sausage links sizzling on a cast iron in front of her. Forty looks at her expectantly and then huffs. "Come on, girl. You know the answer. We *drink*."

Because she's still taking it easy with her shoulder, Grace spends the day working alongside June. Together, they tend to the other horses, but mostly—they do barn chores. It's a good thing Grace knows her way around a barn and all the maintenance that goes with it, because June doesn't seem to be interested in offering any instruction. Or having any sort of conversation, for that matter.

Grace takes it in stride. They work in silence, but they work hard, getting as much done as they can before dinner. Around them, the rest of the hands are all in brighter spirits, smiling and joking more than usual. There's a buzz in the air, like the anticipation of getting to break free of the norm for an evening is its own sort of high.

In the last hour, June's scrubbing a particularly stubborn stain right outside of one of the stables, sweat beading at her brow and chest lightly heaving with exertion. After five minutes of observing this, Grace, already set with her own tasks and putting away her cleaning supplies, walks over. Stains around a barn are a dime a dozen—putting that much elbow grease into trying to get rid of one is a battle not worth fighting.

But June seems to have a personal vendetta against this stain.

Grace grabs a bundle of steel wool from the cleaning-supply caddy next to June, then crouches down until she's eye level with her. "Can I help you with this?"

June's eyes flick upward, meeting hers. "I've got it."

Grace nods, tilting her head. "Doesn't really seem like you do."

With a frustrated grunt, June sits back on her haunches, wiping the sweat from her forehead with the crook of her arm. With a quick, impatient once-over of Grace, she says, "You're like a dog with a bone, aren't you?"

"I'm just trying to help," Grace counters. "You're using soap and water—that's not strong enough to penetrate a stain like that—"

"As I said," June cuts her off. "I've got it."

Grace stands, throwing up her hands. "Fine." She tosses the steel wool back into the caddy and wipes her hands on her jeans. "I need to go shower anyway." Looking down at the stains left in the wake of her palms, Grace can't help but regret not bringing—not *owning*—any nicer clothes than these. Even her cleanest outfit is the same old boring jeans and T-shirt, and she doesn't have any shoes besides her Red Wings.

"Oh, don't worry about that," June replies, not looking at her.

Grace's brow pulls together. "What?"

"No one showers. They'd rather maximize the time spent drinking."

Skeptical, Grace plants a hand on her hip. "Really? They just go to the bar smelling like sweat and horse shit?"

A humorless chuckle echoes from where June is hunched over the spot, scrubbing away. "Welcome to Halcyon," is all she says in response.

With this information, Grace decides to take advantage of the free half hour before dinner once she's done what she can to help Forty. Exhaustion has been creeping into her eyes and body for days at this point; a catnap before a fun evening on the town will do her good.

Thirty minutes seems to pass like seconds, and suddenly, the murmuring of voices and clinking of dinnerware wakes her. She sits up in her bunk, slightly disoriented, to see everyone sitting at the table, digging into their meals. Forty looks up and gives her a bright smile when he notices she's awake. "Morning, sunshine. Didn't want to interrupt your nap, but dinner's ready."

Raymond is already tipping a bowl back into his mouth, scraping the final remnants of his meal with a spoon. He sighs once he's gulped it all down at impressive speed, then looks to Grace. "And you better hurry up. The bus leaves in twenty."

"And by *bus*," Mikey cuts in, "he means Forty's truck."

"She knows what I mean," Raymond says.

"Nobody ever knows what you mean," Caleb counters, his voice muffled by the dinner roll stuffed into his mouth.

Grace grabs a bowl, settles down into the seat Raymond vacates, and is about to tuck into her meal when she does a quick survey of the table. A sinking feeling settles in her gut. Everyone looks . . . clean. It occurs to her then that she's picking up on the scent of aftershave and cologne and maybe even a little bit of hair spray. Alec's doing, if the stiff coif of his hair is any indication. They look *polished*, like they've—

"You guys showered?"

Forty looks at her like she's sprouted a second head. "We do that every now and again. Especially when we're going out in public."

"Gotta look presentable for the ladies," Pierce adds.

Bryan barks out a laugh. "What ladies, exactly, P?"

"The pretty ones at the bar," Pierce says.

"You *know* all the ladies at the bar, darlin'," a female voice coos. Grace's eyes flit to June, finding her with her hair done, makeup on, and a nice, new-looking hat fitted snugly atop her curls. Grace's throat tightens at the sight, twin flames of anger and hurt flaring up in her gut. "They're all either married, old enough to be your mama, or they charge by the hour."

"There could be tourists," Pierce grumbles. "People passing through."

No one seems convinced, and the conversation pivots to who is responsible for buying the first round. An argument breaks out between Mikey and Alec, who both are convinced the other lost at pool the previous month and therefore should be liable, but Grace isn't listening. She's too distracted by the anxiety starting to fester in her stomach. She doesn't want to be obvious, doesn't want to give June even a sliver of satisfaction by looking down at what she's wearing.

Soon enough, everyone is buzzing, ready to get on the road. They all vie for spots in front of the full-length mirror, pushing one another around for a moment to look at themselves and fuss with their hair, despite every one of them grabbing a hat on their way out the door.

Grace doesn't have time to shower. That much is painfully obvious. Instead, she does what she can, changing into a pair of jeans that don't reek and tugging on a T-shirt that has less noticeable pit stains than the rest. She doesn't even want to look in the mirror, certain she'll be disappointed and annoyed with herself for being so gullible, but God only knows the state of her hair right now. Sure enough, it's sticking out in just about every direction. By some small miracle, the universe mercifully throws her a bone and she's able to tame it into a somewhat presentable ponytail.

She pulls on her boots, looks around the room, and hopes none of them call attention to the fact that she's going to look like a hitchhiker they picked up along the way. Caleb, the last of them in the bunkhouse, urges her with frantic hands to grab her things and get to the truck. "Let's go, Grace," he says. "Whiskey ain't gonna drink itself."

At sundown, an overcrowded truck full of ranch hands rolls up to Moe Willie's Tavern. A crooning country song blares loud enough to be heard from the parking lot as they tumble out of the cab in droves, hollering like a pack of wolves kept inside for too long. They cascade toward the entrance like a chaotic wave, a freckled man with a rust-colored beard hanging all the way down to his collarbones nodding them in. The walls are bedecked in neon and old Clint Eastwood movie posters. A trio of pool tables sits near the back, illuminated in fluorescence by dusty beer lamps. The group crowds up to the long bar, and the smell of cigarettes, sweat, and tequila invades Grace's nostrils.

There's an energy that comes over the place as they all move inward. Something like a shock wave—like their presence alone is sending reverberations of unease across the entire room. A stocky red-faced man appears behind the bar with a bus tub and heaves a deep sigh upon spotting them.

"Moe, Moe, Moe," Raymond practically croons, leaning his forearms onto the bar. "You don't look very happy to see us."

Moe lets loose another sigh, tossing a rag over his shoulder. He reaches for a bottle of Jack Daniel's with one hand and starts setting up a row of soap-stained shot glasses with the other. "Oughta shut this place down on the second Friday of the month," he grumbles.

"You say that every month, Moe," Caleb retorts from farther down the bar. With an encompassing sweep of his hand, he adds, "And yet."

Moe points at Caleb, eyes narrowing. "The only reason I don't is because y'all drink more in one night than my regulars do in a week. But I swear to God, Caleb, you go anywhere near the pool tables tonight, I'm calling the sheriff. Don't even *look* at them."

The group laughs, playfully shoving Caleb, who has gone red as a strawberry. Grace smiles awkwardly, unaware of the reason behind the ribbing.

Mikey notices and leans down toward her ear to say, "He got a little carried away with a gal on one of the pool tables last month. Thought he was being inconspicuous, but he was also seven shots deep. I'll let your imagination paint the rest of that picture."

Grace grimaces. "Gross."

Mikey chuckles. "Moe caught him with his trousers halfway off and ran him out, but not before nearly breaking a cue over his bare ass."

Caleb, still pink cheeked, waves everyone off, nodding his begrudging agreement that he'll steer clear of the pool area.

Raymond whips out a wallet from his back pocket, slips out a card, then pushes it across the bar toward Moe with a conspiratorial smirk on his lips. He takes two of the shots Moe's already poured and hands them to Mikey and Caleb, who then turn around and pass them farther back. In an impressively efficient maneuver, they all hold their own shot within seconds. Grace can smell it from where it sits in her hand, and it takes a good effort not to actually gag. In the rare event that she does drink, it's usually beer, maybe a strawberry margarita if the occasion calls for it. Hard liquor has never been her first choice. But all the hands are smiling like kids on Christmas morning as they raise their glasses up. Loudly, proudly, and with a little extra twang added to his vowels, Raymond declares, "All right, boys and girls. Let's get ha-ha-ha-*hammered*."

A retro jukebox in the corner of the bar runs through almost every kind of country song imaginable, from Garth to Kenny to Reba and Shania. Slow songs, two-stepping songs, twirling songs, line dances. The ranch hands filter on and off the dance floor between rounds of beers and shots, and by the third hour at Moe Willie's, everyone seems to be perfectly toasted and relaxed.

Grace stands at a high-top table and watches in awe as Pierce expertly twirls a woman around the dance floor to "Friends in Low Places." The woman squeals in delight when he dips her, her dark curls scraping the floor. Mikey and Alec stand across from Grace, arguing about football, or maybe baseball—some kind of sports statistics she doesn't care about. Caleb is standing dutifully on the opposite side of the bar from the pool tables, sipping a neat whiskey and playing darts with Harrison. Raymond—Grace searches the premises for a moment before finding him with a rope in one hand, a shot in the other, and a doe-eyed girl caught in his lasso. With the look she's giving him, Grace can't help but wonder if Raymond's some kind of local rodeo celebrity.

The half-drunk Shiner Bock bottle weeps condensation while Grace idly picks at the label with her thumbnail, half listening to the guys droning on about RBIs and half scanning the rest of the bar. The alcohol has made her cheeks warm and her limbs a little heavy, and she knows it's probably time to switch over to water, or she's guaranteed to feel like absolute shit in the morning.

The song switches to something slower, a classic Randy Travis, and she's stepping away to head to the communal water jug when a man sidles up next to her at the table. Her first impression of him is he's got a *lot* of cologne on—it isn't bad; it might even be nice if it didn't smell like he applied it with a garden hose. He's tall but not hulking, and his smile seems genuine enough. White teeth stark in comparison to his suntanned skin, and a straw hat tucked over a head of neat, short hair. A Coca-Cola cowboy. Her least favorite kind.

"Hey there," he says, tipping his hat to her.

Grace smiles flatly. "Hey."

"Buy you a drink?"

Her eyes dart over to Mikey and Alec, who have both miraculously paused their heated conversation to intently, *not* subtly, size up the visitor. Grace gives them a covert, tight shake of her head. They accept her signal, and she turns back to the stranger. "I'm switching over to water, actually."

"I see." The man nods. He looks older than her—there are little strands of gray in his beard. He's undeterred by her initial denial, and his smile widens. "A dance, then?"

Grace hesitates. She's danced with men before, and it's never been too pleasant of an experience, especially when it leads them into thinking they've got some entitlement to her time afterward. But "Forever and Ever, Amen" is one of her favorite songs, and three shots of Jack Daniel's are amplifying a voice in her head—one that sounds suspiciously like Maryann—telling her, *Live a little, goddammit.*

"All right," Grace agrees. "But I'm leading."

In the three-minute length of the song, Grace learns the man's name is Vince. Vince is divorced, from Albuquerque, and he's passing through town on his way to an auction. He has soft hands, and his boots are shiny enough that she can almost see her own reflection, but he's a decent dancer, though he only lets her lead for a single verse before taking over. Grace stops herself from rolling her eyes as her feet start to shuffle backward instead of forward, and it's right about then that she starts to tune out his unsolicited autobiography. Her eyes drift across the bar over Vince's shoulder, clocking the starch-pressed, too-neat lines of his button-down. She searches the room, looking for nothing in particular, until she reaches the pool tables and does a double take.

Leaning against the corner of one, pool cue in hand, is Crew.

He'd been out on the porch of the main house with Cooper when they left, and he'd waved everyone off, telling them not to do anything stupid. The other hands didn't seem fazed by him not joining, so Grace hadn't thought much of it.

But she's thinking about it now—because here he is, leaning forward on the table with a long arm outstretched over the cue, laser focused on his target. Cooper stands to his left, shaking his head in disbelief as Crew's lips move, maybe calling the pocket, maybe trash-talking his brother, who seems fully unconvinced that he'll make whatever shot he's about to attempt.

Crew is steady and still until he shoots, and then the cracking echo of the cue ball hitting another sounds throughout the bar. He smirks.

Shot made.

Crew stands, circling the table to work out his next move, and Grace continues to stare at him, blatantly ignoring Vince's hand at her waist and his beer breath wafting between them. Crew chews on the inside of his cheek as he considers, and when he's made his way around to an unobstructed new position, Grace can't help but admire the way he looks in the black jeans he's wearing. She's never seen those before, nor has she seen the black pearl-snap shirt that hangs over his gigantic shoulders. The getup is distracting enough—it takes her a few seconds to realize he's also not wearing a hat. It's a rare sight, his hair; there's no way that man puts any real time and effort into it, but it's somehow perfectly styled, and the inky-black hue of it shines under the ancient Budweiser lamp. He takes another step and then goes completely still. Grace's breathing hiccups when his eyes suddenly leave the table and, in the span of a heartbeat, find hers across the bar.

She chides herself for the reaction for a brief moment—the man was nice to her and helped her pop her shoulder back into place. It's no reason to get *breathless*.

But she also doesn't look away.

He stands, pool cue held lazily in front of him, maintaining her stare.

"So, what do you think?"

She swings her head around to look at Vince, who is staring at her with eyes too eager and slightly bloodshot. "What? Sorry, I didn't hear you."

"I was sayin', we could go back to my hotel if you'd like," he repeats, kinking a brow.

"Oh." She looks down to hide her immediate discomfort at the suggestion. Rejecting men always is such a crapshoot, and she's annoyed that he's putting her in a position to have to do it. "That's kind of you, but I don't think so."

His steps slow slightly, losing the beat of the song. Grace looks up to find him . . . surprised.

"Really?" He laughs, but there's an edge to it. "I mean, of course, that's fine, but—"

Grace's eyes flit to Crew again, almost involuntarily. He's taking another shot at a ball. Not looking at her.

"You just seemed like you were interested."

She looks back to Vince. "In going home with you? Because we danced?"

"Well, yeah," he replies, shrugging. They're hardly moving now, standing near the edge of the dance floor. "That's usually how this goes."

Any pretense of politeness goes out the window at his words. Grace's patience for men who can't accept no for an answer has never been in hefty supply. She drops his hand and takes a step back. "Not with me. Sorry."

This time, the emotion that flickers over Vince's face isn't surprise—it's anger. He steps into her space abruptly, the tip of his nose nearly touching her own. Grace's hands fly up to his chest, pushing backward.

"So, you're the teasing type, then," he says menacingly, reaching for her hips. His pride is hurt, and he's clearly not used to that.

She grits her teeth and bites out, "Don't touch me."

The command only spurs him on, and there's a hand at her bicep now, squeezing roughly. His eyes are wild as he says, "I've never been a fan of being teased. Maybe we should go out to my truck and settle this."

"How about you *back the fuck off?*" a voice booms. It cuts through everything—the music, the murmur of the patrons, the thudding of Grace's heart. Somehow, Crew has found his way across the bar and is now standing between her and Vince. How he got here as quickly as he did is one of nature's mysteries—his impossibly long legs lending to quicker strides, maybe.

"Who's this?" Vince barks, his chest starting to puff out. The effort to look more masculine is comical and futile.

Crew isn't just taller—he *towers* over Vince, dwarfing him into more of a wiry schoolboy than a man.

"This is—" Grace stops short. Her eyes dance back and forth

over Crew's taut features, staring at him as he stares Vince down like a predator in wait. There's a subtle, guarded fury that vibrates off him, something that's only visible if one knows where to look: his hands, fingers flexing and unflexing; his jaw, unsettled and tense.

"It's none of your fucking business who I am," Crew spits back, taking a sidestep to put his body even farther between Vince and her, until Grace can see only the top of Vince's hat over Crew's shoulder. He crowds into Vince's space, and she wonders if it stings, the way the shorter man's head has to angle upward to continue looking Crew in the eye.

"Walk away." Crew seethes.

A long moment passes with neither man saying another word. Crew is still as a statue, but Grace knows instinctively that he's a coil ready to spring at any second. Self-preservation seems to finally rear its head in Vince's case, because after a beat, he throws up his hands in surrender and starts to back away from them.

When he's nearly halfway across the bar, Crew turns around to face her. Grace lets out a long breath as Vince sits down next to his friends, pointedly not looking back at either of them. She glances up to Crew and tilts her head appraisingly. The tension is slowly starting to seep from his body, noticeable in the way his jaw is finally still, and the line of his shoulders is less rigid.

When he notices her staring, he smirks. "What?"

"Did you enjoy that?"

Crew stares at her, eyes narrowing, while the jukebox transitions into "Tennessee Whiskey." They don't join the other patrons pairing up to dance. They stay as they are, a good three feet between them, assessing each other.

From the corner of her eye, Grace notices a head of blond hair moving clumsily across the dance floor. She looks over to see June and Cooper teetering together, Cooper clearly not on the same level as June. She leads him patiently, her mouth moving in what looks like encouragement, if Cooper's bashful smile is any indication.

Crew speaks over the music, following her line of sight to see his brother being pushed around the dance floor. "Guy's not a local," Crew says, eyes still on June and Cooper. "He doesn't know how things work around here. Had to be done."

With a purse of her lips, Grace asks, "And how do things work?"

Crew's eyes pull slowly back to hers. "We come in here once a month and blow off steam. Locals know to steer clear—they know better than to try to go toe-to-toe with us. Drinking or otherwise."

Grace nods, humming in response to his statement. Folding her arms over her chest, she coos, "Big, bad cowboys of Halcyon, scaring everyone out of the bar."

Crew huffs. "Only if they deserve it."

"As long as you weren't trying to be some white knight saving the damsel in distress," she counters, folding her arms over her chest.

The returning laugh he gives her is low, originating deep in his belly. His Adam's apple bobs with the movement, and it occurs to her now just how prominent it is, even amid the wide expanse of his pale, freckled neck. "You don't strike me as the damsel type."

Grace sighs. She's been categorized as a couple of different *types* already this evening, and frankly, it's a little annoying. "What is it with men? Y'all spend ten minutes with a woman and, suddenly, you know what *type* she is."

Crew's brows lift, amusement dancing in his dark eyes. "I've spent more than ten minutes with you. I think I've got a pretty good idea."

Grace scoffs. "Let's hear it, then."

He clears his throat, puts a hand on his hip, and says, "You're—"

She doesn't get to hear what he's come up with—because just before the words leave his lips, a fist collides with his cheek.

Grace's eyes go wide as Crew doubles over and skids backward a few steps. She finds Vince standing before her with his equally drunk-looking friends at his back. "What the fuck?" Grace shouts over the music, and when Crew stands back to his full height and reveals a cut beneath his right eye, her vision goes redder than the blood trickling down his cheek. It's almost like she's stepped completely out of her body, because the rage that fills her at the sheer *audacity* of this motherfucker—

Grace punches him right back.

It hurts. It hurts like few other things in her life have ever hurt. If her knuckles weren't knobby and her hands weren't covered in scar tissue, she might've broken something for how hard her fist collided with his face. It sends him fumbling backward, falling directly onto his ass. Whether by the force of her fist or the shock, she couldn't say, but her teeth are bared as she looks at the rest of his pals, fists curled at her sides, ready to take them all.

Little does she know, she won't need to.

Because the rest of the hands have caught wind of what's happening, and now, she has the entire bunkhouse of Halcyon Ranch at her back.

By the end of it, Grace has a split lip and possibly a fractured rib, but despite the throbbing ache in her side and on her face, she is downright gleeful. Smiling with bloody teeth, she surveys the rest of the group, all in various states of injured and inebriated. It had stopped being a fair fight soon after it started, especially once Crew was back in commission and started body-slamming dudes onto the dance floor. The guys all seemed to have their own specialty—Alec and Caleb with spectacular backhands, Mikey and his strong left hook, June's supernatural sense of how hard to knee a man in the balls to bring him down and *keep* him down. Even Forty had been in the mix of things, yanking up men half his age by their collars and tossing them around like rag dolls. The sound of bottles breaking and tables smashing into pieces had drowned out the jukebox, and only when Moe's desperate scream came over a megaphone, telling them he'd already called the sheriff, did they finally come up for air.

The out-of-towners, though barely walking, had escaped with their tails between their legs well before the red and blue lights started to flash through the bar's tinted windows. The Halcyon group had let them go—the beating they'd put on the four of them was brutal enough. But, as Caleb had so eloquently put it, they had fucked around and found out.

An older man—a stereotypical small-town sheriff, handlebar mustache and all—now stands before them as they half-heartedly attempt to clean themselves up outside of the bar. He's mostly addressing Crew as he scolds, a knobby-knuckled finger pointed in his direction. "You oughta know better by now, young man," he gripes, wagging his finger toward Crew's chest.

Crew's hands are up, and he nods placatingly with a sincere, apologetic look in his eyes. A far cry from what she'd seen flashing in them earlier, all feral and black with rage. "I know. I know. I'm sorry, Jim," he says. "We'll pay for the damages. You know we're good for it."

Out of nowhere, a familiar female voice cuts in. "You mean your mama is good for it," Renata Caldwell spits as she approaches the bar with such speed and intensity that fire may as well be licking the heels of her boots. Where Grace has only ever heard Renata's voice be soft, lilting, and melodic, it now sounds tight, impatient. Like she's gearing up to tear each of them a new asshole.

Any lingering conversation, any remnants of laughter over the whole ordeal completely cease as she steps up to them all, looking like the exhausted, pissed-off mother of this gaggle of unruly idiots. She shares a look with the sheriff, who seems to understand his place in the hierarchy of this situation and tips his hat before walking toward his Crown Vic. Renata slowly turns back to the group and folds her arms over her chest. She looks chic as ever despite the irritation that roils off her in dense waves. Black leather jacket, black felt hat, jeans that probably cost more money than Grace has made in her lifetime. The picture of class and sophistication, she could drop-kick them all into the middle of next week and would still look like she just walked out of a magazine.

"Here's the deal, gentlemen," she says, then gives a pointed stare to June and Grace. "And ladies." They all pick up their chins at the statement, bracing themselves. "I don't care what the fight was about. I don't care who threw the first punch."

Grace tries not to sink in on herself, but the guilt is heavy. Even if she didn't *start* it, she sure as hell egged it on, and the weight of it is so heavy that she has to look away from Renata—eyes drifting until they find Crew, standing with his hands in his pockets. Looking at her. There's a softness to his expression, despite the shitstorm his mother is about to rain down on them. He holds her gaze for a moment, perhaps picking up on her fear, her sense of responsibility for starting the brawl. He shakes his head tightly, quickly, as if to say, *This is not your fault.*

She hates how much better it makes her feel, that one look from him.

"What I do care about is the fact that when you leave my ranch, you're representing me and my family." Her head swivels to look directly at her son. Crew's eyes dart away from Grace's and land back on his mother. He simply nods, knowing—likely from many a talking-to just like this—it's better to just keep his mouth shut. Renata's hard eyes drag slowly back to the group.

"Y'all about gave Moe a heart attack last month with your antics," Renata continues, this time pointing at Caleb. "And now"—she shrugs, shaking her head—"you've trashed his bar. His livelihood."

A long, tense beat of silence passes. No one looks away from her, but no one dares to say anything to the contrary. "I'm docking each of your pay a hundred dollars this month to pay for the damages. Anyone who has a problem with that can find themselves a new job."

A hundred dollars off a ranch hand's salary isn't small potatoes, but no one objects. No one says a damn word. Renata waits for it, but nothing comes. Eventually, she turns on her heel and walks over to Crew. The two share a conversation, too quiet for anyone else to hear, but Grace watches as his face shifts from guilt to resignation to apology in the span of a few seconds. His mother shakes her head, then walks away. About ten steps into the parking lot she stops, turns, and shouts, "What the hell are y'all waiting for? Party's over. Let's go."

Like an obedient herd of cattle, they all stand, grunting with the effort. About half follow Renata to her truck, chins down and hands stuffed in their pockets, and the other half, including Grace, follow Forty's slow steps over the gravel toward his. A few paces behind her, Grace finds Crew lingering, watching them all scatter. She slows her steps, letting him catch up.

The curiosity—and the whiskey—gets the better of her as she asks, "What'd she say to you?"

Crew swallows, his eyes casting downward. "Nothing I haven't heard a thousand times before."

Truck doors slam shut. Engines roar to life. "You do this often?"

He smiles crookedly, his mouth curving upward toward where a bruise over his eye is starting to bloom. "Not so much in my old age. When I was younger, though."

A picture pops into her head at that—a sepia-toned memory that doesn't belong to her, of a boy with a mop of black hair and a split lip, toeing up to men twice his size and smiling through bloody teeth.

They're halfway to the trucks when Grace stops, turning to face him. "Thank you, by the way," she says. Alcohol, it appears, makes her sentimental.

Crew's eyebrows shoot up. "For what?"

"For earlier." She shrugs. "For stepping in."

Another one of those low, rumbling laughs sounds from his chest. It barely moves him, but it rocks her where she stands. "Maybe I should be thanking you."

Grace smiles, or attempts to, anyway, before the cut in her lip forces her face back into something neutral. Crew's eyes fall to her mouth, the humor in his expression fading slightly.

"You all right?" he asks, giving her a quick once-over before nodding toward her lip. "Apart from that, I mean."

She nods. "Got kicked in the ribs, but I don't think anything's broken. Nothing a good night's sleep and some Advil won't cure."

"Shoulder's all good?"

She'd left the brace at the bunkhouse, but, miraculously, no additional harm had come to her shoulder. Even when she'd fallen on the ground after being shoved unintentionally by the brawling mob, she'd mercifully landed on the opposite side. "All good," she replies, rotating it just a little. "Thanks."

Crew nods, satisfied.

Stumbling on her words only slightly, she asks, "Are you—all right?"

The smile she gets in return is warm, like standing in front of a space heater in the dead of winter. "I'm all right," he says softly.

A horn honks. Someone yells for her to hurry up, but she doesn't look away, and neither does he. A few seconds, minutes, maybe hours pass as they stand there, staring at each other. Eyes tracing wounds, old and new, like the scar on the left side of his jaw. The indentation above his right eyebrow. She wonders what he sees when he looks at her. Wonders if he's making up his own stories to go with each one of hers.

Crew lets out a breath through his nostrils, only tearing his gaze from hers when the honk sounds again. He shakes his head in exasperation at whoever it is that's beckoning her. He nods toward the truck and says, "Go on."

She walks away, and only when she gets all the way to the truck does she look back to find him still standing in the same spot. Watching her go.

CHAPTER 7

Everyone's a little worse for wear by the time ten rolls around the next morning. A bottle of Tylenol is passed around at lunch, which consists of the greasiest, cheesiest smashburgers Grace has ever seen, alongside crispy sweet potato fries, pickle spears, and heaps of ketchup. It coats her stomach like something out of a dream, allowing her to keep the pill in her system and, eventually, feel less like she rammed her head into a concrete wall.

Waylon spares no sympathy for her. In fact, it's almost as if he *knows* she's hungover and has chosen to shame her for it. He side-eyes her as she familiarizes him with the saddle they'll be using, letting him get used to the way it feels against his body, the way it smells. Though he does all she asks, it's with an air of judgment. When he grunts at her toward the end of the session because she's repeated the same movement with the saddle nearly twenty times, Grace rolls her eyes. "I don't want to hear it," she grumbles, walking back into the barn to hang up the saddle on its hook. "I'm allowed to have an off day." Waylon blows out an unsympathetic huff through his nose.

Toward sundown, all the ranch hands are gathered in one of the hangars, some shooting the shit while others work on servicing one of the compact tractors. Grace joins them once she's gotten Waylon situated and smiles gratefully at Raymond when he hands her a cold beer upon walking up. She looks around, curiously surveying the state of everyone—all having seemed to sweat out their hangovers for the most part, at least enough that they're already steadily working through a case of Bud Light. One of the first people she notices is Cooper, who is standing near the tractor in question with June and Forty, engaged in a conversation that has his brow furrowed in concentration. He nods intently as they both take turns speaking at him, both with adamant hand gestures. Grace watches the interaction with a slight fascination, trying to decipher what they could possibly be talking about. Caleb ambles up next to her and clinks his beer against hers. He follows her line of sight and nods knowingly.

"It's a bad idea, if you ask me," he says cryptically.

Grace glances over at him. "What is?"

"Trying to train that city boy how to be a ranch hand," he says, pointing his beer in Cooper's direction.

"Is that what they're talking about?"

Caleb nods. "They want him to *shadow* us. Learn the ways of the ranch."

Interesting. Grace didn't realize that was something a Caldwell would need to learn. Seems like it'd be a given considering where he grew up. "Does he not spend a lot of time here?"

Tossing back a couple of glugs of beer, Caleb shakes his head. "Not since he left for college some years back. Word is he flunked out of business school."

Grace takes a swig of beer; it's crisp and tastes like yeast-flavored water, but she relishes in the coldness rushing down her throat. "And now he wants to live here and, what, work on the ranch?"

"Probably just some performative bullshit," Caleb says, shrugging. "The Caldwells are a funny bunch, Grace. The kids all tend to march to their own, very unique drums."

Less concerned about prying Caleb for information, Grace asks a question she's been wondering about since she got to Halcyon. "There's a girl, right? I saw a picture in the main house, but no one ever talks about her."

Caleb nods. "Caia. They're all still bitter that she moved across the country and stayed there."

Imagining any rifts in a family as idyllic as the Caldwells is strange, almost unfathomable. "Do they speak to her?"

He shrugs. "She comes around for holidays sometimes, but it's never for long. Would rather spend her days in board meetings, I guess."

Grace tucks that information away, and then—she can't help it—the curiosity spikes and tumbles out of her mouth without a second thought. "And Crew?" He's absent from the current activity, probably off somewhere barking orders at someone. "You all seem to respect him."

Caleb nods. "It's different with Crew."

"Why?"

"He didn't run off to college in the city to find himself. He went to war. Twice. And now he's taking care of his parents' place. He isn't cruel, or careless, or stupid like too many people in our world tend to be. He's a commander. Of course we respect him."

She'd been rocking back and forth on her heels absently, but at his words, she goes still. "What?" she asks dumbly.

Caleb clocks her surprise, then looks back over to Cooper, who is now hunched over the hood of the tractor next to Forty. He looks like he's studying every part, every coil, every function. Forty points, then speaks, then points, then speaks.

Caleb's voice is a little gruffer when he says, without looking at her, "He did two tours in Afghanistan."

Grace's mouth gapes slightly, lips snapping shut only when she realizes she's staring at him, dumbfounded. "Oh. I didn't know that."

"Not surprised," he continues, seeming to sense her shock. "He doesn't talk about it much. And I wouldn't ask, if I were you."

Grace nods, waving it off. "Wasn't planning on it."

Cooper reaches under the hood to touch something, only to jump backward, flapping his hand and grimacing. Forty shakes his head, exasperated.

Caleb snickers. "Told you," he says, then walks away to join the others.

Grace watches them for a beat longer, surveying the way Cooper looks wholly unaccustomed to the more gritty parts of ranch life. Like when he grimaces as he wipes grease onto his jeans, leaving streaks of black and gray. He looks up from the damage with nothing short of horror in his expression, and Forty throws his head back and howls with laughter.

Though his inexperience—or rustiness, maybe—leads him to stick out like a sore thumb among the other hands, Cooper does seem to put his best effort toward catching on to everything. He sleeps in the bunkhouse and rises with everyone before the sun, which earns him a modicum of respect right off the bat. The beds, though significantly plusher than the one Grace slept on at Braxton, probably feel like plywood compared to his bed in the main house, but he doesn't complain. He does the dishes after breakfast and even cleans out the gunky coffeepot—a task that was horrendously overdue.

Crew snaps orders at him in the same manner he does everyone else, unconcerned that he's speaking to his little brother. In fact, his eyes seem to sparkle when he announces Cooper's tasks for the day—Crew looks almost *gleeful* to send him to pull out a mile-long patch of stubborn weeds with Caleb and Mikey. When they trudge into the bunkhouse for dinner that evening, Cooper looks like he's ready to pass out. Any semblance of neatness he'd come into this journey with is long gone; his clothes are almost as haggard as his hair, and the five-o'clock shadow on his cheeks is quickly ticking toward midnight. He gets a few slaps on the shoulder—a gesture of solidarity from the other, equally unkempt ranch hands. Grace is standing at the stove, warming up leftover chili from the night before in a stockpot, when he ambles up to the sink to wash his hands. "Smells great," he says over his shoulder, eyeing the steam that emanates from the pot. "I'm starving."

Grace chuckles. "I bet. Y'all get a lot done today?"

Cooper flicks the excess water off his hands before reaching for a dish towel. He leans against the counter and shakes his head. "It feels like the weeds are growing faster than we can pull them out of the ground."

Knowing all too well how insurmountable that specific task can be, Grace gives him a conspiratorial look. "That's the point, you know."

Folding his arms over his chest, Cooper asks, "What?"

She shrugs, looking back to her task. "At my old place, weeding used to be at the bottom of the barrel for duties. Reserved for anyone who managed to piss off the foreman." The chili begins to bubble, morsels of onion and tomato rolling to the surface alongside the ground beef and pork. She gives it a good stir and then turns around to face Cooper, who still looks confused by her statement.

She smiles and says, "Crew's fucking with you."

Cooper's mouth hangs a little loosely, but then he sighs and throws his head back. "Of course he is." His jaw tenses, and he looks as though he's scheming on the best way to enact his revenge on his older brother when Caleb and Mikey walk into the kitchen, their stench immediately masking the warmth and richness of the simmering chili. Cooper glances at them, then straightens up. "So, what'd you two do?"

Mikey, gulping down water from a metal canteen, kinks a brow. He gasps for breath once he's sated, and wipes his mouth before saying, "What do you mean?"

"To get put on weeding," Cooper says. He jerks his chin toward Caleb and says, "Apparently y'all did something to piss off my brother and that's why we're out there pulling weeds that will grow back ten times taller by the morning."

"Ah." Caleb nods. "Yeah. We, uh . . ." He trails off, like he's trying to decide if he should even broach the topic. Grace tilts her head, waiting for him to fess up.

"Well, you see," Mikey cuts in, setting his canteen on the counter so he can use both of his hands. "It went like this—"

"They took the compact tractor on a joyride last weekend and blew out the clutch," Grace supplies, knowing that if he had his way, Mikey would tell the story as though it were some epic saga full of adventure and intrigue.

"Wait," Cooper says, looking between the three of them. "*That's* why the tractor is out of commission? That's why I have first-degree burns on my fingertips?"

"Well, no," Caleb argues. "You have first-degree burns on your fingertips because you thought poking at an engine block would get you a gold star with Forty."

Grace looks at Cooper, who is shaking his head slowly. She laughs at the horrid awe on his face and says, "Get it now?"

Cooper honks out a humorless laugh. "I get it," he replies, "I get that my brother is a vindictive piece of work."

"He ain't all bad," Caleb says, yet again coming to Crew's defense. Grace wonders if he even realizes he's doing it, or if it's an instinct born out of years spent working by Crew's side. "Look at it this way: At least you ain't hauling hay in this heat."

"We have a hay baler," Cooper counters. "Why would anyone be hauling hay?"

Mikey and Caleb share a look, then a laugh. There are probably a dozen stories between them about the ultimate ranch punishment—hauling hay by hand during a Texas summer when a perfectly functional hay baler sits thirty feet away in a hangar. That kind of job is reserved for *real* infractions, because it's the kind of job that results in only one of two things: The ranch hand in question either sucks it up and sticks it out, knowing they'll never err so badly again, or they pack their bags and find another place to work.

"C'mon, city boy," Mikey says, wrapping an arm around Cooper's shoulders and walking them out of the kitchen. "There's an ice-cold beer in that cooler with your name on it."

The beer offered to Cooper turns out to be the first of many. Grace partakes, too, nursing her Budweiser and observing the poker setup sprawled across the dining room table. Alec has taken great care to arrange it. His bunk is the messiest of everyone's—rumpled clothes spilling out of every nook and cranny—but his poker set is immaculate. He begins to shuffle the cards, and his tan, sun-leathered hands are a stark contrast to the pristine white of the reverse side. Grace watches them flow through his fingers fluidly, like a waterfall of paper. She zones out slightly while watching, the long day attempting to saddle an obstinate horse catching up with her. Only when the bunkhouse door swings open does she return to herself, glancing over to see who's barged in so dramatically.

It's Pierce—he's holding an open magazine tightly against his chest and his eyes are sparkling with mischief. He's breathing heavily, like he ran here, his hair windswept and wild. "Y'all ain't gonna believe this," he says, approaching the table.

"You're late," Alec barks, still shuffling. "Buy-in is ten."

Pierce waves Alec off. "Shut up and listen to me. Remember how we heard that Easton was doing some modeling out in California?"

"What of it?" Forty asks from his place at the head of the table. His feet are propped up, ankles stacked on top of each other as he counts out single dollar bills.

"Well," Pierce says, his lips bursting into a grin. "Turns out, it was true."

He turns the magazine around, holding it wide for everyone to see.

It's quite a picture. A tanned, smiling man with pearly white teeth sits on a beautiful horse, wearing nothing but a cowboy hat and a pair of very tight-fitting black briefs. His body is ripped, like *never eats carbs and spends four hours in the gym every day* kind of ripped. He has an eight-pack *and* biceps that are nearly as big as Grace's head. She clocks the *Come and get it* look in the man's sparkling blue eyes. How a photograph managed to capture such a clear message, she isn't sure.

"Holy shittin' Christmas," Raymond hollers, standing up immediately to rip the magazine out of Pierce's hands. "How is this an ad for cologne? What about a shirtless idiot riding a *horse* in the middle of the day says, *Yeah, I smell great*?"

The others gather around Raymond, trading their own huffs of bafflement. "What a fucking tool," Mikey grumbles.

"You mock," Bryan counters, "but I bet he got at least 10K for that."

"Take my money, but never take my dignity," Mikey replies, shaking his head.

"I'm sorry," June cuts in. She raises her brows at Mikey and asks, "Didn't you sing '. . . Baby One More Time' at karaoke last month?"

Mikey looks up from the ad and stares at her. "If you're implying that paying tribute to Britney Spears is not a dignified act, I'd have to disrespectfully disagree."

Cooper, who just gulped down the dregs of his third helping of chili, finally joins in the fun. "What's everyone freaking out about?" He walks over to the group, standing on his tiptoes to see over their shoulders and get a glimpse. The second his eyes land on the magazine, the humor and ease of his expression dampens. Ceases, really. He says nothing, simply sinks back onto his heels and walks away from the cluster. No one seems to notice the shift except Grace—she follows him with her eyes as he walks over to an empty chair two seats down from her and slumps into it, looking a bit like he could punch a wall if given the opportunity.

"You good?" she asks, quietly enough that only he can hear.

His gaze flits to hers quickly, and his expression clears a little. With a deep breath in through his nose, he nods. "Yeah," is all he offers in response.

Grace doesn't ask him any further questions, sensing that he isn't interested in elaborating. But, clearly, this *Easton* person is someone Cooper knows. Knows, and—if the look on his face is any indication—does not particularly like.

The evening takes a turn after that. Beer is swapped out for Jim Beam right around the time Bryan is up at the poker table, cleaning out everyone's wallets with a cheeky smirk on his whiskey-flushed face. Mikey is in the hole, trying and failing to use his best puppy dog eyes to persuade Forty to spot him ten bucks. Alec is dealing cards with a cigarette hanging from the corner of his mouth, plumes of smoke wafting toward the screen door and open windows near the kitchen. Cooper is quiet and contemplative until suddenly, he isn't, and then everyone learns very quickly that he's a bit of an obnoxious drunk. Which means he fits in perfectly with the rest of the hands, especially when it comes to an increasing lack of inhibitions once shots start getting poured. Grace checks out right around then, deciding to wait out her turn in the shower rotation in her bunk with her trusty corded earphones and Faith Hill's greatest hits. She's supposed to be after June, who's after Caleb, who's after Pierce, who is currently singing "Hound Dog" in the shower and taking his sweet time. Between the three of them, she might be waiting awhile.

Though Grace probably should've guessed she would fall asleep in the meantime, she certainly doesn't expect a *mouth hanging open, a puddle of drool on her pillow* kind of knockout. A rustling in the kitchen is what yanks her out of that depthless slumber, and her eyes shoot open to see Mikey crouched in front of the cabinet under the kitchen sink, rummaging through various cleaning products. He seems dissatisfied with the Clorox and the Pine-Sol, tossing them over his shoulder quickly, haphazardly. Still shit-faced, if the way he is slightly teetering from side to side is any indication. Grace sits up slowly as a dull, throbbing ache rises in her shoulder. She winces, reaching across herself to rub it, then rotates it slowly against her side. It feels better every day, but it still isn't fully mobile, and it has a tendency to ache after a hard sleep. Once she's up, it dawns on her just how quiet the rest of the bunkhouse is. Too quiet—there's hardly any snoring. She likes all the hands—she really does—but they snore like trains passing over gravel. So much so that she's been woken up by the symphony of snoring multiple times in her short tenure at Halcyon, even had to toss a balled-up pair of socks at Forty's head one night when he was going on so loudly she could hear him *over* her music.

It's too dark to confirm who is missing from their bunk, except the obvious, who is still digging through the cabinet with fervor. Grace pads over to him, still in her work clothes and socks, and whispers when she approaches so she doesn't startle him too badly. "What're you looking for in there?"

He jumps, nonetheless. "Jesus *fucking* Christ on a banana," he shouts, putting a hand to his heart and closing his eyes as he whirls around to face her.

Grace holds her hands up. "It's just me. Sorry."

"Am I being noisy?" he asks in a sort of yell-whisper. A comical attempt at keeping his voice down. "I didn't want to wake you up."

She shakes her head. "It's fine. What's going on?"

"We've got a bit of a situation," he says, voice incrementally raising to a normal volume.

Grace straightens, folding her arms over her chest, and waits for him to elaborate.

He looks guilty, his shoulders starting to slump. "I—uh—I don't know if I can tell you. I was given strict instructions not to wake you or Forty up."

Her cheeks begin to heat. Something about this—the guilt in his face, the secretiveness—an ominous feeling spreads in Grace's gut. "Why?"

Mikey's eyes drift back to the cabinet, and instead of answering, he pulls out a basket of sponges and rags, his face lighting up as he sets it aside. "Thank God." He reaches in again, dragging a red plastic box marked with a cross on top.

Grace's nostrils flare. "Is someone hurt?"

He blinks, then side-eyes her. "Maybe?"

"Mikey," she says firmly, taking a step toward him. "Tell me what's going on."

Mikey winces, then his eyes fall slowly shut, as if all of the will to keep his word to the guys is gone in one single, surrendering breath. "Please don't be pissed."

"Why . . ." Grace closes her eyes, frustrated. "Would I be pissed?"

The next words come out in a jumble, barely discernible. Barely even English. "WedaredCoopertotrytorideWaylonandhebuckedhimoffandwethinkhebrokehisankle."

It takes a moment for the jumbled statement to sink in, but it does, and Grace's eyes are open again, widening with rage. "You did *what*?"

"I said don't be pissed!"

"I don't care what you said! You *dared* someone to ride a wild horse? Are you out of your fucking mind?"

For a moment, he just stares up at her like a chastised child. The look on his face *almost* makes her feel guilty for blowing up, but the feeling is quickly replaced by frustration and shock and pure anger. Reckless. They are all reckless idiots. Dangerous, reckless idiots.

"It was Pierce," Mikey says, holding up his hands in supplication. "I didn't say shit."

"Did you try to stop him?" Grace bites out.

The grimace on Mikey's face is dramatic, the kind of overexpression only a drunk person can manage. "I'm sorry, Grace," he says in a pitch higher than his normal voice.

Grace rolls her eyes, then turns on her heel to march toward the front door to grab her boots. She tugs them on with an exasperated grunt and then asks, "Where are they?"

Mikey stands, first aid kit tucked into his side. "Um—"

"And what do you think *that* is going to do for a broken ankle?" she asks, pointing at the kit. "Grab some duct tape from the junk drawer and find something hard, like—" She looks around, eyes dancing over the dark room. She notices only now, from this new vantage point, that every single bed is empty.

Pointedly ignoring the fact that they purposefully left her out of this stunt so they could do something stupid with *her* horse, Grace continues to search until she lands on the makeshift piece of wood that holds all of their grungy work hats. "That." She points at it. "Get that off the wall—take the hats off and the nails out."

Mikey obeys quickly, throwing open the junk drawer and stuffing the tape into his pocket before rushing over to the hat rack and pulling it off the wall. The nails come out easily, and then they are out the door, speed-walking toward the barn. Grace trails behind him by a half step, and she takes the quarter-mile journey to center herself. There's no point in getting pissed off and screaming at everyone right now—right now, she just needs to make sure Cooper and Waylon are okay.

A shadow moves within the walls of the enclosure, and Grace can tell just from the silhouette that Waylon and Duke are both distressed, pacing back and forth and blowing out loud, impatient breaths through their mouths. Scolding the ranch hands in their own way, just as she plans to do.

The group is huddled near the barn's entrance; only the dim, warm light bulb above the saddle wall illuminates their shapes in the moonless night. There's an antsy murmuring coming from where they sit, but Cooper's groaning is loud enough that she can't make out what anyone else may be saying. She walks up with purposeful steps, Mikey at her side. He stares down at his boots, embarrassed for snitching. She'll tell him later that it was the right thing to do. Much later. For now, she steps into the group with an exacting stare that demands eye contact and acknowledgment, that says a thousand words without uttering a single one. Everyone is looking at her, all growing more sheepish by the second. Because even though they're drunk and stupid, they *know* better than this. Caleb opens his mouth to speak, but Grace holds up a hand, and he promptly shuts it. She takes a deep, calming breath in through her nostrils and asks, "Did he hit his head?"

"No," Caleb says solemnly. "Just landed wrong when he jumped off. Think the ankle is sprained. Not broken."

"Well, thank God for small mercies," Grace spits, shaking her head. She crouches down until she's eye level with Cooper, who is flat on his back with his knee tucked into his chest, writhing in pain. His ankle, from what she can tell in the dark, looks intact. It'll probably swell up to the size of a softball by the morning, but there's no bone or floppiness to worry about.

Cooper lifts up his head to see who has approached, and when he spots her, he groans, "Grace." He lets his head fall back again, defeated. "I think your horse hates me."

She stands, runs a hand through her sleep-tangled hair, and sighs. "He doesn't hate you. He doesn't know you, and he sure as hell doesn't know what to do with a rider. I haven't even saddle-broken him yet," she bites out, throwing her hands up. "And he's not *my* horse."

The words are slurred when he replies, "Of course he is. He only listens to you. Plus, we all like you. You should stick around."

Grace lets the statement roll off her back—she doesn't have room in her brain to consider how kind it is. She takes yet another centering breath and looks up and around the circle. With all the quiet firmness she can muster, she says, "There is no amount of whiskey in the world that excuses this kind of recklessness. He could've died. Or been paralyzed. I'm—" She gulps down a rough swallow, cutting herself off before she tailspins into a lecture. "Let's just get this ankle splinted. Mikey, come on." She waves him over, and he practically jumps forward, plywood and tape in hand.

Cooper's pained groaning grows louder as Mikey tapes his ankle to the board, wrapping around and around until it's fully secure and unable to move even a centimeter. He leans forward to rip the tape with his teeth, then stands and surveys his work. He looks to Grace for approval, and she nods.

"All right," she says, "are any of you sober enough to walk him back to the bunkhouse?"

A cacophony of affirmatives, all in varying coherence, erupts from the group. She's about to tell Caleb that she'll take Cooper's left arm if he takes his right, because he seems to be the only one who can even stand for more than five seconds without wobbling. But just as she opens her mouth, someone else's voice cuts in.

Louder, firmer, and scarier than she could ever be.

"What the hell is going on?"

Her heart sinks in her chest at the sound, because it's a distinctive voice. There's no question whom it belongs to. The irritation in it is thick enough to have them all, even Grace, standing up a little straighter. Everyone except for Cooper, who either doesn't realize or doesn't care that his brother is here now, surveying them all with fury tightening every line of his face. Even in the dark, his anger is bright and unmistakable. His dog, Boone, is at his side, judging all of them with similar levels of disdain.

Crew stands stock-still beside Grace as he looks around the circle, waiting for someone to speak up. When no one does, and when his ire seems to be almost bubbling up from beneath his skin, Grace sighs and turns her body to face him head-on. "Cooper here got himself a real ranch hazing experience," she says, pointedly not looking at anyone besides Crew. "Lost a round of poker and had to do a lap around the barn while singing 'Sweet Caroline.'" She looks back to Cooper, who is staring at her with a mix of disbelief and gratitude. He opens his mouth to speak—refute, maybe—but Grace shakes her head tightly. "Clearly, he was too wasted to see where he was going and tripped on something. Sprained his ankle."

Crew, who has been staring solely at his brother, finally pulls his gaze away and looks at Grace. She can tell he isn't fully convinced, especially by the way his jaw tenses when Waylon lets out another annoyed huff from the enclosure. Crew holds her eyes for longer than feels appropriate, as though he's challenging her, waiting for her to fess up. When she doesn't, his eyes narrow. "That right?"

Grace shrugs. "Yep. Some pain meds and ice and he'll be good as new."

"Hm." Crew nods, then glances back to Cooper. "You tripped?"

"You heard the woman," Cooper grumbles, hoisting himself with his hands until he's sitting up. His hair is in complete disarray, his expression slightly dazed.

Crew's jaw flexes again as he silently offers Cooper an opportunity to tell the truth. When his little brother does not take him up on it, Crew sighs. His face full of impatience and sternness, he looks at Grace again, and the words he speaks next are curt, brooking no argument. "Let's go."

Grace's eyebrows pull together. She looks from Crew to Cooper, who seems equally confused. Back in Crew's direction, she blurts, "What?"

"We're taking him to my house," he replies, then, pointedly not looking at Cooper, adds, "Where I can keep an eye on him."

From the corner of her eye, Grace sees Cooper's chin dip toward his chest.

Grace is on the verge of asking the most appropriate question—*Why me?*—when Crew decides he doesn't care to hear her response and simply dips down to lift his brother up by his armpits. Cooper grunts and hisses at the lack of gentleness, hopping on one foot once he's completely upright. His injured leg sticks out, bound completely straight and stiff by the splint. His gait will probably be clunky and slow for the next week or so. Grace, still unsure why she's been commanded to assist with this task, says nothing as she sidles up next to Cooper, offering her good shoulder to assist with his balance. Together, the three of them hobble over to the golf cart parked near the barn.

Cooper sits in the back, his hurt leg jutting straight out. He leans back, breathing heavily from the effort it took to even walk the few paces. Grace scoots in next to Crew, who maintains a chilly silence as he starts the engine and drives off, not sparing a single glance at the ranch hands he leaves in his wake.

CHAPTER 8

Crew doesn't say a word as they ride up the hill, the cart slowing down only slightly as it plugs away at the increasing steepness. Boone is undeterred; in fact, he's grown rather impatient with the golf cart and its inability to move faster as it climbs. The heeler looks back at them every few feet, his tongue hanging out of the side of his mouth, seeming to urge them with his eyes to *hurry it up*. Grace smiles at him, admiring his natural agility. She hasn't seen him in action yet, but she'd bet he's a hell of a herder. Probably runs the cows and sheep like a drill sergeant, not unlike his owner.

Once they're parked in front of the house, Grace and Crew assist Cooper off the golf cart and up the steps that lead to the wraparound deck. Crew holds on to his brother with one arm and flings the front door open with the other, and the three of them hobble awkwardly inside like some piss-poor rendition of a monkey walk. Crew tosses the golf cart keys onto a table near the door and toes off his boots, all the while still holding up his little brother and ... yep. Still scowling. And not just with his mouth—his entire *face* is somehow downturned into a scathing frown.

"Extra room is this way," he grumbles, starting down the hallway to their left. He gives Cooper a brief scan, his eyes somehow hardening even further as he clocks the way his head has lolled forward like it's on a swivel. Yet, even through Crew's stony exterior, he remains a big brother. A caretaker to his core, especially when he begrudgingly mumbles, "I'll bring you some clothes so you don't ruin my sheets."

They make it to the bedroom at the end of the hall with no small amount of effort, Boone trailing at their heels happily. By the time they sit Cooper down on the bed, his eyes are half-closed. His head drops back, gravity bringing the rest of his body with him, and in what seems like an instant, he is wrapping himself up in the duvet and exhaling contentedly. Crew sighs.

"I'll grab him some pajamas," he says, running a hand roughly through his hair. It's only the second time she's seen him not wearing a cowboy hat, and it's no less jarring than it was at the bar. More so, maybe, because the neon beer signs have been replaced with warm, cozy lamplight that accentuates his natural waves, bathing their feathered edges in swaths of gold. It's silly that any man should have such pretty hair, but *especially* Crew, who hides it beneath a hat 99 percent of the time.

She must have been observing his raven locks for longer than she realized, because Crew glances at her and seems to be waiting for her to say something.

Grace blinks. "What?"

Crew's eyes and mouth soften just slightly, the hand that was tangled in his hair now coming down to scratch at his jaw. "I'll get him changed." He nods toward the door.

Right. Grace nods quickly, cheeks heating. "Yeah," she blurts, beginning her speedy exit. "Of course. I should head back anyway."

"No," he cuts in, turning on his heel to keep her in his sights as she starts to move. "I just meant you'd probably be more comfortable in the living room. Getting him to cooperate enough to change, uh—" He looks back to his brother, who is well and truly snoring now. "It won't be pretty."

Halting her footsteps, Grace cranes her neck to meet his eyes. The way they sparkle amid the room's glowing light is fascinating; there are hints of tree sap and lush forest green. "Oh."

Crew offers her a half smile, a simple, gentle tug of his mouth. "I won't be a minute." He nods toward the door again. "Make yourself at home."

She doesn't argue. Doesn't ask any questions, though there are about a hundred rolling around in her brain as soon as the words leave his mouth. *Why* does he want her to stay? Is it so he can yell at her for lying? Is he going to tell his mother? Does he think that because it was Waylon who they decided to mess with, she was part of this ridiculous stunt? Each question is more dramatic and paranoid than the last, but she keeps them at bay and does what he says, leaving him with Cooper to venture down the hallway and into the living room. Where his parents are connoisseurs of fine, chocolaty leather furniture, Crew has a taste for the softer, plusher variety. A giant sectional—appropriately sized for him, she supposes—is the centerpiece of the room, upholstered in a light gray fabric that looks like it'd melt beneath your fingertips. She's seriously considering falling into it and letting herself drown in the cushions when something on the opposite wall catches her eye.

What she finds is so endearing, her heart squeezes in her chest. Polaroids, newspaper clippings, family photo shoots, all in different, eclectic frames, sitting alongside more masculine tchotchkes than the ones in the main house. A faded autographed baseball protected by a glass cube, a boxing trophy, a large cigar box, and, though mildly disgusting and morbid, a taxidermy raccoon sitting in a canoe, holding a tiny paddle.

A muffled exchange sounds from down the hall, and Grace is emboldened to step closer, wanting to get a better look at the pictures. Some people she recognizes, even at their varying ages—Clint Caldwell with brown hair instead of gray, standing at a beach with his arm around his elder son, who is already almost taller than he is. Crew is all knobby knees and pointy elbows, and he's squinting as he faces the camera, a hand at his brow to block out the beating sun.

Next to that photo is one of three sudsy children in a claw-foot bathtub. On the far left, a girl—Caia, Grace presumes—who is grinning bright as she holds up two fingers behind her brother's head. It must be Cooper, because he's the smallest of the three, and Crew is—even as a child—so distinct. His freckles, his mop of jet-black hair, wet and plastered to his forehead. That stern look, which has evolved over the years but not really, not at its core, conveying a sense of protectiveness and authority over his siblings. He watches over them both from the far end of the tub like a tiny warden. Grace smiles, noting his furrowed brow and pinched mouth. He can't be older than ten here, and already, he's perfecting the signature scowl that will follow him into adulthood.

A framed, faded newspaper article is the next one down. It's a story covering the opening of Halcyon Ranch back in 1918, and there's a picture—faded almost beyond recognition—of an older couple, hand in hand under the original stone gate entrance.

Next to that, a nearly monochromatic photograph, curved at the edges like it's been held one too many times. A vast expanse of sand as the backdrop, and two uniformed soldiers front and center. Crew stands with his arm around the other man's neck, smirking.

It takes a moment, but Grace eventually recognizes the other man in the photograph. Knows him by the pearly white teeth, that movie star grin. Easton. The naked, horse-riding cologne model.

An insistent bump against her shin interrupts her snooping, and she looks down to find Boone staring up at her expectantly. Grace smiles, crouching down to pet him. Uncharacteristically open to belly rubs for a heeler, he flops down onto his back to give her full access. She's scratching his fur, chuckling at the way his tongue has started to hang out of his mouth, when a gravelly voice cuts through the quiet living room. "Hey."

Grace starts, swiveling her head around to find Crew standing at the mouth of the hallway, watching her curiously.

"Hey," she says, slightly breathy from the surprise. She stands hastily, leaving a bereft Boone still on his back with his paws in the air. Grace looks toward the direction from which Crew came. "Cooper all tucked in?"

Crew smirks, nodding as he enters the room fully and leans onto one of the couch's arms. "He'll be hurting tomorrow in more ways than one," he confirms with a little shake of his head. "But he's fine. Mouthy as ever."

Grace smiles, then walks over to the opposite side of the couch and sits down in a gingerly manner, hovering right at the edge. It's such a *nice* couch, and it's fabric, not leather, and the grime on her jeans—it could track or stain. Crew, amused by her stiffness, tilts his head slightly. "You can *actually* sit, you know," he says softly.

She lets herself sink down a half inch. "I know," she replies quickly, though she is still not quite comfortably seated.

He continues to watch her, eyebrows flickering upward, that frequent ghost of a smile returning to his mouth. Like a passing ship in the night, she never gets a good enough look at it. It's always gone too soon, replaced with only a shadow of what it once was. "Grace."

Grace decides to cut his urging off at the pass by asking, "Is that Easton?" She points at the photo in question. "Were you two in the army together?" The words tumble out with no regard for how prying they are, and it's profoundly disappointing to watch Crew's smile fade in response. To be the reason it disappears.

His chin dips to his chest. With a tight nod, he says, "Yeah. We grew up together, too."

At the admission, Grace clears her throat. She's slightly stunned by this, by the peek into the lore of Halcyon. "The guys were looking at a centerfold of him earlier tonight. Apparently he's a cologne model now."

A little huff escapes Crew's nose. "I heard."

When he offers nothing further, Grace makes a mental note—that *two* Caldwell siblings who seem to have beef with Easton. It's curious, though, because having a framed picture of someone in your house doesn't exactly scream *mortal enemy*.

Thighs starting to burn, Grace finally surrenders and stands, stuffing her hands into her pockets and walking awkwardly into the safety of the center of the room. It's as though she can't be too close to any one thing—his pictures, his furniture, *him*. With every little directionless step she takes, Crew watches her with slightly narrowed eyes. There's no judgment in them, at least from what she can see. It's just . . . curiosity. Like she's some kind of puzzle with no picture on the box to guide him in piecing things together. She purses her lips, eyes scanning the room.

"This is a nice place," she says, because she can't think of anything else to say to fill up the silence. She's never been one to talk just for the sake of talking, but she's . . . unnerved. Really, she should head out. At this rate, the longer she stands in his space, the higher the odds are that she'll stick her foot directly into her mouth.

"Thanks," he replies. "I can't take much credit for it."

"No?" She chances a look in his direction, then feigns shock and asks, "You mean you're *not* an interior designer in your spare time?"

Crew's smile returns, this time with teeth. It's a sight to behold, the crookedness that overcomes his mouth when he fully grins. It humanizes him in a way nothing else does, bringing him back down to earth to stand among the mortals. Grace has to look away, but now she's smiling, too. "Was it your mom?"

From the corner of her eye, she sees him shake his head. "My sister. She moved in here when my grandfather died. Forced my dad to give up his credit card for a few months while she swapped out the gun safes and stag heads for all of this." His eyes dance around the room.

"Safes, as in plural?" Grace replies, amused.

Crew chuckles. "I think he had one in every closet."

"A man who liked to stay prepared," she muses.

"Oh, that's not even the half of it." He points at a door on the opposite side of the house, past the little kitchenette. "There's a half-completed doomsday bunker in the backyard."

Grace barks out a laugh. "What was his nonperishable of choice?"

Crew grimaces. "Black-eyed peas."

"Hey," she counters. "There's decent protein in those. Gotta be strategic in the apocalypse."

"You spend a lot of time thinking about the apocalypse?"

Grace snorts. "Among other things."

Unconsciously, she's made her way back toward the wall of pictures and knickknacks. She lands on one of Renata, young and suntanned in a flowy pink dress, sitting in a lounge chair with an easy smile on her face. At the edge of the chair, leaning back onto her mother's legs, is the same little girl from the tub. School-aged Caia's brown hair is roughly chopped, almost like she took a pair of scissors to it herself. Her smile is wide, and her two front teeth are notably absent.

"Why'd she leave?" Grace asks before she can think better of it. Something about this night—this chaotic, ridiculous night—has honest, bald curiosity bubbling up her throat until she can't help but let it free. When Crew doesn't answer for a beat, she turns toward him, embarrassment creeping up into her cheeks and turning them hot.

"I'm sorry," she says. "It's none of my business."

Crew shakes his head. "It's fine," he says, but his smile has once again transformed into something much less bright and warm. There's a sadness twisting his mouth now, and it has seeped into his eyes, too. "She left for the same reasons we all did. Change of scenery. A chance to be just another face in a crowd. To put some distance between her and the *Caldwell dynasty*." The last words come out a touch derisively; Crew looks past Grace to stare at the picture that sparked her curiosity. "She's a VP at a software company in New York now."

With a slow nod, Grace says, "That's impressive."

"Yeah," Crew agrees. "Always been a real go-getter."

"And you?" An internal, exasperated sigh looses in her belly at the question. *Good God on a hot dog, Grace Louise. Stop giving this man the third degree.*

But Crew just chuckles, shaking his head. "I can confidently say I'm the least worldly of the three of us. Getting deployed was the only time I've ever left the country."

"If it makes you feel any better," Grace counters, rocking back onto her heels, "I've never left the state." She admits this to him without considering the implications—he already knows her background, and that the company she kept until recently was less than desirable. But continuing to paint the picture of her past, sharpening it with details like the one she just shared—she wonders if he'll pity her.

But the look in his eyes doesn't speak to pity, or shock, or anything, really. He's simply giving her the opportunity to elaborate, and when she doesn't, he offers a lighthearted shrug. "Well, Texas is as good as it gets, in my opinion."

It's a lifeline. An easy out. Grace gives him an appreciative nod. "Good to know."

Boone lets out a heavy sigh from his place on the couch—all their yammering is disrupting his nap. At the sound, Crew's head swings around to look at the dog, and he rolls his eyes.

"He's become very dramatic in his old age."

Boone's eyes dart to Crew, and Grace doesn't know if it's possible, but it looks like Boone then rolls *his* eyes in response. A beat of silence passes between Grace and Crew, both staring lovingly at the dog as he drifts back to sleep.

Then Crew faces her again, and he must have some want or need to level the playing field, because he asks, "Was your family from Texas originally?"

She knows he isn't asking about Bellamy. And though he's just being kind and offering the same curiosity she's badgered him with all evening, Grace can't help the physical reaction that comes when anyone asks or talks about her family. A crater-size hole in her gut throbs; the back of her neck begins to feel warm.

"Yeah," she says, her eyes falling to the floor, to the supremely dirty boots that she should've taken off at the door.

He doesn't say anything in response, but he keeps his eyes on her, patiently waiting for more. Grace clears her throat, figuring she owes him at least a morsel of detail after everything he's supplied. Grace swallows, and her saliva tastes like battery acid. She has to stop herself from recoiling as it stings her throat.

"Bellamy is my mom's older brother. She grew up at Braxton. My dad was from somewhere close to Lubbock." She can only hope Crew doesn't probe that statement further; the last thing Grace wants to talk about right now is her father.

Crew must sense it, because he pivots with an earnest, unexpected follow-up question: "Were you ever happy there? At Braxton?" Grace can feel the lines of her face hardening. A rush of cold envelops her heart. With his voice rawer than before, Crew adds, "There had to be something to live for, right?"

Like an old friend, grief waves at her as it settles beside, around, and within her. It must've missed her, for how strongly it's attaching itself to every fiber of her being right now. Grace takes a deep breath, psyching herself up to broach this topic. If she doesn't say something to Crew now, she's worried the grief will lodge itself in her throat.

"I had a horse. A palomino. She was my birthday present when I turned seventeen, when my uncle was still parading around like some saint, like he was the most benevolent, generous person in the world for taking me in. Her name was Vesta."

Crew listens without comment, and he keeps his eyes intently focused on her. When he doesn't say anything in response, Grace finds herself needing to clarify something.

"He sold her to the first buyer willing to take her off his hands. To punish me. I—" Grace's throat seizes, that painful grief finally moving in. "I don't know where she is now. I would've taken her with me if I could've."

His face falls, his brows pulling together. Suddenly, he's standing, walking into her space, and he looks devastated. As though, somehow, he can feel the sadness that is coursing through her, and he's taking some of it into himself. Helping her carry it. "Grace," he says, his voice painfully soft. "I'm sorry."

Instinctively, she takes a step back. It's easier to be farther away, and it's definitely easier to put this topic to rest sooner rather than later. "It's fine," Grace says quickly, unconvincingly. "Really." She looks toward the front door, thinking it looks like a beacon, a port in a storm. "I should probably get going," she says, already walking. She only takes about four steps before Crew says something that stops her in her tracks.

"I know Cooper didn't trip."

Grace looks over her shoulder at him. There's no anger or frustration in his expression—he maintains the evenness he's had for their whole conversation, tapping his fingers rhythmically against his jean-clad thigh. "I also get why you lied about it."

Slowly, Grace turns around. Better to face the judgment head-on, chin high.

But his next words aren't punitive or derisive; his next words surprise her. "Is Waylon okay?"

Grace blinks, schooling her face into something neutral. "He'll be fine," she replies, then tilts her head in consideration.

"I'll give him extra cookies tomorrow for not kicking anyone in the face."

Crew smiles softly. "Charitable bastard."

"He handled it better than I would have."

His head tilts slightly. "And Duke?"

Grace can't help the little smile that tugs at her lips. "He seemed pretty pissed, too. Think he's become a little protective of Waylon."

Crew huffs. "That right?"

Grace shrugs, still smiling. "Sure seemed like it."

Then there's another lull, quiet and deeper now that there's more space between them.

Grace tries again. "I'm gonna head back—"

"You missed your shower slot."

It isn't a question. Especially not with the way he does a quick once-over of her, assessing the way she's still in the clothes she was wearing this morning at breakfast. Every insecurity she's fended off since entering his home starts to rear its ugly head again, telling her she's *dirty*, grimy, and unfit to be here.

"Yeah," Grace replies quickly, an excuse and apology at the ready. "I'm sorry if I got anything on your couch or tracked—" She looks back to where she walked in, silently relieved when she doesn't see any boot prints.

"You can use mine, if you want."

Her head swivels around fast enough that she nearly gets whiplash. "What?"

That flash of amusement is back. It makes the tips of her ears turn hot. "Hot water's probably done for at the bunkhouse by now," he explains, looking at his watch. "I have my own tank."

Of course he does.

A hot shower does sound like heaven, but she hesitates. It feels like pity, like charity granted to the forlorn cowgirl. And anyway, ranch hands take cold showers all the time, and she highly doubts he ever invites Forty over to use his personal water heater when he's last on the rotation.

"That's all right," Grace says. "I don't mind them cold." It's not a lie, but there's hardly any conviction in her tone.

Crew gives her no quarter, only maintains that soul-penetrating stare that threatens to peel back all of her carefully placed, protective layers. "It's just a shower, Grace." There's a gentleness to his urging. It's soft at the edges. "Don't overthink it."

She glances down at her hands, wincing a little at the red dirt that's collected under her fingernails. No matter how many times she washes them throughout the day, they never seem to lose that rusty tint. She sighs, then blinks up at him. "All right." With a tight-lipped nod, she adds, "If you insist."

It's actually sinful, how good the shower feels—so good that Grace wonders how Crew manages to spend any time *not* showering. He even has a removable showerhead, which she takes full advantage of, along with an array of hair products ranging from high-end conditioner in a sleek black jar to something called *clarifying shampoo*, which, she's horrified to see when she squirts some onto her palm, is a dark green color. She doesn't dillydally, but she also doesn't rush—and a good five minutes is spent just standing under the showerhead. The heat is turned up high enough that steam rises throughout the bathroom, and Grace's skin is starting to turn pink, but she doesn't care. Her senses feel sharper, her mind more alert, like she's cleansing more than just her body right now.

Eventually, sadly, she does shut the water off and climb out carefully, grabbing one of the giant fluffy white towels Crew left for her on the back of the door. Wrapping it around her body, Grace can't help the contented sigh that leaves her lips at the feel of it. Plushy, soft, and warm. The relief of being clean, the *joy* running through her veins dampens a little when she looks toward the pile of clothes on the floor. Caked in dirt and smelling of horse—she doesn't want to put them back on. But because it's either throwing *something* on or emerging from the bathroom in only a towel, she makes do. In lieu of putting back on all her clothes, she slips on the sports bra and spandex shorts she was wearing beneath. They're modest—she never chooses fashion over comfort when she's working. The bra practically glues her breasts to her chest, tamping them down until they're secure and out of her way, and the shorts, well—chafing is never a stronger possibility than it is in the dead of a Texas summer, so they're on the longer side. The mirror is still completely opaque; even when she uses her T-shirt to wipe down a spot, it fogs back up almost immediately. With a sigh, she scoops up the rest of her clothes, her boots and socks, and walks out of the bathroom.

A dull murmur of voices echoes from the living room. She finds Crew lounging on the couch with his feet propped up on the coffee table. Boone is curled up next to him with his head in his lap, peacefully dozing. There's a baseball game on television, and Crew looks mildly displeased with its current state. He curses under his breath when a player strikes out, waving a dismissive hand at the TV. Grace smiles softly at his exasperation, padding down the hallway until she's just at the edge of his vision. Another player steps up to the plate, twirling his bat around.

She doesn't want to interrupt, but she also doesn't want to stand here awkwardly until a commercial break, so she clears her throat and says, "I'm gonna head out. Thanks for the shower."

The batter swings and hits the baseball with enough force to send it soaring high, far enough into the outfield that it has the potential to go all the way. Crew doesn't look at her, transfixed by the play at hand. He replies distractedly, "No problem," and continues watching the game. It ends up being a home run—a grand slam, no less, and Crew jolts forward, his fist pumping so hard that Boone startles into a seated position, staring daggers at Crew for waking him up. Crew comforts him by reaching out and swiping his hand over Boone's muzzle, but he doesn't accept it. Instead, he walks to the opposite side of the couch, plops down, and then lets out a long, dramatic sigh.

Grace passes the couch on her way out the door, and Crew meets her eyes as she goes, finally pulling his attention away from the game. Something happens then—something that has Grace slowing her steps just slightly.

Crew's eyes lock with hers for a heartbeat, and then he seems to notice she's not wearing the dingy clothing she walked into his house with. Slowly, his gaze travels down her body. He takes his fill of her, unapologetic save for the visible swallow that moves his throat. When his gaze meets hers again, after what feels like whole minutes, there's a darkness in them that wasn't there before. He seems to remember himself quickly, and then he's standing and walking over to her with purposeful steps. For a half second, Grace isn't sure what he's about to do. That look in his eyes—it's unpredictable and enticing and terrifying all at once. But he asks, simply, "Can I give you a ride back?"

Grace shakes her head. Her eyes trail back to the television, and she says, "Can't have you miss the end of the game."

Crew huffs with a half smile, then pads over to the door, which he holds open for her. Grace stares out into the gaping maw of the night, and part of her wishes she didn't have to go. To leave behind the warmth of his house and the lingering scent of his aftershave to return to the coldness of her bunk.

But she does. She steps through the doorway, smiling up at him. "Thanks."

He nods, that sort-of-smile spreading and carving out dimples in both of his cheeks. "Anytime. Seriously."

"Don't tempt me," Grace says, wiggling her eyebrows.

Crew doesn't return the silliness; his expression is sincere, almost imploring. "I mean it. You deserve . . ." He trails off, letting himself take one more look at all of her. He lets out a rough sigh and shakes his head, as if ridding himself of an errant thought. He continues, but his voice is rougher, more restrained. "Your showers should always be hot."

Grace's stomach swoops at his words, but she does her best to not look affected. "Thank you," she says once more, and then she leaves his porch, because she'll be rooted to the spot if he keeps saying things like that. If he keeps looking at her like that.

Her strides are long, and she doesn't check to see if he's watching. She keeps her focus trained on the bunkhouse straight ahead, shrouded in night, set against a backdrop of stars.

CHAPTER 9

"All right now. Show me you can behave like a gentleman." Grace's breathing is steady, but her heart thuds against her ribs in a wary rhythm. She keeps her voice even and soft as she sweet-talks Waylon, turning up all the charm in hopes that it'll coax him into letting her slide the saddle smoothly onto his back. He's been resistant to it since the Cooper incident—the same way he's been resistant to everything. Any finessing she's attempted has been futile up to this point; he's done nothing but snort and sigh at her for the past forty-eight hours despite her plying him with all of his favorite foods.

Unaware of the fiasco entirely, Renata had come by the previous evening under the pretense of "craving Forty's fajitas," but in reality, she'd wanted to get a temperature check on how things were going, on where Grace was in the timeline of saddle-breaking. Grace had been honest—he *was* making good progress and would be ready to ride much sooner than expected. At least, he would be when he decided to stop being ornery and resentful—but Grace couldn't be angry with him for that. A bunch of idiots had invaded his space and grabbed at him when, after nearly two weeks together, he'd only just gotten comfortable enough to let her touch him. She understands his fury.

Renata hadn't seemed especially concerned, but she'd asked Grace to come by the house for lunch the next day to discuss everything in more detail. To Grace—someone who was constantly waiting for the other shoe to drop—that only meant one thing. *Time is running out.*

"I know you're not happy about this," Grace murmurs to Waylon. She's inching around his body at a painfully slow pace, gently dragging the saddle across his hair. "And believe me, I'm not, either. I don't want to make you do anything you don't want to do." Her voice quiets to a whisper. "But I need your help. I need you to do this for me." *Or I won't get to stay* is the frightful thought that follows her plea. Then, she swears Waylon actually *sighs* at her words—whether in annoyance or acceptance, only time will tell. "Thank you," she says as she approaches his other side, the place from which she'll hoist the saddle onto his back. If he cooperates, it will be a fluid movement, less than thirty seconds. If he doesn't and decides he'd prefer to bolt off in the opposite direction, she'll probably tumble to the ground and earn herself a face full of dirt, maybe a broken arm. "Let's see it, Waylon."

She tries not to hold her breath. She really does. Horses pick up on things like that. They echo it. But it's something she does without even thinking, sucking in a long breath through her nostrils and then clamping down her mouth as she lifts the saddle into the air and prays to God he stays still.

By some miracle, he does. For the entire fifteen seconds it takes to lift the saddle and let it slide onto his back, Waylon is a statue of calm. Grace's eyes widen as this unfolds, as the saddle settles and the horse remains still. Her heart, pounding but slightly softer now, squeezes. In this moment, with all of his steadiness, all of his quiet resolve, he reminds her of Vesta. Grace exhales sharply, all the breath shuddering out of her lungs in a gust of profound relief. She smiles, reaches out, and runs a hand over Waylon's shoulder.

"Excellent," she tells him. Admiring the way he looks so experienced and professional with the saddle now sitting comfortably on his back, she adds, "It looks good on you."

They walk around the enclosure for a few laps, Waylon steady at her side. The sun beats down on them both, not even a streak of cloud in the sky for respite. Sweat drips down Grace's back, plastering her white tank top to her skin. Little curls have begun to sprout near her forehead, her ears, and the nape of her neck. This kind of heat—it's the kind that can convince someone they've never felt a cool breeze in their life. The kind that penetrates every molecule and worms its way into the brain. The kind that makes people go nuts.

"All right, now this part I know you're not gonna love. But you're gonna have to trust me," Grace says, forcing her voice to be low and soft. Without giving herself enough time to hesitate nor giving Waylon enough time to second-guess her, she slips her boot into the stirrup and pushes down, then immediately releases her hold. Waylon gives way, leaning over with Grace's weight, and though he looks slightly perturbed by the movement, he doesn't seem angry. She repeats the motion, even leaving her boot in the stirrup and sort of bouncing herself on it to try to get him used to the movement, the feel of having to bear someone else's weight. He is surprisingly compliant, and Grace decides to give it a go, hoping against hope that if he does buck her off, she'll land on the shoulder that isn't freshly healed from a dislocation.

When she fully mounts Waylon for the first time and he does

nothing but accept it—albeit with a little impatient-sounding grunt once she's settled—no one is around to see it except for Duke. The older horse watches them carefully, and Grace swears she sees something like pride flash in his expressive eyes. Grace pets Waylon's neck, giving him a few encouraging scratches, telling him in her softest voice that he's good, he's smart, he's such a quick learner. This seems to work on Waylon; buttered up and amenable, he even takes a few cautious steps with her on his back, and he remains remarkably steady. When Grace dismounts ten minutes later, the grin on her face is wide and wild.

Excitement and pride course through Grace's veins as she washes her hands and splashes water on her face in the barn sink. Since the night before, she'd been dreading the worst-case scenario happening: She wouldn't be able to get Waylon to allow the saddle or allow himself to be mounted; she'd have to tell Renata she isn't nearly as far along as she'd claimed. She'd fail her trial run at Halcyon and be back in that dingy one-stoplight town by sunset. Now, there's a tentative relief that has her quickly drying her hands and checking her clothes for any excess grime. Relief, and a glimmer of hope that getting him saddled today will mean she's secured her place here.

On the walk toward the main house, Grace admires the wildflowers surrounded by a sea of neatly mowed grass. They stand out, vibrant and wild—colorful rebels refusing to conform to the rigidity of the pin-straight blades. She counts the spiderwort sticking upward through patches of better-known blooms, like the runt of the litter trying to get its own slice of affection. But the primroses are her favorite. They're a perfect blend of pink and purple, lush and elegant, never demanding attention but attracting it all the same.

All thoughts of flowers and whimsy dissipate like mist on the wind when the main house comes into view, because sitting in the driveway behind four Halcyon trucks is a government-issued vehicle. The Texas Department of Agriculture, by the looks of it. A flare of unease threads through Grace's ribs at the sight of the logo on the side of the white truck, and, on instinct, her feet stop in their tracks.

Some part of her figured this might happen—if Bellamy was going to go down, he was going to take everyone with him. But she didn't think it would be now. It's too soon. It feels like she just got to Halcyon, and now he's going to take it away from her, the same way he's taken everything else.

Grace gulps down a dry, scraping swallow, the heat suddenly stealing all the moisture out of her body. Her heart races as she clocks the front door swinging open and two men walking out onto the wraparound porch, Renata following close behind them. The three of them stand together for a minute or so, chatting amiably, and then, like something out of a nightmare, Renata's head swivels in Grace's direction. She spots her immediately, and the men follow her gaze. Renata waves at her—they don't.

Grace doesn't know what's supposed to happen next. Does not turning her uncle in for his crimes count as abetting? Can the TDA even arrest people? But then Renata's wave turns beckoning. Insistent. Much to Grace's confusion, she notices after a couple of steps forward that Renata is smiling.

Renata leans onto the porch railing with her forearms as Grace approaches. "How are you, darlin'?"

Grace manages a smile, halfhearted and slightly trembling. "I'm just fine, thanks," she replies. "How are you?"

"Oh, happy as a pig in mud." She nods in the direction of the troopers, and Grace turns to find them both looking at her. "Grady, Tripp, this is Grace," Renata says. "She's workin' on Tasha's stud for us. Grace, Grady and Tripp." She waves a hand between Grace and the two men. "Two of the TDA's finest outreach specialists, who tried and *failed* to ruin my good mood just now. All they ever do is deliver me bad news."

Grace's throat tightens. Here it comes. Her breathing starts to quicken, growing more erratic with every passing second. They start to walk toward her, slowly, deliberately, and it takes every ounce of willpower Grace has not to bolt. To turn tail and run as fast as her legs will take her. They're closing in, now less than an arm's length away, and she considers turning around and putting her hands behind her back. Maybe if she does it without them having to ask, they won't hurt her.

Then something strange happens. Almost in perfect unison, they come to a stop, and then both men tip their hats toward Grace. "Nice to meet you, Grace," Grady says.

It's a miracle Grace can form a coherent sentence, a feat she doesn't even realize she's capable of until "Nice to meet you, too," comes tumbling out of her mouth.

"They were just leavin'," Renata chimes in. She's turned around now and leaning onto the rail with her elbows. "Weren't you, gentlemen?"

"Yes, ma'am," Tripp says, his voice several pitches lower than Grady's. They start to walk toward the cruiser, but as they go, Tripp turns around and says, "Please keep in mind what we discussed, Mrs. Caldwell. Highest temps on the record. Gonna be a mean August."

"Tripp McCade," Renata calls out, standing to her full height and pointing at him with a firm index finger. "If you call me Mrs. Caldwell one more time, after I have politely and consistently asked you to call me Renata, I'll show you *mean*."

Grace hears them chuckle, the footsteps descending the stairs, and the truck doors open and shut. As the engine hums to life, Renata peeks over the railing and sees Grace holding on to the wood of the porch. A strange thrumming in her ears is overtaking all other sound. Her knees suddenly start to buckle, and she's sinking to the ground, landing atop a soft thatch of grass.

"Grace—" Renata is off, rushing down the steps and toward Grace's side. Once within reach, she steadies Grace, helping her stand with two hands on her arms. It sounds like she's speaking from underwater as she pleads, "Grace, look at me."

Grace tries. She really does. But everything feels like it's happening in slow motion. Except her heart—that feels like it's about to burst in her chest, like a balloon floating toward a wall of needles.

Renata's voice is even, soft but imploring. "Honey, I don't know what's happening—you gotta talk to me. Is it those men? They're harmless—they just came by to tell me to move the herd out to the summer pasture sooner than we did last year."

Grace barely hears the explanation. Her vision continues to swim until she almost teeters over again. Renata's grip tightens on her biceps, straightening her back up, and then her hand is suddenly cupping Grace's cheek, cool to the touch.

"Grace, listen to my voice. Listen." The last word is sharper than the rest, like it finally broke through the surface of the water.

Grace nods. A slow, syrupy movement. It's the best she can do.

"Good. Now, I want you to do something for me," she urges.

"I want you to think about your boots. Think about the grass beneath them. Think about digging your heels in. Think about the texture of the dirt against the soles."

Grace nods again, the frenzy in her brain slowly starting to fade into a dull roar. She closes her eyes and sees the grass, the dirt, the heels of her boots pressing down.

"Good. That's it. Now, I want you to breathe in slowly, and when you do, I want you to try to smell everything you can, okay? We can do it together. On the count of three. One, two, three."

Renata's chest rises slowly, and Grace's does, too, but with less vigor. Her breathing is unsteady—like it could easily spiral into chaos at any second.

"What do you smell, Grace? I smell sourdough made with Ronnie's thirty-year-old starter." Renata takes in another deep breath, a satisfied sound leaving her lips at the tail end. "That'll make for a mean turkey sandwich."

Grace breathes in, too, and she picks up on something—just a hint. "Eucalyptus," she whispers weakly.

Renata nods, then gently releases Grace's arms. "That'd be my perfume. Anything else? I can definitely smell horse shit, but that's kind of a permanent thing around here, as you know."

Despite herself, Grace smiles. It feels foreign and wonderful on her lips. She's still here. No one has taken her away from this place. For now, for this moment, she gets to stay in this little corner of heaven.

After a long, calming moment of silence between the two women, Renata sets two fingers under Grace's chin and gently lifts until Grace is forced to meet her eyes. Grace takes in the perceptiveness in her expression, the cleverness, the earnestness.

"Okay," Renata says with a firm nod. She wraps an arm

securely around Grace's shoulders and turns them around, then begins to march them both up the stairs toward the house. "Let's go have ourselves a girls' lunch, shall we?"

Ronnie's sourdough is still warm when Grace bites into it. Her eyes fall shut involuntarily at the first taste of the sandwich; it's all she can do to not *moan*. It's stuffed with turkey, salami, tomatoes, and some sort of spicy mayo concoction that's starting to drip down her palms, and the bread doesn't scrape the roof of her mouth like others sometimes do. The crust is perfectly crunchy, and the center is pillowy soft. After the second bite, Grace decides, with absolute certainty, that she could eat this sandwich every day for the rest of her life and not get sick of it. So focused on the meal, she hardly notices Renata, sitting catty-corner to her at the head of the kitchen table, studying her. Grace catches her eye and gulps down a big bite. She dabs her mouth with the cloth napkin in her lap and smiles.

"This is amazing. Thank you."

Renata waves her off. "Don't thank me, honey. But be sure to tell Ronnie you like the bread. It's a real point of pride for her."

"Of course."

A steaming cup of an undisclosed liquid sits in front of Renata's plate, which has gone mostly untouched save for a few nibbles at the corner. Grace is flabbergasted by this—how is Renata not devouring it with abandon the same way she is? She's staring at the uneaten sandwich when Renata says, "Crew tells me you got to see my youngest in rare form the other night."

Grace's brow hikes upward, and for a moment, she's unsure how to respond. Renata has a way of sniffing out the truth, and Grace doesn't know how much Crew has shared of the ranch hands' sordid adventure with Cooper. She replies simply, "Yes, ma'am."

"They get that from their father, you know," Renata says.

Grace tilts her head, unsure what that means.

Renata's lips turn into a flat line. "The idiot gene. That's all Clint. No DNA of mine would have someone trying to ride a wild horse while three sheets to the wind. He's lucky he didn't break his damn neck."

Grace can't help the little snort that escapes her nose. She nods, amused by the comment, and by Renata's natural ability to be funny even in uglier moments. "Yes, ma'am," Grace repeats.

A companionable silence settles between them for a beat, and then Grace looks up to find the older woman tapping her lips with her index finger. She gives Grace a reassuring look, then lightly puts her hands up, like a book falling open.

In a gentle but notably firm voice, she asks, "Would you like to tell me what happened out on the porch just now, Grace?"

Not really. Not really at all.

In fact, Grace wants to finish eating her sandwich, then she wants to eat Renata's sandwich, and then she wants to go back to the stables and forget it ever happened. But she knows Renata's not really asking—she's prompting. Waiting expectantly for Grace to supply the information she's after. Regretfully, Grace sets down her sandwich.

"The TDA—they used to come around Braxton a lot," she says, looking down at her lap. "My uncle was always being investigated for one thing or another. And when they'd come, he'd make me and the other hands hide any evidence that could get him into hot water. He wasn't good to the animals, and he knew if they saw the way he neglected them, he'd get fined. Or worse. So we covered it up. Strategically placed healthy animals around and kept the others out of sight. It always felt so—" She hates this—hates remembering those awful days when she, too, felt like a criminal for helping him. "It was terrible. There's no other way to slice it. He should've never been allowed to buy them in the first place."

Renata stays quiet, but there's a tightness to her features that wasn't visible before. A tense moment of quiet stretches between them until she finally asks, "So he was abusing his ranch hands, abusing his animals, and lying to the TDA." She shakes her head, a little curl of disgust folding into her top lip. "Anything else?"

Grace considers what she should say next. It would be easy to give him up to Renata, and it would be nice to tell someone all of his secrets. All of his cut corners, his tricks and scams. She thinks about how yellow his teeth would look when he would grin after closing a deal, after swindling yet another poor, gullible bastard. The image is nausea inducing. "Yeah," Grace says, nodding firmly. "There's a lot. But his principal con, his bread and butter, is the stud scam."

Renata's eyes widen slightly at that, and she leans forward, her face turning steely. With that determined, no-bullshit-taking look in her eyes, she nods in Grace's direction. "Go on, then," she says. "Tell me everything."

Grace spends the rest of the hour telling Renata everything she can remember of Bellamy's infractions, from small to massive in scale. Renata listens patiently, and though she doesn't write anything down, Grace has a feeling she'll remember everything in stark detail.

She seems especially intent when they discuss the stud scam—Bellamy's most predatory and lucrative swindle. With the help of experienced forgers and talented snake-oil salesmen of the most sinister variety, he'd sold at least a million dollars' worth of fraudulent horse semen, pushing claims that it was all from prized studs and sure to result in future success and riches for the buyer. He preyed on those new to ranching, those with money burning holes in their pockets, and those with too much whiskey in their system to make sound decisions. He'd scammed everyone from elderly women to eighteen-year-olds with trust funds. And because there were so many variables with breeding, he'd flown under the radar for years, swiftly avoiding any consequences for his thievery.

With every story, every victim Grace recounts, Renata looks more and more like she's calculating something, or many things, while continuing to listen.

Grace is about to ask what kind of master plan she's cooking up when they're interrupted by the kitchen door swinging open. Clint walks in, and he looks a little dazed with his hair and pearl-snap shirt both slightly undone, a cream hat in his hand.

"Well, hi, handsome," Renata greets cheerfully. "Enjoy your nap?" She walks over to him and starts fastening his undone buttons. Clint stares adoringly at his wife as she fixes him up, even as she licks her fingers and presses down on a stubborn cowlick in his silver hair. Watching them, it occurs to Grace that she's never witnessed this sort of natural, settled-in intimacy. The only married couple she's known in her life was her parents, and they were vicious to each other, resentful and violent. When they looked at each other, there was never love in their eyes. Never softness and warmth.

Eventually the two split apart, and Clint nods a greeting to Grace. He walks toward the table and reaches into a bowl of potato chips, popping one into his mouth. While crunching on it, he asks, "How's it going with that horse?"

Grace sits up a little straighter in her chair. Waylon—she'd almost forgotten he was the reason she was coming up to the house in the first place. "Good—real good, actually. I came up here to talk to Renata about our progress."

Clint tugs lightly at the sleeves of his shirt. "Good news, then?"

Grace looks at Renata, and all shades of anger and disgust from their previous conversation have disappeared. She looks excited now, her eyes bright as she awaits Grace's news. With an involuntary grin, Grace says, "I saddled and mounted him this morning."

The look on both of their faces sends a surge of pride through her—it's a lovely mix of pleasantly surprised and not surprised at all. Like they both knew all along that she could do this. The confidence emboldens her, and she adds, "I think he'll be ready for a real ride by next week."

Renata turns to Clint. "Can you believe that? And she was in a shoulder brace for most of last week." She looks back to Grace, incredulously shaking her head. "I should've known Maryann wouldn't steer me wrong. Well, then, Grace, what do you say? Do you want the job?"

She asks it so casually, like she isn't handing over an opportunity that will change Grace's life forever. And Grace knows she just asked it straight-out, but she can't help the disbelief at her turning luck, and her throat tightens with emotion. "Really?"

They both chuckle. Renata says, "Really. We'd love to have you stay on full-time, if you're interested. What do you think?"

Joy, or something very close to it, erupts in Grace's stomach.

She can barely contain it as she responds, almost immediately, "Of course. I accept. Yes."

Renata grins. "Great."

"Well done, Grace," Clint says, and there's pride in his smile, and Grace learns right then that being on the receiving end of such a look is like standing in the warm glow of the sun after months of frigid winter. He looks at his wife, and his smile transforms into a conspiratorial smirk. "You know what that means, honey."

Renata grins, nodding. "I do."

"Grace," Clint says, "have you ever been to a hoedown?"

Despite the full spectrum of emotion Grace has experienced in the span of five minutes, she honks out a laugh. "I grew up in Texas. Of course I have."

"Of course. My mistake. But I'll tell you what—I bet you've never been to a hoedown like the ones we have around here." Clint looks past her with a twinkle in his eye.

Like something out of a movie, Grace looks toward the window to find a line of vans heading for the house.

"You see," he continues, "my birthday is tomorrow. And every year on my birthday, my wife subjects everyone to the most expensive, most over-the-top hoedown on God's green earth."

In the laundry room that evening, Grace is moving all of her clothes from the washer into the dryer when June walks in with a collapsible basket on her hip. Her hair is gathered at the top of her head in a tangled bun, and she looks like she hasn't slept in days. She says nothing as she sidles up next to Grace and sets her hamper on the floor. Grace yanks runaway socks from the back of the washer and tosses them into the dryer, and once everything is out, she slides over, freeing up the machine.

Grace has shared a bunkhouse with only three women in her life. The first, Jackie, was already at Braxton when she showed up as a teenager, and she'd been something of a lifeline for Grace. She'd been rough around the edges and a little mean at times, but she'd also protected Grace from ogling eyes and wandering hands, and chewed out the ranch hands who spoke to her indecently. Protective as she was, she couldn't manage to keep a lid on her temper and was fired less than a year later for punching the foreman directly in the nose.

And then there was Abby, who was much more like June in her disinterest in making new friends. She saw Grace as competition on the ranch and with the men. Despite her animosity, Grace had learned from Jackie that sometimes, on a ranch, you need someone in your corner. Grace took that to heart and protected Abby the same way Jackie had protected her, and there were scars on more than one man's skin to prove it. They never became real friends, but they were eventually reluctant allies, watching out for each other when it mattered. Until Abby fell in love with a bartender in Frasier, packed her bags, and left in the middle of the night.

Though anything Grace says to June will likely be taken the wrong way, or ignored entirely, she can't help but speak up. Whether June wants to acknowledge it or not, there's a solidarity between women on a ranch. An unwritten law by which they must abide. To break it would be to betray something precious, snipping the invisible string that connects them all. She knows what it's like to shy away from the offering of friendship, especially in a setting like this. But she also knows how vital it is, how comforting. She strategizes silently, quickly, knowing she needs to be creative about how to approach this. A simple *How are you?* isn't going to penetrate June's steel-reinforced walls. Instead, Grace goes with "Can I ask you something?"

June is piling all of her white—well, perhaps the clothing used to be white; now it's all varying shades of beige—garments into the washer, tossing the colorful ones to the floor by her feet. She sighs, and uttering the words seems to physically pain her, but she finally says, "Go ahead."

Grace fiddles with the knob on the dryer, telling the machine to bypass the gentle dry. Not a single article of clothing Grace owns warrants anything gentle. "Do you know about this party tomorrow?"

"Clint's birthday party?"

"Yeah."

June reaches for the bleach that sits on the communal detergent shelf hanging over the washer and dryer. "What about it?"

"Is it—" Grace searches for the words, hoping to not convey how nervous she is about the prospect of attending a rich person's birthday party. "Is it like an *everyone's invited* kind of thing? Do you all usually go?"

June chuckles, but there's little mirth in the sound. "Yeah, we all go." She lets the top of the washer slam down, then angles her body toward Grace. "Haven't you figured out by now that these idiots will jump at any chance to get shit-faced?"

Grace smirks. "Right." She presses the start button on the dryer, and the rumbling sound of her clothes beating against the machine starts to echo through the room. She angles her body toward June, too, and folds her arms over her chest. "Let me guess—no one showers? Everyone quits work and walks over in their sweaty jeans and dirty boots?" Grace holds June's eyes as she speaks, never once relenting. There's a sparkle in June's bright blues, newfound and momentary, but the flash of it confirms something in Grace's head: June gives as good as she gets. So, with that in mind, Grace kinks an eyebrow, daring her to refute the statement, to feign ignorance.

Instead, June smiles knowingly and gives Grace a careful once-over, like she's seeing her for the first time. It's the only response Grace gets to her question, and it's all she needs. June continues to appraise her as she says, "I heard you're sticking around."

"You heard right."

June hums. "Well, then." She kneels down next to her clothes, digging around until she grabs hold of something light blue and pulls it out from the colorful pile. She shakes it into its full form, revealing a sundress, simple but beautiful with delicate red embroidery lining the hems. Without preamble, she walks over and presses it against Grace's shoulders, surveying the fit. Grace looks down, the dress falling just below her knee. It smells like June—floral and clean with a remarkable lack of grime and sweat. June hums, seemingly satisfied, then looks at Grace. "You're lucky the party isn't until tomorrow," she says, grimacing. "It's gonna take me hours to make you presentable."

CHAPTER 10

The front lawn of the main house is nearly unrecognizable by lunchtime the next day. Renata Caldwell, unsurprisingly, spares no expense when it comes to a party. She goes full throttle. The hoedown theme isn't subtle—there are picnic tables covered in checkered cloth, stacks of hay placed around the grounds for seating, and two large, rustic wooden bars that sit on either side of the lawn. At the center is a large dance floor surrounded by a border of hay, and at the front of it, a massive stage decked out with streamers, balloons, and a giant banner that reads **Happy Birthday, Clint!** in colorful bubble letters.

Chores and ranch tasks seem to drag on endlessly that Saturday afternoon, with everyone gearing up to spend the entire evening partying. Crew picks up on the antsy energy immediately and decides to be ornery about it, making sure no one is slacking or cutting corners. Grace doesn't get a visit from him until after lunch.

She hears him before she sees him—he's hollering at Caleb, unsatisfied with his work fixing one of the stable doors that had come off the hinges. "I've learned not to expect a whole hell of a lot from you, Caleb," he barks, "but this really takes the cake."

The squeak of the door echoes through the stables out to the arena, followed by a thundering *slam*. Grace grimaces. Crew's voice is dripping with impatience as he asks, "Does that look fixed to you?"

"No, sir," Caleb replies quickly. "I'll try again."

"You do that," Crew says. Grace hears his boots thump against the dirt floor as he walks away, grumbling, "Y'all keep this shit up and you'll work through the damn party."

"Won't happen again," Caleb shouts.

Crew comes into view then, and he looks as distressed as he sounds, his mouth pinched like he's been sucking on a lemon. Grace stands with Waylon on the opposite side of the arena, watching him practically stomp toward the metal bars. When Crew finally makes eye contact with her, his scowl softens by a fraction. "Hey," he grunts.

Grace can't help but smile. The more time she spends in his presence, particularly when he's with the other hands, the more she understands how *dramatic* he can be. Grinning, she says, "Hi."

He notices her smile and, because it's just the kind of mood he's in, his brow furrows. He seems annoyed that anyone in his vicinity could even *appear* to be happy. "What?" he barks.

"Nothing," she says quickly, trying—failing—to force her mouth into a straight line. She looks back to Waylon so she doesn't have to maintain eye contact with Crew. The silence between them stretches a little too long, and Crew's nostrils are flaring, so in a bid to distract him, Grace asks, "How's Cooper?"

His mood doesn't exactly do a one-eighty, but he at least seems to redirect his ire to his brother, the mention of whom makes him roll his eyes. "I told my mother he has exactly one more day of recovery and then I'm tossing his ass back into the bunkhouse."

Grace chuckles. "That good, huh?"

"He got one of them to steal a whistle from the barn so he could *beckon* me," Crew says flatly. "In my own house."

"Well, I'm glad he's taking advantage while he can," Grace volleys back, knowing she's teasing but unable to help herself. He just looks so . . . tense. Like someone zapped all the water out of his body but left behind all the rigid bones. He scoffs at her comment and kicks a cloud of dirt up with the toe of his boot.

Grace goes back to work with a cheeky smile on her face, turning her back to him. She thinks he's taken off to go shout at someone else when his voice surprises her. He sounds slightly less pissed, even a little soft. "He looks good in a saddle." She turns to see him appraising Waylon, admiration and a hint of pride now colliding with his irritation. His eyes drift to hers, and a tiny, almost imperceptible smile tugs at the corner of his ever-frowning lips.

"He does," Grace agrees.

"So they made it official," he says.

"Yep." Grace scratches Waylon's shoulder in the spot she knows he loves. "Guess y'all are stuck with me."

Crew's jaw flexes, almost like he's actively *trying* not to let his smile take full form. "I'm glad."

Her eyes flit to his and linger there. Still and steady. "Me too."

Their quiet exchange is interrupted by what sounds like a metric ton of glass shattering, so loud it echoes all the way to the stables. They both look over to the distant front lawn and see a van with its tailgate up, and a man standing at its edge with his head in his hands. Milk crates are scattered in front of him, shards of glass spilling out of them onto the manicured lawn.

Crew mutters something under his breath, and it's kind of remarkable how quickly the softness of his features turns rock-hard. His lips curl slightly, and it seems a million thoughts are currently racing through his brain, each one angrier than the next.

Grace clears her throat. "Everything okay with you?"

He glances at her out of the corner of his eye but doesn't falter in his stoniness. "Fine," he replies curtly. His chin drops to his chest, and he kicks the toe of his boot against the loose dirt. "Everyone seems to have forgotten this is a *ranch*, not an entertainment venue."

She doesn't get much out of him after that, though in fairness, she doesn't really try. Crew is wound too tightly to unspool today, and the last thing she wants is to accidentally push a button that sends him spiraling into raging oblivion. He storms off a few minutes later toward some of the guys who are up on horses herding wandering cows. Grace watches, amused, as she sees his hands start to gesture wildly. Pierce and Alec immediately snap to attention, whatever joke they'd been bent over laughing at suddenly not very funny. They sit up straighter, and Grace watches the smiles melt off their faces like butter on a hot pan. They've seen this before, probably too many times to count. Crew Caldwell is on the warpath, and he doesn't give a single *fuck* about the destruction he leaves in his wake.

The bunkhouse reeks of cheap cologne. Forty stands behind an ironing board, carefully smoothing out the wrinkles on someone's button-up shirt. They're all in various stages of dress, and everyone looks remarkably presentable, considering the state of them not even an hour ago. Grace is sitting on her bunk, freshly showered hair tied back in a loose low ponytail, and her face scrubbed clean of all dirt and sweat. She is patiently—anxiously—waiting for June to beckon her into the bathroom, where she will proceed to cover her in makeup, douse her in hair spray, and then dress her up like a perfect Southern bumpkin.

There are two reasons Grace agreed to this. One, because June offered it, and it seemed like something Grace shouldn't deny if she had any hopes of further strengthening their tentative bond. And two, because in her twenty-five years of life, she's never once had someone offer to do her makeup and hair. Or lend her clothes. Growing up, she dressed herself in the mornings, brushed her own hair, and always opted for convenience over vanity. A low bun with a plastic claw clip, secondhand jeans, and two-year-old tennis shoes from Payless. Function over fashion, even then.

Grace can see June through the slight crack of the bathroom door, leaning over the sink with a tube of lipstick in hand. Already dressed with her hair looking lovely and effortless, she skillfully swipes the pigment over her lips, taking care to not color outside of the lines. She claps her hands together once she's satisfied, and then hollers, "All right, Grace. Your turn."

It feels like she's grown a new layer of skin. An odd, nice-smelling, slightly tacky layer of skin that has concealed every one of her freckles. June is hard at work, a small makeup brush between her teeth as she stands over Grace, brushing—blending?—furiously at the shadow on her right eyelid. Grace had been commanded to sit on the covered toilet and not move a single muscle unless told to, like when June made her smile with only her cheeks so she could apply an orangey-pink blush.

"You have good features," June says, though it seems like it's mostly to herself, more of an assessment than a compliment. "Shame you never show them off."

Grace tries not to blink too rapidly as June closes in on the corner of her eye, the blending brush now pushing aggressively into her skin. She can only imagine what she must look like right now, and some dark, insecure part of her has wondered more than once if June is setting her up again—if she'll look in the mirror at the end of this makeover and look like a rodeo clown.

"Well," Grace says, her head instinctually starting to lean away from June's ministrations—which June does *not* allow, and promptly pulls her chin back into place.

Grunting, Grace adds, "It's not like I have many opportunities."

"Honey, you're young, fit, and pretty," June replies. She sounds tired as she says it, like it's a fact that Grace should know. Like it's a personal affront to womankind that she doesn't take advantage of these assets. "You gotta make the opportunities."

Grace gives her an unenthusiastic thumbs-up. "I'll get right on that."

By the time June's done with her, Grace's eyebrows, eyelashes, eyelids, cheeks, lips—hell, even her neck is painted with foundation and then dusted with some sort of iridescent powder—are all done up. When June begins to pile everything into her carry-on-suitcase-size makeup bag, Grace thinks she's done, she's finally been released and can go look at herself in the mirror. But as she starts to stand, June pushes her shoulders back down, forcing her to plop back onto the toilet. "No," she says, then reaches behind Grace to gently release her ponytail. She fans her brown locks over her shoulder, the slightly frizzy almost-waves falling down her chest. June kinks an eyebrow, tapping her lip with her index finger. "Now we need to do something about *this*."

An immeasurable amount of time passes before June finally takes a step back from where Grace stands in front of the bathroom sink, looks her up and down, and smiles brightly. "I knew I was good," she muses, shaking her head in wonder. "But I didn't realize I was *this* good."

Grace lets out a little sigh, her patience already far past its limit. When June had started clamping swaths of hair into a curling iron, Grace had realized that *this* is why she never cared to learn how to primp herself. The task itself outweighs the reward by a long shot. She's going to wear this makeup and hairstyle for a couple of hours, and then she's going to come back here and scrub it all away. Three hours of work, gone with one swipe of a washcloth.

But then June gently twirls her around to look at herself in the mirror, and all her internal mutterings—*ridiculous waste of time, can't believe I'm letting her do this, how the hell am I going to keep this dress from riding up*—cease entirely. Because—for perhaps the first time in her adult life—Grace looks like a woman. A real, red-blooded, rosy-cheeked woman with shiny, bronzed skin, unblemished and unfreckled beneath the dewy foundation. Her brown eyes sparkle under the harsh fluorescent lights, and there's a perfectly placed touch of color on the apples of her cheeks. When she turns her head, she finds a glow that crawls up her cheekbone toward her temple—a gold-and-silver-flecked streak that reminds her of a river glistening in the sun.

The chestnut-brown curls she keeps tucked in constant ponytails cascade loosely, freely over her shoulders and past her breasts—they're what June referred to as "beachy," because they're supposed to mimic the effortless waves that form after a day drenched in salt water.

She doesn't realize tears are welling in her eyes until June's face morphs from ecstatic pride to concern in the flash of a second. "What the—" She steps forward, coming shoulder to shoulder with Grace and looking at her in the mirror. "Don't cry. If you ruin that eyeliner, I'll kill you."

A wet little laugh bursts from Grace's throat, accompanied by a sniffle.

"Honey," June says, reaching for one of Grace's hands. "What is it?"

"Nothing," Grace replies quickly, sucking in a deep breath and looking up at the ceiling. "I'm fine. You did a really great job."

"Well, obviously," June touts. Then she squeezes Grace's hand, beckoning her to look at her. When Grace does, she says, "So, why the tears?"

Grace manages a shaky smile. "I, um—" She peeks at herself in the mirror, and the person staring back at her stuns her all over again. "No one's ever done anything like this for me before." She looks at June, swallows down the emotion as it floods back in, this time with a vengeance. "I've never seen myself like this."

Something changes in June's face at Grace's words. It looks like an altering, a glimpse of the woman she is underneath it all. A softness she doesn't let others see. Nurturing. Protective. Warm. "Grace," she says, rubbing her thumb over the back of Grace's hand. "You're beautiful." The statement brooks no argument. She has a way of making statements sound irrefutable.

Like if she were to declare the sky is green, then it simply *would* be. June swings her around by the arm to look at herself again, all the softness turning into supportive resolve. "And it's about damn time you knew it."

The sun is still high in the azure evening sky when music begins to resonate throughout Halcyon. The ranch hands walk over to the lawn in a jumble of pearl snaps and shiny leather boots, some nearly hopping on their heels with excitement. Grace feels decidedly less agile in June's white ostrich boots, which are a size too small for her but—according to June—looked too good with the sundress to leave behind.

Emerging from the bathroom once June finally deemed her *ready* had been quite the experience. The reactions to her new look ranged from silent, slack-jawed awe to loud whoops and whistles. Only Forty had managed to actually form words in response, walking up to Grace once the frenzy had quieted down and telling her, with that gentle sincerity he always carries, "You look gorgeous, darlin'. Don't let any of these idiots get too close—they might drool on your pretty dress."

They arrive at the lawn; the party and all its bells and whistles are laid out before them like a portal into another world. How a team of people managed to plop this perfectly curated scene into the middle of a ranch in the dead of summer, Grace has no clue. But it's beautiful, and, in Renata Caldwell fashion, not a single detail is unimportant.

People Grace has never seen before are mingling among the tables, holding bottles of beer and wineglasses, dressed in expertly starched shirts and felt hats molded with care to perfectly fit their heads. They all look like they share the same tax bracket with the Caldwells, and even in her new state of feminine glamour, Grace can't help but feel a bit underdressed.

The guys all make a beeline toward the bar, Grace following a few paces behind with June. "What do you think?" the blonde asks, clearly not nearly as impressed with all of this as Grace.

"It's really something," Grace replies, still taking it all in. Renata and Clint are near the dance floor talking to a man with a guitar hanging from his neck. He looks familiar, but Grace can't quite put a name to his face.

June follows her line of sight and smirks, nodding knowingly. "That's Bryce Carrigan, in case you were wondering."

Grace looks at her, eyes widening. "Bryce Carrigan, like—"

"The guy who just won a Grammy and did a duet with Kacey Musgraves? Yeah."

"Holy shit."

"Yep," June says, nodding. "Honestly, I'm kind of surprised. He's small potatoes, comparatively."

Grace isn't sure she even *wants* to know what that means, but her eyebrows tilt up in question anyway.

June smiles, her eyes glittering with playfulness. "Last year was George Strait."

Cold beers in hand, Grace and June decide to make a lap around the party. A sea of strange faces stretches out before them, and Grace can't ignore the flare of nerves that rises up in her belly at the sight. She knows her uncle wouldn't come all the way here—the drive would take hours, and what would he even do once he arrived? There are men in all-black attire with walkie-talkies and guns at their hips strategically placed around the perimeter of the party. Close enough to blend in, far away enough to be invisible, depending on where a person is standing. Against that kind of muscle, her uncle would fold like a cheap polyester suit.

Whether June notices her unease or not, Grace can't be sure, but she chalks it up to a woman's intuition when June leans in and starts whispering in Grace's ear about the guests. It's a welcome distraction from her paranoia. Grace indulges her by following her gaze as she looks out at the dance floor. A man and a woman sway near the center, neither really moving their feet. He's silver haired and large in stature, dwarfing his petite companion. His arms are wrapped possessively around her shoulders, and she seems to smile only when he looks at her. Otherwise, she seems like she'd rather be anywhere else. The closer Grace looks, the clearer it becomes that the woman is younger than him. *Much* younger.

"Julian MacArthur," June says, nodding in his direction. She looks slightly disgusted, and soon, Grace understands why. "Oil baron kind of money—richer than the Caldwells. Richer than God, honestly. He's got his hands in all kinds of pots, but mostly horses and sponsoring bull riders. And that's his new wife, Makayla." June looks at Grace, kinks a judgmental brow, and says, "She's twenty-three."

"Ew," Grace replies. "*New* wife?"

June nods. "Left his first wife after forty years or something like that. Four kids, all grown. And—" June folds her arms over her chest, staring once more at the man, who, to Grace, somehow looks colder, more menacing than he did seconds ago. "The real kicker is he made her sign a prenup before they got married. She got to keep the house and one of the Porsches. One. He took the rest."

One Porsche—a cool hundred grand, tossed over this man's shoulder like scraps for a dog. Grace lets out a humorless laugh at the thought.

"Ten o'clock," June says, and Grace's attention blessedly drifts away from Julian, who is starting to sweat through his suit. At the far left corner of the dance floor, she sees two women standing close together, both staring up at a man and listening intently to whatever he's saying. "Carolyn and Marilyn Montgomery," June explains. "Houston royalty. Rodeo princesses."

Grace nods, transfixed by how stunning both women are, in that rare, ageless kind of way, and it takes her a half second to realize they look . . . *exactly* alike. They're twins—dressed the same, down to their shoes. They mirror each other's mannerisms; they both throw their heads back when they laugh, and they both follow it by shaking their heads in feigned exasperation. It looks as easy and natural as breathing when they both reach for the man's bicep—one to the left, the other to the right.

"I've never had the pleasure of meeting them, but, by all accounts, they're lovely. *Never met a stranger, could charm the mortar off a brick wall* kind of women."

An older man with a silver mustache appears a moment later, and he inserts himself between the twins with a knowing smile. They must be familiar with him; they both guffaw at the same time when they realize who's wedged themselves into their circle. Even from a great distance, Grace can see a sparkle in his eyes and the self-assured way he carries himself, as if confidence has never once been a point of struggle.

"I *think* that's the Caldwells' lawyer," June says when she notices him. "I can't remember his name... Flanagan something. Never met him, either, but Forty says he's a real demon in a courtroom. Never lost a case for the family, which, if you think about it, is not all that impressive. If someone was paying me a half-mil retainer, I'd be winning, too." The man, Flanagan, holds his hand out for one of the twins to join him for a dance, and when one agrees, they spin around in fluid, practiced motions, looping arms and sliding bootheels.

While Grace and June have been observing the crowd, the band has been setting up, and soon enough the live music takes over the speakers, replacing the generic country playlist with something more alive, more electric. Bryce Carrigan is a newer name in music but one who has quickly cemented himself as a favorite, and everyone at the party seems to flood the dance floor the second he steps up to the microphone and says, "Howdy, y'all."

Like Whac-A-Moles, Mikey and Raymond pop into Grace and June's field of vision, both holding cans of Bud Light, smiling with flushed cheeks. They insist on a dance, holding out their hands, and for two songs, the four of them laugh until their stomachs hurt, two-stepping and spinning around on the faux-wood dance floor.

Toward the end of the second song, Grace sees Renata staring out at the dance floor, and when they eventually make eye contact, Renata does a double take with bulging eyes when she realizes who she's looking at.

Oh my God, she mouths. She slaps Clint's and Cooper's shoulders without taking her eyes off Grace, wordlessly pulling them both from the middle of a conversation. They turn, both rubbing their arms and looking affronted, but then they follow Renata's gaze.

When Cooper sees Grace, his eyes and his smile light up his entire face. Clint, on the other hand, raises his arms toward the sky and gives her two thumbs up. Then he places his thumb and index finger between his teeth and whistles, *loud*. Grace gives him a weak thumbs-up in return, blushing and trying to hide her face in Mikey's shoulder.

Bryce's lilting voice carries on through the speakers set up on either side of the stage. Grace continues to mingle, to drink, and to dance with all the hands. She tries—she really does—to *not* scan the party for a tall, probably frowning, dark-haired figure.

But he just—he tends to take up a lot of air in any space he occupies. Even when he's grumpy, or stubbornly reserved, he's like a magnet for all the oxygen around him. The second he enters a room, her eyes tend to gravitate toward the vacuum of his presence, even when she doesn't want them to. Which is how she realizes—with a little tinge of disappointment flaring up in her belly—Crew isn't here.

It isn't until about half an hour later that a truck appears on the horizon. Crew's truck. It rolls down the long drive slowly, and the windows all begin sliding down. A woman with hair dark brown and thick emerges from the passenger side. She's hoisting herself up to see over the top of the truck, and then she waves slowly, with a cupped hand, like a rodeo princess in the grand entry. Grace notices Renata start to wave excitedly with both hands.

The closer the truck gets, the easier it becomes to figure out who the strange dark-haired woman is. The resemblance to her mother is uncanny—effortlessly beautiful and elegant. But her smile is all her father, lighting up her eyes and dimpling her cheeks. What *really* gives it away, though, what makes it completely undeniable which family she belongs to, is the hard set of her brow and mouth when the truck suddenly starts bouncing, jostling her from side to side and interrupting her regal entrance. She slaps the top of the cab, cursing like a drunken sailor at Crew for tapping on the brakes. There's not a single doubt in Grace's mind. That's Caia Caldwell. Crew's little sister.

The truck slows to a stop in front of the house. Cooper is there in seconds, remarkably swift considering his still-recovering ankle, and he practically yanks his sister out of the cab and wraps her in a hug. Clint and Renata make their way over, and eventually, Grace turns away, feeling like she's invading a private moment once she notices Clint trying to inconspicuously wipe his cheeks with the back of his hand.

The smell of barbecue wafts through the air, and Grace meanders over to the buffet, ravenous after skipping dinner to get ready for the party. She piles a couple of ribs and a chicken leg onto a plate, then covers every remaining inch of it with coleslaw, baked beans, and macaroni and cheese. Some of the guys are doing the same—Pierce's pile of food is so high it looks like it's about to topple over. Grace follows them back to their designated table and plops down, laying the denim napkin over her lap and praying she doesn't get anything on June's dress. Because she is about to shovel every last bite of this food into her mouth at warp speed.

The next time she looks up, feeling fit to burst, she finds the Caldwells have moved inward, all standing around their table, in the center of everything. Clint has his arm around Caia's neck, and she is patting his cheek affectionately, talking to someone Grace doesn't recognize. Cooper is gesturing animatedly at his mother, who seems quietly amused but only half listening, half laser focused on the cake across the way, which is currently being artfully stuck with small, golden candles.

Grace isn't sure what she expected of the only Caldwell daughter—resentment due to the distance or Caia's choice of career, maybe. But there's nothing but warmth and familial recognition. It's evident, between her and her parents of course, but even more between her and her brothers. Cooper yanks on a piece of her hair while she has her back turned, then points at Crew when she turns around. Caia reaches over and whacks the unsuspecting Crew's shoulder, and he whirls around, indignant, and proceeds to drop his shoulder and lift her over it, sending her feet flying into the air and her fists slamming into his back. Renata and Clint, now standing next to each other with their fingers intertwined, seem completely unfazed.

Crew sets her down eventually, picking his bottle of Dos Equis back up, and tossing back a big swig as Cooper tests his luck once more with a wet willy in Caia's ear. Caia practically tackles him, the two nearly tumbling into the grass. Crew watches them, content, and Grace watches him.

He hasn't seen her yet. Hasn't seen this ... new look. For a brief moment, she contemplates running back to the bunkhouse to change into something more *her*, because—does it look like she's trying to fit in with the rest of these wealthy Texas ranchers? Is the makeup even still on her face? It's hot and humid as hell this evening. Dozens of anxiety-inducing questions start to cascade through her head, and before she even realizes what's happening, she's standing up and leaving the table, removing herself from his line of sight. She orders a beer and then stands at the bar and drinks almost half of it in one go.

The sound of a clinking bottle echoes from her right, and she looks over to see Crew near a trash can made to look like a barrel, and now walking up to the bar. Grace stands frozen, just off to the side with her forearms pressed stiffly into the red-checkered cloth that covers the pop-up bar. She does *not* look at Crew as he steps forward and asks the bartender for another beer. His voice is low and rumbling, and she can pick up whiffs of his scent from where she stands. His weird, spicy cologne is most prominent in his usual mix now, surprisingly intoxicating. *Don't inch closer,* she scolds herself. *And don't you dare inhale as deeply as you want to.*

She keeps her eyes trained on the mouth of her beer, but she can see in her peripheral vision when Crew turns his body and leans on his elbow, awaiting the dressing of his Dos Equis. His stare seems to drift over the party, taking it all in, until he finally spots her. For half a second, his head keeps moving, ready to look right past her.

But then he jerks his gaze back and goes completely still.

Even as the bartender sets the beer in front of him and motions for the next person, Crew doesn't move an inch.

Grace decides then, even if just for a moment, she can be brave. She wants—needs—to see what he looks like, looking at her. Crew has looked at her many times, for many reasons, with everything from irritation and impatience to concern and curiosity. In his gaze now is something else. Something brand-new that she can't quite put a finger on. It's more of a flurry of feeling than one specific emotion—somewhere in the realm of wonder, maybe a sprinkling of awe. She catalogs as much as she can, an exhilarating warmth starting to bloom in her belly.

"Hi," she says, offering up a nervous smile. His appraising stare doesn't falter; he doesn't even *blink*, let alone look away. Instead, his eyes drift down her body swiftly, and the heat in her abdomen starts to boil when she sees his breath catch, his jaw tic.

His voice is slightly raspy when he responds, maybe even a little dumbstruck. "Grace."

Grace smiles. "Didn't recognize me?"

Crew shakes his head. "No, of course I did—I just didn't realize—" His lips pull together in a tight line, and his eyes seem to be moving independently of his brain, refusing to cooperate until they take their fill of her. "New dress?"

She almost laughs at the banality of it. The halfhearted attempt at having a normal conversation. "It's June's," she says, giving a little twirl. Though the action, the showing off, is not something she's adept at, Crew's *still* looking at her. It sparks her confidence a little, and she holds out the hem near her knees, fanning out the flowy fabric. Showing it off, and, in the process, showing off her tanned, toned legs.

Crew's eyes drop, and it happens again—that flexing jaw, unsettled and tense. He clears his throat, and Grace finds she is enjoying this maybe a little too much. This big, strong, stoic man turned fidgety and unsteady by a girl in a dress.

By *her* in a dress.

She's never had power like this before. She may as well enjoy it. "Do you like it?" she asks, because she's enjoying playing with fire. It could be dangerous, calling direct attention to this tension between them, something that's maybe always been there but is now buzzing and insistent, growing thicker by the second. It's risky—it could be catastrophic, if looked at under a magnifying glass. But his eyes have turned wild, like she's a five-course meal after years of bone-deep hunger—and it's delicious, the anticipation radiating down her limbs, all the way to her toes. Crew's mouth opens to answer; Grace sucks in a breath she's unable to release.

"Grace—"

An unfamiliar female voice comes from behind her, closing in rapidly. Crew's mouth snaps shut the second it hits his ears, and Grace can't help but mourn whatever words he was about to say.

"Crew." Grace turns to find Caia, short in stature but, like her mother, a titan of dominating energy. "Be polite and introduce me to your friend."

Crew blinks, a too-long beat passing with him saying nothing at all. Caia grins, then turns to Grace. "I'm Caia," she says, holding out a hand. "Sorry to interrupt."

"Grace." She shakes her hand. "Don't be sorry. We were just—"

What? Grace bites the inside of her cheek. *What were you just . . . ?*

Caia pays no mind to her stuttered sentence; she simply crosses over to stand near her brother and elbows him playfully in the ribs. "Flirting, it looked like. Or whatever crude imitation of it my brother could manage."

Grace watches a subtle redness start to bloom on Crew's cheeks. Caia grins up at him, then, to Grace, she says, "Grace, the magical horse whisperer, right?"

Grace flushes. Bashful and ill-equipped at taking compliments, she shakes her head. "I wouldn't go that far."

"She's done great work," Crew cuts in. "Got a stallion saddle-broken in no time."

Caia nods, impressed, and with a swift clap to Crew's back, says, "Then she's out of your league in more ways than one." Something behind Grace catches Caia's attention, and her eyes bulge slightly.

"Uh-oh, you'd better go, Crew," she says, feigning terror. "Cooper looks like he's one whiskey away from trying to arm-wrestle a state senator."

Crew lingers for a moment, looking between the two of them. Grace, a little—a lot—intimidated by his firecracker of a sister, tries to implore him with her eyes not to go. But Caia gives him no choice when she practically shoves him away with her palm to his chest. "Go, wrangle him before Mom has to." She smiles and winks at Grace, then adds: "We'll be fine."

Crew sighs loudly, tossing his head back. Grace observes this, smiling despite herself. It's odd—and maybe even . . . adorable?—to see Crew among his family. Especially Caia. She seems to bring out another side of him entirely. More expressive, more present. More like Grace imagines he might've been as a kid.

He steps into her space then, and Grace's breath catches slightly. "I'll see you later?" Crew asks, hardly louder than a whisper. He gives her a moment, his eyes boring into hers. Only when she gives him a tight, nervous nod does he walk past her, leaving just the slightest bit of room between them as he goes.

Caia snorts and mumbles something that sounds a lot like *Real smooth.*

Nerves dance in Grace's belly, in her throat. The look in Caia's eyes when the two women find each other's stare is unsettling—mostly because it looks *exactly* like the one Renata gets on occasion when she's trying to puzzle something out.

"Come on," Caia says, hooking her arm into Grace's. "I need a drink."

CHAPTER 11

It becomes evident after one shot and one shot *only* that Grace is not a fan of tequila. And this fact must be all over her face, because Caia spots her grimacing and breathing hard through her nose and trying to keep her dinner from coming back up, and she has to clap a hand over her mouth to keep from laughing. "Oh, Grace, I'm sorry. I didn't realize—"

Grace shakes her head, waving it off. "All good. I'm fine."

"Really?" Caia counters flatly.

Grace hiccups and the taste flickers back into her mouth with a vengeance. Rather than risk talking, she gives Caia a thumbs-up.

Caia chuckles. "All right. Want to sit?"

They sit on a cube of hay near the bar, and Grace is finally starting to feel like she can breathe normally when Caia goes in for the kill.

"So, you like him," she says, knocking playfully into Grace's arm with her own. When Grace looks up for clarification, she follows Caia's glance until she finds Crew with his arm securely wrapped around Cooper's neck, walking him away from a group of annoyed-looking men and waving an apologetic hand in their direction.

Stuttering, shocked, and still nauseated, Grace makes a clipped, unintelligible noise. "What? Crew? No—he's my boss."

"Ah, right. Of course," Caia says. "That boss-slash-employee dynamic never turns into anything. There's *never* any attraction there."

"Well, I'm sure there's attraction for some people, but it's—it's not like that."

"It looked a lot *like that* to me, honey." She shrugs. "But, hey, we don't have to get into it. You don't know me from Adam—of course you're not going to confess your undying love for my stubborn-ass brother."

Grace says nothing, grateful for the out. She notices Caia scanning the scene, particularly spending a good amount of time watching the dance floor. She seems to be looking for someone, something. Grace couldn't say. To keep the conversation healthily distanced from dissecting her feelings for Crew, she asks, "Looking for someone?"

Caia kinks a brow. "Just making sure my mother didn't invite any unsavory types. Con artists. Musicians. Bull riders turned cologne models." Caia sighs, biting the inside of her cheek as her search continues. "She tends to be too charitable about that kind of thing."

Cologne models—Grace remembers that. She swings her head around to look at Caia, and, excited to have something concrete to contribute, she says, "Oh, Easton, right? The guy from the centerfold in *For the Ranch*?"

Caia's search halts. She looks at Grace sharply and abruptly, and for the first time since laying eyes on her, Grace notices a twitch of something sad in her eyes. A chink in her armor. A rare sight, if Grace had to guess.

"You know him?" Caia asks, leaning back and folding her arms over her chest.

It's a self-protective gesture, Grace knows. She learned that from a guidance counselor in middle school. "No, not at all. The guys just made a big stink about it a few nights ago. Everyone seemed to have their own opinion of it, none of them good."

Caia nods, smiling, seemingly satisfied with that answer. "Well, there's not a whole lot of good to say, so that makes sense."

Grace nods, waiting for Caia to elaborate on what clearly seems to be an old wound with an old . . . someone. When she doesn't, a peaceful, unexpected quiet settles between them. Grace glances out of the corner of her eye at Caia here and there, admiring her sharp profile, her full lips, the freckles that span her cheeks and nose. It really should be studied, how beautiful all of the Caldwells are. The gene pool should be at the top of science's list on how to make people pretty, if that's even a thing science does.

The bartenders are still hard at work as night settles in, and Bryce Carrigan steadily and enthusiastically continues to work the crowd with his crooning and his charm. Couples dance, people mingle, all the laughing and cacophonous voices morphing into roars as the alcohol continues to flow.

Around nine, the candle-covered cake is rolled into a central location amid all of the tables. The candles are lit by a team of waiters as everyone crowds around, Clint standing nearest to the table with Renata by his side. Caia bids Grace a quick, sweet farewell, and then the three Caldwell children are standing together, opposite their parents. Caia extends onto her tippy-toes to whisper something in Crew's ear that makes him cup a hand over her mouth, and Cooper ducks his head toward them, hoping to be let in on the joke. Grace tries not to wonder what Caia said, tries not to consider the possibility that it might've been about her. When the last candle is lit, Renata smiles proudly and holds up her wineglass. Without having to say a word, she brings all of the conversations to a gentle close.

"I'd like to say a few words about Clint on his sixtieth birthday," she begins. Her cheeks are wine flushed, but she looks radiant. "You've all probably heard this before, but you're gonna listen anyway."

A light chuckle ripples through the crowd.

"Clint and I met when we were just kids. He was my high school sweetheart."

Grace's brows hike; she had no idea their story spanned so many years. They look at each other like they're still in the throes of passionate, all-consuming love—she never would've guessed they've known and loved each other for most of their lives. She didn't think that kind of love actually existed—let alone *thrived*—in real life.

"We grew up together. He's always been my best friend." She looks at her husband, tilting her head affectionately. "But I didn't know he *like-liked* me until we were in tenth grade, when he bribed the janitor into opening my locker on Valentine's Day so he could leave me a necklace and a letter that confessed his feelings." With her free hand, she fishes something out of the pocket of her sleek black slacks. A folded-up piece of notebook paper, faded and discolored from years of being touched and treasured. "I still have it. You don't get to know what he said—but what you *should* know is that the necklace was from Kmart. It turned my neck green, but I still wore it every single day. I still have that, too, but it's become a bit more fragile over the years. Clint spent his lawn mowing earnings on it, and the reason I always tell this story when I'm talking about my husband is because it's so quintessentially *him*. Even at fourteen, he was willing to work tirelessly for the people he loved. Sweat, blood, tears—hours of hard labor to pull together twenty dollars so he could spoil me in the only way he knew how." Clint's cheeks have gone red, and he's shifting back and forth on the heels of his boots—the man looks about two seconds away from breaking into a full sob.

"We've been through a lot since then," Renata continues. "Colleges on the opposite side of the country—long distance was awful. But then we came back to Texas, made a home for ourselves on my family's ranch. He knew that was my dream and he made it come true. He gave me three beautiful children." She nods in the direction of the three of them, all suddenly looking uncharacteristically sheepish. Renata dismisses their shyness with a tiny, endearing wave of her hand.

"Clint—every single day, you make me happier than the one before. Thank you for being the heart and soul of this family, the unshakable port in my perpetual storm. You are more loved than you will ever know." She raises her glass, and the sea of people surrounding her follows suit. "Happy birthday, honey." The crowd echoes her, and then everyone drinks to a teary-eyed Clint, who has pulled Renata into his embrace to kiss her temple, the two looking very much like two kids in puppy love.

The band returns to their instruments to accompany the "Happy Birthday" song, and Clint's smile grows wider as he approaches the cake, beckoning everyone closer. "Are y'all trying to burn down the ranch? Get over here and help me with these," he shouts. With the help of his family and friends, the candles are extinguished, followed by roaring applause.

As beautiful as the moment is, Grace can't help the darkness that settles into her thoughts as she watches the Caldwells share a long, tight group hug. Clint's smile is blinding, not a shred of melancholy in his eyes. The look of a man surrounded by love so genuine it's almost palpable. Grace has never seen anything like this—doesn't quite know what to make of it once the joy begins to soften. It's like real life comes crashing back, reminding her that *this* is how a family should be. Telling her none too kindly that she doesn't belong in this picture—doesn't fit in with all these shiny, happy people.

Thankfully, the onslaught of self-doubt and hate is throttled by a hand grasping and squeezing her wrist, demanding her attention. She turns to find June at her right, eyes sparkling and glued to the stage. "You ready?" June asks.

Grace follows her stare and sees Bryce on the verge of starting another song. "For what?"

June grins but says nothing.

"All right folks," Bryce says into the mic. "I've been told y'all have a little tradition for Señor Clint's birthday."

A variety of hollering erupts from the crowd, and suddenly, everyone is pouring in, racing past Grace and June and onto the dance floor.

"That's right," Bryce says, nodding. "If you aren't already, come on and get down to the dance floor. Because we . . ." He strums the guitar, taps a boot against the stage, and looks to his band for confirmation that they're ready. Satisfied, he smirks and says, "Are about to *boot scoot*."

A familiar song begins, and the steps to the accompanying

line dance begin in perfect synchronicity. "Boot Scootin' Boogie" is one of those universally beloved songs, and there isn't a person in the state of Texas who doesn't know it, or the steps. It draws people to the dance floor like moths to a flame, Grace included. Because when "Boot Scootin' Boogie" is playing, it's basically sacrilegious to do anything *but* boot scoot.

June renews her hold on Grace's wrist, dragging her out onto the dance floor amid the sea of party guests. Grace looks around, spotting familiar faces with alcohol-flushed cheeks and wide grins as they all make their way into surprisingly uniform lines. She starts to move her feet when she's found her place in a line—the grapevines, the clicks and kicks, all of it comes as naturally as breathing, muscle memory at its finest. Standing in the line in front of them are Mikey, Caleb, and Pierce, who all stumble through the steps and almost knock over a group of elderly women. Grace and June nearly double over with laughter as the three men attempt to regain their footing, the older women staring daggers into them, all the while not missing a single step. The mass of people turns fluidly in a new direction, and then the Caldwells come into view.

While it isn't surprising to see all five of them on the dance floor—as a unit, they seem to have the power to convince the surly eldest son to do anything they want—it is strange to witness just how . . . *good* of a dancer Crew actually is. Grace imagines him being dragged to dance halls across the state with his parents as a child, learning line and square dances elbow to elbow with his mother. His hat is tipped back slightly, revealing a sliver of his hairline. His expression is uncharacteristically relaxed, like he doesn't even have to think about what move to make next. He knows it by heart—could probably do it in his sleep.

Toward the end of the song, Cooper tries to cut his older brother down to size by kicking behind his knee. He laughs as Crew nearly face-plants, and then the two men are tussling in the middle of the dance floor. Caia and Renata both yell for them to knock it off; Clint hollers something that sounds like *Take it outside*—a dad joke if there ever was one, considering they *are* outside. The horseplay ceases as the song comes to an end—Crew's hat has fallen to the floor, leaving his dark hair to sprout wildly in multiple directions. He replaces the hat firmly on his head, then chuffs Cooper's chin with a light fist. A boy's version of getting the last word.

"Y'all look damn good out there," Bryce says when the music has faded out. "What about the El Paso? Anybody know that one?"

The majority of the crowd cheers, but some begin to scatter, heading back to their tables, or the bar, or to the extremely fancy porta-potty trailer bathrooms, which are air-conditioned and smell like a garden in the springtime.

It happens quickly, before Grace even realizes what's unfolding. Caleb and Pierce grab hold of each other dramatically. Mikey tries his luck with a guest, and his eyes light up when she agrees. Cooper playfully slaps Crew in the stomach before turning around and starting slowly, nervously, toward June, and when they make eye contact across the dance floor, she gives him a Cheshire cat smile.

Grace, now by herself amid the buzzing crowd, searches for a familiar face to pair off with before the music gets going. She sort of knows this dance—remembers it vaguely from the teen nights she went to at Midnight Rodeo in middle school. Mostly, she remembers how important it was to quickly partner up with your crush before they got stolen away by another. How scandalous it felt, holding both hands, wrapped around each other, sweaty and tentative and exhilarating.

Now, as an adult, the stakes are much lower. In fact, Grace is content to walk off the dance floor when she sees most of the hands already paired with others. An ice-cold drink sounds like heaven after working up a sweat during the previous dance—and with this hairstyle, there's no respite from the dank heat, no breeze hitting the back of her neck. It takes all the patience she has not to yank the now flattened, frizzy curls into a high ponytail.

Bryce begins to strum his guitar, landing on another cover, a familiar tune. Over the music, a murmur catches Grace's attention as she's making to leave, and what she finds has warmth blooming in her cheeks for a reason other than the summer heat. Clint's and Renata's hands are already clasped, both standing and ready to begin. In front of them are Cooper and June, and next to them, Caia is standing at Crew's shoulder looking adamant about something. Crew's hands are up, and he's starting to back away from his sister, but she appears to care little for whatever excuse he's making to leave.

Because Caia's got Grace in her sights, and the twinkle in her eye tells Grace that her mind is made up. It looks so much like the one in Renata's—but where Renata's is sage and assuring, Caia's is mischievous and confident.

She mouths the word *go* to her brother, then points firmly past him. At Grace.

Crew turns, and when he spots her, his shoulders give a little sag. Whether from disappointment and irritation at his sister's matchmaking, or from relief that it's Grace on the other end of Caia's command and not another politician's wife he has to schmooze, she doesn't know. His expression is as unreadable as ever.

She doesn't know exactly what she expected—maybe a shake of his head, a resigned shrug—*something* that would let Grace down easily when he inevitably exited the dance floor and did not succumb to sisterly pressure. In the variety of scenarios, she hadn't given weight to the possibility that he'd actually listen, and that he'd be walking toward her with purposeful steps, his face transforming from a nondescript mask into something soft. Something sweet.

He sidles up next to her about twenty seconds before the wheel of people will begin to turn. Leans down and says into her ear, "You want to?"

Grace looks up at him, heart fluttering slightly in her chest. "I've only done this one a couple of times," she admits, because it'd be easier to make an excuse and run off than it would be to stand at his side for the next four minutes, holding his hands and moving with him. Easier and significantly less dangerous. "I don't know if I remember it."

Crew is undeterred. He nods, then turns until he's elbow to elbow with her. "That's all right," he says, giving her a little smirk.

Cocky and self-assured about *dancing*? She never would've guessed. "I can keep us in line," he states, like it's the easiest thing in the world. Like it's no skin off his nose to make sure she steps in the right direction. He lifts his hands, starts to reach one over her shoulder. With a slightly playful look in his eyes, he asks, "May I?"

Grace nods, then reaches up to grab both of his hands—the one near her chest, and the one that now lies over her right shoulder. His grip is somehow firm and soft, and his hands engulf hers entirely. Heat seeps from his palms into her skin, and Grace takes a deep, centering breath. Then the circle of people starts to move.

The song somehow simultaneously lasts for an eon and mere minutes. Crew's grip on her never falters. It's all well and good, really, nothing too crazy—but then they get to the bit where she is supposed to stand in front of him and . . . well, by looking at the people on either side of her, it would appear that she's meant to swivel her hips to the beat while he continues to hold her hands. She glances at him over her shoulder the first time this happens, unsure of herself, and a moment passes before she's able to follow along. They go back to marching hand in hand.

"Sorry," Grace murmurs, flushing.

"Don't be," Crew says, squeezing the hand he holds at her shoulder.

When it happens again, Grace doesn't miss it. She turns, giving him her back, holding both of his hands over her shoulders. There's little space between them; she can feel his breath against her hair, the heat from his chest. She sees June a few feet away, laughing as she sways in front of Cooper, giving the move a flourish that's all confidence and allure. Grace sucks in a quick breath and decides she may as well try to do the same.

What occurs then isn't an exact impression of June, but it's not terrible, either. Grace has always had some hint of rhythm, has always been able to keep up with beats and tempo. Dancing is no different—she is nowhere near an expert, but she can move her body to music in a way that doesn't look clumsy or stilted. She sways, lets the song direct her, lets herself momentarily forget who stands behind her, holding her hands, watching. Her body moves toward the floor, then back up again with a natural finesse she has never been more grateful for.

Crew's thumbs brush across the backs of her hands, and Grace shivers.

Toward the end of the song, the uniformity of the crowd begins to dissipate—couples start doing their own thing during the standing-in-front-of-your-partner bit. Elaborate twirls and dips; Mikey's partner even jumps into his arms and lets him spin her around. Grace is more confident than she was at the start, but not *that* confident, so when the last round of it begins, she does only what feels natural, bending the rules of the dance just a hair. Without really thinking about it, she moves their joined hands from the tops of her shoulders to her hips, bringing his arms around her rather than above her. Crew lets out a quick breath, surprised at the adjustment, but he doesn't stop her, doesn't miss a beat. For a brief moment when his hands release hers, Grace panics, thinking she's crossed a line, rung a bell that can never be unrung. Ruined everything with her attempt at being bold and *fun*. But then he grips her hips instead, his thumbs digging pleasantly into the bones there through the thin material of her dress.

Grace's breath hitches in her throat. His hold is so— Nothing about Crew has ever struck her as timid, or meek, or anything but firm. His hold is no different. He holds her like a decision he's made that won't be contested, like a statement of fact rather than a show of desire.

Subtly, slowly, he drags her backward. With only seconds left of this part of the dance, they have little time to continue going off script, but he takes advantage anyway. Brings her flush against his chest, lets his chin dip until his nose brushes against the tip of her ear.

Though she wants to, though every fiber in her being is screaming at her to do so, she doesn't lean back into him. She can't—with the flickering flames being stoked in her belly by his every touch, every caress, she can't be held responsible for what would happen if she were to give in entirely. Not right now. Not here.

So she lets the music pull them apart, moves back to his side, and regrets it immediately when his hands leave her hips and return to their original places at her side and shoulder. They start to march, and she chances a peek up at him, finding him already looking at her.

They don't say anything, but then, they've never had to say much to convey what it is they're feeling. The language they share through eye contact has evolved since they first met—in the beginning, it was a lot of *Are you actually fucking kidding me?* kinds of glares. Then, when they started to warm to each other, the looks softened along with the messages. They became more concerned, more curious, more reassuring.

It seems now they've progressed into new territory again, if Grace's gut holds any truth. Because what she reads in Crew's eyes is simple and direct, the same way he always is, but there's something else, too. Something unexpected that leads to a little throb between her legs.

Something that looks—undeniably—like hunger.

When Grace falls into her bunk that night, it feels like she's floating. The makeup is scrubbed from her face, the curls in her hair are frizzy remnants of their original glory, but it doesn't matter. On this night, she danced. She's still riding that high, wanting to prolong it as much as possible, so she reaches for her phone and earbuds, ready to hear that second song, the one she moved to like water. The one Crew held her through, his grip warm and unfaltering on her hips. But when she turns the phone on, a notification pops up that not only dampens her good mood—it drowns her in a sea of icy dread.

A text from an unknown number, but Grace knows exactly who it is. His utter lack of intelligence practically screams through each letter. And still, her stomach turns at the words, the boldness of them. The recklessness.

> I no u sent tht bitch sniffing round here

> Do u think I can't get 2 u, Gracie? ?

> Did U rlly think u were safe there??

CHAPTER 12

Caia leaves the next morning before dawn. Crew's taillights beam as they drive away from the property, painting the gravel below the tires in a blanket of red. The ranch hands have already begun to scatter, trudging toward the first of their duties for the day. They are a symphony of yawns and hungover groans.

Forty walks with Grace toward the stables. He's been tasked with cleaning the pens and grooming the horses—they've got a group of potential buyers coming in from Fort Worth later in the day, and everything needs to look presentable. Not that it ever doesn't—Crew runs a tight ship—but if a little extra elbow grease gets them a better deal, Forty will happily oblige.

"Have fun last night?" he asks her in a thick morning voice.

Grace, having slept fitfully after staring at Bellamy's texts for hours on end, manages a sleepy smile. Her eyelids feel heavy, ready to shut, even as she plods toward the barn. If given the chance, she could lie down right here in the grass and take a long, hard nap. "Yeah," she says. "It was nice."

Their boots scuff the ground in unison as Forty clicks his teeth. "Get lots of compliments?"

Grace chuckles. "There was a line of suitors hoping to court me. Didn't you see them?"

"Right, right." Forty nods. "The line. Of course."

With a sigh, Grace says, "Everyone was really sweet once the initial shock wore off."

Forty huffs knowingly. He lets a beat pass before speaking again, and his tone is gentle, as if he's trying to avoid spooking her. By the time he gets to the end of it, Grace understands why. "Maybe there was someone in particular you were hoping to get compliments from." It's a question but it isn't—one of Forty's musings that always seem to ring true, even when the person on the receiving end doesn't want to hear it.

Nerves and embarrassment and anxiety all rear their ugly heads instantly, ready to fight to the death to be at the forefront of Grace's brain. She'd bitten her nails down to the quick the night before, replaying their dance in her head more times than she could count. Wondering if she'd been too bold, if she'd misread the moment entirely and made a complete fool of herself. After all, once the song had ended, Crew had practically bolted away from her, retreating to the safety of his siblings without a word. He'd stuck around for only ten minutes or so after that, and then he'd pulled an Irish goodbye and slipped away from the party, Boone at his heels. Grace had stood there, alone amid a crowd of people, bereft and reeling.

Anxiety drips like acid into her stomach. "Not especially," she lies, hoping Forty won't see right through her. Hoping that, even if he does, he doesn't call her on it.

The fib hangs in the air between them, Forty allowing it to sink in, allowing her the opportunity to correct it. When she doesn't, he sighs, throaty and raspy from sleep and age and a past life where he smoked a pack of Marlboro Reds every day. "For what it's worth, Grace," he begins, slowing his steps slightly.

Grace follows suit, and soon, they are facing each other in the dark. He looks younger in the predawn light, like the shadows and moonbeams are working in tandem to erase the years of lines and scars from his face. Even his hair looks brighter, and if she squints, it's less like the familiar shades of gray and more like the sandy blond it once was. "I've been working here a long time." He smiles wryly. "I watched the Caldwell kids grow up."

Grace nods, her thoughts immediately going to those sudsy kids in that photograph in Crew's house. Soap coating their hair and faces, smiling at the camera without a worry in the world. She imagines them running amok on the grounds, grass-stained clothes and scraped knees. And a younger Forty, still spry and able to chase them away from dangerous things like rattlesnakes and rusted wind turbines.

"In my years here, I've seen every version of Crew Caldwell," he states, his smile growing slightly wistful. "The good son, the reliable brother, the brave soldier."

She doesn't know where he's going with this. Doesn't know what she did to deserve this little glimpse into this past, this nugget of knowledge. But she listens intently anyway.

"I've seen the way his view of the world has evolved over thirty years. The way he looked at things before the war and after . . . he was—*is* a different man. There's a hardness there. Some of it he's always carried, as the eldest, the most responsible. A self-imposed duty. But most of it came from a place none of us have ever been. And it came to stay."

It feels wrong, talking about this. Like she's pulling back a curtain and seeing something wholly private. Too precious to gossip about at six in the morning. "Forty—"

He raises a hand to stop her. "Last night, I saw an old version of him. His steps were lighter. His smile was easily earned. When I saw him look at you in that dress . . ."

Grace holds her breath, bracing for whatever he's about to say. She can't hope, or wish, or wonder, because that only ever leads to disappointment. And Crew had run—he'd left like he couldn't get away from her fast enough. Maybe he'd held her, touched her with a strange dichotomy of a firm grip and soft caresses, but it had been the dance. The moment. That's all.

Forty kinks an eyebrow at her, as if to say, *You better be listening.* "I saw a Crew that I thought we'd lost many years ago. I saw it in his eyes."

They approach the barn together once Forty has sufficiently assured Grace that she doesn't have to *do anything* about the observation, but that he'd just wanted her to know. Felt like she had the right to understand her obvious effect on Crew, and to not hold it against him when he shied away from it. "He's a little out of practice when it comes to the fairer sex," Forty had advised. "This place—this life. Not exactly a *chick magnet*."

Grace had snorted at that.

She's content to not pay this any mind. Sure, maybe her feelings toward Crew have shifted away from the general unease he'd caused her at first, but, if asked, she wouldn't be able to put a name to what those feelings are now. There are too many—a complicated and indecipherable mix that spans from physical attraction to downright terror. A fear so potent that she decides quickly to not unearth the rest. If she were to take Forty's words to heart, she'd look Crew in the eye and see a long-lost man who'd returned home simply by looking at her. The consequences of a look like that could be catastrophic. To gain him, to know him, to touch him would mean that when she inevitably lost him somewhere down the line, she wouldn't survive it.

Too lost in her own thoughts, Grace doesn't realize right away upon entering the stables that something's off. Something's wrong. Forty senses it immediately, straightening his posture and speeding up his steps, which yanks her out of her reverie.

It's too quiet—too still for a place full of life. They round the corner and Grace's stomach sinks. "Holy shit," Forty says quietly, his face twisted up in pain and horror.

"Oh my God," Grace says breathily, and she has to lean against a doorframe to keep from falling to her knees. Forty places a hand over his mouth, his eyes widening as he takes in the scene—the horses not upright and eager for breakfast, not brimming with life and impatience. Waylon and Duke are standing, but barely, both teetering on the edge of crashing to the ground at any second. Cash and Marquis, too. But the rest—Grace's heart thunders against her ribs.

"Go," Forty says, not looking at her, the word clipped and hard. "Get Crew. Now."

Two white vans sit parked near the stables. Equine veterinarians, a whole five of them, had piled out about an hour earlier, ready to help. The ranch hands are gathered in little clusters, none speaking louder than a whisper. Grace sits off by herself in the grass, knees pulled to her chest as she watches the doctors shuffle back and forth between the barn and the vans. When she sees one of them emerge with a pained frown, shaking his head, she barely makes it to the giant trash bin before vomiting up her breakfast.

It takes almost three hours for the vets to feel comfortable enough to walk away, and even then, they agree at least two should stay behind to monitor overnight. Whatever it was the horses ingested—a bad, moldy batch of alfalfa, most likely—proved to be too toxic for three of them. Stringer, Abraham, and Carrot had all succumbed in the small hours of the night. The rest were critically ill, now heavily medicated and sleeping.

Renata, Clint, Crew, and Cooper surround the lead vet, and Grace can pick up about every other word or so, enough to know the man is adamant they get the police involved because this doesn't look like an accident. One horse could maybe be explained away, but all of them—it looks premeditated. That, coupled with the fact that it happened on a night when everyone was far away, distracted with alcohol and dancing and birthday cake, leaves little room for doubt. While they were all looking the other way, someone tried to murder all of Halcyon's horses.

Grace watches Waylon sleep from outside his stable. Tears stream down her face as she wonders what they all must've thought, watching each other drop like flies. These beautiful, majestic creatures, cut down by some invisible evil. By someone's cruel heart. Her teeth grind together in pure fury, and she resists the urge to punch a fist straight through the wood of the stable. Forty tells her to go, there's nothing more she can do here. She doesn't want to leave Waylon, but the vets reassure her that he'll be cared for, watched around the clock until he's back to his normal, grumpy self.

After a long, lukewarm shower, Grace is wringing water out

of her hair with a raggedy towel when someone knocks on the bunkhouse door. Strange—no one ever knocks. Especially strange considering it's almost ten in the morning and everyone is out working. Grace slips on her boots and walks toward the door, finding Renata on the other side. She's wearing sunglasses despite the overcast day, and she jerks her head toward the patio surrounding the bunkhouse, a silent invitation.

They sit beside each other in a pair of rocking chairs, and for a long moment, neither woman speaks. When Renata breaks the silence, her voice doesn't sound like her own—there's no lightness, none of her usual breezy elegance. It's firmer, deeper, with an ominous edge. "Grace, I'm going to ask you something right now, and I don't think you're going to like the question all that much. All right?"

Heat encases the porch, buzzing around them like an errant fly. Grace can feel it seeping into her bones, melting away all of her resolve. She knows what Renata's going to ask, knows that it's well within her rights as the owner and operator of Halcyon Ranch to investigate every angle. But she's right. Grace doesn't like it very much at all.

"All right."

The balls of Renata's suede boots press against the wood slats, rocking her chair backward. Her chin dips to her chest, and it takes a long moment before she finally asks, "Do you know anything... anything at all about what happened to the horses?"

The question hooks its claws into Grace's stomach, and the world suddenly feels very big and very small all at once. Countless miles from here, in a hellhole of dead grass and sprawling weeds and malnourished animals, is her uncle. Right now, he's probably reaming his underlings or swindling some poor bastard out of their life savings. It's implausible at best to think he'd come all the way here, sneak onto the property and into the stables to poison the alfalfa. He's a cruel bastard, but he isn't that smart, or sly, or in the physical shape it would take to walk all the way to the main grounds undetected. Even with his vague, threatening texts in the back of her mind, Grace finds it highly unlikely that he'd work that fast or that strategically. So when she answers Renata, it's with a half-truth. A single word shrouded in fear and omission. "No."

"I hope you don't take this to mean that I am suspicious of you," Renata adds, perhaps sensing Grace's unease. "Because I'm not. I know you didn't hurt them. I know you would've stopped it if you could have."

Grace swallows, and her throat feels dryer than soil baking in the sun. "I would have."

"But is there a chance that someone could be trying to send us—you—a message?"

Grace feels the urge to tell the truth warring with the paranoid, insecure side of her brain. She has too much baggage—too much for the Caldwells to tolerate for a lone horse trainer, especially when hundreds of more experienced ones would be lined up to take her place. If she tells Renata about the texts, there's a very distinct possibility Renata will deem her not worth all of this trouble and send her packing. Grace stares out at the barn, watching as the vets walk back and forth from the van, hoisting plastic cases, half-empty Gatorade bottles, boxes of latex gloves. On a shaky exhale, she says, "I don't know, Renata. I wish I could say no without a shadow of a doubt, but I can't." Her jaw tics; her hands curl into fists at her thighs.

Renata presses back again, then swings forward, the movement as clipped and restricted as her tone. "You think your uncle would punish you for leaving?"

Grace looks down at her boots, her sockless feet and haphazardly tied laces. "I think anything is possible when it comes to evil. There's no rulebook."

Grace looks at Renata processing all of this, noticing the line of her jaw is a much straighter edge than usual. The veins in her neck are more prominent for it, and for the first time since she's known her, the woman actually looks her age. The fear, the stress, the unknowable danger—it has erased all her lingering youth.

Renata claps her hands together and sits up. "Here's what we're going to do." She reaches out, grips the handle of Grace's chair. "I'm going to bring in some extra security for a while. It's something I should've done a long time ago. Clint will be over the moon—he's been begging me to get around-the-clock patrols for years. I'll make another phone call to the troopers, too. Paul Freeman has some explaining to do as to why they didn't haul that man into jail last month."

Grace blinks, stunned. "That might—" The thought alone has her stuttering. Catastrophizing. Seeing her uncle's train of thought even from hundreds of miles away. Her thumbnail digs into the skin of her palm, and she clears her throat and tries again. "That might make things worse."

Renata looks invigorated by the statement, and it should've occurred to Grace that telling this woman she *shouldn't* do something would only make her want to do it more. Backtracking may be a futile effort, but she attempts it anyway. "I just mean . . . adding fuel to the fire could be dangerous." Grace clamps her mouth shut, tears forming at the corners of her eyes.

She won't let them fall, even if the bastard isn't here to see it happen. Her nostrils flare. "I don't want anyone else to get hurt. Maybe it's better if I go—"

"Stop."

Grace doesn't look at her, doesn't want to see the look on her face. That stubborn Caldwell resolve. "What if it isn't the animals next time? What if—"

"There won't *be* a next time, Grace. Enough. It's out of the question."

Grace laughs at that, but it's watery and humorless, more baffled than anything else. "How can you be so sure about this?" Finally, she turns to the matriarch of this gilded Eden and finds nothing but certainty in her dark eyes. The kind of self-assuredness that tells Grace, *Sure, you can argue. But you won't get very far.* "How can you think that I'm worth all of this trouble?" She nods toward the veterinarians and thinks about the security detail they'll have to pay handsomely to guard the grounds at all times. "All this *money*."

"Grace," Renata says calmly, and she reaches out to halt the manic motion of Grace's rocking chair. Though completely still now, Grace feels like her body is somehow still moving, buzzing and antsy and ready to bolt. "Look at me," the woman demands.

Grace does, through gritted teeth and red eyes.

"When I offer someone a job at this ranch, there are certain . . . *unwritten conditions* that go along with the agreement," she explains carefully, slowly. "One of those conditions is that, upon accepting, you are acknowledging that my family and I are a selfish bunch. We don't like to share, and we're very particular about who we choose to bring into our lives. Because of that, there's an expectation that when you agree to be here, you're also agreeing to stay. It's a long-haul kind of commitment." Grace searches her face for some sign of hesitation, some signal that she's rethinking her resolve. She finds nothing. "My point is," Renata continues, now reaching for Grace's hand, then gently unfurling her tightly wound fist, "you aren't going anywhere. This is your home." Renata squeezes Grace's hand. "I expect you to protect your home. In return, we'll protect you. You hear me?"

Grace looks down at their intertwined hands, staring at the way Renata's knuckles are slightly bulging from the tight grip. She squeezes back and gives a single nod. "I hear you."

"Good." The woman releases her hand and pats the top of Grace's thigh as she lifts off the chair. The heel of her boot clunks against the wood slats of the front porch, and for a moment, she just stands there, looking out at the scene before her. A queen surveying her kingdom. "You know, my son didn't even want me to have this conversation with you."

"What do you mean?"

Renata turns, folding her arms over her chest. She leans back against one of the unvarnished support beams placed evenly beneath the eave. The decisiveness in her expression has shifted into something a bit softer, more open. "He didn't like that I was going to question you." She smiles now, looking down at her boots, remembering. "Didn't like that I was insinuating you had something to do with this."

Grace swallows roughly, unsure of how to respond. Picturing Crew coming to her defense, irritated with his mother for even considering this line of questioning—the thought fills her with a welcome warmth, an unexpected balm to the morning's bitterness.

"He's a lot like me in that way," Renata says, her smile turning into a knowing thing, like she's in on a joke of which Grace is wholly unaware.

But she has to know. "In what way?"

Renata chuckles. "Protective, sometimes to a fault. A compulsive need to turn himself into a fortress to guard the people he cares about."

Grace shakes her head, a knee-jerk reaction to such an implausible declaration. "He doesn't—"

"He does, honey," Renata states, tilting her head as she looks at Grace. Her smile is a little sad, perhaps with an echo of unintentional pity. Grace wants to look away, but she doesn't think that'd go over well. Renata sighs, somehow knowing her words won't penetrate the way she wants them to. "Crew cares about you," she repeats. "They all do."

The hard wood slats of Waylon's stall are unforgiving against Grace's back, pressing roughly into the knobs of her spine. For nearly three hours now, she's sat here, knees pulled to her chest, forehead resting on her kneecaps. Listening to Waylon's steady but slightly shuddered breaths. The vets are on the opposite side of the stable, both engrossed in their phones, but they've been diligent in monitoring the horses, keeping them hydrated, and noting any changes in their behavior. Though they will all recover, the three stalls that once housed Stringer, Abraham, and Carrot now sit like ominous maws, dark and deep and devastatingly empty.

Grace talks to Waylon on and off, quiet murmurs to not interrupt his sleep or be overheard by the vets. She recites stories from her childhood that once helped her escape into a different world, allowed her to leave behind the mess of reality and believe, just for a little while, in magic and happy endings. The spoiled princess with the pea under dozens of mattresses, the girl dumb enough to sneak into a house owned by bears, the mouse eating too many cookies. They're a patchwork of out-of-focus memories, strung together by Grace's ad-libs—some less fitting than others, like the girl getting eaten by the family of bears, because what kind of idiot thinks she can just commandeer the furniture of an apex predator? She talks and talks, and Waylon doesn't so much as snort, uncharacteristically quiet and tolerant of her ramblings. She files that away for future reference—only when he's sick and exhausted beyond belief will he entertain her without comment.

Dinnertime comes and goes. The sun descends, and in its wake, a sky of lavender and bubblegum pink meets in the middle to form a thick streak of mauve, crossing the expanse like a giant racing stripe. She'd skipped lunch, unable to conjure any sort of appetite after the harrowing morning, but now her stomach rumbles, loud and insistent that she find sustenance. She ignores the sound and the pangs in her gut. She'll fight her body until she no longer can—refusing to leave until she knows Waylon is going to be okay, until he's upright and grumbling at her with those judgmental sidelong glances. Then, and only then, will she give herself permission to eat and sleep.

Half an hour after sunset, the sky begins to bleed out its warm colors, giving way to the charcoal black of night. The vets are elsewhere, likely enjoying a delicious Ronnie-supplied dinner in the main house, and in their absence, the stables feel eerily quiet. They take on a dreamlike quality in the night. The light bulbs hanging from exposed beams are dull and yellow, casting the space in a hazy, surreal glow. Grace can feel herself growing more tired by the minute, but she swims against the tide of sleep with all of her strength.

The sound of gravel crunching beneath boots cuts through the silence. Closing in, getting louder with each step, and Grace is no longer fighting to stay awake. Her eyes are wide open, her back ramrod straight. She doesn't care who it is, but she will care if they try to coax her back to the bunkhouse for a meal, a shower, and a good night's sleep. She pushes the heels of her boots into the dirt, adhering herself to the ground. Clamped into the earth with such force, they'll have to drag her out by her hair to get her to move even an inch.

When Crew comes into view, it's a bit alarming, the wave of breath that rushes out of her. Her limbs seem to relax despite her efforts to keep them stiff and unbudging, and her head falls back against the wood of its own accord. Her traitorous body seems to be under the impression that she won't have to fight him, that he is safe, that he will understand her plight. Because of this, she can ease up and let herself uncoil. He stands over her like a looming giant, ready to *fee-fi-fo-fum* a helpless village under his gargantuan feet. For a beat, they say nothing to each other, and Grace watches Crew's eyes scan her form, from the haphazard bun on her head to the dusty toes of her boots. His lips fold into a straight line as he studies her, until finally, his eyes find hers. She's distracted by the weight of his stare and doesn't notice the plate in his hand until he's holding it out to her, until the aroma of smothered beef tips and mashed potatoes and bacony green beans hits her nose and her stomach lurches in demand once more. "You need to eat," Crew says by way of greeting.

Tucked into his palm beneath the plate is flatware folded up in a paper towel, and she notices now that he has two bottles of water in his other hand, dwarfed by his palms into looking miniature. Grace takes the plate and the flatware and sets it gently on her lap, then watches as Crew places the water bottles at her side. She thinks, for a moment, that he'll leave, having done his duty to keep his ranch hands fed and hydrated. But he doesn't— he looks into Duke's stall for a long moment, face tight but otherwise unreadable. Then he turns and grunts as he slides down the stall door to sit next to her, stretching out his long, denim-clad legs.

Grace looks at him, waiting for . . . something. She doesn't know what. A reprimand, maybe. A statement of doubt to echo his mother. An exit strategy. But he just looks at her plate, nods toward it with a single, firm movement. "Eat."

She tucks in and practically inhales the food. It's delicious, but she hardly gets the chance to savor anything, considering how quickly she devours it. She downs almost an entire bottle of water in one go. The dramatic gasp of air she takes after crackling the plastic beneath her fingers is loud and ridiculous, but the water tastes uncommonly good. The best water there ever was, maybe.

Sufficiently fed and watered, Grace lets herself sink back into the door, a wave of exhaustion now flooding through her, taking all the space left by hunger and thirst. Crew turns his head and watches her, and eventually, she meets his eyes, feeling a bit sheepish. A bit like a fool, to let all of her resolve crumble the moment someone shoved food and water in her face. He must pick up on it, must see a flash of shame in her eyes, because the corner of his mouth crooks upward. "It's okay," he says, even though she's spoken none of her worries aloud.

"It is?" Grace asks.

Crew nods. He bends his legs, lets his arms slink atop his knees, and blows out a long breath. "It's been a day."

"No shit."

He breathes out a laugh at that. With a dip of his chin, she loses eye contact and decides to follow suit. Together, they stare straight ahead.

"You talked to my mother."

It isn't a question. A ranch often operates like a small town; there's always someone watching, and even the most banal acts are supervised in one way or another. It isn't surprising that Crew has already been briefed.

"This morning." She looks down the line of stalls, stopping her journey before she gets to Carrot's. "After."

"I didn't want her to do that," Crew says darkly, gently bumping his head back against the door. Like his frustration has to manifest itself physically, like he can't let it simmer inside without somehow inflicting it on the outside. "I asked her not to."

"She mentioned that," Grace replies. She lets a beat pass, a beat of quiet consideration, before saying, "I appreciate you going to bat for me. You didn't have to do that."

"I know I didn't have to," he says. "I wanted to."

Maybe it's the hour, or the fading twilight, or the smell of burning cedar in the air, she couldn't say—but something makes her brave enough to pry open that statement. "You wanted to."

He nods once, and she continues.

"Because..."

Crew smirks, turning his head. Grace lets him look at her for a moment, not returning the stare, keeping her focus across the way. For the span of a breath, a heartbeat, a lifetime, he just looks. Breathes.

Finally, he says, "Because I didn't want to put any more doubt in your head. I didn't want my mother to make you start questioning your place here. Not when you just . . ." He trails off, and Grace finally gives in and turns her head. He's such a striking man, a paradox of gentle sharpness with features that shouldn't work but *do*—a face from which it is difficult to look away. "Not when you've just started to feel at home."

And God help her—when he speaks those beautiful words, Grace can't help but let her eyes fall to his lips to watch them move, watch them change shape around each vowel and consonant.

A stifled but rational voice in her head barks, *There's trouble this way*, and makes her abruptly turn away so she doesn't tailspin into complete delusion. Because this man, in all of his strange beauty, in his disjointed but enchanting charisma—

He is *trouble*.

For her sanity.

For her heart.

CHAPTER 13

With the dog days of summer fast approaching, the bunkhouse begins packing up shop, preparing for the annual move to the summer pasture. Late July is when it starts to get real—when the heat becomes less of an annoyance and more of a safety hazard. Left to roam beneath the blistering sun, the cows could suffer a multitude of temperature-related maladies: dehydration among the mildest, and heat stress—which can lead to infertility and decreased milk production—among the most lethal. Because of this, most ranches have a designated place where they set up camp for a brief period, somewhere near the summer pasture, which is typically more shaded by trees or hills. Halcyon is no different from any other ranch in this regard. But aside from the obvious upgrades in equipment, tents, and toiletries compared to Braxton, there's one feature in particular that sets this summer camp apart: About a quarter mile east, nestled within a ring of lush oak trees, is a watering hole.

This piece of Eden is the first place they go after dumping their things at the campsite and tying up the horses. When Grace walks up to the water's edge, she's flanked by Mikey and Alec—who are hastily stripping off their shirts and bolting past her. Grace laughs at the scream Mikey lets out when he nearly trips on a branch, and then she looks to her left to find Cooper jogging lightly to catch up with her.

Once at her side, he slows, panting. "Hey, Grace."

"Hey, Cooper," she says, looking sidelong at him curiously.

"How are you?"

Grace's brow furrows slightly. "I'm . . . great. A little hungry. How are you?"

He nods, but it's animated, a bit over-the-top for small talk. "I'm hungry, too, yeah. Forty'll start cooking dinner soon, right? Want me to ask him what's on the menu?"

She barks a laugh. "That's all right. I'll wait and be surprised."

"Right," he says, a little deflated.

A moment of awkward, loaded quiet sits between them, and then Grace decides to show him some mercy. The guy doesn't seem to know how to voice whatever it is he's after. And he's clearly after *something*. This is the most they've spoken in all the time she's been at Halcyon. "Was there something you needed, Cooper?"

His hand flies to the back of his neck, and he rubs at it nervously. "Yeah, um—listen, I was wondering . . ."

They come to a stop at the edge of the pond. The water looks absolutely divine. It sparkles, dancing glimmers of light that skip to and fro atop the concentric ripples. The trees are tall enough that it's perfectly shaded, a guarantee it will be like dipping into euphoria after a day spent in the heat. The guys are already splashing around, standing thigh-deep in just their briefs. They're like children without a jungle gym, the way they crawl and hang all over one another.

Grace turns back to Cooper, who seems to be mustering up

the courage to finish his sentence. She helps him along with a soft, "You were wondering..."

He nods quickly, like he's finally, sufficiently psyched himself up. "I was wondering if you'd happen to know if June is seeing anyone."

A smile erupts on Grace's face. After their dance at Clint's party, she might've predicted this would happen, but seeing it play out in real time—being even a small part of it—fills her up with warmth and affection for them both.

"I don't think she is," Grace says honestly. Smirking, she adds, "We don't get a whole lot of time to socialize, if you haven't noticed."

"Right." Cooper's eyes fall shut on an embarrassed exhale. "Duh. Of course."

A game of chicken is happening in the pond, but it's quickly ended when Raymond topples over into the water from atop Pierce's shoulders, and the opposing team of Mikey and Caleb are cheering at the quick victory, wading around the pond with Caleb's ankles hooked into Mikey's armpits. Alec is readying himself to duck so Bryan can lift up onto his shoulders, and Forty is adamantly shaking his head when Harrison tries to bring him into the mix.

Cooper sighs loudly, dramatically—like a Caldwell—and says, "Do you think she'd be interested in going out with—"

Then a voice echoes across the pond, familiar and mischievous. "Oh, *boys*..."

Cooper's mouth snaps shut, and all the surrounding chaos quiets at the melodic, sultry sound.

Like they are puppets tied to strings, every single head lifts upward to find the blonde sitting on a branch, nearly to the top of the highest tree in this little patch of forest. June's feet swing back and forth, dangling absently, like it's not absolutely insane that she's twenty feet above a waist-deep body of water.

"Guess we know who's taking the record for highest climb this year," she says with a grin, then starts to unbutton her shirt with one hand.

"Holy shit," Cooper says under his breath. Grace rolls her eyes.

June dangles her shirt outward once it's off her body, and everyone continues to stare up at her, dumbstruck. She lets the shirt fall, and Mikey catches it just before it hits the surface of the pond. He wraps it around his neck and looks back up. "Cowabunga, Junie," he calls.

"Cowabunga, indeed," June parrots with a laugh.

"June," Forty cuts in. "If there was a trophy for highest climb, I'd hand it to you, fair and square. Now c'mon down before you break your goddamn neck."

June considers this dramatically, tapping her chin with her index finger. "I suppose I could try to climb down the way I came." She looks down, grimacing as she stares at the path down the tree. "I don't know. Seems more dangerous than just jumping in."

Grace and Cooper glance at each other, then both take a step forward, looking frantically among the men in the pond and waiting for someone—anyone—to argue that statement. Forty, the most rational of all, has already stated the danger—why isn't he screaming for her to shimmy down the trunk until she can get to a reasonable height? Anyone who has ever climbed a tree knows that's the safest way to get down.

June doesn't make any moves to do so, and instead looks

down at the watering hole, surveying. Cooper shakes his head, aghast, and cups his hands around his mouth to call out when someone sidles up next to them.

Crew's arms are folded over his chest, the navy blue T-shirt he wears doing *nothing* to conceal the heft of his biceps, the sinewy lines that run across his muscles.

Grace is startled at his sudden appearance, partly because of the unexpected gun show, and partly because she has no idea where the hell he just came from.

"Are you seeing this?" Cooper asks, pointing upward to where June is now carefully getting to her feet, using the branch as a balance beam and relying far too much on its sturdiness. She's bafflingly steady and graceful, almost on her tiptoes as she takes tiny steps toward where the limb drops off.

"Mm-hm," Crew replies, now looking at his phone. "They bring the toilet paper?"

It's Grace's turn to be aghast now, and her mouth falls open in shock and horror that he's thinking about something as inane as toilet paper when June is at risk of breaking a bone, or worse. "What? Yes! Raymond did—you need to get her down, Crew. She's going to get seriously hurt if she jumps from that height."

Crew huffs, attempting to do something with his overly large thumbs on his phone and apparently failing. "You're probably right. Be a real shame."

Cooper's eyes widen. "Crew, what the fu—"

Grace gasps. "Oh my—"

They're both cut off by June's scream, and they whirl around to see her lithe form heading straight for the water, arms tucked at her sides and her feet pointed down. A zinging bullet aimed perfectly at a target. She'll break her ankles like that. Maybe fracture her hips. It's going to be catastrophic—

But then she dips beneath the surface like a hand sliding into a glove, the water parting and swallowing her all the way up. Grace is dumbfounded, the panic and anxiety and pure *confusion* hitching her breath. A heartbeat later, June jumps up, hair plastered to her forehead and undergarments drenched, a beaming grin on her face. Cooper is so relieved it looks like his knees are about to buckle. Despite the misplaced shock and horror, Grace can't help the little squeeze her heart gives at the sight.

"You fuckers will *never* top that," June yells, and then she's moving, whipping her arms as quickly as she can, splashing every one of them with a wall of water. The guys groan and fight back, and soon, it's an all-out brawl as water flies in every direction. Mikey dunks Alec under the water; June makes a show of diving beneath the surface only to emerge with someone's boxers in her hands. Caleb's cheeks have gone perfectly pink as he slinks toward her, sheepish and—apparently—naked as the day he was born. Cooper eventually decides to join in the mania, stripping off his clothing as he stomps into the pond.

Grace turns on her heel to find Crew still behind her. Smirking. Now finally deigning to give her his full attention. "There's a submerged cave," he tells her, pointing to the back corner of the pond where June had jumped. "Nearly a hundred feet deep."

Her eyes pinch together in suspicion and irritation, because how hard would it have been to just *tell her* that before she nearly had a panic attack? Grace scoffs, stomping off, away from the pond and Crew. Her tent needs to be set up, and she may as well start gathering everything she and Forty will need to make supper. A self-satisfied laugh rumbles from behind her, and Grace whips her head around to see Crew's shoulders bouncing, his head shaking. All too pleased with himself. *Dick.*

They keep it simple for dinner—burgers and dogs grilled over a fire, a vat of brown sugar beans, and a smattering of pickled veggies soaked in Forty's homemade brine. Everything hits the spot, the perfect meal for a summer night spent outdoors. After everyone's good and stuffed, they sit around the fire in camping chairs, working their way through a case of Coors while also taking swigs of a communal bottle of Jameson. By the time the sun has dipped below the horizon and left the world covered in hues of navy and violet, they're all perfectly toasted.

Mikey clears his throat, sits up a little straighter in his chair. "So, who's going to start?"

A collective chuckle runs through the group, but no one raises a hand. On the opposite side of the circle, Cooper, Grace's fellow newcomer to the summer and all its traditions, pipes up. "Start what?"

"Evidently, there is a universal need for everyone on this ranch to know *everyone* else's sexual history and business," June gripes, using her turn with the whiskey to take an impressively long pull. She exhales once she's gulped it down and asks, "Whatever happened to truth or dare?"

"No," Caleb says from across the fire. His eyes are glassy and he's got a boyish smile permanently etched into his mouth. Drunk and content. "You know the rules."

"Fuck the rules," June bites back.

Raymond snorts. "Just because some of us have more embarrassing exploits than others doesn't mean we just toss tradition in the trash."

"But you already know *all* the exploits!" June barks, throwing her hands up.

Pierce cuts in now, and he must be tiring of all the bickering, because his voice rises above the crowd at a volume Grace has never before heard him reach. "The game," he says, looking between Cooper and Grace. He waits until the rest of the murmurs die down completely before finishing his sentence. "Is called 'Never Have I Ever.'"

"Not sure I've played that one before," Grace admits. There aren't many group drinking games she *has* played, come to think of it. Parties and gatherings and any sense of camaraderie and inclusion weren't exactly Braxton's style.

"That's fine," Pierce says. "We'll teach you. Now, everyone, please." He urges everyone with a beckoning hand, then holds his up, fingers stretched out like he's ready to give a high five. Everyone complies.

Even Crew, who sits to Grace's left, though he does so with a throaty sigh that tells her he has probably been subjected to this game one too many times.

Pierce, satisfied with everyone's participation, nods. He keeps his focus on Grace as he says, "All right, now—how it works is, we'll go around the circle, and when it's your turn, you'll tell us something you've never done. For example"—he holds up his hand to emphasize that it's *his* turn—"never have I ever . . ." He considers for a beat, then his gaze moves toward Caleb, and he smirks. "Hooked up with a cougar."

Smug laughter sounds throughout the circle, and Caleb sinks

back into his chair after dramatically pulling down his index finger. "I hardly think forty-five is a cougar," he mutters.

"It is when you're *twenty*," Pierce counters. "So, you see"—he turns back to Grace, then points at Caleb—"because this fine young chap here has in fact hooked up with a cougar, he puts a finger down. The first to have all fingers down has to do something decided on by the group. Last year, Mikey had to roll down the hill naked. He was picking sticker burrs out of his ass for a week."

Mikey, clearly remembering this all too well, rolls his eyes.

"All right," Grace says, though preemptive seeds of embarrassment have begun to sprout in her belly. There's so *much* she hasn't done. And even with the beer and liquor, she isn't sure she's ready to dive into the *why* behind her general inexperience. But she figures she'll likely get more questions, more resistance, if she doesn't play. So she holds up her hand and nods.

"Okay then," Pierce says, grinning. He kicks Forty's boot with the toe of his own. "You're up, old man—though I can't for the life of me imagine there's anything you haven't done in the centuries you've been roaming God's green earth."

Forty cuts him a look, then smiles, saccharine sweet, as if to say: *Game on*. Pierce seems to recognize his mistake before Forty even begins speaking, and his eyes fall shut. "Never have I *ever*," Forty declares dramatically, "shit my pants on a date."

Pierce's eyes squeeze together. "I deserve that," he says quietly, shamefully pulling his thumb into his palm. The group is cackling, clearly all well aware of this story. Grace smiles, though she sits on the outskirts of their memory, not fully able to enjoy it.

Beside her, Crew leans in, and in a voice only loud enough for her to hear, says, "He ate some very questionable beef chili in town. We tried to tell him not to, but he learned the hard way. She ran for the hills, then told all her friends. He hasn't had much luck with the girls in town since, as you can imagine."

Grace looks at him, finds his eyes full of warmth and soft, golden hues, accentuated by the fire. She smiles, now able to picture the scene. "That's disgusting," she says quietly, and Crew grins, leaning back into his seat.

The game continues around the circle, and Grace learns some very interesting things about everyone. To Crew's chagrin, Cooper reveals he's never had a threesome, which prompts Alec to dramatically put a finger down and boast about the fact that he has. Mikey has never sent a nude, a statement that is loudly, vehemently refuted by Raymond, who swears up and down that Mikey sent an unsolicited dick pic to someone on Tinder once. Mikey denies this, then points around the circle and demands fingers go down. Grace watches everyone except Crew, Forty, and Pierce comply.

When it's Harrison's turn, he lets out a deep, considering sigh, sinking back into his chair. Everyone stares at him while he contemplates and then smiles across the circle at June and Grace like they're easy targets. And when he says, "Never have I ever kissed a guy," Grace realizes they are. She and June look at each other, June's face a map of irritation, and both put a finger down.

"Weak," she barks at him. "Should earn you a shot."

Grace's eyebrows lift as Harrison denies this with waving hands. "A shot?" she asks.

Pierce nods. "I forgot about that. You see, propriety is not something we accept in this particular game. If you choose to say something as tame as . . . I don't know—*never have I ever been on an airplane,* you have to take a shot. Salacious confessions only."

Grace's stomach knots up even tighter, especially considering there's only two more people until her turn. She's running through the potential options, scraping her brain for something that's spicy enough to please the group, when Raymond speaks his piece. "Never have I ever . . ." He purses his lips, thinking. Then, like a light bulb has blinked on in his brain, he grins. "Had a pregnancy scare."

This earns him a few well-deserved groans. A couple of the guys seem to be reliving it, curling into themselves as that long gone terror sets in. Grace chuckles at Alec's literal shudder.

When Crew clears his throat, readying to take his turn, the group leans in, a hush falling over them. They are rapt, quieter than Grace has seen them, as though missing even a syllable out of Crew's mouth would be a grievous error.

"Never have I ever . . ."

Out of the corner of her eye, Grace sees a slight movement around the circle, like everyone's leaning even *farther* in. Crew must be stingy about sharing nuggets of information about himself, must maintain a hefty professional boundary between himself and those on Halcyon's payroll. She wonders if perhaps he'll take the easy way out, offer something tame and choose to toss back a gulp of whiskey. But he surprises her by instead saying, "Never have I ever had a one-night stand."

"Bullshit," Mikey yells almost immediately. "I call bullshit."

Crew shrugs. "Call it whatever you want," he says with a hint of aloofness. "Doesn't make it any less true."

"You've *never* hooked up with a woman and then never spoken to her again?" Mikey argues, remaining unconvinced.

"Weren't you like . . . a football star in high school?" Caleb asks, eyes narrowed.

"So?"

"So," Caleb parrots, looking at Crew as if his implication should be obvious. When it clearly isn't, he scoffs. "What kind of D1 linebacker doesn't have a single one-night stand?"

Again, Crew shrugs. "The kind who had a girlfriend."

June chimes in then, "And in the military?"

"Look." Crew leans forward, elbows resting on top of his thighs, and stares all of them down. Everyone stops murmuring and looks at him. Everyone except—Grace notices—Forty. He sits across the circle with a soft, knowing smile on his face. Like this back-and-forth is all silly to him, like he isn't going to waste his time trying to disprove something he clearly knows to be true.

"If I'd known y'all were going to try to fight me like a pack of hyenas, I wouldn't have said anything at all. But since you're so damn *curious*, I'll say one thing and one thing only, and then we drop it." Crew speaks with such comfortable authority. There isn't a shred of doubt in his mind that everyone will comply. When everyone stays obediently, expectantly quiet, Crew blows out a breath. "I don't have any interest in casual sex. I never have. Intimacy shouldn't be something you can check in and out of like a fucking motel. There should be a connection. Otherwise, it's just bodies in repetitive motion."

There's a pause as they all process the statement, then Pierce cuts through the quiet with a lighthearted, "All right, Romeo. Whatever you say. But all you fuckers"—he points around the circle accusingly, eyes narrowed—"better put a finger down." And they all do. Even Forty, though he looks a little wistful as he folds his thumb toward his palm.

Grace's head is drowning in the echo of Crew's words. She tries not to be too terribly obvious that she's watching him, but it can't be helped. Once the attention has moved away from him, he leans back in his chair and exhales, then tosses back a healthy glug of whiskey. There's a melancholic tinge to his features now, and Grace wonders if it pains him, being honest like that. Vulnerable and open, especially with those he's entrusted to lead. He stares at the fire, looking but not seeing, and idly taps his fingers against the side of his leg.

A not-small part of her wants to tell him that she *gets it*—what he said about casual sex. Though it isn't something she's ever put into words, she understands what he means about bodies in repetitive motion.

But, if she's being painfully honest with herself, she didn't really think there was an alternative. Sex, for Grace, has always been a favor, a box to check, an unspoken rite of passage that would allow her to cross over the threshold of girlhood. It's never been something to truly enjoy, or relish, or look forward to. It's never brought her closer to someone. It's never been something she's done because she's in love.

Her thoughts begin to take the shape of something she's never known—something that has her stomach tightening and her cheeks blooming with intrigue. A man and a woman coming together again and again, learning each other, loving and talking and laughing. A current of pleasure so strong it runs through them both, pulling them under the surface and into a pool of golden warmth. Dark hair twined within her fingers; freckles spread out unevenly, unpredictably over muscular arms; a smile so slow and hard-won that it melts her into a puddle of want.

Grace leans toward him slightly, gearing up to speak. What will roll off her tongue is anyone's guess, but she has to say *something*. She has to know what he means when he says not checking in and out of a motel of intimacy. She has to understand how it can ever be more meaningful than that, and if giving it meaning gives it the power to actually feel *good*. Because it has never felt good, and she's had nearly a decade of thinking it simply isn't supposed to.

He notices her before she can utter a single word, and she must be absolutely radiating her fascination and curiosity, because he gives her a soft, barely there smile, as if already aware of the thoughts racing through her brain. Her nostrils flare under his gentle gaze, and whatever unintelligible mess was about to leave her lips is stymied entirely by this look—this comforting, reassuring gaze. *Does* he already know? Has he already figured out that she is just like him? It seems impossible, and yet—

She gives in and hopes for the best. "Crew, I—"

"Okay, Grace," Pierce interrupts joyfully, loudly, "your turn. And remember: no PG-13 bullshit. We want the stuff they keep behind the beaded curtain you can't get to without showing your ID."

"You really show your age when you talk about video stores," June says.

The circle seems to wait with bated breath, much like they did for Crew, and Grace begins actively trying not to panic. She could make something up—they wouldn't know, couldn't verify. But it feels wrong when so many turns have been taken with such intimate, personal details. The group doesn't seem to hide much from one another, and she likes being part of the group.

Something enters her field of vision, and she looks down to see the Jameson bottle. Crew holds it out for her, encouraging her with a nudge.

"This will help," he says quietly. "At the very least, it'll stop you from remembering what you fessed up to in the morning."

Grace nods, taking the bottle and immediately tipping it back to guzzle down a couple of warm, bitter mouthfuls. She winces upon swallowing, but the burn is almost immediate and surprisingly pleasant. Then, she clears her throat, racks her brain for a good fifteen seconds, and sighs. "Okay," she says to the circle. She stares at the dirt, at the kindling at the base of the fire curling at the edges, the ashes of logs that have already succumbed to the heat. If she tells them what she really wants to say, what's at the forefront of her mind in giant, neon letters, it would reveal something about her that she's never told anyone. It would reveal her bad habit of swallowing her voice when she should speak up, and that she's never been brave enough to fight for the satiation of the gnawing hunger that's been lingering in her gut since she was a teenager.

But the whiskey must be working its magic quickly, numbing her conscience and punching holes in the barriers of her truth, because—

Fuck it, she thinks, then finishes her statement, clear as day and as unashamed as she can manage. "Never have I ever had an orgasm."

The reaction, or the lack thereof, is not what she'd expected. Hardly anyone moves, let alone speaks; they all seem to be processing the bomb she just dropped. They stare at her for a beat, and then awkward eyes begin to dart in different directions.

June is the only one who speaks up, and only once she has turned her entire body to face Grace with an incredulous expression. "You mean, like . . . with someone else, right?"

Grace takes another good, long sip of whiskey. She'll need as much as she can handle if she's going to have to answer *follow-up questions*. With a wince and a sigh as it settles in her stomach, she shakes her head. "Nope."

"Oh, honey," June says, and the pity in her voice makes Grace want to sink into her chair and disappear.

From across the circle, Caleb barks, "What kind of selfish bastards you been sleeping with?"

The sound of mumbled agreements ripples through the rest of the guys. As they all stare at her, it feels a bit like she's a subject in a lab, being so thoroughly studied like this, poked and prodded to see what reactions may occur. Grace won't let things get too personal—*can't* let the questions go any deeper than this. So, she manages a wry smile and says, "Only ranch hands, actually. In my experience, y'all aren't the giving type."

Caleb puts a hand to his chest, wounded by her statement, but it's Mikey who asks the million-dollar question, or at least attempts to. "And what about by yourse—"

Maybe it's on her face, a flash of terror or shame that signals she does *not* want to get into this, and she regrets even bringing it up, because June cuts him off quickly. "What a lady does in her alone time is none of your business, Michael Chapman."

Mikey's mouth, hung open and ready to finish his question, promptly snaps shut.

Grace takes another swig. She's pleasantly numb and warm now, embarrassment dulled in her belly and a blooming affection for June in her chest. Especially when June snatches the bottle from her and says, "My turn."

The guys all shift their attention from Grace to June without further comment. They smile and wait for whatever is about to be revealed, and it's suddenly completely fine that Grace has shared something so private, so revealing. Because while they may be curious, they aren't altogether interested in understanding the logistics. Not a single one of them gives her a second glance once June has the floor—no appraising looks, no curious or hungry eyes scanning her, mapping out the ways they could remedy this . . . ailment of hers.

"Never have I ever had sex while someone else was in the room," June declares, a slow grin spreading onto her face.

Multiple heads dip down in shame; multiple fingers fold down, and groans of disgust sound from everyone whose hand remains unchanged. Those innocent of this seem to recall the exact situation that makes the others guilty, and are evidently still as put off by it as they were when it occurred.

"Naughty, no-good boys," June tuts, shaking her head. She tosses back a sip from the bottle and then stands. "I'm beat, y'all. Let's continue this tomorrow."

Some protest, but enough are in agreement that the game is put on pause. Pierce puts the fire out as Harrison and Caleb toss empty cans and paper plates into trash bags. A couple of guys wander off to relieve themselves. When Grace stands to join the exodus, she realizes very quickly how drunk she is. Just rising from her seat has her tilting over, nearly plummeting into the dirt, but then there's a hand at her elbow, keeping her upright. She glances up to see Crew, who isn't even *looking* at her, but has somehow managed to keep her steady nonetheless. She studies him unabashedly, the hard set of his jaw, the stoniness that bleeds into every line of his face as he watches the last golden ember in the pile blink out and turn to gray.

Grace snorts, then chuckles to herself. Crew looks at her, his brows pulling together to make him look even more serious than he did seconds before. It makes her laugh even harder.

His eyes narrow. "What?"

She catches her breath and says, "Well, it's just . . ." She looks at the ashes, barely visible in the moonlit night. "We *can* build another fire tomorrow. You don't have to look so upset about this one being put out."

The shape of an eleven forms between his brows now, and it's amazing that he's able to pull them together so tightly. The incremental descent of his face into pure rage, or disbelief, or frustration—whatever color is best suited for the moment—is fascinating.

"I'm not upset," he says evenly.

He's still holding her elbow. She realizes this and begins to wiggle in his grasp until he releases her. "You look very sad. Or maybe pissed. I can't ever really tell which one it is until I see your eyes. But s'too dark right now." And maybe she can't see the light brown, caramel-swirled-with-forest-green irises in the darkness, but she can certainly see the way his body straightens at her words. The way he is staring at her in that relentless manner of his, intense and unforgiving.

But then Crew's voice is a little softer, lighter, when he speaks. "That right?"

"Mm-hm," Grace hums. She starts to walk away from him and is almost successful until she's about a foot past him, and then her boots decide to tangle up with each other—stupid, old, run-down boots, can't even walk in a straight line—and gravity decides it ought to team up with her boots to yank her down to the ground. Knees first. She falls with a grunt, a loud and breathy *oof* as she hits the crunchy grass.

From behind her, she hears something that sounds like *All right* in a conceding, impatient tone. She doesn't have long enough to dissect what it means, because in the span of a blink, there are two hands gripping her arms and hauling her up. She's only on two feet for a split second before she's being hoisted up and tossed like a bag of flour over a large, sturdy shoulder. It all happens so fast that she barely has time to process it, but once she realizes how far she is off the ground, how she's hanging *upside down*, and how there's an absurdly large hand holding her thigh to keep her steady, she gasps in horror. "This is ridiculous," she protests, knocking a fist into his back. "You can't just throw me over your shoulder like a duffel bag and carry me around."

"I'm just helping you to your tent," Crew says, and it pisses her off, how not drunk he is at this moment, how he's rescuing her and speaking to her like the damsel in distress he said she *wasn't* all those days ago.

"I don't need your help."

He is unfazed. "I'm not letting you sleep in the dirt."

"Maybe I like to sleep in the dirt."

"You'd prefer to wake up with a colony of fire ants crawling all over you?"

An absurd memory pops into her head at his question, and she starts giggling to herself. Six-year-old Grace, stringy hair and lips red and sticky from a lollipop. Said lollipop dropped onto the sidewalk, and a legion of fat, dark red ants marching over it, celebrating the bountiful offering from above. A gentle hand stopping her from touching them—*They're different from regular ants. They hurt a lot more. Like burning.*

"What's funny?" Crew barks.

Catapulted back into the present, Grace lets her laughter peter out with a sigh. "I was just thinking about when I was little and my mom told me about fire ants. She said they burned, so I decided to call them *spicy boys*." She finds this just as funny as the memory had been, and once again bursts into a fit of giggles and snorts.

"Cute," Crew says curtly, but Grace can hear the hint of amusement in his tone.

Soon enough, she's being gently lowered to the ground, set onto her feet and held in place by strong, unmoving hands. To her left, she sees her tent. Her bedroll is laid out, looking inviting even if it will only supply an inch or two between her and the hard ground. In front of the tent sits a blue-lit lantern and a smattering of shared camping supplies. The other tents at the campsite are spread out nicely, but close enough that the glow from the lanterns within softly breaks through the darkness outside.

"A*ha*." She grins, then swings her head dramatically to look at Crew. "I see we have arrived at my front porch."

Crew huffs a breath through his nose. "Indeed."

Grace nods firmly. "I appreciate the lift, good sir."

"Hm. You were singing a different tune about ten seconds ago."

She tilts her head, considering, then pokes her index finger into his chest. "A lot can change in ten seconds, you know."

"Sure."

"This is . . ." She pokes in a different spot, pushes inward as much as she can despite the resistance of the muscular expanse. "You've really got some heft here."

A deep, rumbling laugh sounds from his chest, and it pulls Grace's attention from his chest back to his face.

Her finger, however, does not stop its exploration.

Crew watches her, amusement flashing in his eyes. "Enjoying yourself?"

"I think yours might be bigger than mine." Grace snorts.

"Ah," Crew says with a sigh. "Time for bed, Grace."

Grace pouts, then lets her hand drop to her side. "Party pooper."

"Afraid so."

Then, almost as if on cue, a giant yawn escapes her mouth. She shudders toward the end of it, her eyes growing sleepy and weary in its wake. "Fine," she relents.

"Go on," Crew says softly.

Grace sighs, then bends down to pick up the lantern. With it in her hand, Crew is fully visible, and she takes a brief moment to study his face. That face—how she wishes she could stare at it for hours without interruption. Learn its peaks and valleys, its sharp and soft edges, and name the constellations of his freckles and moles until she's invented a whole new star system. A thought crosses her mind, and damn Jameson and his Irish brashness—but it leaves her lips, too. As if her brain is now attached to her mouth with a liquor-soaked adhesive, one unable to operate without the other.

"I think you're so beautiful," she says dreamily. Dazedly.

And then, about two seconds later, clamps her mouth firmly shut.

But she doesn't take it back. Doesn't apologize. Because even if it is only whiskey-induced honesty, it's honesty nonetheless.

And frankly, she thinks, now resolute in her decision, Crew deserves to know. To hear it out loud. Even as he stands there, silent and still, she doesn't concede.

Grace has felt many different kinds of touches in her life. Some—too many, perhaps—originated from anger. Roughness. A sense of urgency so intense it manifested itself into brutal physicality. Some of them were gentler, born out of love, like her mother's lips on her forehead, or Maryann's bony but reassuring embrace.

But she's never felt a touch like Crew's hand coming up to her face, never once experienced the contrasting, delicate caress of rough, work-torn fingertips. Never felt a shiver run down her spine like the one that does as he tucks a piece of hair behind her ear and then rubs his thumb softly over the apple of her cheek. A stuttered breath leaves her lips before she can stop it.

His face, lit harshly by the lantern, is all shadows and stark highlights. But it makes her ache, the way his eyes seem to be boring into her, like it has suddenly become his mission to peel back all her layers of protection and burrow himself into the depths of her soul. She feels exposed. Raw.

When his entire hand cups her cheek, only a whisper of a touch, Grace can't help but lean into the warmth of his skin.

A quiet hum sounds in Crew's throat.

"Good night, sweetheart."

He leaves her then, turning away and walking toward his own tent.

But his touch stays—it lingers long after he's gone.

It radiates, like a burning sun after weeks of cold.

CHAPTER 14

When Grace wakes the next morning, all she knows is *pain*. Throbbing, ceaseless, and sharp enough to yank her from a heavy, dreamless sleep. In the small confines of the tent, she sits up slowly, sucking in deep, hot air through her mouth. Aches have settled in various crevices of her body, each one more demanding and urgent than the next, all vying to be the center of her attention. The center of her universe.

Neck—from the ancient, pathetic lump of cotton disguised as a pillow.

Back—from the firm, uneven terrain beneath her bedroll.

But worst of all, head—from the copious, *stupid* amounts of liquor and beer she consumed the night before. It is the most blaring of all, so insistent and violent that there doesn't seem to be a way out of it. This is the headache to end all headaches. She might have to call in sick. Do ranch hands get sick days? She might have to quit the job full stop and move into a dark, cold cave. A perfectly silent, neutral-smelling black hole.

But instead, she's attacked by the sound of singing crickets, the smell of manure, and the thick, humid air that has already begun to warm to the point of discomfort. Summer heat spares her not—it won't even give her the luxury of waiting until dawn to begin its cook.

The headache becomes a stomachache—a stomach *turn*—quickly. Despite her deep breaths, she can feel all of last night's mistakes bubbling up in her throat, threatening to out themselves all over the tent floor. She has to do something. Find water. Coffee helps, doesn't it? And bread? Maybe there's a leftover hot dog bun somewhere that can soak up the residual stream of alcohol still coursing through her veins. Whatever the case, she can't sit in this tent, in this world of hurt and nausea, for another second.

Stumbling out past the unzipped flap, she's relieved to see it's still completely dark out. No inkling of the rising sun has yet begun to lighten the sky. Standing straight is a challenge—the soreness of her back and neck becoming more intense with each attempt at movement. She takes a moment to try to stretch, carefully rolling her head around until there's a semblance of mobility, and then arching her back gently, hissing as hot pain shoots up her spine. It's ridiculous, really—she's slept in much worse conditions than a bedroll and a worn-down pillow. Damn Halcyon bunk beds have clearly made her soft.

A cooler sits about twenty feet away. Shiny red plastic salvation. There's bound to be a couple of lukewarm bottles of water within, and, if she's lucky, a hot dog bun or two that haven't drowned in a pool of melted ice. She steps carefully in its direction, not wanting to overdo it and end up face down in the grass *again.* Images of the night before creep into her head, but she shoves them away, not yet ready to remember in full detail. Not when projectile vomiting is still a very real, very likely possibility.

Just get to the cooler. Get to the hydration and carbohydrates.

But then her bare left foot collides with something on the ground, sending it toppling over. A loud rattling sound echoes from below.

"Shit," she whispers, crouching down.

Only when she's holding it right in front of her face can she make out what it is.

Despite the heinousness of her awakening, Grace smiles.

A bottle of Advil sits in her palm, left outside her tent by someone who knew she'd need it.

The day that accompanies the hangover to rival all hangovers is particularly grueling. Whether Crew already had this planned, or he's doing it just to spite them all, Grace doesn't know. About a month ago, about a quarter mile of the south fence had been destroyed, leaving the summer pasture and the entire south quadrant of the ranch vulnerable. They can't risk losing cattle or having trespassers stomping around on the ranch without realizing they're on private property.

And so, it's up to the ranch hands to repair the fence, and every single hand is needed to expedite the process. They start early, well before the sun begins its boiling ascent, but it matters little. The humidity is the real kicker, and that thicket of hot, moist air waits for no sun.

Grace's headache and nausea clear up by midmorning, which is nothing short of a miracle, because this work is a special kind of brutal. Barbed wire, even with heavy-duty gloves, is a cruel mistress. And manipulating it with tools and grit has her sweating through her shirt.

The guys seem less exhausted—they're all significantly better at holding their liquor than she is—and almost *jolly* as they work, and Grace learns this isn't the first time they've done something like this. Last year, it was the east fence nearest to the back road entrance, and they fixed it quickly, but not before a few memorable incidents occurred due to the opening.

"Those sweet, innocent kids," Mikey laments, shaking his head. "They probably just wanted to get their exploration or wildlife badge. They still do badges, right?"

"Yes, Mikey," Caleb grunts. "Boy Scouts do still earn badges. But your memory is shot. It wasn't Boy Scouts—it was a church group. Remember the crosses on the bus?"

"Boy Scouts, church group, whatever," Mikey spits back. "Point is, I've never seen a group of teenage boys all shit their pants at the same time."

Crew, sitting at his piece of the fence, working in silence, finally snaps. "Every time you tell this story, it gets worse—first it was Swedish tourists, then a church group, now Boy Scouts?" he barks, waving the pliers in his hand toward Mikey animatedly. "It was a football team. College. Old enough to know better. They wanted to take the scenic route and didn't listen to me the first time I asked them to stay on the other side of the fence."

"But they listened the second time," Pierce adds, snorting. "When you fired your shotgun into the sky and scared them so badly they were calling the sheriff the next day to complain about— What did they call you? 'A hostile, murderous cowboy'?"

Crew shrugs. "Law's the law."

"That's right, Grandpa," Cooper tuts. "You keep those kids off our lawn."

Grace smiles at that, and especially at the glare Crew pins his brother with in response.

It takes all morning and afternoon to get the fence back to its original glory. They eat cold cuts and toss back bags of Doritos as they work, and all the while, they continue to reminisce, rib one another relentlessly, and laugh until their stomachs hurt. Grace finds listening to them and giggling at the growing atrocity of their stories makes the monotonous task of bending and shaping thick, sharp wire not as daunting. Though her neck and back ache more than they did this morning, the routine of snipping, bending, and welding becomes muscle memory after a while. About an hour before dinner, they're able to call it quits and admire their work.

"No Boy Scout is getting through that," Cooper murmurs as they walk the line, checking the sturdiness and finding it consistently firm and unbudgeable.

Crew sighs. "Let's go," he declares, satisfied with the job they've done. "I'm starving." He shoulder-checks Cooper on his way back to the campsite, and Cooper laughs cheekily as he sways from the collision.

They have breakfast for dinner, and while Forty and Grace flip pancakes and bacon on a portable griddle, the guys all take a dip at the watering hole, tossing around the communal body-wash and two-in-one shampoo and conditioner. Grace is looking forward to doing the same after dinner. Her hair has certainly seen better days. She already washes it infrequently due to the time it takes in the shower, but the exertion of the day has left it especially oily and unpleasant. Dipping her entire head into cool water and washing out all the grime sounds like heaven.

Everyone ravenously inhales their food, complimenting the chefs on the banana–peanut butter pancakes and expertly crisped bacon. Grace finds herself equally as starved, and in her haste manages to accidentally dip the tip of her ponytail into a well of syrup. She frowns, still chewing a mouthful of pancake, then sucks it off until it's no longer dripping down her T-shirt. But the sugary stiffness remains, adding to the already chaotic state of her hair. They all get seconds, then thirds, and continue to eat until a symphony of satisfied, overly full groans sounds around the circle.

Those who did not cook all pitch in to clean up, and then everyone scatters into their own preferred evening activity. With the sun only at the midpoint of its descent, it's too early for a fire, and instead the majority of the guys walk out to the large clearing to toss a football. June stays behind with a book while Forty and Pierce break out a chess set. Grace has to squint from where she stands in front of her tent, but she's pretty sure they're using screws and hex bolts in place of some of the chess pieces.

It's as good a time as any to go sink into the cool water of the pond. The day has produced a sheen of grime and stale sweat over Grace's skin, the kind that feels like she could actually *peel* off if she tried. It's itchy and heavy and irritating, and she is in dire need of a good scrub. She grabs an extra set of clothes, a towel from the pile, and the bucket of toiletries on her way out. Her back and neck protest with each step she takes, and it's becoming progressively more difficult to even turn her head. Now that the adrenaline of the day has worn off, it feels like she's racing some invisible clock to get ahead of this pain. She hopes the bath will help—she'll use the time to massage the aching muscles into submission. She can't be incapacitated tomorrow. Not when she's going to ride Waylon for the first time.

The trees surrounding the pond come into view through ripples of heat, like a beckoning oasis on the precipice of disappearing. She's stripped of everything except her bra and panties by the time she reaches the small opening between the trunks, and she can hear the water as it collides gently with the rocks scattered throughout and the foliage that lines the perimeter. A smile blooms on her lips at the thought of being *clean*—and in less pain—in the very near future. With any luck, she'll sleep like a baby later. Setting her belongings at the top of a small hill, Grace reaches behind her back to remove her bra, winces at the way her back spasms with the movement. She's nearly there, nearly completely naked from the waist up, when someone clears their throat.

Grace yips, jumping an inch off the ground. Leaving her bra where it is, she turns around slowly to see who has dared interrupt her bathing time. She should've guessed—should've *known* simply by the gravelly sound that escaped his mouth. Crew stands waist-deep in the middle of the pond. Shirtless. Possibly bottomless, too, but she can't see anything below his belly button.

Despite herself, her mouth goes dry at the sight of him.

Obviously, she knows Crew is big; she's five foot five and her eye level is at his bicep. She also knows he's strong; she's seen him lift a half-full horse trough off the ground without breaking a sweat. But observing these things from afar while he's fully clothed and just doing his job is entirely different from standing before him now, with all of his physical . . . assets proudly, openly, *nakedly* on display.

There's no washboard abs, no overly bronzed skin like so

many guys sport on television and in magazines. His biceps aren't the size of watermelons, and his trapezius muscles don't look like an Elizabethan collar around his neck, but even if he doesn't outwardly check all the boxes for *fit*, or *jacked*, it's clear that he is. He's built like a weight lifter—strength billowing out of every inch of his body, and absolutely no regard for eating like a bird to maintain an eight-pack.

It looks like he may be speaking. Grace refocuses on his face, on the present moment, and silently reprimands herself for staring—for admiring. He seems to be waiting for her to answer, but whatever question he asked is lost to the ether of her ogling. "What?"

Crew smiles faintly. "I said I'm nearly done. I just need to grab my things," he says, nodding toward the pile of his clothes and boots on the opposite side of the pond, "and I'll be out of your way."

"Oh," Grace blurts, suddenly and confusingly against that idea. "You don't have to leave on my account. I was just going to wash up real quick." She holds up the end of her ponytail, the strands barely moving for how much syrup still remains tangled within. "Got syrup in my hair."

He smirks. "That happens when you don't slow down to actually chew your food."

Grace begins to yank at the hair tie, wincing as she pulls it out. "Are you judging me?" Her hair falls down around her shoulders, long—too long—and heavy from the buildup of sweat and sunscreen. "You're the one who worked everyone to the bone today," she grumbles, futilely attempting to run her fingers through the strands. "I had to make up the calories somehow."

"Ah," he says. "I figured we'd get the most taxing thing done early in the season. Have more time for easier stuff."

"Hm," Grace chirps. "I don't hate that strategy."

"Thank goodness."

Keeping her eyes pointedly on the water and not on the man mere feet away, Grace walks into the pond, locking her mouth shut as it attempts to release a euphoric groan at the sensation. Immediately, it feels like she's begun to shed the first layer of her skin. More loosens up and floats away as she continues to walk, just to the precipice of where she'll no longer be able to touch. She's neck-deep now, and she spends a good minute or two dunking her head in and out, sighing loudly each time she breaks through to the surface. To be fully submerged in this pool of cold, refreshing water is a luxury she didn't realize she needed this badly.

Crew keeps his back to her. He lathers his hair with shampoo, and Grace studies the practiced way his fingers massage his scalp. For a man so gruff and unfussy, he is surprisingly gentle with himself. Leaving no crevice of his head untended, then rinsing thoroughly in chunks of dark strands until all of the suds have escaped into the water.

Eventually, Grace makes her way back to the shallower part of the pond. She grabs the bucket of shampoo, conditioner, and soap that conveniently floats next to her as she begins to bathe. They're standing parallel to each other now, and it's strange and quiet and intimidating to be in such close proximity to him as she runs a soapy washcloth beneath her bra to scrub under her breasts, then her ribs and belly. She doesn't look at him, even if she is curious what part of his body he's attending to now. The water makes a gentle, conceding noise as it laps against him, as he moves within it, as though it has learned that resisting him is a fool's errand. It will mold itself to fit his needs, not the other way around.

After about five diligent minutes of cleaning every inch of her body, she refrains from doing any more, realizing that if she continues, she'll leave raw, red cloth-burns in her wake. Next, she has to tackle the mane atop her head. But as she reaches up to lather it up in shampoo, a seizing pain shoots up her neck and back. "Fuck," she hisses, dropping her arms immediately. She blinks through it, letting it subside with a deep breath. Her neck has given her issues before, when she decides to become her own worst enemy on nights she sleeps in compromising positions. But it's never been *this* bad. She tries again and is met with the same resistance. The same flashing ache radiates all the way down to her toes, only letting up when she's staring straight ahead with her arms at her sides.

In this moment, even with Crew nearby and definitely within earshot, Grace feels the weight of the day tumbling down onto her. The anxiety of getting drunk the night before and making a fool of herself. The splitting headache that woke her from a dead sleep. The charitable bottle of Advil left outside her tent because she would *clearly* need it with how hammered she was. The brutal, daylong task of mending the fence. She's never felt incapable of handling life on a ranch, but right now, she feels a very specific shade of inadequate. Too delicate, too easily breakable to be rubbing elbows with these ranch hands.

With this foreman.

Hot, frustrated tears begin to well in her eyes. Difficult as it is to conceal the sound of her breath shaking in her throat, she tries, because she doesn't want Crew to hear her, let alone see her falling apart. Stubborn through and through, Grace reaches upward again, resolving to fight through the pain and get it done. Tears slip down her cheeks with every inch her arms rise, but, slow and shuddering, she breathes through it. If she can just get through the shampoo part, that'll be enough. She doesn't *need* silky-soft conditioned hair—not if it means she may stiffen up irreparably and be permanently stuck in this position. Lathering the shampoo is tough; she needs the assistance of the water to activate the suds, but leaning back—and then coming back up—with her body in this state would be next to impossible.

She gets angrier with herself with each passing second. Countless times in her life, Grace has pushed through awful, traumatizing situations and come out on the other side. She's seen more terrible things, felt more terrible things in her twenty-five years than most will experience in a lifetime. And yet somehow, by some cruel trick of the universe—by the whims of a vengeful god who is clearly laughing at her in the heavens—shampooing her wild hair, it seems, is what will ultimately be her undoing.

A few more seconds, she tells herself. *Just work it into your hair for a few more seconds, and then you can dunk under the water and stay there as long as you like.*

So distracted is she by this plight, the fact that another person is sharing this pond with her becomes a distant memory. That is, until she hears the *whoosh*ing of moving water. Her eyes widen, red rimmed and still teary, but she sniffles and tries to compose herself as ripples begin to spread out in front of her, and a large presence finds itself at her back.

A soft voice asks, "Did you hurt yourself?"

As if on command, Grace hisses at a red-hot stab of pain in her lower back. "No, I—" Another hiss, followed by a little contorting until she finds relief. "I just slept wrong, I think." But she continues, wholly certain that the middle section of her hair is coated in shampoo while the top and bottom remain untouched. "It's fine."

"It's not," Crew argues, and his voice sounds closer now. "You're in pain."

Grace sighs, struck by the need to keep his attention elsewhere, so she says through a watery laugh, "My pain tolerance is pretty high, if you recall."

He doesn't take the bait—and when he speaks again, it's directly into her ear. As though he's standing *right* behind her. And now that she's homing in on it, she thinks he is—thinks she can feel the heat of his chest against her bare back. "Let me help you," he commands gently.

Despite herself, despite the radiating aches coursing through her limbs, she scoffs. "You know, you don't always have to come to my rescue. I can take care of myself."

He's quiet for a few heartbeats. "I know you can."

Grace nods. "Good."

"But I've seen those scars on your hands," he says unceremoniously, and Grace tenses up, eyes squeezing shut at the pain that follows. "And I know you didn't so much as whimper when I reset your shoulder. But I also know you're crying right now."

"It's the water," she lies, eyes remaining shut. "It feels great. They're happy tears."

"Don't," Crew interjects. It's faint, barely there, but the press of his chest against her back has her movements halting. Her hands freeze in her hair; her shaky breath catches in her throat.

His lips are touching her ear now. She can feel them, hot and insistent as they caress the skin on her lobe. He breathes against her, and the sound—the *feeling*—makes her knees weak. "Don't lie to me."

"I—"

It's a futile effort, trying to contradict him. Crew Caldwell is not a man to be toyed with or manipulated. He has always seen right through her to the darkest, rawest parts. Now is no different.

"Let me help you," he says again. His lips travel downward, and when they move across that wondrous spot between her ear and jaw, Grace lets her arms fall. She couldn't stop them if she tried.

Crew is there first, wrapping one of his own arms around her torso, so when Grace's land, they fall atop his sinewy forearm. He pulls her tight against him, keeping her upright, which—thank God, because all of her bones have suddenly transformed into jelly.

He breathes hard against her neck. "Can I, Grace?"

She hums, lets her head fall back onto his shoulder, and then, finally, gives in. "Yes."

A lot of things happen very quickly once she gives him permission, but Grace keeps her eyes closed to it all. She knows Crew must retrieve the shampoo bottle and somehow get more of it into her hair, because now he's massaging her scalp with that same level of care and expertise he used for his own. It's sinful, how good it feels. When he uses his short nails to scratch at the base of her neck, she lets out an indecent sound, and maybe she should be embarrassed—maybe she should apologize and run like hell away from the pond, but she doesn't.

He rinses her hair by gently lowering her into the water with one hand secured behind her neck, and it surprises her how safe she feels in his grasp. How confident she is that he won't let her fall.

The aches and pains in her back and neck have subsided at his ministrations, and Grace is left with only the feeling of being clean and boneless, a lump of clay for him to mold at his will.

She silently rejoices at the sound of him opening another bottle; he clearly has other ideas about skipping the conditioner, and she's glad for it. If he were to stop touching her right now, she might actually combust into a million tiny molecules of wanton dust.

Crew's fingers are adept despite the size of his hands. He pulls them delicately through her tangled, now-clean hair, smoothing out the neglected bed of chaos with ease. When he's worked the conditioner into her ends, he proceeds to braid her hair down her back, then plucks the hair tie from her wrist and secures the end. A little smile folds into her lips, even through the haze of serenity. "Did you just braid my hair?"

Crew hums, then lays the braid over her shoulder. The tip of it grazes her left breast, still concealed by her bra, which is now completely soaked and heavy with pond water. Quietly, he says, "It'll keep your hair out of the way while the conditioner works."

She can't help but ask. "Is that why your hair is so wavy and shiny? Because you braid it?"

The laugh that rumbles in his chest vibrates onto her back, and it's a tantalizing combination of sweet and arousing. Grace leans a little farther into it, testing, seeing how far she can go before he calls her out. Before he backs up and calls it a job well-done. Her hair is washed, after all.

He doesn't. Instead, he situates her until there's just enough room between them that he can shift his attention to her neck. For a moment, it feels like his entire palm is encompassing it, his thumb grazing her hairline. Grace's breathing stutters again, caught off guard by the change in grip—by the unexpected possessiveness. In a gruff voice, he asks, "Is this where it hurts?"

"Mm-hm," she manages.

With his other hand, he stairsteps his fingers down her spine. He presses just slightly between the grooves, adding pressure and making her shiver. "And here?"

"Yes," Grace breathes. She feels weightless in his hands, like her entire body has been reduced to only the parts where he touches her. She is no longer a thinking, breathing human, and instead is a maelstrom of sensation blanketed by feverish skin.

Silently, he works. He kneads her neck and her back until the rigid, aching muscles are pliant and devoid of tension. Grace has no concept of time; she can only register their synchronous breathing, heavy and warm.

"There you go again," she tells him after he tames a particularly difficult knot.

His voice is soft, with a hint of amusement. "What?"

Grace sighs, letting her head fall forward as he works his hands into the top of her spine. "Fixing me. You're always fixing me."

For a beat, he says nothing, and Grace worries she's crossed some invisible line. Some arbitrary boundary between them that didn't exist seconds ago. But then he breaks through the silence and his voice is a shade firmer than it has been since she joined him in the pond. He sounds more like himself and less like this rugged but soft cowboy masseur-slash-hairdresser.

"For me to fix something," he says, pushing his nails into the hair at the base of her neck.

Grace's lips fall open in an involuntary silent cry for *more*. He hears it, somehow, and scratches there, while also pulling her head back gently and closing the distance between them once again. Pressed flush against her, he speaks into her temple.

"It would need to be broken. You aren't broken, Grace. You never were."

Grace's eyes blink open at the affirmation. He says it so plainly, without even a sliver of room for argument. Though she knows he's wrong on so many levels, she doesn't argue. She lets herself live in this reality for a precious moment, where she is strong and capable and respected by this man. Where she is wanted and welcomed and home.

Crew must be in a giving mood. Something in the water must have him ready to spill all of the feelings he keeps tightly under lock and key, because without prompting, he continues. "I never got to tell you what I thought about your dress," he begins, as one of his hands moves slowly to her hip. It's a question more than an action—a tentative, slow request to break through the pretense of massaging her aches and just *touch* her.

Grace bites back the *What took you so long?* that wants to break from her lips and nods. He grips her there, no longer gentle. When he pulls her even closer to his body, she feels something hard against her backside.

"At the party."

The dress—the party—Grace swallows, nodding again. It feels like it was ten minutes and ten months ago all at once, coming back to her in a kaleidoscope of colorful, misshapen memories.

"Uh-huh," she attempts, then swallows down the only remaining saliva in her mouth. "You—you ran away before you could."

"I think it's more appropriate to say I was dragged away," he counters. "But if I hadn't been—"

The hand at the back of her neck comes to her other hip. Another question, followed by another quick answer, another quick, silent insistence that *Yes, you can touch me anywhere you want to.* His hands are big enough that when he spreads them across her belly, his fingers can intertwine. He uses this woven grip to keep her in place, speaking now into the apple of her cheek.

"I would've said you were stunning. That I always thought you were beautiful, but in that dress—it hurt to look at you. It hurt to look away."

Oh. This man and his beautiful, honeyed words. Grace doesn't know whether to smile, or laugh, or cry at this, and so instead she simply accepts it, letting it wash over her skin alongside the spring water.

"I like it," she eventually murmurs, words slurred with desire, "when you look at me."

Another deep, reverberating rumble. "You do?"

"I didn't know it at first," Grace admits. "Didn't know— what this was, what the feeling was when I felt your eyes on me in a crowded room."

He strokes up her torso, teasingly soft. "But you know now," he says. "What it is."

"I think I do," Grace exhales, scraping the recesses of her brain for logic and sense. "But it isn't just one thing." She swallows hard. "It's attraction . . . but also curiosity, and maybe some terror. All swirling together."

Crew's hips barely, almost imperceptibly rock into her. Grace's eyelids flutter as he grunts with the movement, the newfound friction. "You want to know what it is for me?"

Grace nods. She can't think of anything she wants more at this moment.

He rocks into her again, but this time, he's less delicate about it. Any trepidation he felt about pressing his hard length into the crevice of her bottom is long gone. Grace arches into him as he says, "It's want." He exhales hot and thick onto her skin. "It's need."

A distant, muffled alarm bell sounds in her head when his fingertips graze just beneath the elastic waistband of her underwear, and some ancient instinct arises, telling her that if they keep going like this, Crew is going to make her come. He's going to give her the first orgasm of her life, and she'll never come back from that. The thought of being wrecked to oblivion has her next words stuttering out of her mouth like a protective reflex.

"Is this—is this a bad idea?"

The cadence of his hips slows and she immediately wants it back—the pressure of his body moving into hers. His fingers stop their downward trajectory into her underwear. She hates herself for making him stop.

"You tell me," he says breathily, and his grip on her hip softens, becoming less urgent and more soothing. Grace knows in her bones that if she asked him to let her go, to walk away from this and never speak of it again, he would. Without hesitation. He would respect any boundary she constructed.

And it's that reassurance that makes her brave. Makes her want him all the more.

"It doesn't feel like a bad idea," she says honestly, and then, because she thinks she may actually die if he doesn't keep touching her, she presses her hand against his and guides them both into her underwear. He cups her gently, his fingers barely sinking into the folds of her, and groans.

He begins to explore, grazing her clit with intention and precision. When a thick fingertip presses lightly into her, he grunts, a whispered *fuck* falling from his lips and onto her cheek. His mouth is open, hot breath spilling out in huffs against her skin. "You're so wet," he says, a hint of wonder in his tone.

Grace moans. "I am," she affirms, her hand sliding up his forearm and leaving him to his own devices. "It feels so good—you touching me."

"I—" Crew attempts, but swallows his words roughly. He plays with her clit with his thumb while he dips just the tip of his finger in and out of her, slowly and purposefully.

Grace's breathing picks up as she clenches around it, as though her body is trying to pull him within, to bring him even closer.

"I want to make you come," he says after a particularly hard squeeze. "Can I do that for you?"

"Please," she cries. A pleading, desperate imitation of a word. "Please, Crew."

He sinks his finger all the way into her, and the tight, invasive, *full* feeling that follows makes her eyes roll back. "Shit," Crew grunts. "You're so fucking tight."

As he begins to fuck her with his finger in earnest now, Grace surrenders entirely to his control, letting him keep her body upright like a needy, overheated rag doll. She is right up against it now—that cliff's edge of euphoria.

"Let go, Grace," Crew tells her, somehow knowing she's toeing the precipice, hesitating before she jumps. "I'm here. I've got you."

She obeys. She couldn't stop herself even if she tried, and what follows is a flurry of sensation so intense her knees buckle under the weight of it. Grace cries out, and Crew clamps a hand over her mouth at the growing volume, the unhindered vocalization of a bliss so pure and relentless that it may actually kill her. Her heart pounds against her ribs as pleasure rushes through her entire body, syrupy thick and heavier than anything she's ever known. A pinpoint is placed in her life, in her soul, at the moment it crests—a marker that indicates who she was before this, and the person she will be after.

"Good," Crew sighs as he holds her up, as he fucks her through the wave with his thick, deft finger and plays with her clit all the while, sending aftershocks of crippling ecstasy through her.

She trembles in his grasp, a vibrating mess. An exposed, raw nerve.

"Fuck," he shudders. "You're perfect."

It takes minutes—hours—*years* to come down from the high, and he holds her through all of it. When he extracts himself from within, she feels the loss acutely, missing it and instantly wanting it back. He crosses his arms over her body, and she can feel him still hard against her—rigid and hot and insistent. She rubs her ass over the tent in his briefs, and he groans, tightening the cage of his arms around her.

"I want to bury myself in you," Crew says, and he moves a hand to her hip to pull her backward into him.

Grace wants that, too—desperately—but she can't speak. All

that falls out of her mouth in reply is an incoherent moan. Crew moves his other hand to her jaw, gripping her gently and turning her face to his. His eyes are wild and blown black with desire, his lips parted and pink and begging to be kissed. She cranes her neck to do just that, and their lips brush together lightly—the beginning of something neither of them will be able to come back from—when a sound shatters the haze of their shared Eden.

A whistle.

A jaunty tune falling from Forty's lips as he breaks through the trees surrounding the pond with a towel around his waist, completely oblivious to what he's just walked in on.

When he spots them tangled together and panting, the whistle abruptly stops. He freezes, takes about five seconds to realize what he's interrupted, and then turns right back around and walks away.

Crew and Grace are suspended, both silent and unmoving as they watch his hasty retreat. Once he's out of sight, they look at each other, grimacing.

"Great," Grace says.

"Yeah," Crew sighs. "We're never going to hear the end of that."

CHAPTER 15

Storm clouds roll in the next morning, bruising the sky with billows of gray, purple, and green. Weather of such nature is a blessing and a curse; the temperature is ten degrees cooler, which makes the workday seem less daunting, but that they'll have to trudge around in mud, and sleeping, eating, and working amid the downpour and soaked earth is less than desirable.

Grace, however, cares little for the incoming tempest. Neither excited nor dreading its consequences, she eats breakfast with a swarm of butterflies taking up residence in her belly. Once he'd rinsed the conditioner from her hair, Crew had walked with her back to camp after they'd been caught by Forty, smiling at her with an achingly soft look in his eyes that had nearly compromised her once more, nearly made her drag him right back to the pond to finish what they started. He didn't shy away from her when they rejoined the group, and didn't care about creating a berth between their arrivals to keep the others unaware. They'd gotten a few curious looks, but for the most part, no one seemed all that surprised that they'd been off somewhere alone.

For the rest of the evening, the not-quite-secret lingered between them, remembered through shared looks over dinner and the campfire, when instead of picking up where they'd left off with Never Have I Ever, they sat around and sang old country songs while Pierce strummed away—poorly—at an acoustic guitar. Grace and Crew sat next to each other, and more than once, their hands had brushed, featherlight and intoxicating touches that carried the same charge as they had at the pond. But surrounded by people, they were only fleeting, teasing, temporary reminders of an incendiary moment that had ended too soon. They couldn't explore each other any further, not with an audience of chuckleheads around, and so they'd gone off to their separate tents at the end of the night, but only after Crew had escorted Grace to hers with a hand at the small of her back. In his touch, there was gentle reassurance that he felt it, too. And in the sweet hint of a smile he'd given her before they'd parted, there was longing. There was desire and comfort and the promise of something Grace couldn't quite put into words.

He sits across from her now with his own plate of bacon, egg, and cheese breakfast tacos, and though Caleb is animatedly telling a story about getting arrested on a decades-past Mexico spring break trip, Grace isn't listening to a single word. She can't concentrate on anything except Crew's hands. Staring at them doing something even as mundane as holding a taco and a coffee thermos has her in a daze—in the throes of a heat-laced memory. Sharp and vivid across all of her senses. It doesn't help that he keeps looking at her, glancing up from his breakfast every few moments and holding her eyes, like he's replaying their tryst, too—watching the same conductive scene and remembering the way his hands felt as they learned her body. Learned exactly how to use them to make her keen.

Any doubt or residual fear she'd held for the possible blowback of this development between them had been mostly assuaged the night before, but flashes of that alarmed, muffled voice still linger, even now, as she sits on the receiving end of Crew's kind eyes. It's dull and warped, as if speaking to her underwater, but it remains nonetheless, saying the cruelest of things. Things like *He doesn't want you for anything more than sex,* and *You must be delusional if you think you're good enough for him.* And worst of all—loudest, clearest of all: *He'll never look at you again once he finds out what you did.*

Grace compartmentalizes those errant voices as much as she can and goes about her morning—alongside the rest of the group, she battens down the campsite for the oncoming torrent, feeds and waters the horses, and tells Waylon they'll go on their promised adventure once the storm passes as she tries to ply him with a particularly fat red apple, to no avail. Crew saddles Duke, which only makes Waylon more agitated. Why Duke gets to go on an adventure but Waylon doesn't is a frustrating mystery to him.

"You could at least do it in private," Grace murmurs out of the side of her mouth, just loud enough for Crew to hear from where he stands on the other side of Duke.

Crew huffs a laugh through his nose. "Someone needs to learn the value of patience," he counters, giving Waylon a challenging look.

Waylon, uninterested in lessons, snuffles and turns his cheek like a bratty teenager.

"Grumpy," Crew says to the horse, a smile tugging at the corner of his mouth.

"Where are you all off to?" Grace asks, crouching down to

scratch behind Boone's ears. He's panting, antsy, ready to bolt off with his dad to whatever end.

"Gonna scope out some of the more neglected zones," he says, nodding in an all-encompassing way at their surroundings. "See if there's anything we need to deal with while we're staying out here."

Grace nods. "More fences to fix," she muses.

Crew's smile blooms into more than just a corner tug. He stares down at her with something that looks frightfully like adoration—and the butterflies in her stomach begin to swarm. "Probably so."

Grace sighs, feigning exhaustion at the future task. "At least the come-along works now."

He's quiet for a beat. Looking at her with those soft eyes, his expression so warm it makes her heart squeeze in her chest. "When I get back," he eventually says, leaning into her space only slightly, "I want to take you somewhere."

Craning her neck a little, Grace blinks up at him. "Somewhere," she repeats quietly.

"Mm-hm," Crew replies, and then he bends down even farther, closing the distance. His lips are at her cheek before she can take in another breath, and the inhale stutters in her chest at the contact. "After the storm passes." He breathes into her skin.

She can't stop her eyes from fluttering closed, especially when he presses the softest, faintest kiss to her temple. It's the sweetest goodbye, the most lovely *I'll see you later*.

And then he's off, trotting away atop Duke into the endless, darkening gray horizon, Boone biting at his heels.

· · · · · · · · · · · · · · · · · · ·

Grace is grateful for being busy with various tasks around the pasture. She takes Waylon with her, though he's less than ecstatic to chauffeur her around to do menial chores like weeding and hacking at thickets of sticker burrs that can get wedged like tiny knives into skin and leather alike. It's all easy, repetitive work, and it leaves her little room to think about Crew—how much she misses him despite his only being gone for a handful of hours. How excited she is to venture off to this mysterious *somewhere* once the storm has passed. It's a strange, foreign feeling, one Grace has never really experienced before. She'd had crushes in school before dropping out, but nothing like what she saw in movies—nothing like what she saw when Clint and Renata looked at each other. Nothing so warm and wild and wholly consuming.

He's still away when lunch comes around, but it's of little concern to the group, who assures her he probably brought along something to eat for himself, Duke, and Boone. She takes their word for it and eats her turkey sandwich, piled with tomatoes and slathered in mayonnaise and mustard until the meat is practically an afterthought between two pieces of Wonder Bread. They snack on Doritos and bread-and-butter pickles and slurp down cans of Dr Pepper; they tell their usual stories full of chaos and debauchery through full, impolite mouths, and all the while, Grace keeps her eyes steadily on the horizon.

She thinks she's being subtle about it, but concern must be written all over her face, because Forty eventually lowers himself into the chair next to her with a grunt and knocks her knee with his own.

"You look like a wartime wife waiting for her soldier to come home," he chides, and Grace's cheeks immediately bloom with heat. He smiles at the flush that spreads over her face like a wildfire, knowing full well that he's embarrassed her, and then knocks her again playfully. Apologetically. "It's all right, kiddo. We've all been there at some point."

Grace's voice is low and quiet when she responds. "Does everyone know now?"

He chuckles, and it brings out the creases near his eyes, accentuates the way his patchy, wiry beard moves with his wide smile. Grace can't help but feel a surge of affection for him despite the ribbing—this silvery, solitary guardian to a gaggle of adopted children. "With these idjits, who can say. But to anyone who actually *looks*, yes. I didn't tell anyone about the watering hole of it all, though," he says, eyebrows raised.

Mortification rings through her entire body at his words, and Grace wants nothing more than to curl into a ball and be buried beneath the thirsty dirt. "Forty," she manages, grimacing, "I'm sorry about that. It was dumb and it just *happened*—"

He laughs for real now, a belly-deep, jovial sound. "Stop, darlin'," he says once he's gotten the barking laughter out of his system. "Your apologies aren't needed here. You know I'm rooting for y'all—always have been."

Grace's mouth hangs open as a million questions clog her throat. *Always have been? What does that even mean? How long has he—*

A loud, heavy crack of thunder interrupts her spiraling, and it startles everyone with its abruptness. Evidently, they'd all been distracted with time-old tales and cold cuts, because upon looking up, they find the clouds have swelled to the point of bursting. They have an hour, probably less, before the sky opens up and swallows them whole.

Grace turns her attention back to the expanse of the property, squinting in the direction Crew went this morning, but finds nothing. Only sparse trees and unwalked plains. Murmurs begin to sound among the group, and there's an edge of concern in everyone's questions, but no one is panicked. They're all confident Crew will come back before the storm; it's far too dangerous for him to stay and ride it out in the open.

But he doesn't.

When the storm begins half an hour later, it's as though a knife has slashed through the blanket of clouds, releasing all the rain at once. It's unrelenting and deafening, and they crowd under a large tree near the campsite to discuss what—if anything—they should do. It's difficult to see through the sheet of water that surrounds them on all sides, but Grace tries anyway. She keeps her eyes peeled in every direction, waiting with her heart beating as loud as the thunder to see Crew's blurry figure in the distance, riding in on Duke, weighed down by his sopping wet clothes.

"He's probably holed up somewhere, waiting it out," Cooper reasons. His arms are folded tightly over his chest as he looks out through the rain alongside Grace.

"Probably," Grace says, but there's no conviction in her agreement. It's a distracted, halfhearted sentiment that neither of them actually believes.

Forty, having overheard them, chimes in. "Of course he is. He probably found a tree or something just like this before it started to get bad. He'd have felt it coming on." Grace says nothing, does nothing to concur. She just watches the panorama of precipitation surrounding them, hoping to see something—*anything*—beyond the endless streaks of rain.

When another hour passes by with no emergence and little reprieve from the storm, anxiety in its purest form settles deep in her belly. It becomes difficult to stand still, to think rationally, and alongside that blooming sense of dread, that cruel inner voice returns. It's singing a different song now, tinged with tragedy and self-pity, but carries the same level of vitriol.

He's dead, it murmurs. *He's gone, just like Mom. He's not coming back. Nothing good in your life ever comes back.*

If she lets herself catastrophize, things could get ugly. She can't let that happen right now, not when Crew could be in danger. So, Grace shuts the voice down—stomps on it with stubbornness until it's barely a whisper.

They've hatched a tentative plan to go look for him on foot, but in the climax of this downpour, it would be a fool's errand. The visibility is too low; they wouldn't see him in this until they practically stepped on him. The only option is to wait for it to die down, and then launch into action as soon as they're able.

But all of that goes to shit when a small figure comes racing in from the east.

Though they can't quite make it out, Grace knows in her bones exactly what—who—it is.

Boone. Alone. Running toward them faster than she's ever seen a heeler run.

"Oh shit," Forty grunts, stepping into the rain to meet Boone as he approaches the campsite. Grace can hear his high-pitched whine even over the roar of the rain, and as soon as he knows he has Forty's attention, he's already making to run back in the direction from which he came. To lead them away, toward something.

Someone.

"He's hurt," Grace shouts, and Forty looks at her with a furrowed brow, barely able to keep his eyes open amid the storm.

He hesitates, looking at the dog growing more and more impatient, and then out into the soaked plain ahead.

Grace looks in Boone's direction and yells, "He wouldn't have come back without him unless there was a reason. You know he wouldn't, Forty. We have to go."

"We're coming with you," a voice says from behind her, and soon, she's flanked by Cooper, Caleb, and Pierce. They begin jogging, trailing behind Boone, who has already taken off. "The others will stay with the herd," Caleb yells back to Grace. "Come on."

It takes nearly forty minutes, and with every single second that passes, Grace begs the universe to not be the cruel and merciless thing she's always known it to be. It doesn't make any sense, but the longer they follow behind Boone, crossing the plain with the rain still beating down on them, the more she blames herself for whatever it is they're about to witness. She is quicksand. Always has been. Everyone she tries to keep close ends up hurting in the end.

She should've known better than to start anything with Crew. He's too good—too gallant and kind to be associated with her. It was never going to pan out well for him, becoming part of the land mine of tragedy and chaos that is Grace's life.

The rain lets up before they find him. Hard, ceaseless, fat drops fizzle into a whisper, a gentle sprinkle that allows them to actually see what lies ahead—and as soon as Boone starts barking, they know they must be getting close. Grace's heart is in her throat as his barks get louder, more insistent, and when she eventually spots something in the distance that doesn't fit in with the landscape of dirt and dead brush, she squints, trying to make it out. When it's finally clear enough to see, Grace gasps, and then she starts to run.

CHAPTER 16

The fear that courses through Grace's entire body when she spots Crew lying beneath Duke's prone, massive form is sharp and unadulterated. It moves her feet, pushes her legs, steadies her breath so she can sprint toward him with abandon. Her eyes are riveted to his face looking skyward, giving her that angular, enchanting profile she's seen in dreams and stared at for far too long. His eyes and his mouth are open—and though the movement is stunted by the hulking, nine-hundred-pound animal on top of him, his chest is rising and falling.

He's breathing. He's alive.

Grace gets to him before anyone else, crashing to his side on her knees like she's sliding into home base. Crew glances at her, and his face is strained, his features tight and twitching. "Hi," she blurts out, and something in her soul knits itself back together when the corners of his mouth pull up.

"Hey," he rasps, barely audible.

Suddenly, she's not alone—the guys appear at her side, surveying the situation. Forty crouches down to Duke's front left leg, shaking his head. "Gopher hole?"

Crew nods, sucking in a shuddering breath. "Didn't see it in the storm. He stepped right in and took me with him."

Forty's already moving, and so are the others, positioning themselves evenly around Duke, who looks more annoyed than distressed about this situation. Grace stays next to Crew—she won't move. She can tell he's playing tough, forever in the role of valiant, unbreakable protector. But it's a mask. He's in pain. He's afraid—she can see it in the wild honey of his eyes as they dart to hers.

Grace doesn't have room in her brain to rationalize what the others may think when she reaches out and cups Crew's cheek, much like he did with her the other night. Soft and tender, she sweeps her thumb over his cheekbone and blinks down at him. "You're gonna be okay."

Crew nods, leaning into her touch.

"All right, men," Forty grunts, reaching down into the gopher hole to grip Duke's sunken leg. "On three, let's slide him off. He's gonna get up quick, so be ready to give him room."

Grace backs up as little as she can, not wanting to leave Crew but also not wanting to be in Duke's line of fire when he's upright. Forty counts, and then, as one, they lift his body and slide it off Crew's, while Forty relieves the animal of its trap gently, methodically. As predicted, Duke is up within seconds, shaking off the fall and groaning a little as he trots away from them. With the horse situated, they shift their focus to Crew, who still lies in the same position, spread out atop the wet ground. Grace kneels next to him once again, and Cooper drops down to his other side, scanning him for any visible injury. "Anything broken?" he asks.

Crew shakes his head. "I don't think so. Just—"

"Wind knocked outta ya," Forty supplies, standing over them.

"Yeah," Crew grunts as he attempts to sit up.

"Slow," Cooper urges, reaching behind him to grab on to his shoulder. Grace does the same, and together, they help him into a seated position.

Crew breathes deeply, one after another, until he seems to relax slightly, the tension in his shoulders dissipating. Cooper's hand is back at his side, but Grace keeps touching him—his shoulder, his chest, his thigh. Without even realizing what she's doing, she's patting him down for wounds, for protruding bones or sprains.

Satisfied, she looks up to find him staring at her.

"Well, Doc, am I gonna make it?" he asks, a twinkle of amusement in his eye.

Grace could cry with the relief that floods through her. He's fine. Snarky as ever. She exhales, sinking fully onto the ground next to him. The others back away, Caleb and Forty running off to reel in Duke, and Cooper and Pierce comforting Boone, thanking him for being such a good dog.

"You got lucky," Grace says, shuffling up until their thighs are touching.

When he answers, there's no humor left in his voice. "I know."

She looks over his form once again. "Can you walk?"

He nods, and together, they slowly get to their feet. Though he seems steady at first, he stumbles slightly upon being fully upright, and Grace reflexively latches on to his middle, keeping him in place. "Hold on to me," she says softly, and he wraps his arm around her neck. They walk back like that—all the way to camp, she holds him up.

The hands who'd stayed behind clap when they see them approaching, and while it's meant to be a lighthearted gesture, she can see the relief in their faces. The care they all have for Crew, for one another, is a powerful thing—if one of them is hurt, they're all hurt. Grace doesn't know if she's been fully integrated to be part of that collective outlook, but she certainly feels it when it comes to Crew. The second his safety was in question, she'd launched into action, sprung like a feral animal, and stopped at nothing until she'd gotten to him.

In the commotion of relief and questions and claps on the back, Grace doesn't notice that one of the trucks is now parked behind camp, and she also doesn't see Renata leaning against the tailgate, arms folded over her chest, watching. Crew, who still clings to Grace despite seeming to have fully regained easy mobility, sees his mother first and walks them both over to where she stands. Renata's welcoming smile is less bright than normal—twisted with residual worry. She pins her elder son with a look that says a thousand words, a lifetime of conversation, lessons taught, warnings given. Eventually, once they seem to have exchanged whole sentences without uttering a word, she sighs and asks, "Did you think you could *stop* the storm? Control the weather like some ancient deity?"

Crew huffs a laugh through his nose. "I thought I'd beat it," he replies. "And for the record, I would have."

Renata shakes her head, marveling at how even now, his stubbornness is on display. His unrelenting conviction that he'd mapped it all out in his head, that his plan *was* going to work. His refusal to be anything less than exceptionally reliable. "You can't try to outsmart Murphy's Law, son," Renata says, reaching out to pat his chest. With a knowing look, Crew nods sullenly, as though this is a battle he's been waging for a while. "Dad's coming out to get me," Renata says, jerking her thumb over her shoulder. "The guys unloaded all the supplies."

"Good," Crew says.

"You need to rest," his mother adds, brooking no argument with her statement.

"I'm fine, Mom," Crew grumbles. His hold on Grace tightens just slightly.

"I can see that," Renata counters, giving him a quick scan from his toes to the top of his head. "But my statement still stands." She looks to Grace, and that sparkle in her eye has returned as she leans in and, conspiratorially, says, "Make sure he stays off his feet, will you?"

From the corner of her eye, Grace can see Crew turn to look at her. "Of course," Grace replies resolutely. She glances up at Crew and says, "We'll take it easy."

There's a tug at the corner of Crew's mouth at her implication. He'll comply now, if it means they can do so together.

"Good," Renata says. She squeezes Grace's shoulder on her way past, walking into the fray of the ranch hands.

Crew and Grace stay behind, and he slides his arm away from her neck so he can turn to face her fully. She hates that she already misses the warmth that enveloped her within his hold—hates that she feels unrooted now, like she could float away without him to tether her to the earth. "Take it easy, huh?" he asks, smirking.

Pursing her lips, Grace looks up at him, craning her neck back to keep his eyes locked with her own. "Yeah," she says, rocking back on her heels. "You know how to play rummy?"

Crew's eyes narrow. "You want to play cards?"

Grace cocks her head. "Do you understand what the word *rest* means?"

"Well, yeah," he replies, then clears his throat. "I just thought—"

"Thought we'd go hang out in your tent and *not* rest?"

He looks . . . caught. Smug. A little too confident. Grace tiptoes up until their mouths are level. With hers inches from his, she says, "Seems ill-advised. What if you overdid it?"

"That was my plan," he says, low and rumbling, his words laced with a heady promise.

Grace smiles. "Soon," she declares.

He lets out a little sigh, a defeated expression crossing his face. "Okay, but," he adds, leaning forward. His hand finds her jaw, tilting her head upward farther. His thumb strokes the bone there, caressing all the way back toward her ear. "I still want to take you somewhere later."

"Does this journey require any strenuous activity on your part?"

A real, genuine smile blooms on his face, and it's a beautiful sight. A lovely, warm balm to the horror of the afternoon. He's here—he's real—he's okay.

He's with her.

Crew shakes his head. "Shouldn't be too taxing."

"All right," Grace agrees. "But for now, let's go." She nods toward his tent. "I'll grab the deck, you go settle in."

"Yes, ma'am," he says, still smiling.

They part ways then, and with every step she takes from him, a longing deep in her chest becomes more potent than ever before.

It doesn't make any sense—frankly, none of this does—but

she misses him the second she isn't standing within arm's reach of him.

She misses him even knowing she'll see him in mere minutes.

She misses his eyes, his mouth, his touch—in the very fabric of her soul.

"You're such a sandbagger," Crew grumbles as Grace lays five different sets of cards down onto the tarp-covered floor of Crew's tent.

Grace grins, carefully placing each one, fanning them out so there's no confusion on *how many* points she's about to rack up. Crew holds only two cards, but he's been holding on to them for the better part of fifteen minutes, itching to play them so he could use the large fan of cards she'd held in her hands against her with his win.

But Grace is no stranger to rummy tactics. In fact, she's quite an expert.

"Don't be a sour sport," she volleys back. When she's done laying out the riches of her hand, and only one card remains between her thumb and index finger, she looks at him, feigning innocence. "You're up."

He tilts his head, glaring at her. "I am aware."

Grace's smile widens. She's growing fonder by the second of how cute he is when he isn't getting his way. It must be something that doesn't happen very often.

Scanning the cards in front of her for an out, Crew groans when he finds none. He reaches for the deck to pull a new card, peeks at it, then shakes his head in frustration. "You've rigged this deck," he proclaims, tucking the card into his hand. "I'm certain of it."

Grace places a hand to her chest. "Are you calling me a cheater?"

"You heard me," he says, then he nods toward her one card. "Go."

"It's not nice to call people cheaters. I, for one, am full of integrity when it comes to rummy. You're just mad that I'm better at it." Grace reaches for her own card from the pull pile. When she picks it up to reveal a king of diamonds, she keeps her poker face as neutral as possible. He doesn't *need* to know that unless he gets lucky this turn, she's about to beat him.

He doesn't get lucky. He just gets ornerier, in the most harmless, adorable way. He mutters under his breath and sneaks little glares in her direction when he thinks she isn't looking. Grace tucks this information away for safekeeping: Crew Caldwell is a sore loser.

When she places her remaining cards down onto the victory-scape of her sets, she does so with gentle but purposeful force. And she doesn't take her eyes away from him as she does it, clocking his expression as she lays the last one down and says, "Rummy."

Instantly deflating, Crew hangs his head. "Jesus."

"Look, you gave a valiant effort," Grace says, sweeping up the cards. There's no point in actually counting them—she was already beating him by a wide margin and definitely would've gotten past their agreed-upon two-hundred mark with this hand. "I just happen to be really, really good at this game. I used to play it with my grandma almost every day."

Crew looks up at this, a glimmer of softness washing over him. "Yeah?"

Grace nods. "Yeah, she was the one who taught me the art of sandbagging. I used to get so pissed when she'd win after hoarding half the deck for the whole game."

He chuckles. "Sounds like you were cut from the same cloth."

"Yeah," Grace says quietly. It surprises her, how casually she just brought up her family, how easy it was to tell him something about her life before. Pangs of wistfulness ache in her belly at the memory, but she doesn't feel the urge to tamp it down, or shove it into a drawer in her brain and throw away the key. Instead, she wants to keep telling him about the woman who was once one of her favorite people in the universe.

"She died when I was still a kid. She was the best," she adds.

Crew stares at her for a beat, and then leans back until he's fully horizontal on his bedroll. He scoots over just enough for her to burrow in next to him, an offer he makes with his eyes as he settles in. When Grace hesitates, he gives her that painfully soft smile that she is very quickly beginning to love—beginning to understand on a molecular level. It means so much more than any other smile, carries so much more weight.

I'm with you, it says. *I see you.*

She lifts up onto her knees and crawls in next to him, and for a moment, it's slightly awkward. She's on her side, he's on his back, and she doesn't want to drape herself all over him the way she knows she should in order to be comfortable in such a tight space. But they haven't—there's been no real *touching* since the previous day. Nothing as definitive as an all-out cuddle like this would be. Grace bites her lip, contemplating, holding herself still and stiff.

Crew makes the decision for her. Ever the steadfast, confident leader. He gives her no room for any further doubt when he slides his arm under her head, letting her use his bicep as a pillow. He takes one of her arms and wraps it around his torso, then sets his hand atop her elbow and begins to rub soothing lines up, down, up, down. It instantly puts her at ease, and it doesn't feel odd or ill-fitting, the way they've tangled together so quickly. It feels like the shape of his body was carved specifically for her to fit against him.

He ducks his chin down and his lips are at her forehead; he presses a kiss there, lets it linger, and Grace's eyes flutter shut. "Tell me more about her," he says.

And so she does.

She tells him more than she's ever told anyone. How her grandmother used to watch her on summer days when her mom was at work, and she'd lie on the couch and watch Mr. Rogers, and she can still smell the cup of coffee her grandmother perpetually drank—she took it with milk and cinnamon, and it was somehow always lukewarm.

She tells him about the hushed conversations her mom would have with her grandmother when she came to pick up Grace, the frustrated, animated way they'd talk to each other outside of the car, too muffled for Grace to know what they were saying. She'd figured it out eventually—it was about her father; it always was. Her grandmother had known from the start that it wasn't a good match—that he was a sinking ship that would bring them down with him.

"'Love makes you dumb,'" Grace says, quoting her. "'Dumb and blind.'"

Crew stares down at her, wordless. His eyes search hers, and for a moment, it seems almost as though he'll argue. When he doesn't, Grace looks away, and fills the space with more memories. Talking about the past, somehow, seems easier than addressing whatever look he was just giving her. Whatever declaration he may have been about to utter.

She tells him about falling asleep in her grandmother's arms as she spun her around in a rickety chair at the dining room table, reciting a lullaby that wasn't a lullaby but simply a string of proclamations said with the softest lilt of a melody: *Mimi loves Grace; Mommy loves Grace; Papa in heaven loves Grace; Miss Winters loves Grace; Goose and Lulu love Grace.* She'd always made sure to include Grace's teacher and her two old, chubby cats because, of course, they all also loved Grace. Six-year-old Grace never doubted she was loved. She'd been told she was every single day.

Tears sprout in her eyes at that particular memory. And then, before she can stop herself from saying the next words, they tumble out of her mouth, as if Crew has hooked them with a reel and is pulling them out of her. "It was kind of soul-crushing when I realized as an adult that there was no one left on that list," she says, slightly hoarse from all the talking. "No one left in the world who loved me."

She doesn't realize she's actually crying until Crew is wiping her tears away with his thumb. He doesn't say anything—he doesn't have to. His eyes are full of something Grace doesn't want to try to decipher, for fear that she'll find pity. She lets out a watery laugh, turning away from him.

"Sorry. Didn't mean for that to turn into a sob story."

"Hey," Crew finally says, breaking his prolonged silence. He gently turns her head to face him again, and they're so close now. Their mouths are inches apart. He swipes his thumb across her bottom lip, watching the motion, and then finds her eyes again. "You have nothing to be sorry for." His eyes search her face, like he's trying to memorize her every freckle. "I don't know what happened to you, Grace, and you don't have to tell me. But I do know this—"

He swallows hard, then leans forward to one of her cheeks, placing just a whisper of kiss there, then doing the same with the other. He leans back, cradles her face in his hand, and says, "You deserve to be loved. You deserve to be happy every single day of your life. If I would've—" His lips flatten in frustration, and his eyes drop. He stops himself abruptly, but then seems to shake off whatever was caught in his throat and returns her stare with renewed conviction. "I can't change the past. I can't hold you through all of that lost time and tell you how precious you are. I wish I could." He lays his forehead against hers. "But I can hold you now."

The tip of Grace's nose grazes his as the words settle between them. As they sink into her bones, her every iota. He's making good on his promise—holding her like she's something inexplicably special to him—and there's no other way for her to thank him but to tilt her head up and press her lips into his. It's tentative, a quiet, fleeting question she asks on instinct, then pulls away as quickly as she'd leaned in. Crew's eyes are fluttering when she looks at him, but when they open, they're glassy, searching hers with a darting wonder.

"Grace." He says her name on an exhale. Like the very word is a relief.

And then he spreads a hand to encompass her jaw and neck, and he descends.

Grace has been kissed before. Enough times to know that no kiss is the same—there isn't a rulebook anyone follows, or if there is, most seem to disregard it entirely. She's experienced everything from a hard, dry push of her mouth into another person's to a sloppy, tongue-forward lick fest that left her chin sparkling with saliva. Everything in between had been forgettable, a mechanical, uneventful locking that did nothing for her, physically or otherwise.

This is nothing like any of those kisses. This kiss is singular; it's raw like an exposed nerve. It could raze cities; it could start wars. It is everything good and warm and intoxicating, and she wants to live and die in it. To let her bones rot beneath the weight of its intensity.

Crew groans when Grace leans into it, a fervor she's never known taking over her body and calling the shots. He reaches down to grab her thigh, then yanks until he's hooked it over his hip. Within the space of a pounding heartbeat, he's halfway on top of her, settled between the cradle of her legs. He kisses and kisses and kisses her, worshipping her lips with his own. When he swipes his tongue across the seam of her mouth, she lets out a keening sigh, loud and unexpected. It just—it feels so good. To be kissed so hungrily. To be wanted like this.

The sound breaks him from the spell they've both been under, and he picks his head up to look at her. When the rushing, pulsating blood in her ears dies down, she realizes what he's doing. He's listening, intently checking what's going on outside the nylon—and extremely *thin*—walls of the tent.

She hears it then. A familiar, sobering, moment-killing sound.

A collective, knowing chuckle.

Crew sighs, letting his head fall onto her collarbone. After a long moment of silence between them, he starts to kiss her throat softly, hesitantly. When Grace starts to squirm, her mouth falling open, he seems to pick up on it. To understand they're never going to be able to do this quietly. He picks his head up again, pushes a strand of hair behind her ear, and smiles.

"Let's get out of here," he says, his eyes sparkling. A little mischief, a little adoration. She wants to kiss him again, nearly does—but instead, she refrains, knowing if she complies, they might have a moment to actually be alone.

"To *somewhere*?" she asks, calling back to his promise from earlier.

Crew nods, then brushes his lips across hers in the most teasing, lovely way.

And then he's up, pulling her along with him.

CHAPTER 17

Somehow managing to avoid any curious, prying eyes, Grace and Crew sneak out of the tent and pile into the truck. Whether because everyone is graciously giving them an out or they're just lucky, she doesn't know. Doesn't particularly care. Especially not now, sitting in the passenger seat with the windows rolled down and Crew's hand on her knee. "Folsom Prison Blues" plays on a spotty radio station, Johnny Cash's deep croon tuning in and out, accompanied by dull static. Though Grace knows Crew is driving toward something, his route feels aimless and unpredictable. He veers off between trees and brush, wholly trusting in the four-wheel drive of the truck to get them over the uneven, rocky terrain.

"Are you gonna tell me where we're going?" she calls out, voice rising over the radio, the wind, and the thrumming engine.

Crew just smiles, looks over at her, and winks.

It makes her stomach swoop, that cocky little action. That mix of playfulness and self-assured ease that she's beginning to understand is the *real* Crew Caldwell. She used to think he was a man of opposing forces—able to be split clean down the middle. One side, the grumpy, chilly, ever-scowling foreman. And the other, a devoted big brother and a loyal, hardworking elder son. A warm, protective, and understanding man of whom she only ever saw sporadic glimpses. Those rare, quiet moments she'd hoarded into her memory for safekeeping.

She understands now that he's somewhere in between. Not quite as clear-cut, but a swirling mix of beautiful, frustrating attributes, the sum of their parts coming together to form this magnetic man she can't seem to look away from.

So distracted by the enigma that is Crew, Grace doesn't even notice that the truck has started to slow down. When she looks out the windshield, what's spread out before them is . . . somewhat anticlimactic. Her brow furrows. "It's a field."

Crew nods, also staring out at the clearing.

"You took us from a field . . . to . . . another field?"

He chuckles. "Notice anything different about this particular field?"

Grace squints, trying to understand, playing a *spot the difference* game she isn't quite grasping. But then it dawns on her, and when she pokes her head out the window to confirm her suspicions, she plops back down, her eyes beginning to sparkle with excitement. "Mud."

Crew winks at her again, and then, without warning, he slams his foot onto the accelerator and takes off, sending mud in every direction with the force of the tires. The slap of it hitting the truck's exterior is loud, and Grace barely has enough time to roll up her window before she's covered in it. She's laughing, screaming, yelling at him to be careful as he starts to pull maneuvers that have the truck nearly tipping over. But it never does, even as he does a series of figure eights, each growing wider than the last.

Grace's stomach hurts from how hard she's laughing, especially when he gets pelted in the face by a rogue splash of mud flying in through the crack in his window. Crew brakes and puts the truck in park, assesses himself, and then blows a raspberry to get the residue off his lips. Grace is practically *snorting* in hysterics now, which attracts his narrow-eyed attention, and then he's launching into action—leaning over without ceremony and rubbing his face against hers, leaving mud on her cheeks, forehead, and chin. She squeals as he begins to also tickle her in retribution, and it's futile to try to push him off. No matter how hard she shoves, he's impervious to her efforts. So easily, like she's made of putty, he molds her to his liking until he's hovering over her as much as he can with the center console between them.

When Grace's laughter eventually dies down, they both begin to still, breathing heavily.

A moment that had, seconds ago, been full of mirth and silliness quickly shifts into something else entirely. The air between them grows thick with a charge so powerful it hums right along with the idling engine. Crew's eyes search her face until they find her lips. Unfazed by the mud and grime, he stares at them for a long moment, studying them. Maybe trying to decide his best plan of attack. Whatever the case, Grace is growing increasingly impatient, so she takes her bottom lip into her mouth, catching it between her teeth. A signal—a message for him she hopes is loud and clear: *I want you to kiss me. I want it so badly I can't see straight.*

Crew lets out a shuddering breath, and then he obliges.

Inexplicably, through some miracle within the fabric of the universe, the second kiss Crew Caldwell gives her is better than the first. Before, when they had yet to know the shape of each other's mouths, there was apprehension and gentleness, shifting hesitantly into hunger and heat. There had been a clandestine quality to it, given their surroundings—doomed from the start to be dampened or interrupted. But here, now, they aren't hiding. They don't have to be quiet, and they don't have to be delicate.

Because if the way Crew's mouth slants over hers is any indication, there are no longer any questions of intent lingering between them. They've all been definitively answered.

With a hand at her neck and the pad of his thumb tracing her jaw, Crew opens her up, physically and emotionally. He strips her bare of all doubt with his tongue, rolling it against her own, and—surely—there must be sparks igniting in her mouth, because electricity is humming throughout her body. The damp, heated spot between her legs—the power source of it all—begins to throb with his ministrations. Crew groans into her mouth, and the sound has her hips rocking on instinct, a begging motion, a need unmet, desperate for the friction of his body against hers. But it's awkward in the cab of the truck—the space is too small, and Crew is *far* too big to do anything comfortably besides kiss her. And even that won't be a sustainable practice if they keep going like this, because with each brush of his tongue against hers, the growing need within Grace's belly to touch, to feel, to be held by him is becoming overwhelming.

She wonders if he's thinking the same thing, because his fervent kisses begin to slow, his grip on her neck loosening. A longing she's never known spreads in her chest when he pulls back, separating himself from her. He's breathing hard, his lips parted and swollen. His eyes are heavy lidded, nearly concealing the way his pupils are blown black and wide. Grace leans forward reflexively, the rope between them growing taut with the wreckage written all over his face. A sudden need, starving and urgent, takes over—she wants him to *always* look like this; she wants to put her mouth on him and hear him groan her name.

She's about a half second away from climbing over the console and settling onto his lap when Crew manages to utter a string of raspy, rumbling words. "Wait. Hang on."

Still in a bit of a trance, Grace murmurs, "What?"

Crew exhales roughly, staring down at her contemplatively. He leans up on his arm, looks out the windshield, then starts chewing on the inside of his cheek. Grace is about to ask him what he could *possibly* be thinking about when he looks back at her and says, "I want to strip you of these clothes and kiss every single inch of you."

A wave of heat crashes through her and she's nodding before she even realizes it—suddenly needing that more than she's ever needed anything.

Crew smiles, his expression shifting into a mix of amusement and adoration. "But I also haven't had a real shower in days and I—" A minute slip of his confidence, a softening of his eyes into something more vulnerable. "I want to make this good for you. Every part of it."

Reaching up a hand, Grace traces her thumb over Crew's bottom lip. "It already is."

He presses a kiss there, then sighs. "Come back to the house with me," he says quietly. He nips at her thumb, and his eyes darken slightly when he adds, "Come shower with me."

There's no logical reason why Grace should be nervous about this, but something about the idea of standing beneath a showerhead next to a very naked Crew while they bathe feels frighteningly intimate. He's already washed her hair, massaged knots from her muscles, literally *reset* her bones, but this—the nakedness, proximity, the steamy, low-lit shower—it makes her almost shiver in a wild combination of nerves and anticipation.

And maybe because she doesn't answer him right away, or maybe because he's got a habit of being his most honest self during these heated exchanges, Crew seems to need to reinforce his request, to solidify and vocalize his intentions.

He leans down and says, deep and rough in her ear, "And then I want to fuck you in my bed." He bites the lobe, dragging it upward for a beat before releasing it, and Grace is temporarily blinded by stars bursting in her vision. Hot, needy, exploding stars.

"How does that sound, baby?" he asks, teasing, already knowing the answer. It sounds perfect.

It sounds like everything she's ever wanted. And still, he toys with her, dialing up her arousal until it's edging close to a fever pitch.

"Will you let me fuck you?"

Grace nods, unable to say—scream—the only word that can possibly follow that question. She nods and nods and nods until Crew is finally up, lifting himself off her and putting the truck into gear. She's dazed, barely aware they're moving until they've reversed out of the clearing entirely and are swinging around to catapult forward in the direction of the house.

Grace leans back into her seat and rubs her hands down her thighs, doing what she can to keep her mind occupied. Crew's hand finds her knee, and Grace latches on to it with her own.

She sighs, grateful for the anchor of his touch—grateful that he somehow knew to reach out and ground her before she floated away on a cloud of sexual frustration.

They waste no time once they're inside. Grace doesn't wait for Crew to romantically peel the layers of her clothing away, and she doesn't pay any mind to the state of her hair when she yanks it out of its ponytail and lets it fall down her shoulders. She simply, quickly bares herself, physically and otherwise, almost as soon as she walks through the door. Somewhere behind her, she hears the jingle of keys being dropped on a table, hears the shifting of boots being removed and slid over the hardwood floor. When she turns around, not a single piece of clothing remains on her body, and she finds Crew in his socks, frozen midway through unbuttoning his shirt. His eyes are the only part of him able to move, and slowly, they scan her up and down, then once more, and when he swallows after taking his fill, the lump in his throat is visible.

He holds her eyes as he rids himself of his shirt, then unbuckles his belt and toes off his socks. His jeans hang loosely at his hips, the elastic of his black briefs peeking out, and as Grace takes him in, she's surprised at how *drunk* she feels, despite having not a single sip of alcohol. It's *Crew*—he's her own special brand of 90-proof. The massive, strong body built like he was supposed to be leading ancient armies into epic wars instead of running a cattle ranch. The fair skin contrasted by the dark beauty marks and freckles all over his shoulders and chest. The soft, depthless eyes that can say more truth with one look than most can utter in a lifetime. That sinful, beautiful mouth. That talented tongue.

He is everything that is good and right and perfect in the world, and Grace cannot fathom spending one more second not touching him.

She crosses the distance between them, caring little for the jeans that still remain on his person, and launches herself into his arms. He bends ever so slightly, catching her beneath her thighs, and hoists her up until her legs are bracketed around his middle, holding him tightly as she leans down and kisses him with everything she has. Everything she is and ever will be.

With Grace in his arms and her bare center rubbing against his lower belly, Crew moans, and his tongue slips into her mouth with languid purpose. He somehow has the wherewithal to walk them out of the foyer, through the scattered piles of Grace's abandoned clothes and toward his bedroom, where the shower—and, more importantly, the *bed*—awaits.

The moments that follow are blurry, shifted out of focus by the blinding desire and arousal that hums beneath Grace's skin. A flurry of skin, water, soap, and wandering hands. Crew stands behind her in the shower, lathering her breasts and taking extra time on her nipples, plucking at them even when they are far past the point of *clean*. He's been hard against her backside since they walked into the bathroom, but with him now free of his jeans, the heat of his length radiates into her, and all Grace can think about is how easy it would be to bend over and invite him inside. To place her hands against the tile of the shower and let him bury himself within her, to feel the fullness she so desperately needs.

Her sense of urgency becomes clearer to him when she starts to whine with impatience as he rinses the conditioner from her hair, and then his own. He runs his fingers through her long brown locks thoroughly, testing her, challenging her will to wait, to hold on for just a little bit longer. Only when he's reached past her to shut the water off does he finally give her *more*, pressing her backward until she's flush against the glass door and cupping her entire cunt with his hand. The tips of his index and middle fingers dip shallowly into her, and they both groan. Grace with relief and impatience and excitement, Crew with awe at how wet she is, and knowing it isn't the shower's doing. As methodical and careful as he'd been during the washing up, Crew seems to abandon all pretense now, as though this tiny glimpse of how turned on she is, of the hot, soft wetness that awaits him has depleted all of his patience. He lifts her up by her waist, encouraging her legs to encircle him once again, and then he walks them, still dripping from the shower, to his bed.

He doesn't lay her down, doesn't tuck her into his mattress and climb on top of her like she thought he would. Instead, he turns around until the backs of his thighs hit the bed, and then he slowly lowers himself, letting her rest atop his thighs.

Grace hums, arching her back until her chest is pressed into his. Instincts, she's learning, are her best friend—her most reliable resource. Undoubtedly, she has a severe lack of experience for this type of congress, and with anyone else—someone she trusted less, cared about less—she'd probably be bumbling and awkward, apologetic for her naivete. But with Crew, that critical, doubting part of her brain switches to standby, stepping into the darkened background and allowing the more primal, impulsive urges to take center stage. She moves without thinking about it, letting her body take what it wants. And right now, all it wants is to see him undone. To watch this pillar of a man become unmade.

Crew's hands push up her back, settling at her rib cage, and Grace shivers from the rough texture of his hands, the path of warmth drawn by his fingertips. When her head tips backward at the sensation of it, a whimpering sound vibrates in his throat. She feels his lips at her neck, his teeth scraping her skin. "God, I want you," he says on a shuddering exhale.

She looks back down at him. "You can have me," she declares, and punctuates the sentence with a roll of her hips, a burst of intense friction between the aching crease in her legs and the thick hardness between his. "You *do* have me."

Crew growls into her collarbone, and then he's moving, shifting backward until he's closer to the middle of the bed, her still secure in his lap. He lies down then, but when Grace goes to follow him, to let the magnetic pull of his lips and his eyes drag her down, Crew shakes his head. Instead, he grips beneath her thighs and drags her up, up, *up*, until she's covering him entirely. She's sitting on his face without reservation, and though she's never done anything like this before, she isn't worried or nervous—especially not when Crew's hands move to her hips while his mouth encompasses her dripping cunt.

They both groan loudly at the first touch of his tongue, and then he begins to *feast*. He eats her pussy with the same level of careful determination he reserves for everything else in his life. Never anything in halves, only ever giving his full, undivided self. He situates her to his liking more than once, using his hands on her hips to guide her, rocking her back and forth over his mouth and changing angles and techniques anytime she's venturing too close to the edge. His tongue flattens out against her clit, then delves inside, then spends a maddening amount of time tracing her lips, just barely grazing the border of that sensitive, swollen little nub. He repeats that, mixes it up, listens for what makes her scream, and keeps going until she's practically sobbing with the need to come. When he finally decides to let her, it's with the assistance of two of his fingers pressing deep inside, making a scissorlike motion and caressing a part of her that she's never been able to reach on her own.

"Come on my tongue, baby," he slurs when he comes up for air. "Wanna feel you gush."

She's breathless and trembling with her mouth hanging wide open on a silent scream when she does, and it's almost painful, how good it feels. Her head falls back as she regains enough breath to let out a long, broken moan, the shape of his name mixed somewhere in the middle.

Grace is only partly aware, only slightly coherent as Crew gently lifts her off him and settles her onto her back. He hovers over her, leaning onto his elbow, and stares at her with deep, brazen affection as she breathes deeply, steadily making her way back down to earth. When he dips his head down to kiss her, it wakes her up a little more, and she can taste herself on his lips. Maybe it should be embarrassing, but it isn't; it's devastatingly intimate and she is suddenly hit with an onslaught of emotion, of appreciation and care and something staggeringly close to love for this man and the way he moves her—not just her body, but her mind, her heart, her very soul. Their kiss quickly grows deeper and more urgent, their tongues delving into each other's mouths, saying everything they need to say without words.

I need you.
I want you.
I'm with you.

Grace, fully aware that physical intimacy with Crew makes her insatiable and demanding, breaks from the kiss to tell him, "I'm on birth control."

Crew blinks at her, darts a quick glance downward, and then back up. Hesitantly, he says, or *tries* to say, anyway, "So, I don't—" He coughs, clearly overtaken by the implication, unable to form the words to even ask the question. "You're sure you—"

"I want you to fuck me without a condom," she confirms, and in any other setting, her unearned confidence would probably be laughable. But here, with him, it's unshakable. With Crew, Grace can finally say exactly what she wants, when she wants, without the worry of being told her desires don't matter. With Crew, she can be brave.

Something that sounds very much like *fuck* slips from his lips, and then he's on top of her, settling himself between her legs and kissing her, hard and rough and finally starting to match the impatience she's been feeling since they were surrounded by that field of mud. Crew grabs both of her legs beneath her knees and pulls them up until they're slung around his hips, and that's when she feels it—the blunt, smooth head of him right *there*, right at the place where she will take him in. "You'll tell me if it hurts," Crew says roughly, his lips tracing her jaw. And though Grace nods, Crew says, "Promise me you'll tell me."

"I promise," she says, wrapping her arms around his neck.

Satisfied, he drops a quick kiss to her lips, and then he's breathing long and hard through his nose as he reaches down and positions himself. He keeps himself gripped securely as he pushes in, the tip of his cock breaching her entrance. In the space of a heartbeat, Grace's senses are overloaded. Her eyes widen slightly at the feeling, and it *does* hurt, but not enough for her to want him to stop, especially not when she looks up to find him staring down at her, his eyes scanning every inch of her face. He gains a couple more inches and his mouth, which had been pressed into a firm line, parts, a heavy exhale falling from his lips. Grace grinds her teeth together as he pushes in farther, and if she were any less wet, if he were even half an inch larger, it'd probably be too much. But he'd taken the time to make sure she was soaked, drenched in arousal for him, not only to bring her more of that blinding pleasure, but to ease this passage. It's working—between the wetness of her pussy, that look of awe in his eyes, and the feeling of his cock burying itself within her, the discomfort begins to quickly subside. It takes a sharp left turn into something much more enticing, hovering in that sweet spot between pain and pleasure. And then Crew captures her mouth with his, and pain becomes an afterthought entirely. Grace moans into his mouth as he reaches the hilt, and together, they breathe the same air, lips pressed together but neither of them moving.

Crew picks up his head slightly to ask, "Okay?"

Grace reaches up, pulls him back down, and says, "Better." And then she kisses him again. She tightens her legs around him, unintentionally causing him to grind into her, and Crew grunts, his hand flying down to her thigh to hold her there as he starts to move.

Grace's vision starts to blur—the room is fading out of view, leaving everything in a haze except for Crew. He's in full color, high definition. She wants to burn this image into her brain—

the way his mouth falls open when he pulls nearly all the way out only to plunge back in with more force.

"Crew," she moans when she sees his eyes roll back, just as turned on by *his* pleasure as she is by her own. Maybe more.

"Fuck, Grace," Crew grunts, and it's like the words are punched from him, like saying them finally gave him the ability to breathe again. He continues to roll his hips into hers, never fully leaving her but stretching her out with each thrust.

He rises then, sitting back on his haunches and gripping her hips, pulling her body into his. His breath stutters as he pulls one of her ankles up onto his shoulder, holding it there as he pumps in and out. Grace's head lolls back, and she can feel it, that telltale spark of something hot and all-encompassing creeping at the base of her spine. With each pump of his cock, it gets bigger, more insistent. She whines at the feeling of it, lost to the sensation of it all, and for maybe the first time in her life, she is fully in her body. Fully present, fully rooted to the earth, anchored by the weight of the man she loves.

The realization of that hits her like a derailed train, unexpected and catastrophic. She is overwhelmed instantly by the knowledge, by the fact that she's known long before this moment. She blinks up to find Crew staring at her again, those pink, plush lips parted in a haze of pleasure as he moves inside of her, expertly, exquisitely splitting her open.

"Say it again," he demands, his breaths growing shallower. Grace reaches up to touch his stomach, his chest, runs her fingers over his nipples. Crew groans and picks up his pace, fucking her steadily into the mattress now. "Say it, Grace. Say my name like you're mine."

Grace manages to get what she wants—pulling at him in any

way she can until he's inches away again, his mouth hovering over hers. "Crew," she says, and as it leaves her mouth, he gives her a particularly hard thrust, causing her to elongate the word with a moan. "Crew," she repeats, and then again, "Crew, I—"

She feels it before she realizes what's happening; his thumb flicks at her clit and white flashes spark in her vision, hurtling her to the precipice of another orgasm. Crew is panting, almost wheezing as he fucks her. He blinks, coming back to himself for a brief second, realizing he'd cut her off. "What, baby? Tell me."

She has one foot out the door when she tells him—one foot on an entirely different plane of existence. One where only euphoria exists, one where her body feels like an endless ocean and stardust and molten lava all at once. But she stays just long enough to say, "I am yours." And then she's free-falling, her vision going completely white. She can't think, or scream, or cry—she can only feel. She feels him squeezing her tighter as she falls, she feels him plunging even deeper into her, prolonging her ecstasy, and she feels his breath on her face. The way it comes out in disbelieving huffs. She clenches around him even harder at the sensation, and that's what does him in.

Grace comes back to her body just in time to hear him let loose a long, broken groan as he pushes his face into her neck and begins to pulse inside of her. She clenches around him at the feeling, and it steals his breath, makes his hips jerk. He breathes loudly, raggedly, her name falling from his lips like a prayer as she drains him of every last drop.

They both come back to earth slowly, in an unhurried flurry of drugging kisses and blissful sighs. He pulls out of her eventually, grunting as he goes. Grace can feel their combined fluids dripping out of her, a warm reminder of the love they just made.

Because there's no other way to describe what happened—*fucking* would be too crude, too simple, too ordinary.

Crew just made love to her.

And Grace knows now, without a shadow of a doubt—nothing will ever be the same.

CHAPTER 18

Of all the firsts Grace has experienced over the past seventy-two hours, this—lying next to a man in a dimly lit room and doing absolutely nothing apart from enjoying each other's company—is by far the most unexpected. She's lived decades without knowing any intimacy at all, and now she's getting a crash course in it and all its different forms. This one, she thinks as she lies with her head on Crew's stomach while his thick fingers stroke her hair, might be her favorite. Obviously, the orgasms, the sex, the kissing—all of it had been otherworldly, a flood of ecstasy in which she was happy to drown. Being as close to him as she physically could has done something irrevocable to her—it's rewritten the part of her that was certain she was only meant to have shallow, unsatisfactory encounters. She understands now that her body is so much more than a vessel to be used for someone else's pleasure; her body is capable of becoming a shatter point of sensation and satisfaction.

But this . . . just talking, learning, enjoying each other, it's different. They may not be physically as close as they had been earlier, but that doesn't matter. He's still holding her flush to his entire body, her heart on top of his. She still feels adored and heard and cared for.

"Tell me something," Grace says quietly, holding Crew's free hand in both of hers, outlining the knobs of his knuckles and the shape of his nail beds with her fingertips. Crew indulges her, his hand limp and malleable.

She can't see his face from where she lies, but she can hear the smile in his voice when he says, "Like what?"

Pulling his thumb to her mouth, she puts the tip between her teeth and nips lightly. His other fingers stroke her cheek. "Like ... why did you come back here? After your last tour, why did you decide to settle down here and not go off on your own?"

He's quiet for a moment, and Grace tilts her head to the side to look at him, but all she can see is the underside of his chin, the flex of his jaw.

"When I left for my first one, I was the worst version of myself. I was aggressive and cruel to the people I loved. I was so angry. I had a lot of resentment for my parents—my dad, mostly. We stopped getting along right around the time I started high school. He was never easy on me, made me work the ranch basically from the time I could walk. He'd get me up at four in the morning and send me out to the bunkhouse, and I had to follow Forty around until it was time for me to go to school. And when I didn't have school, I was out there all day. By the time I was a teenager, I knew Halcyon better than he did." Crew stretches out his fingers, laying his palm flat against hers. There's a rigidity in the movement, and Grace weaves her fingers into his, beckoning him to let his hand—himself—relax once more.

"After that, I got this idea in my head that he wasn't worthy of my mom, that the only reason anyone respected him was because he married her. I remember telling him during a nasty argument that he lucked out when she sat next to him in that tenth-grade biology class, and that if she hadn't, he'd be nothing and nowhere. He laughed in my face and said it was rich for someone *born* into this to call him lucky. I enlisted not long after that." He dips his chin at the same time that Grace turns her head, and their eyes meet. Crew squeezes her hand, a wistful smile tugging at his lips. "I didn't come home between the first and second tours. It was selfish—I wasn't here for Caia's graduation or the blowout that happened after. My mom will never say it out loud, but I know she's still angry with me about that. She thinks if I'd been here, Caia wouldn't have left. She thinks I could've talked her off that ledge, which—I don't think anyone can talk Caia out of anything once she's got her mind made up, but I understand why Mom's brain has crafted that story for her. It's easier than facing the truth, which was that my siblings and I were suffocating under the weight of her legacy."

Grace wants to know more but suppresses the urge to ask for specifics. The blowout, Caia leaving—from what she could see at the party, she'd seemed to be on good terms with her parents, sharing hugs and smiles and tears of joy at her mother's toast. But she also recognizes that the Caldwells, a family that has always been public facing with a reputation to uphold, have to look a certain way to the outside world. Picture-perfect, close-knit, and loving—only when one starts to scratch the surface do they begin to see the cracks in the facade, the unraveling of ties that bind.

"By the time the second one was over, I'd become someone else. All that time spent away—everything I'd seen and done—it put things into perspective. Toward the end of it, Easton and I had made a pact that if we made it out in one piece, we'd stop fucking around and go live the lives we were meant to. For him, that meant throwing everything he had at becoming a professional bull rider and getting away from Halcyon. For me, I—I don't know how to explain it, and I can't point to any specific reason, but the only thing that made any sense after being in Afghanistan, being so isolated, being subjected to so much evil—was to come back here. I don't know what I thought I'd walk into—I should've known that even though time felt different—slower—for me, it was passing like normal here. Faster than normal. When I got home, it was like walking into a parallel universe. Cooper was getting ready to go to college out of state; Caia was basically unreachable. She didn't pick up my phone calls for the first three months that I was back. I had to go to New York and show up on her doorstep to get her to talk to me. My parents were sleeping in separate rooms. Two people who, for my entire childhood, couldn't keep their hands off of each other, could barely say two words to each other at meals. All I'd wanted to do for so long was get away from this place, and I realized that I'd carried this... childish notion that everything would stay the same, no matter how long I was gone. Static, like Halcyon and my family had been frozen in time, and I could just break them out when I was finally ready to face it all. Every instinct I had that had screamed at me to leave all those years ago started urging me to stay, to pick up the pieces and rebuild. To let some light break through the past five years I'd spent in darkness."

It's difficult to picture Halcyon and the Caldwells any other way than how Grace knows them to be presently—and it's especially strange to think about there ever being distance between Clint and Renata. Every time Grace is around them, they seem almost fused at the hip, wary of letting each other get too far away. She thinks about Crew coming home from his second tour and walking into a place unrecognizable from his childhood home—the construction the same, but everything inside completely different. Going from being one of three to being the only remaining child in a house full of newfound silence.

"That must've been really hard," Grace says. "But you did it. You rebuilt it."

"I don't know if that's true. I tried for a while, but eventually I realized there was a lot of truth to people saying *you can never go home again*. We'll never be what we were; Halcyon will never look the same as it did when I was a kid."

Grace nods, her nostrils flaring. "It's one thing about being an adult that I didn't anticipate would be so difficult. Coming to the realization that the best parts of the past are just that. The past. You can never have them back—no matter how hard you try, it won't be the same because you aren't the same. And neither is anyone else."

He hums his agreement, and the sound is more resigned than sad. He understands what she means; he's also come to terms with the way life begins and ends over and over again throughout time. One door closing and all that. She feels his fingertips at her temple begin to softly trace her hairline. For a few long moments, it's comfortably silent between them, but he keeps touching her, keeps his hand secured to hers. Then, quietly, he asks, "Will you tell me something now?"

Grace swallows, letting their joined hands fall gently onto her stomach. She tries not to allow any anticipatory dread to seep into this moment, but it's difficult. She clears her throat and nods. "What?"

Crew's hand drifts down to her face, turning her until she's looking at him. He brushes her hair back once more, then lets out a long breath through his nose. "Why did you stay for as long as you did?" The question is asked roughly, like it almost pains him to put it into words. "You could've left when you turned eighteen. Before that, if you'd told someone how you were being treated. So, why stay? Why put up with it for all that time?"

Reflexively, Grace looks away from him. She can't hold his eyes if she wants to answer his question in a way that doesn't provoke a follow-up; something about Crew makes it difficult for her to lie and twist the truth. A talent she's had all her life, a defensive weapon she uses regularly, and he dismantles it just by looking at her.

And the thing is—she should've seen this coming. She should've known that avoiding it and keeping Crew wrapped up in this blissfully ignorant bubble wouldn't last forever. He was always going to ask the most obvious question, the one everyone wants to ask the second they learn her story. But what they don't know, what no one can ever know, is that they don't actually want to hear the answer.

It isn't complicated—it isn't thoughtful or intentional like Crew's mission to rebuild his family. It's all based on one thing and one thing only. Fear.

Grace swallows thickly, then dons the nonchalance she's feigned for most of her life when asked this question. "There are a lot of reasons," she says. "I didn't know what else to do. I didn't have a GED, couldn't drive, didn't have any prospects of employment. And it wasn't—" She stops herself before she says something unforgivable, something close to *it wasn't that bad*, because that is a lie she cannot force from her lips.

Instead, she parses her words carefully and says, "There were good days. I had a mentor, Hal, who taught me everything about horses. He was kind to me. I spent most of my time with him or in the kitchen with Maryann, who wasn't necessarily *kind*, but she was never cruel. She taught me how to cook and clean, and the quickest way to break someone's nose."

Crew huffs out a laugh. "Jesus."

"Only had to put it into practice once," Grace adds, smirking at him. "But Hal and Maryann made it better. It was never home, but with them, it felt safe. When Hal died, I didn't want to leave Maryann—they'd been really close, and she took his death hard. Then Bellamy offered me Hal's job, and it was supposed to come with more money and—I thought—more respect. It was just . . . one of those things. You keep telling yourself one day you'll find something better, one day you'll make it out, and then you look up and you're twenty-five and still in the exact same place as before."

He doesn't say anything in response, and whether because he's waiting for her to continue or because he's accepting her answer, Grace doesn't know. She stays quiet, hoping he won't poke any holes in her very roundabout way of explaining what happened. Omission may be just as bad as lying, but she doesn't *want* to lie to him.

Grace takes advantage of the break in conversation, rolling over onto her stomach and resting her chin atop his chest. "Tell me something else," she says, happily shifting the conversation back to him. "Tell me something no one else knows."

He stares down at her with sleepy eyes, and for a moment, she thinks he sees right through her. Grace's smile falters slightly—he could call her out right now, could demand to hear every detail she left out. But he doesn't. He smiles back, tilts his head, and says, "You know we can't play hooky tomorrow, right?"

Grace's grin quickly shifts into a pout. "Even if the boss gives his blessing?"

Crew laughs. "The boss has a reputation to uphold, and we'll never live it down if we spend the whole day in bed while everyone else works."

With a groan, Grace concedes. "I hate that you're right."

He chuckles again, then reaches for her arms. "C'mere." He pulls her into him effortlessly, like she's light as a feather, and situates her by his side. They lie face-to-face, and as soon as Grace settles her head onto his bicep, her eyelids immediately start to feel heavy. Crew strokes her cheek, her neck, her arm, and his touch is drugging in the best way, sending her hurtling toward unconsciousness. Her eyes eventually slip shut, and he leans forward and presses a barely there kiss to her lips. As she hovers at the precipice of sleep, she hears him whisper, "Grace." She hums, trying to cling to the sound of his voice—tries to force herself to stay long enough to hear whatever he has to say. Her eyes remain closed, and the darkness is pulling her deeper and deeper, but she manages to resist long enough to hear him say, "It didn't feel like home again until you got here. No one else knows that."

The words reach her ears, her heart, her *soul*, and before she is completely lost to the world, she smiles.

Sometimes, when Grace dreams of her mother, her eyes are greener than she remembers. They were beautiful, bright and curious, but Grace always thought they were closer to brown. In this dream, they're a muted sage. Milky, like Maryann's blues, desaturated with age. It doesn't make sense in reality—her mother never got the chance to grow old. Like so many of the dreams she has of her mother's face, they are short-lived, fleeting images Grace tries to grab on to with both hands, only to watch them slip through her fingers like water, like sand, like all of the goodness that used to live in the world when her mother was still part of it. It always hurts, leaving her behind, even after all this time. It never gets easier to wake up and remember that she's gone; it never gets easier to stomach the sharp, gnawing ache that settles in her chest as soon as she opens her eyes.

But when she wakes in the dead of night this time, with the echoes of those pale green eyes still haunting her thoughts, she doesn't immediately feel that familiar pain—she's too confused, too distracted to let it sink in. Disoriented and sweaty, Grace picks up her head, blinking until her eyes have adjusted to the pitch darkness of her surroundings, and a few things become very obvious, very quickly. Wherever she is, it's air-conditioned, and even though she feels slightly feverish, the temperature is heavenly compared to sleeping outside in her tent—and, in stark contrast, whatever she's lying on is hot to the touch, like a space heater kicked up to full blast.

It takes only a handful of seconds for it all to come back—for her to remember exactly where she is, and exactly what—*who*—she is lying on.

Beneath her, Crew snores softly, the even rise and fall of his expansive chest raising her up, and then lowering her back down. Grace stares at the outline of his face in the darkness, wishing there was just a little bit more light in the room so she could really see him, see what he looks like when he's fully at rest, at peace.

As she looks at him, memories of the events that led to this moment begin to rush in, and Grace's cheeks start to heat as she watches it play back—sweet words from kiss-swollen lips, Crew buried deep inside, gasping against her neck. She shivers as the images sharpen, and it suddenly seems impossible not to crane her neck forward so she can nuzzle at his jaw, if only to catch his scent, to feel his skin beneath her lips and really reinforce the idea that she's *here*. In his bed, in his arms.

Crew murmurs something unintelligible when her lips make contact, and his hands are automatically at her hips, squeezing hard. Grace moves to the other side of his jaw to give it the same attention, and she smirks when his breath becomes notably shallower. Something begins to harden against her stomach, and Grace knows he's awake—or at least on the verge—when he lets out a sigh, throaty and rough with sleep.

Crossing her arms over his chest, Grace picks up her head to look at him, and she can see his eyes blinking awake. He glances down at her, and a ghost of a smile tugs at the corner of his mouth.

"Please tell me it isn't dawn yet," he rasps. His sleepy voice goes straight to that sensitive place between her legs—the place she's realizing is rather sore, but not in an unpleasant way, now that it's coupled with this newfound arousal.

Her eyes flicker to his nightstand, where an alarm clock straight out of the eighties with red, boxy numbers tells her it's only a quarter to three. She can't remember exactly when they stumbled into bed after the mudding and the shower, but it feels like centuries have occurred since then—since the time before she realized she loved Crew and now, when it is the most obvious truth she's ever known. The only sure thing in a lifetime of uncertainty.

"It isn't dawn yet," Grace says, tapping the tips of her fingers against his chest. The hair there is sparse and wiry, and she traces the thin tendrils near his nipples, grinning when he hisses at the unexpected touch. "We have a little time." Her voice is full of implications, of wants, of requests she hopes he can hear. When a hum sounds deep beneath his sternum, she knows that he has.

This time, he situates her on top of him, holding her steady by her thighs, securing them in his big hands. When she takes him in for the second time, there's a pinch of pain, and for a second, she thinks it may be too much, too soon. That maybe he'd split her too far open the night before, despite his carefulness and his thoughtful preparation. But then she hears Crew sigh, sees his neck stretch as his head falls back against the pillow, and pain, discomfort—all the unpleasant things that have ever existed—cease to matter. "Grace," he rasps. "You feel so good. So fucking perfect." He bounces her slowly, lazily on his cock, and when she comes, it's almost out of nowhere, hitting her like a tidal wave of sensation the second the edge of his thumb grazes her clit. She doubles over and moans, but he doesn't let her go far—he holds her face in his hands, keeping her steady as she rests her forehead against his. "Look at me," he demands, and Grace opens her eyes, bleary from the onslaught of this syrupy, delicious orgasm. "Let me look into those pretty eyes while you come."

Grace gasps, obeying his request, and it's so far from anything she's ever known—staring into his eyes, his *soul* as he fucks her through the white-hot heat of it, keeping her hips in motion and groaning as she throbs around him. His hand sinks into her hair, fingers threading through the strands until he finds purchase, and then he pulls *hard*, and Grace's moan morphs into a scream—an unintelligible, high-pitched cry of bliss. At the tail end of it, his name bursts from her lips like a prayer, like a breathless exultation.

Crew grunts, holding her steady as his thrusts start to stutter and slow. He holds her attention with his grip, and then his words. "I'm yours, too, baby," he says, the confession escaping in staccato sounds through his gritted teeth. "I'm yours."

Grace clenches *hard* at that, hit with another towering wave of ecstasy. Crew groans and then his entire body goes completely taut, seizing up until the veins in his neck are protruding and he's seemingly lost the ability to breathe. She feels him pulse and twitch inside her, feels the warmth filling her up until she's leaking, and only when she leans down to press her lips to his does he finally exhale. It's a loud, broken sound, more beautiful than anything she's ever heard.

As the aftershocks of his orgasm fade, she settles herself flush against his chest, both of them dazed and panting. She lies in the sound of his rapidly thumping heart—relishing it, memorizing its rhythm—until she dozes off once more.

CHAPTER 19

In retrospect, they probably should've known they'd never get away with this completely scot-free. Wishful thinking doesn't even cover that kind of ignorance—it was always a statistical certainty that the ranch hands were going to, in some way, shape, or form, give them a rash of shit for becoming . . . involved. The day after their escapade in the mud that turned into a whirlwind of mind-altering orgasms and quiet confessions, things had been suspiciously normal. They'd returned to the summer pasture without ceremony, offering little in the way of explanation for where they'd been, and no one had questioned them. There'd been *looks*, yes—Cooper had even whistled as they'd ambled up to camp together right in time for breakfast. They'd earned a few smiles, an approving nod from Forty, but nothing more than that. It was like they were already old hat.

But that evening, after the fire has died down to embers, whatever lid they'd been keeping sealed on their urges to crack jokes pops off. Completely. Like a teakettle sat on a burner for too long and needing to finally *sing*.

It starts when everyone is beginning to scatter toward their own tents, but Crew stays seated, only moving to grab Grace's hand and halt her departing steps. He stands, giving her a quick nod in the direction of his tent, to which she bites her lip and smiles.

This action, evidently, is the catalyst.

The undeniable, too-cute confirmation that—yeah. They're fucking.

Grace knows it's more than just that, knows feeling anything casual toward Crew was never going to be possible, but from the outside looking in—

If the roaring desire in Crew's eyes is a mirror of her own, it probably looks like they want to eat each other alive.

Cooper's voice cracks through their silent moment, and it's a bucket of ice water dumped on both of their heads. The graceless popping of a delicate bubble. "*Jesus Christ*, you two," he bemoans from where he stands at the campfire, stomping the remaining embers into dull, lifeless ash. "That's gotta be some kinda HR violation."

Crew's nostrils flare. "I'm HR on this ranch, Coop." He steps closer to Grace without a single shred of regard for his brother's or anyone else's opinion. "And since when is looking at a beautiful woman considered a violation?" He keeps looking; his eyes are unapologetically tethered to hers.

"Well, *I* feel violated," Cooper grumbles.

The floodgates open after that, as though Cooper broke through a rusty latch and gave everyone the permission they needed to express their own thoughts.

"Say, Crew," Mikey says. He's shirtless, rubbing aloe vera onto his sunburned chest, a shit-eating grin plastered onto his lips. "Does this mean we get to pack it up early this year?"

Still undaunted by their seemingly growing audience, Crew

keeps looking at Grace. He's drifted closer, an unconscious sway into her space. "Why would we?" he asks, reaching out to tuck a piece of hair behind her ear.

"Well, first—so we don't have to all be subjected to watching this *puppy* love," Mikey replies, and though the words themselves may be cutting, there's nothing but mirth in his eyes as he says them. "And second, because these have thin walls," he adds, gesturing with the bottle of aloe toward the tent behind him. "Unless you're okay with giving everyone a show."

At this, finally, Crew sighs. It's a raspy, irritated sound. He looks away from Grace, and it's like he has to physically force his eyes to move from her face. Like he is ripping them away against his will. He seems to contemplate Mikey's statement, chewing on the inside of his cheek and *glaring* at him. Eventually, his eyes flit around the campsite, finding an audience that neither he nor Grace had noticed until this moment. Everyone's faces show some variation of amusement, all waiting with bated breath for Crew's response.

"If you idiots can't keep it together for a couple more nights, you can sleep with the cows. What I do—" He stops, glances at Grace, and then affixes his pinning eyes back on Mikey. "What *we* do in private is none of your business. We pack up on Friday."

Mikey's shoulders slump a little in disappointment, like a chastised adolescent. Grace doesn't feel bad for him—he knew what he was getting into by playing with the fire that is Crew Caldwell. But she does understand his plight; the time leading up to the end of their stay at the summer pasture, to going back to the air-conditioned bunkhouse where they can shower and sleep on actual beds, has seemed to stretch on for eons.

"I, for one, think it's cute," a female voice chimes in. Grace looks to her right to see June walking up to camp, clad in only a bra, shorts, and a button-down shirt tied around her waist. "It's about time Grace found her a cowboy who can actually satisfy a woman." She looks around the circle with faux disdain. "Lord knows none of you could."

Caleb's mouth drops open, indignant. "Hey!" he shouts, throwing his arms up. "You don't know that. You can't just *assume*."

June chuckles. "I can and I will," she argues. Walking past them to get to her own tent, she winks at Grace and says, "Don't pay them any mind, honey."

Appreciating the reassurance, Grace nods. Crew watches the interaction, seemingly happy to focus on something—anything—else other than the hecklers still gawking at them.

Though it becomes increasingly difficult to keep their hands off each other, Grace and Crew keep it together for the next four days. Rationally, Grace had known sleeping in his tent would only lead to stripping down and losing themselves in each other night after night—maybe during the day, too—and inevitably giving the group more reasons to giggle and poke fun at them at every opportunity. So, she'd bitten the bullet and decided for both of them that she'd stay in her own tent, even if walking away from him at the end of every night was torturous—leaving her unquenched and starving for his touch.

They spend their remaining time in the summer pasture buttoning up everything they can, and in the evenings, they play drinking games, sing along with the guitar, and stuff themselves full of s'mores. Grace finds she might be in love with s'mores made out of Reese's cups instead of the standard chocolate bar, and unashamedly eats four in one sitting. When she comes up for air with chocolate at the corners of her mouth and marshmallow-tipped fingers, she finds Crew across the circle staring at her with a soft, amused smirk on his lips. He looks impressed and maybe a little horrified, but above all—he looks adoring. Grace wipes her mouth and smiles back, wishing she could walk right over and sit on his lap. But neither of them moves, and even though he leaves lingering kisses on each corner of her mouth while saying good night to her, they still walk into their own tents alone.

By Thursday evening, their last night before they pack up and head back, Grace can feel the anticipation buzzing beneath her skin. The idea of going back to the main ranch grounds, of returning to Crew's house for the first time since that night—it makes a shiver of hot anticipation run down her spine. It tugs at the unresolved tension that's been hanging over both of them, leaving Grace in a constant state of dulled arousal. Just thinking about that night makes her *itch* with the urge to re-create it—to hear the groan Crew let out when he pushed inside her for the first time, to feel the mattress beneath her back as he fucked her into it, to see the look on his face when he came inside her, a beautiful mix of bliss and shock and unadulterated satisfaction.

Crew, who'd miraculously managed to stay away from Grace for most of the day, doesn't shy away from being near her in the evening. He sits next to her at dinner, then at the campfire, and he must be feeling the same level of antsiness she is, because when all eyes zone in on his hand as it lands atop her thigh during a particularly terrible rendition of "California Dreaming," he doesn't move away. He doesn't give anyone the satisfaction of acknowledging their stares—simply squeezes lightly with his all-encompassing grip and settles back into his chair. Grace stops herself from placing her own hand on his and dragging it up and *up*. With a shuddering, frustrated exhale, she remains still, letting herself be comforted by the fact that he's touching her at all.

She decides to distract herself with more s'mores, figuring it's as good a time as any to try a Snickers version. Sugary, chocolate goodness smothered in charred marshmallows can't make anything worse. She returns to her seat with a feast on a paper plate ten minutes later, fully pleased with herself and her creations. Four s'mores of varying sizes, made up of Reese's, Snickers, a good old-fashioned Hershey's bar, and—purely for experimental purposes—a Butterfinger. The group continues to sing around her as she devours them all, barely noticing when Crew's hand comes to rest at the back of her chair.

When she's done, she makes a valiant effort to wipe at the corners of her mouth, hoping she's removed any excess chocolate, especially because Crew is leaning over to her now, that same sparkle of awe and amusement in his eyes as when he first saw her house a family-size serving of campfire treats. Under his breath, he asks, "Wanna go somewhere?"

Grace blinks at him, gives the circle a quick once-over, then makes a face. They've shown such restraint over the past couple of days, and she hadn't asked a single probing question about *Why?*, figuring the answer would be something along the lines of *Not mixing business and pleasure*. But now, as Crew stares at her with hungry eyes and slightly parted lips, she wonders if he's reached his limit, too. If he's been getting himself off in his tent thinking about his hands on her body the same way she has.

He must pick up on her hesitation, because his expression softens and he says, "We'll be good." With a quick look around the circle, he adds under his breath, "They're all two sheets to the wind anyway."

It's true—they'd decided to go shot for shot in a particularly sloppy game of quarters after dinner and haven't stopped drinking since the activity shifted into loud, off-key campfire songs. None of them are paying Grace and Crew any mind, the initial novelty of PDA having faded. If they keep going like this, not a single one of them will remember anything about this evening in fine detail, if at all.

Grace grins upon the realization, a gleeful affirmative that *hell yes*, she does want to go somewhere with Crew. She wants to go anywhere and everywhere with him.

They slink off without notice, staying quiet and keeping their footsteps light until they're completely out of ear- and eye-shot. In a nearby copse of trees, they find themselves in the clear, and before Grace can even breathe out her relief, Crew is pushing her into one, pressing her back into the wide, ridged trunk, and slanting his mouth over hers.

The sound that echoes from his throat when she grants his tongue entrance into her mouth is broken and beautiful. Grace wants to lie in it forever. His hands are frantic, spanning across her body in erratic patterns, trying to make up for lost time. But his mouth is determined and concentrated, and with each slide of his tongue against hers, Grace melts into him. She keens, wanting more and more and *more*, and if they keep kissing—if he keeps making those sounds and grabbing at her body like he's trying to own every inch of it, she won't be able to refrain from taking this further. Already, her hands are itching to reach for his jeans, to pull down his zipper and take him in hand just to feel the weight of him, the hard, hot length that takes up so much of her grip.

And if she does that—well, it'd be far too easy to pull her own jeans down and let him push inside, let him go deep and hard until they both are crying out their shared relief.

But the universe seems to have plans for them other than this—much to Grace's chagrin—because just as her hand starts to inch its way downward, Crew's left pec starts vibrating. They separate with a smack of lips, Grace's head rearing back to stare at the little rectangle of light beaming in his shirt pocket. Crew's head falls back with a little groan, and he reaches for the phone and answers it—voice clipped and audibly tense—without even bothering to see who's calling. "Yes?"

The murmur that sounds on the other end is unintelligible, but Grace can make out one key feature: It's a woman, and by the immediate shift in Crew's demeanor upon hearing it, she thinks she has a pretty good idea of who it might be.

"We pack up in the morning," he says, markedly less strained than before. "And I gave them a rash of shit the other day for asking to head back early." His lips fold into a straight line, and then his eyes narrow, and all the while, the voice warbles through the phone, seeming to pick up in tempo and pitch.

"Mom," Crew cuts in—flares of agitation quickly returning—and confirms Grace's suspicion. He waits, then sighs dramatically. "I *do* understand that, but we're also exhausted, and Grace just took down like . . . four s'mores in twenty minutes," he says, then glances down at Grace, eyes flashing with amusement. Her eyes go wide with embarrassment, and he *smirks*. Bastard. "I don't think she's gonna be hungry anytime soon."

She reaches out and pinches his pec, aghast at being so thoughtlessly thrown under the bus. Crew chuckles under his breath, pulling the phone away from his mouth, then takes his revenge by pinching her side, and Grace folds over with a squeak.

"Okay, Mom," he concedes impatiently, too concerned with tickling and pinching her to continue their conversation. "We'll be up in a little bit, but we're not staying."

Grace is panting from defending herself when he finally hangs up, and she stands with her hands on her hips, looking at him expectantly. "Up?"

"My parents are going to Victoria in the morning for the Blue Barrel Auction. It's an annual thing—they go every year and make a weekend out of it. My mother insists on seeing us before they go."

A pang of nerves throbs in Grace's belly. "Us?"

Crew lets his head rest against the tree as he pulls her toward him by her hips, holding on to her loosely, lazily. He stares down at her with soft, smiling eyes. "Nothing that happens on this ranch ever gets past my mother. I used to be convinced she had hidden cameras everywhere. Porches, trees, fence posts. But I think it's more likely she just has the undying loyalty of a very nosy staff. It's safe to say she knows about the other night."

Grace's cheeks feel instantly flushed. "And you think . . ." She starts, but realizes quickly that she doesn't know quite what she wants to ask. Or, rather, she does, but she isn't sure she really wants to know the answer. Crew stays quiet, waiting for her to elaborate. Encouraging her to be honest with his discerning eyes, his kind smile. "You think she's okay with it?"

At this, he lets out a quick, rumbling laugh. It isn't in mockery but surprise, and the toothy grin that follows is a balm to Grace's anxiety. "Of course she is." He squeezes her hip, dragging her closer. "Sweetheart," he breathes. "Why wouldn't she be?"

Grace lets herself be pulled, lets herself be distracted by his closeness. She shrugs, leaning into him. "I don't know. I'm no one special. And I'm on her payroll."

Before she can get the statement fully out of her mouth, Crew is pushing off the tree, closing any remaining distance between them, and wrapping himself around her. "Don't," he says hoarsely. He looks deep into her eyes, searching between them. His mouth hovers near the tip of her nose, and his hot breath fans over her face as he stares and *stares*. "You have no idea how special you are, Grace. You're—" He exhales, deep and shuddering, and presses his forehead into hers.

Grace feels her heart burst into a thousand sparks in her chest at his next words. They're whispered and breathy. Reverent.

"You're everything."

In the dining room of the main house, a dying fire and warmly lit sconces cast shadows across Clint's and Renata's forms at the table, where they sit with two large, half-full wineglasses between them. Renata is leaning on her elbow, bent toward Clint, smiling flirtatiously. He's laughing under his breath, absently rubbing her shoulder from where his hand rests at the back of her chair. The energy between them is effortless but potent, almost decadent, like a century-old cherrywood whiskey. Grace has trouble reconciling the pair before her with the one from Crew's story; it's hard to fathom them ever running out of things to say to each other, let alone separate long enough to sleep entire nights in different rooms. Crew holds Grace's hand, thick fingers interlocked with hers, as they enter the dining room. The two lovebirds are aware enough to recognize they're no longer alone, and when they turn to see the two walk in, their faces both light up with complete delight. Their instantaneous grins are brighter than the room's evening glow, brighter than the flames flickering in the fireplace.

"I swear to you, son, I was just telling your father that I was starting to forget what you look like. Wasn't I just saying that, darlin'?" Renata leans back in her chair, smacking Clint's arm. He affirms this statement, also leaning back, but keeping his grip steady on the back of Renata's chair. "Can't believe you had the nerve to come all the way back up here and couldn't spare a second to drop in on your mother."

Crew stiffens slightly next to her—Grace can see the way his shoulders lift a little toward his ears. When Renata shifts her glare from Crew right to her, Grace's mouth goes a little dry. But the firm line of Renata's mouth softens, the brightness of her eyes and smile returning in full force. "Hi, honey. I missed your face, too."

An impatient, irritated sound erupts from Crew's throat as he clears it, then sighs. "I already told you, there just wasn't a good time. You would've skinned me alive if I knocked on your door at 4 A.M. just to say *hi*."

"You don't know that!" Renata volleys back, but there's no heat in her tone. It's light, a little self-deprecating, even, which is an odd—but not bad—look on her.

"I do, actually," Crew says. "Anyway—y'all gonna offer us a glass, or just make us stand here and watch you drink?" He lifts his chin toward the bottle on the table.

Grace peeks up at him at this, feeling a little prickle of admiration at the back of her neck—and maybe somewhere else farther south—at his tone. He knows they have to be up early, knows they can't stay up here for too long without risking a crappy morning, and they have *way* too much to do in not a whole lot of time before the sun is at its hottest. But he also knows there are sacrifices you have to make in the name of keeping your family happy, perhaps better than anyone. Grace, who has never had to learn that lesson, finds herself enjoying watching Crew thread the needle of being a good son *and* a good foreman. He makes it look easy, but then again, he's sharper than steel and quicker on his feet than most men could ever hope to be. He's unbelievably competent, and Grace is learning very quickly that the quality is a massive turn-on.

"Well, of course we are," Renata says in a singsong voice, waving them over. She stands, walks to the swinging door that leads into the kitchen, and pushes it open. "Mia, will you bring us another bottle of the '82 Château and two more glasses?"

"Yes, ma'am," a voice calls from within.

And soon, a woman who looks almost identical to Ronnie but twenty years younger walks into the dining room with the bottle and glasses in hand, offering Grace and Crew a polite smile as she sets them on the table. She starts to open the bottle, but Renata reaches forward, gently stopping her and taking the corkscrew into her own hand. "You don't have to do that, honey, but thank you. And remember what I told you about calling me *ma'am*."

Mia looks sheepish, letting her head hang for a moment before nodding. "Renata," she corrects. "I apologize."

"Is your mom still here?"

Mia nods, jerking her head in the direction of the back door. "Cleaning the grill."

Renata scoffs, shaking her head as she leans up to get eyes on Ronnie out on the porch, scrubbing away at the enormous grill with a large pair of tongs topped off with half of a white onion. "That woman, I swear to God. Did she send Luc home again?"

"She did."

"I hired him specifically so she *wouldn't* have to clean up after spending the whole day cooking, and she never lets him actually do the job I hired him to do."

Crew smiles, reaching out a hand, into which Renata drops the corkscrew. He begins to open the bottle as she rants—and by the looks on everyone's faces, Mia included, this is not a new gripe. Instead, it sounds like an age-old argument between two women who have been challenging each other for years. Two women who refuse to give up the last word. Grace finds herself wondering what it must look like when Renata and Ronnie go toe-to-toe.

Renata picks up her wineglass and drains the rest, then says to Mia, "Tell her to get out of here—if she's late to another date night, your dad is going to make good on that promise to move her out to the Florida Keys." Mia grins, clearly aware of this threat, and nods before turning around and walking back into the kitchen.

When all the wineglasses have been filled and refilled, Grace takes a sip of hers, managing to keep a straight face when she realizes instantly she does *not* enjoy the taste of wine. Red wine, at least. The sweet pink stuff June keeps in the fridge with the little footprint on it? That, she can get behind. But this—it tastes like rotten grape juice and rubbing alcohol's abominable baby.

"Y'all got your eyes on anything in particular this weekend?"

Crew asks as he sips the wine, and there's no evidence on his face that he shares Grace's contempt.

Clint drums his fingers against the white tablecloth. "Not really. I was thinking I might try to bid on Geronimo just to piss off Bruce, though," he says with a conspiratorial smirk.

"You wouldn't dare," Renata says, gaping.

Clint shrugs, grinning like the cat that ate the canary. "No, I wouldn't. But he could stand to be knocked down a peg, don't you think?"

"That man's been eyeing that horse since 2017. He needs a win."

Grace listens to the exchange without comment, unable to contribute. The rumor mill of the horse auction world isn't one she's familiar with in the slightest—she's never been on that side of ranching, only ever met the horses once they were purchased and ready to be trained. She doesn't think she'd enjoy it much, deliberating over the animals like pieces in some game, like pawns to be played only at the whims of careless buyers and sellers.

Whatever is on her face as she considers this must not be pretty, because Renata leans forward and says to her, "We don't actually bid like that. I don't want you to think we do anything when it comes to our animals without real thought and preparation."

It's strange and unexpected, the way Renata seems to feel the need to defend them, but Grace appreciates the clarification nonetheless. She never figured the Caldwells to be reckless buyers, but in her limited experience, most people aren't as careful with their purchases. Braxton was more of a dumping ground than a cattle ranch, a place where Bellamy unleashed and then forgot about all of his impulse buys, his flavors of the month, everything from zebras to ball pythons.

Grace realizes Renata is still looking at her and nods, waving it off. "Of course not," she says. "When are y'all leaving?"

With a sigh, Renata leans back and takes another sip of wine. "We have to be in the truck by six, according to this crazy person."

Clint, who has been wrapped up in conversation with Crew, seems to hear this jab, and turns to his wife mid-sentence to say, "I am *not* missing the pancake brunch again. It's the only thing that makes this godforsaken auction worth going to anymore."

The minutes pass, the wine depletes—everyone's except Grace's, that is—and Grace learns about the Blue Barrel's history, the Caldwells' involvement and sponsorship, and that they've been trying to slowly relinquish all ties they have to the event for half a decade, partly because it's far away, but also because they're tired of seeing the same faces and having the same conversations year after year. By the time the second bottle is empty, Grace is giggling at their dramatics, at the fantastical schemes they consider crafting to get out of going entirely, at the way they try to convince Crew to go in their stead, even going as far as to try to bribe him with a thousand dollars. He only laughs, saying he can't be bought, and if he could, he'd cost way more than a grand.

It's nearly midnight when they finally leave the table, and neither Grace nor Crew is particularly happy about having to go all the way back to the summer pasture, but they know they'll never hear the end of it if they spend another night at Crew's house when they're *supposed* to be at camp with everyone else.

His parents both stand as they make their way out, and Renata walks around the table on slightly wobbly knees to wrap Grace in a tight hug. She smells like roses and vanilla and spicy, clean soap. Her black shirt is soft under Grace's touch, and she returns the hug with equal fervor, enjoying the extra affection, no doubt induced by the wine.

Renata leans back after a long moment, keeping Grace in her grip. She smiles at her easily, her eyes slightly shiny from the alcohol. "You'll tell me if my son is ever anything but a gentleman to you, right?" she asks quietly, only loud enough for Grace to hear. A few feet away, Clint and Crew are hugging, exchanging a few of those loud back claps that men do whenever they embrace.

"Of course," she says, and then, "but you raised him right, Renata. I doubt I'll ever have to tell you anything like that." Grace says it to make her happy, to make her smile, but she realizes as the words leave her lips that she also says it because it's true. Renata raised a good man—a wonderful, loyal, intelligent man.

"Oh, honey," Renata beams, pulling Grace into another hug. She rubs Grace's back, a much gentler, softer showing of affection than those *claps*, and Grace smiles, pressing her cheek to Renata's shoulder. It's quiet, what Renata says next, and there's less humor in it. Instead, her words are thick with promise, with hope.

But above all, with love.

"I think we're gonna have to keep you."

CHAPTER 20

To celebrate all the work they accomplished at the summer pasture, the ranch hands decide to have themselves a good old-fashioned movie night. According to Caleb, it's a rare, special event that only occurs maybe once a year, mostly because hardly any of them can stay awake through an entire movie. Once camp is packed up and everyone is settled back in the bunkhouse, the guys start buzzing around animatedly, getting things prepped before the sun goes down. They move the bunks first, arranging them against one wall so the main floor is mostly cleared out, then they yank everyone's mattresses off their beds and toss them into a haphazard pile. Mikey rearranges them neatly into rows as Pierce pulls out a projector and a rolling cart from the utility closet. Once it's placed strategically in the middle of all the beds, he opens his ancient-looking laptop and rests his hands on his hips. To no one in particular, he asks, "Who gets the honors this time?"

They're all in the midst of various tasks—Forty standing at the microwave popping a sixth bag of popcorn, June lounging on her mattress and playing a game on her phone, Caleb and Raymond both changing into pajamas, Harrison preemptively tossing back a couple of antacid tablets, and Bryan stocking a

Yeti cooler with Coors—when the conversation erupts, a roar of bickering with movie titles tossed in. Grace observes it all with a kind of awe—as organized and efficient as the setup had been, it seems to all go to hell in a handbasket the second they start arguing over genres and Rotten Tomatoes scores.

Eventually, Forty shuts them all up with a loud slam of the microwave door, and, once he has their attention, says, "I believe I am up next for picking."

Mikey opens his mouth to argue, but Pierce shoots him a glare. "Shut up and let him pick. If we don't, it'll be midnight before we even start a damn movie." He turns to Forty and points at him. "You have one minute, or your turn is forfeited."

Forty rolls his eyes, reaches into the microwave for the steaming bag, and dumps a pile of popcorn into one of the many bowls that are strewn about the kitchen counter. He purses his lips, thinking, and then smiles—wide and wry. "I quite liked Tweedledum and Tweedledee having to hold on to each other through the entirety of *The Babadook*," he muses with a mischievous glance in Mikey and Caleb's direction. "So, let's keep with that theme and go scary. What about . . ." He taps his chin, then snaps, a light bulb clearly going off. "Wasn't there a movie a few years back about a gal who watched a tape and then weird stuff started happening? Ghosts crawling out of the television and such?"

"*The Ring*," Raymond supplies flatly. "He's talking about *The Ring*."

Forty snaps again, pointing victoriously at Raymond. "That's the one."

Grace watches with endless amusement as Mikey and Caleb share a brief, concerned look, and then do their best to swallow their collective concern. "Sure," Caleb says, a little too chipper. "Great. Fantastic. *The Ring*. An early-2000s classic." He clicks around on his laptop for a few minutes before seeming to find what he's looking for, and then everyone starts to make their way to the center of the room to find their place. Grace looks around, knowing she won't find Crew among them but missing him all the same. He'd gone into town to grab a few things but encouraged her to come up after the movie was over and spend the night with him. It takes a surprising amount of willpower not to just go *now*, to drag him into bed and have her way with him without the looming dread of a 4 A.M. alarm. But this little gathering is a special, sacred thing—that much is extremely evident—and she doesn't want to miss it.

Grace drags her mattress toward the back of the room and lies down on top of her comforter, happily taking a small bowl of popcorn when Forty offers it. Once everyone's settled, they flip the lights off and start the movie, and Grace learns *very* quickly that she, too, is perhaps not a scary movie kind of person. But she doesn't have a Caleb to her Mikey to grab on to, so she grimaces and covers her eyes, trying her best to not look up when anything too creepy is happening. It's a difficult feat—*The Ring* is pretty creepy all around.

About a quarter of the way through, she nearly launches fully off the mattress in shock when someone crouches down next to her and invades her space. Scared and tense as she is, she'd been engrossed and hadn't heard the bunkhouse door open or noticed the hulking figure lumbering over until he was right next to her. Grace gasps, then swings her head abruptly to look at the offender, only to find Crew staring at her with a cheeky little smirk on his lips.

"Rude," she whispers.

"Sorry," he whispers back, but he doesn't look very sorry at all.

Grace decides to forgive him, mostly because she's so pleasantly surprised that he's here. "Couldn't stay away?" she teases.

He shakes his head, then gives her an earnest look. "I missed you."

Something warm blooms in her belly, and she bites her lip to resist the need to kiss him. He nods toward where she sits, and Grace understands instantly, scooting over on her mattress and making room for him beside her. Crew moves in, wrapping a long arm around her shoulder. He reaches into his shirt pocket with his other hand and pulls out a little yellow bag of *something* that has Grace's full attention—cursed video tapes and creepy ghost children be damned. He holds the bag flat on his palm and offers it to her, and she's pleased as punch to find it's peanut M&M's, a king-size bag of them. "Salty-sweet is the best combo," he says, gesturing with his eyes toward the bowl of popcorn in her lap. "Try it."

She does, and it's delicious—so much so that she lets out something like a *moan* upon popping the kernels and candy into her mouth.

Out of nowhere, popcorn begins to rain down on them, one piece hitting Crew directly in the center of his forehead, another bouncing off Grace's cheek. They look up to see Pierce glaring at them, his hand in his popcorn bowl, ready to launch more their way. He shushes them aggressively with a finger pressed to his lips, then turns back to the movie.

They manage to stay quiet after that, but it's not easy. Crew runs his fingers through Grace's hair, chuckling every time she hides in his bicep during the scary parts. Soon enough, Grace finds herself happily blocking out the movie entirely, tucked into Crew's side with her nose pressed into his neck. It's possible her body has been rewired to actually, biologically need Crew's scent—his cologne, the clean soap smell of his laundry detergent, and that man smell, which is his and his alone. It's intoxicating, and far more alluring than the movie, and when Grace presses her lips to his throat, it feels like an instinct, a choice her body made independently of her brain.

Crew's arm tightens around her. The tendons in his neck bulge slightly, and Grace looks up to find him staring at her. Fire is catching in his eyes as they drift down to her lips, and for a brief moment, they aren't in the bunkhouse surrounded by people, and there isn't a weird, sort of depressing scary movie playing at an ear-shattering volume. For the space of a heartbeat, it's just them, standing on the precipice of something, each waiting for the other to move. His eyes dance between hers—wanting, desperate, questioning.

They speak at the same time, softer than a whisper.

"Not here—"

"Let's go."

Grace's cheeks are warm. She rubs her legs together without thinking about it, exhaling a heavy breath through her nose at the friction. Crew's eyes trace down to her legs, and he watches with a tense jaw as she does it again. With his teeth gritted, he pulls her closer into his body, his hand finding new purchase on her hip. If he wanted to, he could pull her leg up and over his—he could give her something to rock into.

Something happens in the movie—Grace couldn't have a single guess—that has the hands audibly reacting with screams and shouts of varying pitches. The roar pulls Grace back to reality, reminding her exactly where they are. Crew seems less affected; his eyes are still lingering on her mouth, and his hand is hovering right at the hinge of her thigh like he's two seconds away from pulling her on top of him.

"They'll see us leave," Grace whispers.

Crew blinks, finally breaking free of the haze for a moment to scan the room. "They won't," he says, then looks back to the door behind them. "They won't even know we're gone. Follow me in two minutes."

The truck is parked a few blessed paces from the front door—far enough that someone would have to walk right up to it to see anything happening inside. The windows are tinted, too, which is good—because Grace is completely naked and writhing in Crew's lap about ten seconds after they pile into the cab.

Crew's grip on her hips is unyielding, but it's the only part of him that seems to be maintaining control. The rest of him is wild. His eyes blaze when they connect with hers, fiery even in the dark, and his mouth is a needy, restless thing. He presses it to every inch of her he can reach, coaxing breathy sighs out of her when he pays special attention to each of her breasts. He licks a thick heavy stripe over one of her nipples, then takes it between his lips and sucks. Grace moans, her head falling back at the sensation. She buries her hands in his hair and tugs, just enough for him to feel it. His hips buck in response, and he releases her nipple to let out a grunt, panting hotly against her skin.

"You're so fucking sexy," he rasps, and only takes a brief moment to recover before returning to his task, this time with her other breast.

In such a short period of time, he's figured out exactly how to make her keen, how to make her body move on instinct alone. He draws out a primal, unselfconscious side to her, strange and unfamiliar but far from unpleasant. In his arms, in his grip, she can let herself simply feel, giving way to sensation alone.

"Grace," Crew breathes against her neck. "I need to be inside you."

Grace nods, a lolling movement that she repeats, over and over.

Yes, yes, yes.

He releases her hips to find purchase on her ass, which he squeezes, pulling her body into his. His next words are halfway to a groan. "I want to come in you again." His breath catches when her bare center rubs directly against the hard ridge of his cock, still trapped in his jeans. "Let me fuck you, baby. Let me feel you."

Grace moans, and her hands are already moving—overwhelmed with the same need to have him closer, as close as he can possibly get. She gets his shirt off first, then unbuckles his belt, wasting not a single second before reaching into his black briefs to cup as much of him as she can manage with one hand.

A wheeze rattles through Crew's chest. "Grace, *yes*. Take it out." He lifts up, giving her the space to push his jeans and underwear down until they sit at his thighs. The sight of his cock, bared to her completely now, hard and leaking, makes her clench in anticipation. A rush of pleasure shoots through her abdomen at the mere thought of sinking down onto him.

But before she does, she closes the space between them, wrapping her arms around his neck. The fever running through both of them is all-consuming and impossible to ignore, but she wants to remember herself, remember him, remember them, even if just for a second. "Crew," she whispers, her lips brushing against his.

You're here. With me. We're together, she says with a desperate kiss.

He gets it. Of course he does. He's always understood what she wants, needs, even when she doesn't say it out loud. Especially then. His tongue rolls against hers, and only when neither of them can breathe do they break apart, gasping. "Yeah, baby," he says, remarkably soft. "I'm here."

Grace presses her forehead into his and pulls herself upward at just the right angle—she rubs herself over the length of him, soaking him as she goes. Crew groans, his breath fanning against her face, and then his head falls back onto the seat cushion. With a few adjusting blinks, she's able to see him clearly in the darkness—eyes screwed shut, lips parted, neck muscles tensed. She keeps her eyes on him as she reaches down to position herself over him, and tries to memorize his face as she sinks down, inch by overwhelming inch. Pleasure is etched into every muscle—the tug of his eyebrows, the flex of his jaw, the flare of his nostrils. He looks like a man unmade, like he's barely clinging to the surface of sanity. He looks beautiful in ways Grace could never put into words.

When she's fully seated, aided immensely by the pool of want dripping from her center, they both release a heavy, full-body sigh.

It isn't like before, this time. They don't have the luxury of Crew's king-size bed or hours to spend exploring each other. They have only this truck, a handful of minutes, and a potent, unrelenting need. It makes them both bold, the urgency of it. Crew is louder than she's heard him be, especially when he takes her hips and starts properly bouncing her on his cock. And Grace—she happily lets him drive, arching her back and pressing her breasts into his face, surrendering entirely to the raging waves of pleasure.

On a particularly hard thrust, a raspy, loud *"Oh"* is punched from her lungs.

Crew grunts, squeezing her harder. "That feel good?"

She lets out an unintelligible affirmative, too overcome to say actual words. Her head hangs backward, her body suspended in his hold, completely at his mercy as he fucks her. He splits her open, takes her apart, and builds her anew. Over and over and over again.

The pad of his thumb pressing to her clit brings her back to this plane of reality—it pulls her up, up, up, until she's moaning into his mouth.

"I'm close," Crew says, breathless. "Fuck—Grace, I'm—" His eyes screw shut, and she can see the desperate way he's clinging to control, the way his body wants—needs—to let go. Grace leans forward and kisses his face, all over, every inch. She lands on his mouth, and they stay like that for a beat, his thumb at her clit, his tongue in her mouth.

She makes it to the same cliff at which he's standing, both of them now teetering on the edge of oblivion.

Grace lets her head fall, resting against his shoulder, and Crew's hand is at the back of her head, rubbing his blunt nails into her scalp. "Grace—come on, baby," he says, and there's a touch of madness in his plea, an insistence even the sweetest voice can't hide. "Come for me. Let me feel you clench."

Like a puppet on a string, she does. She lets go, lets herself fall headfirst into an orgasm to end all orgasms. Her legs are vibrating with the immensity of it, and she clings to Crew as hard as she can as it rocks through her, stealing from her all sense, reason, logic.

She squeezes around him like a vise, moaning in his ear.

Crew lets go almost instantly—he'd been waiting for her, and his patience is obliterated with each throb of her cunt around him. "Oh shit—Jesus, fuck," he bites out, and then words are no longer an option; he can only groan his pleasure against her temple, breathing heavily as it relentlessly surges through his body.

They hold each other in place for a long time, just breathing.

Only when the quiet is interrupted by the squeak of a door opening do they finally return to themselves, both of their heads swiveling abruptly to the bunkhouse, where they find Caleb standing in the doorway with his hand on his hip. "In case anyone out here would like to know," he says, "Mikey got too scared when that chick crawled out of the TV, so we're gonna watch *Happy Gilmore* instead."

The door bangs shut behind him, and Grace and Crew slowly turn, holding each other's eyes for a split second before bursting out laughing.

Back inside, both with syrupy limbs and contented smiles, Grace and Crew eat popcorn and M&M's and watch *Happy Gilmore*, which is a significant improvement from *The Ring*. She likes it especially because it makes Crew laugh—a rare and lovely sound. The crinkles at his eyes are more visible when he's giggling, and Grace finds herself wanting to trace them with her fingertip, to feel every nook and cranny of him.

The movie is nearing its end when Grace's phone starts to vibrate in her pocket. She reaches for it, absently hitting the silencing button, and thinks nothing of it. She cuddles farther into her man and pays little attention to the movie, even as the action starts to pick up and the stakes grow higher by the second. She's too content in Crew's arms, too distracted by his comforting hold on her, by the way he seems to know exactly where to run his nails across her scalp and neck to make her entire body shiver.

Her phone buzzes again, and Grace sighs, fishing it out of her pocket. She doesn't recognize the number, and hits the button that sends it to voicemail once more.

When it happens a third time, they are pelted with another few kernels of popcorn, but this time, it's Caleb, and he glares at her sternly, tilting his head as if to say, *Really?*

Grace grimaces, mouths her apology, and then lifts herself reluctantly off Crew. In his ear, she whispers, "Someone's clearly dying to talk to me. I'll be right back." Crew, in the middle of shoving a handful of popcorn into his mouth, nods.

The night air is thick and unpleasantly warm—a stark contrast to the air-conditioned bunkhouse, and a reminder of how good it feels to be *done* with sleeping in tents during the summer in Texas. She's outside for less than a minute before she feels herself starting to sweat. Her phone is buzzing in her palm, another call coming in on the coattails of the previous, and Grace flips it open roughly, frustrated by whatever spammer this has to be to call her ten times in a row.

"Whoever this is," she spits, ready to lecture the person on the other end about calling unlisted numbers, "I'm not buying what you're selling, so you may as well give up the relentless calling. You're interrupting my evening."

When she hears a chuckle through the crackling speaker of the decades-old phone, Grace's blood goes cold. The heavy breathing, wet and thick, the sinister undertones of the voice—she knows it instantly. Her stomach twists, her eyes widen. "What—"

Bellamy cuts her off, his voice low and icy. "I warned you, Gracie." He lets that hang between them for a moment, and Grace looks around, scanning her immediate surroundings. "You didn't listen. Now, you're going to understand that actions have consequences."

Grace swallows, her nostrils flaring. "I couldn't stop them—"

On the other end, he laughs again. "Here's a lesson for you, Grace: Consequences don't always hit you directly, but they'll always hit you where it hurts. I can promise you that."

Her heart begins to hammer in her chest as panic starts to overtake her senses. She's still scanning the area, not sure what exactly she's looking for, when he says, "Or Trey can, actually—he's the one who tailed your precious Caldwells all the way to Highway 46 tonight."

Time freezes then. The entire world cracks open, and Grace is free-falling into its depths, never to recover. The breath leaves her body in a shudder and she gasps, desperate to fill her lungs, to regain the ability to speak so she can ask *exactly* what he means.

She doesn't have to. He tells her happily.

"That Suburban of theirs . . . it rolled and rolled and rolled like a tumbleweed. Didn't even look like a car by the time it was done."

Grace's knees give out, and she falls to the ground roughly, nearly toppling over. "Please," she wheezes, but the plea isn't to Bellamy. Her eyes squeeze shut and she says it again, and again, prayers falling from her lips before her brain even has the chance to process what's happening. On the other end of the line, Bellamy sighs.

"What are you gonna tell them when they wake up in the ICU—if they wake up at all? What are they gonna think when you tell them you could've stopped this? You could've, Gracie. Could've called them off, after all I did for you, all I saved you from. And this is how you repay me."

"I didn't know it would—"

"Of course you did, and now you'll have to live with that. And that boyfriend of yours? If you think he's safe from all this, you've got another thing coming."

Grace's head swings in the direction of the bunkhouse. She can see the light of the movie flickering through the closed blinds, changing the windows from white to blue to gray and back again. Crew is in there, completely unaware, and all Grace wants is to rewind to twenty minutes ago when she was, too. When she was safe in his arms and happy and in love. "You leave him out of—"

"*You* don't give *me* orders, you ungrateful bitch," Bellamy snarls. She hears his panting breaths, the rattle of phlegm in his chest. It disgusts her, makes the nausea in her gut that much sharper. "Meet me outside the north entrance at midnight, or I'll put him in the hospital, too. Think I'm bluffing?"

The line goes dead, and the phone falls from Grace's sweaty hand, crashing to the ground and flipping shut upon impact. Geysers of chaos and despair continue to burst in Grace's head, each bigger and more devastating than the last. Worst-case scenarios of every variety pile on top of one another, and for a long, indeterminate amount of time, she cannot breathe, or speak, or think of anything besides the terror she's wrought on this family simply by choosing them. By letting them get close to her.

She doesn't hear the swing of the bunkhouse door, nor the running footfalls of Crew's boots as he races over to where she sits, nearly catatonic from the shock. Only when he's right in front of her face does she realize he's outside, he's with her, and the storm brewing in her gut implodes—tears pour down her face in hot, endless streaks. He's wiping them away before he even asks what they're for, and Grace is shaking her head, wishing she didn't have to do what she's about to—wishing she could go back and never darken the door of Halcyon at all. This man she loves, this man who didn't try to save her but instead gave her something so much bigger. So much more than she ever thought possible. Her heart feels like it's literally being ripped to shreds, piece by agonizing piece, as she stares into his fearful eyes.

Sound comes back to her ears in gradual waves, Crew's voice growing louder until she can finally make out the hurried, "What's wrong? Talk to me, baby. What's going on?"

Grace's head falls forward, and she gives herself over momentarily to the sob wracking her body. As it desists, she breathes deeply, then gathers up whatever courage she has left and looks him in the eye again.

She's never hated herself more than she does in this exact moment. She should've known she was always going to end up right here. She should've known that outrunning the past was a luxury reserved only for those who deserved to escape.

"I need to tell you something."

"Tell me," Crew says quickly, nodding, so wholly unaware of

the bomb that's about to be dropped in his lap. The bomb that's already detonated on some darkened highway outside of Victoria. "Tell me," he repeats softly.

"I lied—when you asked me why I stayed at Braxton, I lied."

The concern on Crew's face shifts minutely into something else, but then he's brushing it off, immediately reassuring her. "That's all right. What's—"

"It's not all right, Crew. I lied, and there's a reason for that. There's a reason I never left after I turned eighteen. I—I did something. When I was young, I did something really awful."

A wrinkle forms between Crew's brows, his eyes narrowing slightly. "What?"

Grace swallows, glances away from him to center herself—she knows she needs to look him in the eye when she tells him, but every atom in her body is screaming at her to look down instead, to keep her eyes on the ground where they belong. She doesn't listen; she picks up her chin and looks at him as tears continue to flow down her cheeks.

"I killed my father when I was sixteen."

The bob of Crew's Adam's apple is visible, and it's the only part of him that moves for a moment—for an eternity, it feels like. Then his face contorts into confusion, and he's shaking his head like he can't quite make sense of what she's just said. "What do you—"

Grace doesn't give him the chance to wonder or speculate. "It was during the summer before my junior year—I woke up one night to my parents screaming. They screamed a lot—I could usually sleep through it. This was different. My mom—she wasn't screaming at him, she was just . . ." Grace's eyes go sightless, and she's back there, in that tiny bedroom, listening to the sound of her mother screaming for her life. "I went out to see what was going on and he—he was stabbing her. Over and over and over again—and she—" She gasps, and her entire body trembles with it. "She stopped screaming."

Crew's hands are at her forearms, and it occurs to her then that he's holding her up, keeping her in place. She didn't even notice that she was at risk of falling, but it makes sense. She can hardly feel her body at all.

"I don't really remember what happened after that. From what I've read on the internet, it was some kind of trauma response. My brain's way of protecting me. But I remember coming to and holding a knife of my own, and my dad lying on the ground next to my mom, holding his neck. Staring at me. There was so much blood. It was—it was everywhere. He died in less than a minute. His eyes were wide open, just like hers."

"Grace—"

Grace shakes her head firmly. "No—you don't—no. I'm telling you this because Bellamy took me out of that house and made sure that I didn't get picked up by the police. He said they'd be able to tell from the forensics, or whatever, that my mom was already dead by the time I stabbed my dad, so that would make it premeditated murder, which means first-degree. And because I was sixteen, they'd probably try me as an adult, maybe even give me the death penalty, since we're in Texas."

She hears something that sounds like *Jesus Christ* from under Crew's breath, and she finally lets herself look down, letting the weight of it all rest atop her head.

"He promised me if I ever did him wrong, he'd out me. Your mom could tell when those TDA guys showed up that there was more to the story than animal abuse—she saw me lose my shit, and I— Rather than telling her the whole truth, I told her I'd been scared they were coming to question me, and that's when she started looking into Bellamy's dealings. I don't know how he got my number, but he did—and he texted me about a week later, saying he knew I'd been the one to send her sniffing around. He asked if I really thought I'd be safe here." Despair seeps into her voice, breaking it into warbles, but she catches her breath and soldiers on. "And three days after that, the horses got sick."

The realization begins to dawn on Crew's face, and any pieces of Grace's heart that remain intact shatter completely. Anger, shock, disbelief—it all builds in his eyes, his mouth, the set of his jaw, and she knows, right then, that this is it. This is the moment she loses Crew forever.

"When they said it was probably just a bad batch of alfalfa, I didn't argue with them." Her sobs become hysterical then, as the reality of the current situation comes tumbling back. "I didn't think it was him. Logistically speaking, it didn't make sense. I didn't think he'd hurt—"

Crew's voice is firm, unflinching when he cuts her off. "Who did he hurt?"

Grace stares at him, takes a brief second to memorize his face. She tries to burn it into her brain so she can always remember how beautiful it is. After this, she'll never see it and all its loveliness again. "Your parents—they were in a car accident—I think he made one of his ranch hands run them off the road on Highway 46."

Crew's launching into action before she can even finish her sentence. He's turning away from her, reaching into his pocket for his phone, and then he takes off, running at full speed toward his house. Boone is right next to him, and only the dog spares Grace a backward glance as they go.

She follows, unsure of what she's trying to accomplish, but something in her makes her go—forces her to get to him, even if it's the last thing he wants. The front door is wide open when she reaches the porch, and Crew's pacing frantically around the living room on the phone with someone. His hand is at his brow, covering his eyes, but his mouth is twisted in anguish. "Where are they now?" he asks, switching directions so his back is to Grace. He stomps into the kitchen, unaware that she's even in the same room. "Get the fucking chopper out there right now, Martin. The only trauma center worth its salt is in Victoria and that's an hour away. *Right now*. Call me back." He hangs up, then turns and spots her in the foyer. He freezes, and a look of fury and disgust flickers over his face. It feels like a punch directly to Grace's gut. He says nothing as he walks out of the kitchen, doesn't stop to acknowledge her at all as he walks toward his bedroom. She follows him once more, standing in his doorway with splotchy cheeks and swollen eyes, watching as he begins haphazardly throwing clothes into a duffel bag. He yanks his phone charger out of the wall by his bedside table and shoves it in, then disappears into the bathroom and does the same with his toothbrush. Zipping up the duffel, he flings it over his shoulder and then makes to leave. She doesn't know why she does it, isn't remotely sure what her end goal is, but she moves into the middle of the doorway, blocking his exit.

Crew stops, but his eyes remain straight ahead. The only outward sign that he's even aware of her presence is the way his jaw flexes hard and stays taut. He's breathing heavily, and the hand that isn't wrapped around the duffel bag's strap is balled into a white-knuckled fist at his side.

Grace is almost trembling with the panic and anxiety and desperation of the moment, and the words escape her mouth before she can stop them. Her heart, it seems, has different plans than her brain. "Crew, you have to know that I—"

Upon hearing her voice, his eyes fall shut.

"Get out of my way, Grace," he says, and it's so quiet, so devastatingly emotionless that Grace feels her knees threatening to buckle once more.

"Please, just let me say—"

"I can't even look at you right now," he says, and when he opens his eyes, he makes good on that statement, keeping them on the wall behind her.

She doesn't fight him anymore after that. She moves, and he leaves, the door slamming behind him. Grace remains in the empty hallway, and when the rumbling sound of his truck engine fades into the distance, she slides down a wall and buries her head between her knees. She cries harder than she has in years, hard enough that she makes herself sick and throws up undigested kernels of popcorn on the hardwood.

One glance at the clock on Crew's bedside table—that same clock she counted his heartbeats against—tells her it's almost eleven thirty.

It's almost time to leave.

It's almost time to walk away from Halcyon, from Crew. From this life that was so painfully beautiful but never really hers to begin with.

CHAPTER 21

An ancient black pickup rumbles and groans as it waits for Grace on the gravel shoulder of the highway bordering Halcyon's left quadrant. It's parked less than a mile from the entrance, and it takes her only fifteen minutes to reach it. A thousand steps between heaven and hell.

With her backpack slung over her shoulder and her eyes on the toes of her boots, she approaches the truck's passenger side and finds its window down. Bellamy Whitlock sits behind the wheel, wearing his standard uniform—black felt hat; once-black, now-gray jeans; and a crisp, salmon pearl snap, so stiff from being overly starched that it forms right angles at his shoulders. Since she's now seen firsthand what old Texas money looks like, it's never been more evident to Grace that her uncle is anything but. He reeks of newness, of try-hards and wannabes; he is a shade of green that is reserved only for snakes in the grass. The thick, sweet scent of his cologne assaults her nose, and she suppresses the urge to gag.

A cigarette hangs from between his teeth, and he jerks an impatient nod toward the passenger door. "Well, look who finally came to her senses. Let's go." Grace tosses her backpack into the bed and opens the door, which greets her with a painful-sounding creak. Across the seats, there are rips in the leather and stuffing threatening to spill out, and the whole cabin smells like cigarettes and mildew. Grace folds her arms tightly over her chest as she scoots as close to the door as she can—putting as much space between her and Bellamy as is physically possible.

He says nothing as he shifts the truck into gear and sets off down the road. With every mile driven, darkness envelops them. Out here, there are no streetlights to guide the way—there is no reprieve from the unforgiving night. Grace stares out at the void, face-to-face with oblivion. Right here, in this moment, she wishes it would swallow her whole. It looks almost peaceful in its endlessness—as if, perhaps, it stretches into a place where light can thrive—where things are better. Happier.

Bellamy's throaty voice cuts through the rattling hum of the truck's engine, reminding Grace exactly where she is—and also that better, happier things have never been within her reach. There's no use in trying to grab on to them now.

"You'll thank me for this later," he drawls. "One day, you will."

The urge to laugh in his face at the absurdity of the statement is overwhelming. Instead, Grace turns to pin him with a glare. "Enlighten me, please. Because I can't fathom a future where I do anything but despise you."

A dark, rumbling chuckle is his reply, and it quickly turns into an ugly, loud cough. He has to roll the window down to spit, and Grace's lip curls at the sight. There is not a single iota of this man that doesn't disgust her. When he's sufficiently cleared out, he sighs. "Think about this rationally for a second, honey. Did you think you were gonna live out the rest of your days happily ever after at Halcyon Ranch?" He elongates each syllable, disdain dripping off his tongue.

Grace continues to stare at him, and as she takes in his graying skin and thick, uneven facial hair, it occurs to her that he's not wrong. Halcyon had felt like home. She'd belonged there, among the sprawling hills and juniper trees. She'd belonged with the horses, and the ranch hands, and—

"You did, didn't you?" Bellamy says. "You really did. And, what? You thought you'd tie up loose ends by telling that Caldwell bitch a bunch of lies about me, about my ranch?"

Anger sparks bright and red in Grace's chest. "Don't call her that."

Bellamy barks a laugh, and the sound is more horrible than she remembered—sinister and piercing and the principal instrument in the soundtrack of her nightmares. "She thought she could send the law after me and I'd go down without a fight—like I'd just roll over and let those sons a'bitches ruin everything my family built." He scowls at her. "You would've liked that, wouldn't you?"

"You did that yourself," Grace spits. "You and your greed."

"*My* greed? You just walked out of the biggest, most profitable ranch in the country and you want to talk to me about greed?"

"They aren't making money by scamming people. They aren't abusing their animals. They're good, hardworking people—"

Bellamy cuts her off. "The Caldwells are a plague. All they do is take and spread."

"You don't know what you're talking about," Grace says tightly. She has to look away from him, can't take even one more second of staring at his decrepit face.

"You don't even see how they've dug their claws into you," he says. "Made you into one of their little puppets."

Nostrils flared, fists balled at her sides, Grace stares daggers into the windshield and bites out, "I'd rather be their puppet than your slave."

Bellamy chuckles at this, and it's a mocking, derisive sound. Grace can see from her peripheral vision he's shaking his head, then turning to look at her. "My sister—God rest her soul—would be ashamed of what you've become. What you've done." He clicks his teeth in disapproval. "Braxton was her home."

Grace growls, "Don't. Don't you *dare*."

He shrugs. "It's the truth."

"The Braxton my mother called home is not your Braxton. You ruined everything that was lovely—everything good. It's *you* she'd be ashamed of."

The truck jerks hard, veering abruptly onto the surrounding expanse of brush and rocks. It's such a sharp yank that Grace's head knocks into the passenger window, and she's disoriented for a brief moment, unsure of what exactly just happened. That is, until a clammy, calloused palm is pressed up against her throat.

Bellamy's voice is low and menacing—it vibrates with vitriol. "You've always been an ungrateful little shit, even after I did the saintly thing and took you in all those years ago. Remember that? Remember when it was me, the system, or the streets?" He squeezes, and Grace croaks, pushing at his arm and failing to gain purchase. His hold is surprisingly firm for someone with such arthritic-looking hands. Grace attempts to argue but her words come out stilted, spitting. Bellamy sneers. "Remember how I kept your little secret from the cops when they came knockin'? Coulda handed you over to 'em right then. Coulda told 'em you stuck a knife in your daddy's neck after your momma was already dead. You didn't do it to save her. You did it because you wanted to."

Tears begin to form in Grace's eyes—from the lack of oxygen, from the abundance of shame. Shame for having done it, and more shame for knowing she'd probably do it again if given another chance. Though her father had never put his hands on her, she'd witnessed, up close, the abuse he subjected her mother to day after day. The kind of pain he inflicted on her could've only originated from a soulless place—a place of bone-chilling indifference. Grace remembers seeing her mother's lifeless eyes staring up at the ceiling. She lay sprawled out in a pool of her own blood on the kitchen floor; the skin on her stomach had been carved into bloody ribbons.

"But I didn't, did I? I kept you from the streets and I kept you from getting locked up, and this is how you repay me. You try to rob me of my livelihood."

Grace struggles against him, using her weakening arms to try to shove him away, but he retaliates by yanking her forward and then slamming her back, his iron grip fully robbing her of breath now. Suddenly, he's in her face, close enough that she can see her distorted reflection in his silver-capped tooth. "Now, you've got about eight seconds left before you're almost guaranteed brain damage. So, you be a good girl and sit still, and I'll tell you how this is gonna go."

Slowly, begrudgingly, she stills. Every part of her body goes limp, except her eyes, which are still blazing with contempt.

"Good," Bellamy says, nodding slowly. His grip loosens just enough that Grace is able to suck in a vital amount of air, and it's a glorious, short-lived relief. "It's a long drive back, as you well know. You're not gonna give me any lip. You're gonna sit there and keep your goddamn mouth shut." There's a dangerous promise in his words—she knows there's more to them; whatever he's cooked up for her will be brutal and merciless. "And when we get there, you're gonna get to work, and you're not gonna complain. You're gonna listen to me and the rest of the hands, and you're gonna make up for the shitstorm you caused while you were out gallivanting with that highfalutin cowboy family. You hear me? Not a word, and not a single stone left unturned. And if you don't—if you defy me . . ." His voice is lower still, just on the verge of a whisper. "I'll make sure that Caldwell prince of yours gets the same treatment as his parents. But we'll finish the job this time."

Grace's heart punches against her ribs. She wants to scream, to claw her nails down his face. She wants to push him out onto the road and drive over him a couple of times in his own truck—but she does none of that. She stays still, but her eyes must be bright with rage, because Bellamy smiles at her with a mirthless and horrible stretch of his mouth.

"Think I'm bluffing? Try me. Try one fucking thing," he warns, eyebrows pulling upward, "and he dies. I can promise you that, Grace."

She doesn't. She won't. If it means Crew stays safe, stays alive, she will do nothing at all. And with each mile put between Grace and Halcyon, she feels the light inside of her grow dimmer. With each mile that brings her closer to Braxton, she feels all the gifts Halcyon bestowed upon her—every ounce of hope, love, friendship, and belonging—begin to expire, until nothing remains but a rotten, festering crater in the soil of her heart.

Dawn has broken by the time they roll down the gravel road, under the rusty iron arch that used to bear the Whitlock family crest. The engraving is unrecognizable now, distorted by time and neglect and the elements; the structure looks, as it always has, like a gateway into purgatory. Like something out of the most uneasy of nightmares, where there's no sense of place or time, but there is certainty of one thing—only darkness lies ahead.

CHAPTER 22

When the phone rings at 1:15 A.M., Caia Caldwell is just on the verge of her second orgasm of the night. A head of light brown, shaggy hair is between her legs under the duvet, a pair of strong hands gripped around her thighs. With a mouth full of enthusiasm and the desire to please, Landon—Lawrence? *Lucas*, it's definitely Lucas—has performed admirably, making good on the promise he'd made at dinner.

"Let me be clear," she'd told him over a plate of burrata and balsamic vinegar and plump, juicy cherry tomatoes. "I'm not going to fuck you unless you know for certain that you can make me come. And if you aren't certain—which would be fine, most men aren't—we can have a nice dinner, and then we can part ways. Unless, of course, you are. Certain."

Like a greedy, overeager barnacle, Lucas had latched on to the challenge, practically salivating at the chance to prove himself. To set himself apart from the rest.

So, she'd ordered a decently expensive bottle of cab to go with her short rib tagliatelle, drank one generous pour of it, and then sat back and watched patiently while he settled the bill. The card he'd fished out of his wallet wasn't black, didn't look particularly sturdy, and for a moment—half a heartbeat, at most—

she'd wondered if she should feel guilty. If she should start offering to go dutch. Her net worth, not including the inheritance waiting for her later in life, would probably astound 90 percent of her dates. She could've ordered the *entire* wine list—reserves included—without blinking, and the cost wouldn't even make a dent. But it was simpler if they didn't know. It was better if they didn't look too closely at the person she actually was, and instead focused on her well-worn projection of stern confidence.

And because the man between her legs right now has no clue who she is, not *really*, it's easy to let herself get lost in sensation, to fall into the heady spiral of pleasure and pain and want. It's easy to shut her brain off and pretend there's nothing more important in the world than crashing headfirst into a delicious, throbbing climax.

But life, apparently, has different ideas.

When her phone buzzes on the nightstand, it halfway illuminates the otherwise pitch-dark room in swaths of blue and white. She lets it ring, doesn't even look to see who it is. When it goes dark and quiet again, she exhales, squeezing her eyes shut, mentally hammering down any errant thoughts that don't involve this conventionally attractive but torturously dull man and his skilled, spirited tongue. The call had chased away her orgasm, sending all inklings of it into an ether of lost things, and she's determined to find it once more.

But then the buzzing starts again, and Caia groans and lets one eye crack open. Lucas, who either doesn't hear the phone or simply doesn't care about its interruption, is undeterred. He continues to lick and suck and bite without missing even a single beat, but while he remains nestled in the moment, Caia has been plucked out of it entirely. She reaches for the phone, slapping her hand across the screen with a grunt, first silencing the buzzing, then bringing it closer to see who exactly thinks it's okay to call her at this hour. *Twice.*

When she sees the name and the accompanying picture, a bud of potent anxiety blooms in the pit of her stomach. Sharp and heavy, like a punch from within. Because it's Crew staring back at her, his name in big, bold letters, and a picture of him on his thirtieth birthday, wearing a pink party hat and a sash that says *Thirty, Flirty, and Thriving*. That her brother is calling her is concerning enough—but calling her this late, more than once, can only mean one thing. Something happened, and it isn't good.

With little regard for Lucas and his cunnilingus endeavor, Caia answers the call. "Crew?"

His response is immediate. And on his lips, her name sounds like a plea. "Cai."

"What's wrong?"

Distantly, she realizes the motion between her legs has ceased. Only half paying attention, she notices the covers pulling back, watches as a pair of green eyes blink open expectantly as Lucas emerges. When he opens his mouth, seemingly to speak, Caia holds up a finger.

"There was an accident," Crew says quietly, and she can tell he's on the verge of tears.

Caia's heart begins to pound. Impatiently, she asks, "Crew—what happened? Who was in an accident?"

"Mom and Dad."

Nausea roils in her gut. Some awful part of her brain wonders if this is it—this is how she finds out her parents are dead.

Sitting in her bed, thousands of miles away, with a stranger between her legs. This is how a kingdom falls.

Caia rids herself of the thought with a quick shake of her head and lets her pragmatic, problem-solving side take the wheel. She asks the most important question, the one she needs an answer to before any others. "Are they alive?"

"Yes," he says, and Caia's shoulders slump, all the breath in her body leaving in a sweeping *whoosh*. "Dad's fine, they're stitching him up right now. But Mom—" His voice breaks. He doesn't continue right away, and an image flashes in Caia's head with bright, startling clarity. Her big brother, a paragon of strength and fortitude, the backbone of her family, standing outside a hospital room with the frightened eyes and trembling lip of a little boy. A giant cut down at the knees. Eventually, he sucks in a shuddering breath and says, "It isn't good. I think—" He clears his throat, and she imagines him smoothing out the desperation in his face, redonning that mask of courage and Caldwell stubbornness. His next words are clear, concise, and offer no room for rebuttal. "You need to get down here as soon as you can."

The closest airport to the hospital is almost forty miles away, and it's a small one—hardly any direct flights, especially from out of state. When Caia arrives after a layover in Dallas, she's running on half an hour of sleep, a quad almond milk latte, and pure adrenaline. Not trusting an Uber driver to go well above the speed limit, she rents a car, tosses her carry-on into the truck bed, and sets off on I-10 at a cool ninety miles per hour. It isn't lost on her that reckless driving could be part of the reason she's in this situation in the first place, but that voice of reason and logic is quieted by the overwhelming need to just *get* there.

When she'd called Crew upon landing, there were no critical updates. Her father's wounds were superficial and had been stitched and dressed, and they'd released him to be with his family while her mother was in surgery. It would be at least a couple more hours before she was out—Renata had a collapsed lung, a fractured pelvis, internal bleeding, and multiple broken ribs and fingers. Somehow, she alone had taken the beating from the accident, had borne the brunt of its crushing steel like a stubborn shield.

It both shocks and doesn't surprise Caia in the slightest that her mother has collected a laundry list of potentially fatal injuries while her father bears only scratches. She's always been the first line of defense for the family, the one ready and willing to sacrifice her own well-being for the sake of her kids, her husband, her ranch. She's the reason the phrase "If you want them, you'll have to go through me" exists. The very definition of protectiveness.

And while perhaps Caia should admire these qualities in her mother, it would be more accurate to say she resents them. Especially now, as her foot turns into lead against the accelerator and she flies down the interstate. She's always hated her mother's lack of self-preservation, her seemingly overwhelming desire for martyrdom. Caia's never seen it the way everyone else does—the noble endeavor, the motherly instinct—and instead can see through to the uglier, truer heart of it. What it boils down to when looked at through a magnifying glass is this: Her mother wants what every Halcyon heir has wanted, spanning back a century. She wants to be a symbol—to carry Halcyon's name with pride, and to earn the right to her place in the family plot, where explorers and war heroes and politicians lie deep in the soil. Dead or alive, she wants to be revered.

It's total bullshit, and though it's irrational to think that her mother's tendency for self-sacrifice is the cause of this situation, Caia can't help but wonder if she would've wanted it to go this way, had she been given a choice.

That sentiment heats her blood, gives her the push she needs to go just a little faster, with no regard for the decreasing speed limits in the small towns she passes through. She makes it to the hospital in just over twenty minutes, eighteen less than GPS had accounted for. Crew is waiting for her outside when she careens into a parking spot, his arms folded over his chest with that classic, disappointed dad stare he's mastered over a lifetime of dealing with his younger siblings. He knows—whether by doing the math or just having a keen sense for *her*—that she sped the entire way here. Frowning, he walks over to the driver's side and opens the door. But when Caia steps out, feet landing on the warm asphalt, he doesn't scold her. Instead, he pulls her into his arms and hugs her tighter than he ever has.

Caia returns the embrace, taken aback momentarily by this outright affection, but the longer he holds her in place, the more she sinks into it. His shoulders are shaking—his whole *body* is trembling. Distracted by Crew's uncharacteristic vulnerability, Caia doesn't notice another figure rushing toward them. Suddenly, both Crew and Caia are being embraced tightly by another set of arms, and Caia angles her head around Crew to find Cooper pressed into his back. Her little brother's hands are at her biceps, desperately squeezing her, like he isn't completely sure she's even real.

"Hi, guys," Caia says, unshed tears shaking her voice.

Both boys sniffle and hold her tighter.

In the waiting room, they sit, Caia and Cooper next to each other and Crew catty-corner to them. Caia has a now-lukewarm Diet Coke between her legs, and Cooper's been idly munching at a bag of Gardetto's for the past fifteen minutes while Crew gives Caia the rundown of what happened. He is notoriously terrible, as most men tend to be, at including pertinent details, so she's spent most of this time asking follow-up questions and prodding, needing to get the full picture.

At some point during the catch-up, her father walks into the waiting room. The sight of him is a gut punch—he's limping slightly, bandages at his forehead and the left side of his neck. Caia tries not to think about what her mother must've looked like when she arrived, if her father's wounds are considered minor.

"She's still in surgery. No updates yet." Clint lowers himself into the seat next to Crew. "But that's good. No news is good news."

Cooper, less than satisfied with this assumption, shakes his head. He restlessly leans forward and rubs his hands over the tops of his thighs. "They said they would update us regularly. I'll go see if I can find someone who knows what's going on." Then he's up, and his determined steps echo loudly down the hall until he reaches the nurse's station.

Caia watches him go, clocking the tight line of his shoulders, the rigidness of his neck. He is a rope pulled taut, nearing the point of splitting in two. She knocks her shoe into the toe of Crew's boot. He blinks up at her, an eyebrow slightly kinked. "How is he?" she asks him, nodding in the direction in which Cooper disappeared.

"You know," he says, his mouth tightening. "Trying to hold it together. Failing."

"What happened?" she asks, looking between her father and brother. "You didn't exactly give me a full rundown on the phone."

Crew looks at their father, who is staring sightlessly at the carpeted floor of the waiting room. His eyes are blank, dull abysses. Shallow oceans of blue, a stark contrast to the richness, the vibrancy that typically lives within them.

"I don't remember a lot of it," he says finally, his voice sounding far away. "Not in any real detail. But someone ran us off the road on our way out of Victoria."

A bulky, impenetrably twisted knot forms in Caia's stomach. "Someone—" She shakes her head quickly, trying to make sense of this nonsensical development. "Someone did this on purpose? Why?"

Clint reels backward like he's been stung. Crew tenses, and Caia realizes he's trembling, but it's more of a rigid vibration, as though born not out of nerves and fear but complete fury. He looks ahead, over her shoulder, and his eyes are full of all the answers she seeks. All the answers it clearly pains him to utter.

"Crew," Caia says firmly, her glare unrelenting, beckoning him to look at her. Talk to her. He flicks his eyes back to hers.

"Tell me what's going on. Why would somebody want to hurt us like this?"

Crew looks down, refusing to meet her stare, and when he speaks, his voice is gravelly, equal parts pained and pissed off. It takes him a good thirty seconds of gathering himself before he finally says, "There's a lot you don't know. A lot that I don't really want to get into until we know Mom's okay."

Caia doesn't push him after that, and for a long, long while, they sit in the waiting room in tense, complete silence. Cooper returns after half an hour, having walked around the hospital badgering doctors and nurses alike until he was able to track down someone who knew of their mother's current state.

"It could be hours more," he tells them, slumping back into his seat. "The damage is . . ." He bites the inside of his cheek—a tell Caia knows means he is on the verge of tears. "It's extensive. They said we should all try to get some rest and they'll find us as soon as they have news."

It's not what any of them want to hear. Clint has to physically put a hand on Caia's shoulder to stop her from pestering *more*, to figure out a more specific, concrete timeline. He explains to her in his most soothing, fatherly voice that in these types of situations, sometimes concrete timelines aren't possible.

With nothing left to do but wait—impatient, terrified, and exhausted—the three Caldwell kids and their father all fall asleep in the waiting room, curled up uncomfortably into hard vinyl chairs.

Caia dreams of too many things too quickly to remember anything in vivid detail, but one scene stands apart, sharper than the rest: an SUV, destroyed beyond recognition, the taillights flashing in a horrible cadence, telling a story through their blinking of a remarkable woman, twisted up and destroyed, ripped limb from limb until all that remains is an unrecognizable blur of skin.

CHAPTER 23

Rocks pop and ricochet beneath the tires as Bellamy's truck crawls through Braxton, and with every inch gained toward the bunkhouse, Grace can feel herself slowly reverting into the urchinly teenager she once was. A wiry, malnourished beanpole of a girl, all knees and elbows and dirty fingernails. She remembers baring her teeth when she first arrived anytime someone would get too close. A feral animal in a cage, fending off fascinated spectators.

As an adult, she understands now that kind of resistance is futile. With years of experience at Braxton under her belt, she knows intimately how much easier it is to just let them look, let them laugh, to remove the bars of the cage and let them poke and prod her. Better to give them what they want than have them snarling and starving over the thrill of the chase.

The thought of walking back into that all-too-familiar pit of hyenas makes her sick to her stomach, and when they pull up to the bunkhouse, Trey is already waiting for them, cocksure and grinning. At the sight of him, Grace nearly doubles over and pukes.

"Well, well, well," Trey says in a menacing, singsong voice when the truck comes to a halt and Grace pushes the passenger door open. "If it isn't Gracie Lou. Back from the dead." He closes in as Grace's heels sink into the gravel, indecorous as ever without a bit of regard for her personal space. He stands over her, staring down his nose at her with those empty blue eyes.

Grace holds his glare, even when his lips distort into a smirk and he huffs out a quick, barking laugh.

"Couldn't stay away for long, could you?"

Grace feels the skin beneath her left eye start to twitch, but she doesn't relent in maintaining eye contact with him. Best to show him right out of the gate that she will no longer bow to this false king. This detestable mountebank. "No place like home," she deadpans.

Trey's smirk blooms into a soulless, unsettling grin. "You missed me, didn't ya?" He winks, reaching out to chuck her shoulder with his fist. Just shy of too hard.

Grace hums a vague assent, walking around the truck and reaching in for her bag. Bellamy's dismounting the driver's side and hobbling over to where they stand, lighting a fresh cigarette as he approaches. "Y'all get done what needed to get done?" he asks Trey.

Trey doesn't look away from Grace as he answers. His smile only grows, stretching out to either end of his face in a way that looks almost painful. "'Course we did, boss." His eyes flicker down her body, spending a second too long at her breasts, the tops exposed by her tank top. "It's Gracie's homecoming party, after all."

At this, Bellamy snorts. "Good." Gesturing toward the backpack slung over her shoulder, he says, "Take her shit."

He must read the flash of confusion on her face as Trey rips her bag away, because he smiles and holds her eyes, as if daring her to question his command. It's a rare sight, that smile—easily the most off-putting of all his expressions, because having to look at his teeth without the cover of his lips is the visual equivalent of nails on a chalkboard. Rotten, so yellow they're nearly brown, uneven and crowded. Neglected and ruined to the point that he'll have none left by the time he dies. In their place will be only a gaping, putrid maw. A vitriolic black hole.

"Let's go," Bellamy says, and he doesn't wait for her to follow before he's walking away, flicking a tube of cigarette ash into the brown, overgrown grass.

When they arrive at the clearing, the sun is teasing the horizon with its arrival. It radiates its rays subtly, coloring the sky a muted indigo. Just light enough to see the flat land stretched out before them. It's nondescript and unkempt, but even with the lack of visibility, there is one obvious characteristic of this piece of Braxton.

It's covered in rocks.

An uneasy, fearful seed begins to root itself in Grace's gut. It spreads as she slowly swivels her head from left to right, estimating the clearing's size—about a mile long, maybe a quarter mile wide. When she spots a large bucket sitting at the edge of the clearing a few yards away, her hands fold into protective fists, like they know what is about to be asked of them, and they are prematurely recoiling from the task.

The thing is—she knows this piece of Braxton. She knows every corner of Braxton like she sowed every seed, planted every blade of grass, dug every fence post herself. She knows this part isn't one they utilize; especially during the summer, its lack of trees and shade makes it basically unviable, and therefore, it remains overlooked and ignored.

But if the blaring alarm in her brain is correct, that is about to change.

"Gonna get some millet growing here this season," Bellamy says. He takes a moment to spit a thick, brown loogie through his teeth and onto the ground below. "Seems like a loss to not use the space we've got. But we can't till nothin' while it looks like this." He nods vaguely toward the field. "All them rocks . . . they'll break the blades. You know that, don't you, Gracie?"

Grace swallows, but it's a dry, painful motion. She gives a single, curt nod in reply.

From the corner of her eye, she sees Bellamy pivot until he's completely turned toward her, staring her down. "Clear them out," he says, low and deep, but terrifyingly clear.

Grace's nostrils flare. It will make no difference, this she knows without a shadow of a doubt, but she has to try—so she says, "The tractor has a rock rake."

Bellamy's responding laugh is a shade of familiar evil, full of spite and unhinged glee; he's excited about what he's about to do to her. He takes a step closer, and his rank breath hits her face as he says in a cold, deep voice, "You think, after everything you've done, you're gonna get the easy way out of this? Out of anything?" He almost growls the last question, and the distance between them shrinks with every word out of his mouth. Grace's eyes squeeze shut when she feels the shift of the air at her cheek as he nearly presses his nose into her face, ready to enact revenge in the worst, most brutal way he can conjure up. "You're gonna clear out every goddamn rock from this field, and you're gonna do it by hand. If I find even a pebble by the time you're done, I'll break one of your fingers for each rock you missed. Send you to clean out the snake pits with shattered knuckles."

It doesn't make sense that less than twenty-four hours ago, she was sinking into the most comfortable mattress she'd ever felt, her bare, tanned skin wrapped in soft, warm blankets, and her cheek resting atop the chest of the man she loved. Sharing secrets and confessions and whispered words of adoration, making promises through lovestruck smiles; she should've known she could never keep them. Keep him. Now, standing this close to her uncle, picking up waves of his familiar, horrible scent—tobacco, crème de menthe, dirty water—it physically hurts to think of Crew. It hurts the same way it does when a needle hits bone, that breath-stealing, all-encompassing kind of ache. Because when she thinks of him now, the face that flashes through her mind isn't the one full of reverence, or the one beautifully contorted in pleasure, or the one with that devastating half smile he seemed to reserve just for her. Instead, it's the one full of shock and disbelief, giving way quickly into regret and—worst of all—disappointment. In her, for proving his initial suspicions right, and in himself, for being so naive—for thinking she was someone worthy of his devotion. The vividness of that particular memory hits her directly in the center of her chest, knocking the wind out of her. She won't forget his face in that moment for as long as she lives. To the grave, she'll take with her the hardness of his eyes as he saw her finally for who she really was. Burning, golden amber, turned crystallized and gelid.

A *thunk* of something heavy landing at her feet pulls her back to the present, tamping down the gnawing devastation of losing Crew with something equally as horrific: reality. She looks down and finds a dented, metal canteen lying near her left boot. The only life raft she'll receive through this trial. Food, a shower, a bed—she's smart enough to know, been a prisoner of this ranch long enough to know those are luxuries afforded only to the deserving. She'll be lucky if Bellamy lets her dine on slop with the pigs.

"Get to work," he growls in her ear, and then he stalks off. He flicks the butt of his cigarette as he walks away, and Grace follows its arc until it lands upon the uneven, rocky terrain. Its ember glows, the orange hue brighter amid the lavender haze of dawn. The tiny speck of light begins to fade, and Grace watches, still as the thousands of stones that lie before her, until its fire has been snuffed out and all that remains is ash.

CHAPTER 24

The next morning, a chattering, excited family the size of a small army comes into the waiting room of the hospital with balloons in the shape of a baby bottle, a pacifier, and a giant pink heart declaring **It's a Girl!** in bubble letters. They look lost—crowding onto the ICU floor like a litter of lost puppies. Caia watches through sleepy eyes as a nurse redirects them to the elevators, a hand kneading at her neck to soothe the knot formed from sleeping in such an uncomfortable position. She looks around and takes in the other people in the waiting room—an older man pacing on the phone, his voice gradually growing in volume as he argues with his insurance company; a tired-looking woman and her three young, restless children, who have declared one of the rows of seats their own personal jungle gym.

When she looks over to her own family, her heart squeezes in her chest. Her father has taken to the floor, where he lies with his head resting on a balled-up flannel shirt, one he must've taken from Crew, who sleeps in the chair beside her wearing a white undershirt, his legs stretched all the way out and his ankles crossed. Cooper has his head on Crew's shoulder, and his mouth is hanging wide open, allowing him to leave a perfect circle of drool on Crew's shirt. She's momentarily overcome with affection for these three men she loves so dearly—and she's overcome just as suddenly by the terrifying possibility that this may be what their family looks like from now on. That they'll be four instead of five—that she'll be the only Caldwell woman left to take care of them.

Not long after she wakes, a doctor in a rumpled coat and navy scrubs walks through the swinging double doors at the end of the hall and straight toward them. Caia grabs Crew's arm and shakes it, and he shoots up, knocking Cooper off his shoulder and waking him up in the process.

Crew follows Caia's gaze, then leans down to shake Clint's boot. "Dad."

Clint's eyes blink open, and Crew nods in the direction of the doctor. He sits up with a grunt, and for what feels like an eternity, they wait for the doctor to reach them and tell them if Renata is okay. To tell them if their lives are about to change forever.

By the time he makes it to them, they're all standing.

"Doc." Clint nods, and the doctor—Dr. Hannover, his coat says—returns the nod with a flat, tight-lipped smile.

His face is neutral, giving away not even a shred of evidence one way or another, no matter how hard Caia tries to decipher his every feature.

"I know you've been waiting a long time. I apologize that we weren't able to update you more frequently," Dr. Hannover says.

"Just tell us," Cooper pleads, his voice rough with sleep, and with desperation.

Dr. Hannover nods. "I'm not going to sugarcoat this for

you—the road to recovery is going to be long and difficult. Her body endured catastrophic levels of trauma. We had an entire team of people working on her in that OR. If she was any less of a fighter, we'd be having a very different conversation right now. It wasn't easy, and it wasn't quick, as you know. But she pulled through."

A breath of relief punches from Caia's lungs, bending her over with the weight of it. Her father falls to his knees, and Crew's hands go up to cover his crumpling face as he lets out a wrecked, loud sob. Cooper launches forward and hugs Dr. Hannover, whose eyes bulge slightly before he graciously pats him on the back. When Cooper pulls away, his eyes are red and his cheeks are splotchy.

"Thank you, Dr. Hannover," Caia says, her hands trembling and tears sprouting in the corners of her eyes. "Thank you so much."

"Of course," he says. "We'll talk later about what the next few months are going to look like. She's going to need all of your support."

"She has it," Crew says, completely resolute. He's got a hand on Clint's shoulder, and he squeezes it reassuringly as their father cries and nods adamantly in agreement. He starts to stand, and Crew grabs his elbow, steadying him once he's fully upright.

"When can we see her?" Clint asks.

"Two of you can go back now," Dr. Hannover says. "She's a little groggy from the anesthesia, but she's awake."

Crew and Caia share a look, a silent agreement. He turns to Clint and places a hand on his shoulder. "You and Coop go."

Clint nods, then looks to Caia. She musters up the bravest

smile she can and says, "Tell her we're here. Tell her we love her. So much."

In the cafeteria, over steaming cups of black coffee, Crew tells Caia everything. How he'd fallen in love with Grace, how they'd fallen in love with each other—a fact by which Caia is unsurprised; she could've guessed that all the way from Manhattan. The puppy dog eyes he'd given Grace at their dad's birthday party had been a dead giveaway; her brother was down bad, worse than she'd ever seen him—not that he'd had a ton of girlfriends growing up, but when he had been in relationships, in high school and then post-military, there'd never been that kind of unencumbered *yearning* from his end. That was a new look on him, and Caia had enjoyed witnessing it.

What she doesn't expect to hear is the tangle of lies Grace has found herself caught in, a sticky web of corruption and spite. Not to mention the darkness of her youth—Caia can't spend much time thinking about that right now—chills her to the bone even trying to imagine it.

When she's processed it all enough to form follow-up questions, about a hundred pile up in her brain, each warring with the others to be the first to tumble out of her mouth. Leaning forward, elbows resting on the small table between them, she asks, "What exactly did Forty say when you talked to him?"

Crew is quiet for a beat. There's a contemplative, pained look on his face, and she watches his hands ball into tight fists. "He said he saw her walking to the west entrance with her backpack," he finally says. He sounds wistful and resigned, like there's a full-body ache accompanying his every syllable. "Said he called her name a dozen times but she never turned around, so he got on the Gator and caught up with her." He drops off into silence, though Caia knows there's more.

She swivels slightly to peek back at him, chin still resting in her hands. "And?"

Crew's eyes flit to hers. They're shiny—barely holding back the cascade of tears threatening to fall. "And she said she wanted to go. Apparently, she said she doesn't belong at Halcyon, and it would be better for everyone if she left."

"But you two—"

He cuts her off. "It doesn't matter, Cai."

Caia leans forward, grabbing on to his wrists. "Of course it matters."

"How can it? She's gone," he rasps, his jaw tightening.

Caia takes a deep breath, recognizing that her brother is in a highly emotional, highly *irrational* state right now. She keeps her tone even, pulling back on any incredulity or vehemence in an effort to keep him—and herself—calm.

"Let me get this straight," she says, releasing him to lean back in her chair and fold her arms over her chest. "Grace came to us from a really bad situation at her uncle's ranch, where she lived for nearly a decade because she didn't have anywhere else to go. And she didn't have anywhere else to go because—"

Crew's eyes flick up, and he's looking her dead in the eye as he braces himself for the hardest, most brutal truth of them all.

Caia takes another deep breath, this one markedly more shuddering than the last. "Because she killed her father after he murdered her mother."

Crew's mouth folds into a tight line. His entire body is vibrating with tension. "That's right," he says quietly.

Caia nods, tamping down the sadness, the grief, the fury she feels for Grace as she recounts her story. This girl she doesn't really know, who has made her brother come back to life, who has brought color into his cheeks and reignited the spark in his eyes. She loves her without knowing her, and without reservation, for that alone. "She spent nine years there because she figured that if she left, he'd blacklist her and rat her out to the cops."

Crew nods slowly, as if digesting it himself once again. "Yes."

"But then he—and the group of demented frat boys he calls ranch hands—started to get more and more abusive. They sabotaged her, got her in major trouble, and she was punished for it by her uncle selling her horse."

His jaw flexes again. "Vesta."

"And that loss made her finally snap."

Crew nods, biting the inside of his cheek. When his head turns slightly away from her, the fluorescent ceiling light illuminates the shine of a tear streaking down his face.

"And then a few months went by before someone called Mom to let her know there was a talented horse trainer floating around somewhere in Minetta."

"Your ability to repeat stories verbatim—stories you've only heard once—is so unsettling," Crew grumbles. He leans back into his chair and scratches his unshaven jaw. "But yeah. And then I picked her up and took her to the ranch."

Unfazed by his barb, Caia pushes on. "Right. And after that, everything seemed perfectly normal, except *you* were a bit of an asshole because you were suspicious of where she came from, even though you *knew* from Mom that she'd had a really hard time and that there were literal scars on her body. But in the end, Mom hired her anyway."

Something leaks into Crew's eyes at that statement. A strong cocktail of regret, disappointment, and anger. It twists into something darker, making his irises nearly indistinguishable from the blackness of his pupils.

Caia goes on. "Grace eventually opened up to Mom about what Braxton was really like—told her about the scams Bellamy ran to make money. The scams he ran, the animals he hurt. This—of course—pissed Mom off, and she decided to tap into her connections with law enforcement, and *the state*, to start really investigating everything going on at Braxton. And she wasn't subtle about it."

Her brother closes his eyes, and the beginnings of a wry smile tug at his lips. "Is she ever?"

Caia smiles through the piercing pain in her gut at the thought of her mother sitting behind that ancient mahogany desk, talking to the director of the Texas Department of Public Safety on a landline because she's too stubborn and technophobic to use a cell phone. She tries not to focus on the image of her mother's determined face, the stern but melodic quality of her voice as she kindly orders the man at the helm of the state troopers to do her a favor. Caia knows that phone call must've been no more than ten minutes, and she also knows Paul Freeman was on the other end of it scribbling down notes and nodding furiously, adamant that he'd send his best men to do the job. And Caia *definitely* knows her mother probably followed up that statement with something along the lines of *Maybe send your best women instead, Paul. We tend to do things better. And faster.*

"No," Caia replies after the painful visual has receded. "She isn't."

"They did what she asked," Crew supplies, reaching up to rub his thumb and forefinger over his brow, smoothing the worried creases. "They always do."

"And that's when Bellamy texted Grace," Caia replies.

Crew swallows thickly. His eyes open to mere slits, and he stares downward as he nods. A grim, curt movement, like it hurts to confirm. His nostrils flare. "She lied."

"She was scared," Caia cuts in. "I think she lied because she didn't want to be forced to leave the only place she's ever felt safe."

"And now?" Crew turns to look at her, his gaze pointed, unforgiving. "Mom could've died because Grace was too scared to tell us that Bellamy was a real threat. If she would've just been honest, we could've had the bastard locked up before he even had the *thought* to go after them in Victoria."

Caia's quiet for a moment, allowing him to suck the venom out of the bite in his heart, to get the blame and resentment off his chest. Her heart aches, knowing Crew had to come to terms with Grace's confession at the same time as learning their parents were in the hospital. "You have a right to be angry, Crew," Caia says.

Crew scoffs, mirthless and bitter.

Caia leans forward and grasps his forearm tightly. "I mean it. I'd be pissed, too. But you have to see what's happening here. Grace is going back to Braxton. She's probably there by now." Crew's face slackens slightly, and there's a nearly imperceptible twitch under his left eye. Caia doubles down, knowing he's actually listening now. "She's going back—and not just because she thinks it'll keep everyone safe, but because she thinks *you* don't want her anymore. After all of this. By getting angry and blaming her, you've reaffirmed every terrible thing she's ever thought about herself: She isn't good enough. She doesn't deserve to be at Halcyon. She's a liar and scammer and her actions caused animals to die and people to get hurt. She's going back to Braxton because she thinks it's where she belongs."

Crew is quiet for a long time, and Caia notices his eyes dart back and forth quickly, a motion she knows means he's watching something unfold in his head.

"If she goes back to Braxton, he's going to hurt her. Maybe worse," Crew says.

He looks away, off to some unknowable place, tension building in his jaw. Caia stays quiet. Having grown up in the same house as him, she knows when it's time to speak, to advise, and when it's time to let him puzzle it out on his own.

His shoulders slump slightly as he continues. "I don't like that she kept things from us." Looking down at his hands, he stretches out his fingers, only to curl them back into fists. "I don't like that she didn't trust me enough to tell me what was going on. I thought—" Crew bites off the sentence, seeming to think better of it. Then, in a defeated, breathy kind of voice, he says, "I want her to trust me. Even when the truth isn't pretty. Especially then."

A soft smile tugs at Caia's lips at the admission. At Crew confessing his true feelings and, for once, letting his heart win the never-ending battle against his head. His legs are long enough that they're bent on the outside of the table rather than under it, and when his knee starts to bounce, she knows his mind is made up. But since he seems to be in a forthcoming mood, she can't help but ask. "Do you love her?"

Crew's knee ceases its restless movement. His head falls forward slowly, his chin dipped toward his chest. It hangs as if in prayer, a reverent, instinctual kind of reaction to such a question. The answer is one they both *know*, but she wants to hear it anyway. It feels like the right time to say it out loud—like a period at the end of a very long, very complicated sentence. The corner of Crew's mouth quirks upward, and Caia's own smile grows at the sight, at the stubborn line of his mouth helpless and defeated by the joy arising in him. Amid all the terror, he can't help but smile when he thinks of Grace. "I didn't know it was possible," Crew says quietly, with an awed, slow shake of his head. "To love someone this much."

With a single, resolute nod, Caia says, "Well, all right, then."

Crew glances up at her, then tilts his head. He seems to be waiting for her to finish that statement, and Caia rolls her eyes, throwing her hands up.

Men.

"Go get her, you dumbass."

CHAPTER 25

By noon on the second day, Grace is partway convinced that the sun is singling her out for its wrath. Her body is unmade by its relentlessness, and there's no solution—if she keeps her clothes on, the heatstroke will come for her, and all alone out here, she'd likely die. So, she takes off her clothes, walks in meticulous, painfully slow lines up and down the field, and the sun continues to enact its particular brand of torture by beating its red remembrance onto her skin.

Her fingers and hands are dry and brittle, covered in rock dust that she can't fully get off. Any nails she had are now jagged or ripped down to the quick, and a couple are bleeding at the cuticle, freckling the stones with dots of red as she tosses them haphazardly into the wheelbarrow at her hip.

The previous night, in the ramshackle tent they've given her to sleep in, she'd cried. An ugly, wailing kind of cry—she'd known she was far enough away that no one would hear her, so she'd let herself scream and whine and whimper, a rare moment of allowing self-pity to overtake all other emotions. She'd wallowed and lamented her life, angry and spiteful toward whatever cruel cosmic force had intervened and shown her what she *could* have had—shown her the beauty that lay beyond this barbed-wire-lined hell. *Halcyon*, she'd thought, as her throat grew hoarse from the sobs. The sun never hurt at Halcyon. And how appropriate its name felt then—a long gone oasis—a place that, for Grace, would live on only in memories. She'd given herself the space to mourn its loss, but then had quickly come to realize that crying would only dehydrate her faster, and after endless hours without laying eyes on a single soul, she'd figured it would be smart to conserve any water that was still in her body.

The next morning, she'd started counting the rocks as she tossed them into the wheelbarrow, and she had gotten to about fifteen hundred when she had the thought to stop talking altogether, to stop exposing her mouth to the dust and exacerbating her thirst. But she'd mentally done the math after hitting that number, and a dark realization had begun to settle into her gut: This was going to take *weeks*.

During that magical stretch of time at the summer pasture at Halcyon, she'd taken away a few heat-safety tips—the kind she'd never before been offered, because Bellamy never gave two shits if the people on his staff were healthy and knew how to protect themselves. But Forty cared. Forty cared for every single person and animal on Halcyon grounds. Forty was protective and loyal and kind; he'd become more of a father to Grace in those short months than any other man in her life, dead or alive. And when a little voice in her head had encouraged her to be strategic about her time, to seek the shade of trees, to sip water slowly and sporadically to encourage absorption and not urination, she realized it was *his* voice. Deeper than the hollers of the Hill Country, raspy and gentle and seasoned with decades of life and pain and love under his cowhide belt. Once that realization had set in, she'd listened, carving out times throughout the spread of the day to work, rest, and drink. All in the name of not overheating and dying alone out here, not becoming a corpse left to sizzle and shrivel up beneath the baking sun.

She's counting in her head now, using each *clunk* of the wheelbarrow to stay on track. She nears the edge of the left-hand quarter of the field, and behind her, piles of discarded rocks continue to grow taller, spread out evenly beyond the perimeter. A cairn sits at the front of each one, all of them different but serving the same purpose—to remind Grace every time she looks at them that she is a *person* and not merely a pawn in her uncle's demented schemes. She's the person who moved these stones. The person whose blood and sweat and tears coats them. The person who has tried to construct something lovely, even in the midst of a waking nightmare.

Trey brings her a hunk of overcooked steak and a dry, undercooked baked potato on a plate wrapped in foil at dinnertime. He refills her canteen from an old Igloo cooler sitting in the back of the Gator, and denies her with a laugh when she asks him to leave the whole thing. He drives off with a dismissive wave after remarking on how shocked he is with the little progress she's made. Grace sits in the sad excuse for shade she's found beneath a dying oak and eats, chewing the meat until her jaw hurts and taking tiny bites of the potato to avoid getting overly thirsty from its graininess. Her stomach begins to hurt upon finishing the meal, the result of hastily scarfing everything down. She should've known better—should've taken her time and rationed it out—but she was so *hungry*. So hungry that she couldn't sleep. She lies down on her back and breathes through her mouth for a while, hoping the pain will pass. Eventually, it does, and she gets back to work, because there is nothing else she can do. She returns to the field, to the unforgiving sun, to the rocks that seem to sprout from the ground like weeds.

CHAPTER 26

The hallucinations begin midway through the third day. At first, they're subtle—little tricks of light, fleeting apparitions that disappear in a blink. Then, Grace notices a rock that's sprouted legs and a tail, and a face that looks uncannily like Boone. The rock-dog even seems to be panting, as if it, too, is suffering in this perilous heat. But when Grace steps closer to get a better look, it morphs back into stone, faceless and unmoving. She doesn't think much of the various weird occurrences, chalking them up to exhaustion more than anything.

She certainly doesn't anticipate them turning vivid and lifelike and unsettlingly *real*, the way they do at daybreak on the fourth day, when a mirage in the shape of her mother takes form in the middle of the field. Grace does a double take upon seeing her, and she freezes midway through hauling a particularly heavy boulder into the wheelbarrow. She drops it at her feet and stares, confused by the scene—her mother, ten years younger than she was when she died, kneeling down and delicately, methodically picking wildflowers from the ground. And the thing is—Grace *knows* on some level that it isn't real. She also knows that seeing this in such detail is a telltale sign that she's on the verge of succumbing to the heat. But some other, more demanding part of her refuses to let her be rational. It claws its way to the surface and commands her: *Go. Go see. Go be with her.*

Grace walks toward her mother on gliding feet; the rocks disappear and are replaced with soft, thick grass. Her boots are cushioned and held with each footfall, like she's stepping on tufts of green, bladed clouds. Her mother does not look up as she approaches—she stays focused on her task, and there's a contented little smile on her lips as she pulls a particularly vibrant bluebonnet out of a thatch of its brothers and sisters. She stares at it admiringly, then blinks up at Grace and says, "Do you remember what I told you about picking wildflowers?"

Lowering herself onto her knees, Grace settles two feet away from her mother, close enough that she could reach out and touch her cheek, her daisy-patterned sundress, but too scared that she'd ruin it with her dirty fingertips. Too scared that she'd disappear if something from this outside world, this terrible reality, touched her. Grace's voice is raspy and weak when she responds, thick with unshed tears.

"They have to seed first," she says, staring at her mother's hands—olive toned and calloused with nimble fingers, lithe and long and topped with unpolished, well-kept nails.

"And why do they have to seed first, my saving Grace?"

Grace's eyelids drop shut at the endearment. A tear falls down her cheek—hot and unexpected. *My saving Grace*, her mother used to call her, even when it couldn't possibly have been true. She'd say it for reasons as benign as clearing the dinner table and washing up, or sweeping the front porch when the leaves overtook everything in the fall. She'd say it routinely—when she kissed her good night, when she kissed her goodbye, when she needed a favor. Grace's nostrils flare as she resists the urge to give in and let herself sob, and she takes a deep, steadying breath before opening her eyes again. Her mother is still here, still in such high resolution that Grace can see beads of sweat gathering at her hairline. Chestnut-brown strands giving way to deep chocolate.

"Because if you pick them before they seed, they won't grow back next year. You have to let them live first."

Her mother nods, satisfied and proud of Grace's answer. "That's right, honey. Wildflowers have to be allowed their wildness." She caresses the tops of the remaining bluebonnets, ones she will leave unplucked. "It isn't illegal to pick bluebonnets in Texas. That's a myth. But you still have to be gentle with them."

"Even if they're wild," Grace adds quietly.

Her mother smiles. "Especially then."

Grace's jaw tightens. Her hands itch to reach out; her body yearns to fall into her mother's arms and cry into her neck. "I miss you." Her voice is thick with all the cries she continues to suppress. "I miss you every day."

Though her smile does not fade, her mother's eyes take on a hint of sadness. An almost imperceptible wrinkle forms between her brows. "I haven't gone anywhere, Grace."

"You have," Grace counters. "You aren't here. I'm alone."

"Never," her mother says, and it's then that the smile on her lips begins to dampen slightly, the corners pulling down the tiniest bit. "Not for one second."

Grace shakes her head, disbelieving and frustrated. "Don't do that—don't offer me that mystical *I'll always be with you in your heart* bullshit. You aren't *here*, Momma. I am here. I am alone. I'm in hell, and I can't escape it."

The wildflowers fall from her mother's hands, landing softly atop the grass. Before she realizes what's happening, Grace feels a soft, warm palm at her cheek. Her mother is touching her, caressing her—she doesn't understand, can't make herself rationalize this, so instead, she leans into her grip, letting her wipe away a few errant tears with the pad of her thumb. "Brave girl," her mother whispers. Her smile is gone entirely now, replaced with the kind of sadness that is felt by all mothers and daughters separated too soon.

Grace lets herself cry then. She sobs into her mother's palm with abandon; she lets herself feel the pain she so diligently hides away alongside the rose-tinted memories of her life when it was just the two of them. "Please," she begs, though she does not know what for.

"My tamer of horses. My wildflower." She strokes Grace's cheekbone with the edge of her thumb in gentle, repetitive motions. "Who tames you?" Her fingertips embed themselves softly into the hair at Grace's temple. "Who protects your wildness?"

Grace's sobs begin to subside at her mother's questions. Her watery eyes reopen, and she sees something like a smile returning to mother's face. Her lovely, freckle-strewn face, unmarred by the fists of evil incarnate.

"The gardener," her mother says matter-of-factly. Like it's the most obvious answer in the world. For a brief moment, she looks over Grace's shoulder, staring past her, and that hint of a smile on her lips turns knowing. "His shift begins soon."

Grace hiccups, her head tilting in confusion. She's never been very adept at deciphering metaphors, and she certainly isn't in a state to make sense of her dead mother's cryptic words. But then, behind her, a voice cuts through the quiet chirping of crickets, the rustle of deadening leaves.

"Grace."

Her heart skips; her breath hitches in her throat, lodging a hiccup on its way to her mouth. She knows that voice—knows it from her dreams, from her fantasies, from the whispers of its warmth into her ear, her skin. Her lips. The sound of it, the tone and pitch—it's so much more than just a voice. It's a fresh cup of steaming black coffee before dawn. It's the river song of gentle lapping waves hitting the mossy banks of a beloved creek. It's the sweetest kind of authority, the command to be still, to trust, to feel, to *love*. It's home in the form of a sound.

It's Crew.

Grace's head swivels around at breakneck speed because her mother's strange prophecy suddenly makes perfect sense, because there's only one person who understands how to thread the needle of Grace—there's only one person who can quiet the screaming regret, the blaring anxiety, the echoing shame. One person who knows how to stand aside and let her wildness spread its wings, all the while keeping a steady, gentle hand at her back to remind her she can always fly back home. Back to him.

Grace's heartbeat begins to pick up speed, begins to squeeze pleasantly in her chest at the thought of seeing him. Laying her eyes on him after almost a week without, letting them feast on the sight of his big hands and shoulders and his perfect, crooked smile.

But when she turns, she doesn't find Crew standing behind her.

She finds nothing at all. A vacant, sun-drenched field still covered in patches of rocks.

And when she looks back to her mother, ready to scream, yell, and cry at her for such a cruel trick, she finds nothing again. The space her mother had occupied, the flowers she'd tended have all disappeared, contorting back into something uglier, harsher. Realer. The grass below her feet is no longer soft and welcoming. She is, once again, completely alone.

CHAPTER 27

Renata is moved out of the ICU roughly twenty-four hours after surgery, and preparations begin almost immediately. Her room—which is more of a suite than a hospital room—becomes a base of operations of sorts, with phone calls being made to every resource in the Caldwell contact list who could possibly assist with not only getting Grace out of Braxton as soon as possible but also ensuring Bellamy Whitlock spends the rest of his life behind bars.

It's late afternoon on the second day of their mission—Clint is in the midst of an email exchange with a few other ranch owners, gathering intel on what they know of Braxton; Cooper is on his laptop tracking down any notable sales related to equine reproduction in the area over the past five years; Renata is on the phone with Paul Freeman, assuring him she's recovering just fine and would like to waste no further time pushing forward this operation. Caia, having just gotten off her own phone call with Henry Flanagan, the family attorney, watches all of this in quiet awe. Her family could bring down an entire government if they wanted to.

When Crew walks back into the room, he's wearing a smile

Caia hasn't seen since she's been back in Texas. He looks genuinely pleased, maybe even a little proud. She tilts her head, surveying him. "Good news?"

Crew nods. He slips his phone into his back pocket, walks over to give Renata a kiss on the cheek. Their mother angles her head to let him, then waves him off, still speaking firmly—but politely, always politely—to Paul. Crew's smile turns into a grin, and Caia throws her hands out, more than ready for whatever good news he has to offer. They could all use some good news right about now.

"I talked to Reese," Crew says. "They think they know where she is."

"You're kidding," Caia says, shaking her head in disbelief. "That guy is more connected than Mom. Trying to find a single palomino in Texas is like trying to find a grain of salt in a sandbox."

Crew nods. He looks like he's about two seconds away from being outright giddy. "I know."

"All right, honey," Renata says to Paul, holding up a finger to signal to her kids to stop the conversation lest she miss any more of it. "We'll be ready. Thanks for putting your foot on the gas with this. I'll make it up to you somehow." She nods, smirking. "All right. Bye now."

Renata hangs up, then looks between Crew and Caia. "What'd I miss?"

"Reese has a lead," Crew says. "He thinks it's a good one."

There's a sparkle in Renata's eyes as she smiles at this. "Good. One more thing to check off the list. What'd Henry say?"

"He'll be here this evening," Caia says. "He doesn't seem too concerned about anything—sounds like whatever he was able to dig up about Warren and Melissa Underwood was dated and basically forgotten. Graywood PD didn't even know who they were. And with what Coop and Dad have already found, we've got enough to hand over to the cops to bring him down."

"Great," Renata says. She claps her hands together, glances over at Clint and Cooper, both still deep in their own investigations, and says, "Paul's ready to move as soon as tomorrow morning. He's already spoken with the Everlake police. They'll be ready, too."

"So, it's happening," Cooper says, pausing his furious typing. "We're gonna get him—get all of them. We're gonna save Grace."

Renata's eyes flit to Crew, whose bright grin fades into something more earnest, more pained. Even with everything coming together, the ache in him at not yet having Grace here, safe, with him, is written all over his face. He nods, his jaw flexing. "Yeah. We're gonna bring her home."

That evening, Caia meets Henry outside of the hospital and walks him to Renata's room. They discuss the legal logistics of Bellamy's crimes, as well as Grace's, and make sure they are all on the same page about what happens next. As a public-facing family, they have to be careful about this—nothing can fall through the cracks that could come back to haunt them.

When everyone is confident the case is airtight, Caia excuses herself to the hallway for a brief moment. She needs a second to herself to breathe, to be surrounded by something other than the strategizing chatter. She leans against a wall, lets her eyes fall shut, and zones out completely to the idle sounds of the surrounding rooms. The beeping of machines, the low murmur of the nurses' station, the mechanical hum of the elevators.

"You okay?" a voice asks, and Caia's eyes flutter open to find Crew staring at her with big-brotherly concern.

Caia nods. "Just needed a minute."

"It's been a lot, I know. I . . ." He trails off, and his eyes fall to the floor. "I wanted to thank you. For being here, for doing all of this."

Caia's brows pull together. "I'm not doing—"

"Cai, I mean for all of it. For helping me see that she's worth every plan, every phone call, every favor. Grace, she—" He swallows, then shakes his head quickly as if to rid himself of the urge to cry. "She's worth this fight. She's . . . everything."

It's a lovely sentiment, and Caia feels her heart warm, hearing her brother speak of someone with such reverence. He's never been particularly soft, or open, or willingly vulnerable, especially after the tours—but Grace has clearly brought out something in him that was long dormant, if it was ever there in the first place. She's softened his edges, and it's striking, this evolution of Crew who is standing before her.

"That's what we do," Caia says, offering him a reassuring smile. She steps forward, stopping right before she gets to him. "Us Caldwells. We fight for our own. And if Grace is yours, then she's ours, too."

Crew nods, then opens his arms and wraps Caia in a tight hug. Caia rests her forehead against Crew's sternum, feeling hopeful about the next twenty-four hours and about her brother's future. But then Crew suddenly tenses, squeezing Caia hard enough that she squeaks. "Fuck," he blurts out. Caia tries to pull back, but Crew keeps her in place.

"Crew, what the—"

"Listen," he says in her ear, and his voice is miles away from the way it has sounded up to this point. Talking to her now is the brother who tried to ply her with Starbucks and new shoes after he dropped her favorite headphones in the creek. The brother who would barter with her for the last piece of Ronnie's apple cinnamon cheesecake, offering to do her chores for the following week—a deal she never took him up on because that cheesecake was simply *too* good. Caia's hackles start to rise at his tone, because she can't even imagine what could bring it out now. "There was something that I had to do, when I found out Mom and Dad got hurt. I made a promise and I had to keep it. But you're . . . well, you're not going to like it. Just know that I'm sorry."

Caia tenses. A thousand possibilities race through her head, each worse than the last. She catastrophizes for a few seconds before replying to him with a firm, "What?"

And then she hears a voice, and her question is answered.

"Well, that certainly looks cozy."

Caia's entire body floods with ice at the click of bootheels accompanying the question, growing louder and louder with each step. She digs her nails into Crew's back, hard enough to hurt. It's partly on purpose, and partly reflex—her claws are out, ready to protect her. He hisses, but doesn't pull away from her. He *knows* he deserves it.

The voice speaks again, all crooning and lilting and perfectly charming. The affectation of it makes her want to vomit. "Got room for one more?"

Slowly, Caia releases her brother, and though every molecule of her body is shouting at her not to turn around, *not* to look into the eyes of the man standing behind her, she does it anyway. When she finds Easton Beckett's all-too-familiar shit-eating grin, it takes every ounce of composure she has to not reach out and slap it right off of his face.

Caia levels Crew with a glare that could kill a man dead, and her next words are practically spit. "What the *fuck* is he doing here?"

CHAPTER 28

Trey brings Grace kitchen scraps again, but by now she's lost all sense of time. It could be the third day or the thirtieth that she's been out here, being drained of life by the sun and this endless task. She eats slowly, carefully chewing each bite of bone-dry chicken breast and savoring it on her tongue. With her hunger tempered and no stomach pains radiating in her gut, Grace feels the exhaustion set in—her eyelids begin to droop, her body begins to rock heavily back and forth. She's tired beyond reason, barely able to stay upright on the sad excuse for a bedroll they supplied. Eventually, she falls back, out cold by the time she's horizontal, and—for the first time since arriving at Braxton—tumbles into a deep, dreamless sleep.

A steel-toed boot kicks her awake. It hits her in the elbow, sending a jumping, lightning-quick flash of agony through her arm and then her entire body. Pain sings in her blood as she hisses, eyes shooting open and body whirling around, reaching for a knife that no longer rests beneath her pillow. There is no pillow, and that knife is somewhere in Bellamy's possession or, more likely, buried deep in a trash bag on its way to a landfill.

"Fuck," Grace spits, still hovering on the edge of sleep. She rubs at her elbow, cradling it in her palm, but she barely has time to process how much pain she's in before another blow lands at the side of her leg, knocking directly into the edge of her kneecap. "Jesus fucking *Christ*." She seethes, then looks up with a withering glare to the offender standing over her. A black, looming silhouette made faceless by the blinding sun.

"It ain't nighttime," the figure snarls. "The only reason you should be sleepin' is if it's nighttime, or if you're done with the job. And since the sun is still out, I guess you're saying you're done."

Grace shakes her head, wincing as she tries to sit up, reaching out with her free hand to grab her throbbing knee. "No—I didn't say that—"

"Shut up." The figure recedes, walks toward the field, and crouches down with a grunt. "Let's see just how good of a job you did."

Grace lifts up onto her knees, ignores the screaming pain that protests the movement, and begins to crawl toward the figure—her uncle, reaching out to pick up a handful of acorn-size rocks. She's a foot away from him when he stands and turns to face her. "If you're claiming to be *done*, then what the hell are these?" He opens his palm and lets the rocks cascade downward, falling near her spread hands and sending clouds of dust puffing up into her eyes. Grace falls back onto her haunches, shaking her head adamantly.

"I didn't say I was done, I was just so tired—"

"I don't want to hear it," Bellamy barks, then steps onto the rocks on his way to her, abruptly invading her space as he reaches down to grab her left hand, yanking it off her thigh and holding it roughly between both of his. "I told you what would happen if I found rocks. I *told you*, Gracie, and you didn't listen. You just...*never*...listen." He singles out her index finger, holding it in his fist while his other hand grips her palm. With a quick snap, one swift motion backward, a *crack* sounds. It takes a moment for her to process what he's done—it takes a split second of seeing her finger bent back at that terrible, unnatural angle, and then the pain sets in. Heat races through her entire being, and the hell of it overtakes her in the span of a breath. As the pain unloads itself into her system, Grace screams.

He moves on to her middle finger, but this one, he holds at the middle knuckle, fumbling around until he gets a grip he's satisfied with. "You could've been a good girl, Grace," he tuts, pursing his lips. "But you never could *quite* figure it out. Little slow, I guess. Figures, your momma wasn't the sharpest, either." He snaps the knuckle within his fist, and when he releases her finger, it curves harshly to the left at the midpoint. Grace groans, but as the sight sinks in, as that pain comes to join its lesser companion, she screams again. Her throat begins to burn.

"Quit crying," Bellamy shouts, and, without ceremony, he breaks her pinkie, pulling it almost parallel to the edge of her palm. "Fucking pathetic."

Only her thumb and ring finger remain unharmed, and her hand takes the shape of a distorted claw, bound by the pain and unable to do anything but curl in on itself. His eyes dance as he grips her thumb, spreading his legs and digging his heels into the dirt below to maintain a good position. He needs the leverage of holding her hand between his thighs. For the pain he's about to enact on her, he must prepare himself. "This is for running your loud fucking mouth," he croaks, squeezing her thumb hard, suffocating it. "This is for how ungrateful you are, even after all I've done for you. This is for being a disrespectful little bitch."

A few things happen at once then.

First, Bellamy's eyes shift away from the large, maniacal circles they'd become during his tirade. They widen with something more surprised, more fearful, transforming rapidly into ovoid orbs of distress. Second, though his grip on her thumb has loosened infinitesimally, she still screams, already mentally in a state where she's lost that digit, too. The pain has morphed into a singular, devastating being, and she cannot tell the difference between one finger's lament and another. She screams and it sounds like wailing; it sounds like the scrape of rubber on asphalt; it sounds like a cast-iron kettle sitting atop a bright red burner.

The realization happens slowly—too slowly. He lets go of her thumb, stumbles backward, and stops paying attention to her altogether. Grace slumps forward, but she doesn't understand right away what's happened—she thinks, surely, he's tired himself out. He'll be back within seconds, vigor renewed and ready to turn the rest of her fingers into mere fragments of bones, swimming within skin.

But he doesn't come back.

Not for five seconds, then ten, then twenty.

At thirty, Grace begins to understand that the wailing in her ears is no longer hers. It is not the screech of tires. It is not a whistling teakettle.

It's police sirens.

CHAPTER 29

There isn't just one police cruiser driving toward them, bouncing up and down as it rolls over the uneven, untended terrain. There are five.

At first, Grace doesn't allow herself to believe it's actually happening. Despite the lights and sirens on full display, despite the quickly closing gap between her and this black-and-blue cavalry, she refuses to let her brain make a fool of her once again. It had tricked her so harshly with the vision of her mother, with the sound of Crew's voice—creating this facade in the form of a rescue seems on par with its savagery.

Even as the cars come to a stop and doors begin to swing open, she still does not fully accept it. A distant, muffled-sounding voice makes its way to her ears, but it sounds like words being shouted underwater. *Put your hands where I can see them, Whitlock*, Grace swears she hears—but there's no way. She mustn't get her hopes up, mustn't for one second believe that her uncle is finally going to be brought to justice.

Through squinted, swollen eyes, Grace stares out as a perimeter of cars begins to form around them, but her vision is blurry and unfocused. She's still on her knees, cradling her hand against her chest. She's still crying, because the pain is somehow worse now—the tiniest of movements reduces her to the three shattered fingers, allowing her to focus only on them, on the agony they radiate. Nausea begins to overtake curiosity, and the desire to lie down, to close her eyes and try to sleep, to forget—do *anything* but feel—is overwhelming. She begins to vomit without realizing she's doing it, doubled over and balancing on her good hand. Strands of wet hair plaster to her forehead and fall into her eyes. Sweat and tears and sick coat her skin. Strange noises are happening somewhere in her vicinity—she can hear them but can't make them out. It sounds like grunting, heavy breathing—she picks up a phrase that sounds suspiciously like *Back the fuck up*, but she can't be sure. A loud *thump* follows, and a croaking groan after that. Now only coughing up bile, Grace gasps, the bitterness on her tongue making her eyes cross. She's teetering, ready to give in to the urge to collapse and evade consciousness for a long while, and it feels like she's on her way down when something—*someone*—grips her arms, pulling her upright.

"Grace."

It sounds so much like— *No*, she won't let this happen again. Won't let her stupid, overprotective brain gift her this fantasy, this false comfort. Grace shakes her head, tries to yank her arms out of this imitating hold.

"Baby, look at me."

There's something different about the voice than before. In that beautiful, masochistic vision, it had been perfect—exactly what she needed to hear, as commanding as the day she met him. No decipherable emotion, just calm, careful authority. It had been Crew, or her mind's best imitation of him, but without the authenticity and depth of his actual voice. His real voice—

the one that can carry a dozen different emotions in a single syllable, the one that can be harsh and sharp and intimidating in one breath, then kind, soft, and warm in the next.

That voice, she slowly begins to realize, is the one talking to her right now. "Grace," it begs, watery and broken. "Please, sweetheart. Look at me."

Grace stills, no longer trying to pull herself free of his grasp. Her lashes flutter as she opens her eyes, fighting through the overwhelming desire to keep them screwed shut. The blinding sun hurts her eyes, but she doesn't care. She has to see.

What takes shape before her is like a reflection in a rippling pond. Distorted at first, unrecognizable, but becoming clearer as the waves drift away. Grace's breath hitches when he comes into focus, as every detail of his face begins to sharpen. It's strange—though she knows it's him now, can see and hear him clearly, it feels even less real that he's here, on his knees in front of her, his hands leaving her arms to cradle her face. He catches her head as it lolls forward, and she feels his thumbs wipe the corners of her mouth. She has no energy to be ashamed or embarrassed at her state, at the sickness he just cleaned from her skin. She's too busy trying to figure out not how but *why* he's here. After what she did, she was certain she would never see him again. That he's here now, holding her up and looking at her with those soft but frenzied brown eyes, doesn't make sense. He couldn't look at her at all the last time they were together, and now, it seems, he refuses to look anywhere else.

"You're not . . ." Grace mumbles, leaning involuntarily into his palm as her head continues to fall in random directions. The exhaustion, the heat, the pain—it's getting the better of her now, threatening to pull her under the surface. She takes a deep breath and manages, hardly coherent, "You're not supposed to be here."

Crew's nostrils flare. He inches closer to her, pushes her hair back in smooth sweeps until it's all out of her face. "Neither are you," he says resolutely, his head dipping down so he can look her dead in the eye. "I'm taking you home."

A weak smile forms on Grace's lips, and her eyes drift to somewhere far away, someplace beyond this field of stones and blood. "Home," she repeats wistfully.

"Yeah," Crew says, nodding. "Home. Back to Halcyon."

Grace's brow furrows. "Can't go—can't be there, isn't safe—"

She begins to lose the fight with her body, growing weaker by the second, and before she realizes what's happening, Crew is scooping her into his arms and holding her against his chest. With his lips at her temple, she hears him say, "Nothing's gonna happen to you. I promise. After today, you'll never have to see this place again. You belong at Halcyon." He breathes, pushing a hard kiss to her skin. "You belong with me."

Grace sighs, lets herself sink into the promise of his words, and nods. "Belong" is all she says in return, all she can muster. It's the most beautiful word she's ever uttered.

Her eyes drift upward, looking hazily at the police cars, the ambulances bookending them on either side. Police officers stand beside them, looking stiff and ready to pounce. They're all holding out some type of firearm, using their car doors as shields.

"Bullshit," a cold, withering voice calls. It's one Grace knows well; she's been subjected to it for most of her life. Its menacing tone, its poisonous pitch—she has adhered, toiled, and bent under the weight of it. "She ain't going anywhere with you people."

Grace frowns, upset by the statement. She latches on to Crew with whatever strength she has left, hoping her uncle's words don't change his mind about taking her back to Halcyon. If she clings to Crew hard enough, maybe her uncle won't make her stay.

"Only place she belongs is right here. With her family."

Crew's grip on Grace tightens, and she realizes a beat too late that the voice is growing louder. She can hear wheezing breaths erupting from tar-soaked lungs, and Grace's eyes flicker open to confirm her suspicion. Her uncle is zeroing in on them, closing the distance with violence flashing in his eyes. Crew's voice is laced with a growl when he warns, "Take one more step and it'll be the last thing you ever do."

As if on cue, to further assert and validate Crew's threat, a figure emerges beside him. Not quite as tall but on his way to becoming just as broad, Cooper Caldwell wears a hardened scowl, and his chest is rising and falling quickly as he stands beside his brother with clenched fists. Bellamy's lip curls, and it's painfully obvious that though he wants to call Crew's bluff, he knows this is not a battle he will win. He's surrounded. But that doesn't stop him from considering it. And when Cooper recognizes that, he practically snarls.

"Try it, motherfucker," the younger Caldwell says. "Just try it."

An officer's voice suddenly bleats through a speaker, echoing its command across the field. "Step away from them, Whitlock. Now."

Bellamy, still too close, takes a wobbly step to the left, then another, until he is far enough away that Grace can no longer catch whiffs of the malodorous mix of cheap cologne, sweat, and alcohol. He stands completely still, with his hands at his sides. Though his body is unmoving, his face is a war zone of emotion—panic, fear, anger, and shock all battle it out.

"Put your hands behind your head," the officer says. "Get on your knees."

"Fuck you," Bellamy bites out through gritted teeth. Then, because he is nothing if not the worst, most detestable person on the planet, he hawks a golf ball–size loogie and sends it flying in the direction of the police cars. "You can't come onto my private property and bark orders at me. I ain't done nothin' wrong."

"Well, that's just not true at all, is it?"

Grace's head swings around—more of a slow swivel, because everything she does seems to be in slow motion right now—the familiarity of that voice pulling her attention like a magnet. Female, crystal clear, brooking absolutely no argument. The younger, crisper, less accented version of one Grace knows very well.

Like Moses and the Red Sea, a wide berth forms between the officers, a path cleared without anyone needing to be asked. Through it, with purposeful steps made in tall, black alligator boots, walks Caia Caldwell. She carries a thick stack of manila folders under her arm and a self-satisfied smirk on her lips, and a random thought occurs to Grace—inappropriate given the situation at hand, but she can't help but wonder if part of the reason Caia left is because she and her mother had started to become almost indistinguishable. They must've gotten mistaken for each other constantly—and right now, with Grace's vision blurred and hazy, it could very well be Renata walking toward them.

Renata—a pang of sorrow clenches in Grace's gut. Is she all right? Will Grace ever have the chance to tell her how sorry she is? How *stupid* she was? How she'll regret not speaking up every day for the rest of her life?

Caia's perfume hits Grace's nose, pulling her back to the present. The middle Caldwell child is standing just in front of Bellamy now; she's practically toe-to-toe with the bastard, and though she is a little shorter, she towers over him in every way that matters. She folds her arms over her chest as she appraises him, nostrils flaring as her eyes make their way back up his old, run-down form. She tilts her head, considers for a beat, then says, "I thought you'd be bigger."

Bellamy grits his teeth. "You must be the daughter," he spits, echoing Caia's look with one of his own. "How's Mommy doin', by the way?"

A growl rumbles in Crew's chest—Grace can feel the vibration of it against her skin. She peeks up at him to find him enraged, a murderous look on his face. She burrows farther into his arms on instinct; she doesn't want him to give Bellamy the satisfaction of knowing he's pushed the right button. Cooper, equally as furious, rocks back and forth on the balls of his feet like a coiling spring, ready to be unleashed.

Caia is less affected by Bellamy's question—or, rather, she's better at hiding it than her brothers. A smile blooms on her lips as she says, "Actually, you'll be relieved to know she's recovering quite well. Out of the ICU in record time, considering her injuries."

He's quiet for a half second too long, clearly surprised by the update. "Isn't that just the sweetest blessing," he says darkly.

Caia nods, her expression even. "My mother is very dear to me and my family. She's very special to a lot of people, actually.

So, yes—it's a blessing that an entirely preventable accident didn't take her from us. And you know what else is a blessing, Mr. Whitlock?" Bellamy jerks his head upward, keeping his chin high. He grunts in acknowledgment. The smile on Caia's face shifts into something more sardonic, something slightly more terrifying. "My mother's social circle." A silence settles throughout the swaths of people gathered around them, all enraptured by Caia's speech. "Growing up, I thought it was the pointiest, sharpest thorn in my side. Always getting stopped at the grocery store, the mall, the playground. The *gynecologist*, for crying out loud." The theatricality of it all—the dramatic shake of her head, the huff of indignant laughter—is masterful. All eyes are glued to her; everyone around them is enamored with the way this spider of a woman is spinning, *trapping* Bellamy in her web. "Everybody wanted to talk to Renata Caldwell. It didn't matter that I was tugging on her arm and begging her to stop. She never did." Caia smiles, a little wistful, a little mischievous. "She never cut anyone off. She never lied and said she had to run. She greeted everyone like an old friend, even if she didn't remember meeting them in the first place."

Something dark and fast-moving breaks through the westward thicket of trees, and once Grace realizes what it is, her breath shudders in her throat. The entrance is less dramatic than the local police had been—their entire battalion could be counted on one hand—but some things clearly need no ceremony or introduction. Black SUVs roll onto the field in a neat, methodical line. They hum as they close in, and murmurs begin to echo throughout the crowd. Caia has yet to look over her shoulder, but she doesn't have to. She knows exactly what's unfolding behind her.

"She's always been great at listening. *Networking*, as the fancier kind would say. And you want to know what makes her so good at it? It's not some big secret, I'll tell you that. It's not about the money, or the name, or the legacy."

Bellamy's eyes are wide as he watches men in bulletproof vests and blue raid jackets begin to climb out of the vehicles. Twenty or more, all armed to the teeth.

"It's about kindness," Caia says, firm and unmoving. "Generosity. Community." With this statement, she takes a step forward, and all pretense of decorum slips out of her expression. She wears the same face as her brothers now—icy and cutting and battle ready. "Things you know nothing about. You abuse people, lie to them, cheat and steal from them. It's all you've ever done." Her lip curls, as if she's letting all of the disgust she feels for this monster of a man finally come to the surface. "You'll rot behind bars for the rest of your life for what you did to my mother, and what you did to the thousands of people you scammed." She lets that sink in, and her tone is darker and more scathing when she adds, "But if I had a vote, I'd put you in front of a firing squad for what you did to that girl." Caia doesn't look at Grace as she says this, but she points to her with a stiff, exacting finger. "What you made her believe. What you *stole* from her."

Crew holds Grace tighter, but something about Caia's words ignites a vestige of strength Grace must've been holding on to, because she wiggles in his arms, and he seems to understand— seems to get that she wants to be on her own two feet for this. To face it standing up. When her boots hit the ground, she is slightly wobbly, but Crew's already there, straightening her up, and then lacing his fingers with her own.

"I *saved* that ungrateful brat," Bellamy argues, flecks of spit flinging from his lips. "Without me, she would've wound up in foster care. Think she would've had some normal, apple-pie kind of life then? She would've gotten it a lot worse than she ever got it here."

Caia huffs out a mirthless laugh. "Of course. How noble of you to pull a child out of school and turn her into your own personal slave. They should give out medals for such selflessness. I'm sure the check you collected every month had nothing to do with it."

With a snarl, Bellamy lunges forward. "You don't know what you're talking about, bitch."

Caia is unmoved. Unfazed completely by this act of hobbled aggression. "I do, actually." She pulls the folders from under her arm and holds them up. "You see, *this* is a highlight reel of your greatest hits, Mr. Whitlock. Spanning all across our lovely state, from Saracen County to the Rio Grande. There's enough in here to put you away for five lifetimes. And I'll let you in on a little secret." She takes a step closer, not caring at all for the way Bellamy is practically heaving now, a pathetic excuse for a growl sounding on his every exhale. "There's not a single thing in here about a little girl in Graywood murdering anyone. But we kept digging and digging and *finally* found a dusty case file in an abandoned file cabinet at GCPD." Caia swallows, then looks directly at Grace. She holds her eyes as she says, even and clear, "Warren Underwood's death was ruled accidental nine years ago. No suspects, no investigation. Case closed."

An onslaught of emotion races through Grace's ragged body at the words. The declaration that would've changed the entire trajectory of her life. She doesn't look at Bellamy, sees only from the corner of her eye as his head begins to bow, his chin dipping to his chest. Whether in shame or embarrassment, she doesn't know—doesn't care. What he *took* from her, what he planted in her young, trusting, vulnerable mind—she can't see straight through the vermillion that seeps into her vision. The red rage of indignation, of horror and understanding. Her lips tremble with all the words she wants to say, all the loathing she wants to unleash. But she stays silent, breathing roughly through gritted teeth, and Caia seems to understand. On some molecular level, she seems to *get it*.

And so, she takes it home. For Grace, for Renata, for every woman and girl who has been taken advantage of by a cruel man. By a cruel world.

"You're going to die in Everlake County," she promises. "And you'll be forgotten. Just like this place will be. No obituary. No legacy." With one final look of detestation, of lip-curling abhorrence, Caia Caldwell makes her kill shot. "And when they incinerate your rotting corpse, not a single soul on this planet will mourn."

CHAPTER 30

The image of Bellamy Whitlock on his knees and in handcuffs stays with Grace for a long time after she leaves Braxton. Even as she weaves in and out of consciousness, wrapped up in a blanket in the back of an ambulance, the outline of it forms behind her eyes. It echoes into the dream she has on the way to the hospital—she's standing in the front yard of the house where her mother was killed. Dark, syrupy blood drips from the eaves, creating red puddles across the rickety porch. Bellamy's there, but he's standing outside, staring through a window, pressed against the glass with his hands cupped around his face. Satisfied with whatever he sees, he tries to walk toward the front door, but his left leg yanks him back. Grace, in whatever shapeless, nonbeing form she's taken in this dream, an observer and not a participant, looks down at the same time he does to find a thick, rusty shackle at his ankle, secured tight enough that it will cut off his circulation if he struggles against it. He shakes his leg once, twice, then pulls it with all of his might. A futile effort, because the chain doesn't seem to have an end. It goes beneath the porch, and when Grace crouches down to follow it, she sees that its start is underground. Deep within the earth, too deep to ever dig out. This, she knows, somehow.

Bellamy starts to scream, starts to bang his fists against the house, but no one comes to his aid. He pulls at the shackle hard enough that he breaks into a sweat, and only when he is too exhausted to continue does he finally look up into the yard. He seethes when he spots her, starts to spit vitriolic remarks, vehement enough that he's nearly foaming at the mouth. He points at her, lunges for her, but he remains rooted to the same spot. And though he shouts, though he seems to take deep breaths in between bouts of screaming, Grace cannot hear him. She stares for another minute, watching him crumble in a kingdom of his own making, and then she turns around. She walks away from her father's house, a house she lived in but never called home, and she doesn't look back. She leaves Bellamy Whitlock chained up in the past, where he should've always stayed.

When Grace wakes up, the first thing she sees is a window with open blinds. Wherever she is, it's nighttime. The glow of streetlights coalesces with black and gray clouds, gilding the sky in tinges of gold. Grace blinks, clearing her vision more each time, until the heaviness of sleep no longer threatens to pull her back under. She swallows and quickly notices how dry her mouth is, how horrible it tastes. Grimacing, she looks around, hoping for water, but what she finds instead sends a pleasant warmth swooping in her belly. Her heart squeezes and seems to double in size with all the love that immediately overtakes her as she absorbs the sight of Crew, fast asleep in an uncomfortable-looking chair right next to her bed. His cheek rests on the palm of his hand, and his lips are parted slightly. His hair is a mess—he's probably been running his hands through it nonstop. He looks paler than usual, like he hasn't been outside in a couple of days, and his skin has already started to retreat to its natural fairness. His other hand is beneath her own on the bed, and though he is completely asleep, his thumb strokes back and forth over her palm, unconsciously rubbing random, gentle semicircles into her skin.

Grace takes a moment before waking him to take in her surroundings—a dimly lit, private hospital room, bigger than her last apartment by a wide margin. A mauve, vinyl love seat up against the farthest wall, with duffel bags strewn across its stiff-looking cushions. A collection of flowers sit on various flat surfaces throughout the room, some arranged elegantly in beautiful, bow-laden vases, and others—well, the green plastic pitcher with sunflowers haphazardly sticking out of the mouth looks a lot like the one they use in the Halcyon bunkhouse for sweet tea. Tears well in her eyes at the thought of the guys being here, and she wishes she'd been awake to see them, wishes she could've squeezed each one of them until it hurt.

As for herself, she's hooked up to an IV, and the steady beep of a monitor sounds beside her. There are oxygen prongs attached to her nostrils, though she isn't sure why. The pain she was in before—that searing, brain-altering pain—is dull and manageable now, but still present. Lingering in a way that lets her know it isn't going anywhere anytime soon, despite the fact that she's probably on some high-dose meds. As the memory of it all begins to seep back into her consciousness, Grace's gaze darts to her hand, and the desert of her mouth goes somehow dryer at what she sees. It's stiff and unmoving in a thick cast that stretches halfway up her forearm and elevated on a firm pillow. She tries to move her fingers from within, but is met with a blinding ache that sends a roil of nausea through her gut. Grace lets out a harsh exhale as she stares at her hand, and memories begin to come back in flashes—unnaturally bent fingers, a hand hanging limp and immobile, the crackling sound and sensation of knuckles being dislocated beneath cruel, brutish thumbs. She isn't breathing normally anymore; she's hyperventilating as the picture becomes clearer. The past four days spent withering away in that rock field, certain she would die out there, alone and left for the coyotes to feast upon. It's impossible in the *now* to forget the *then*, to rationalize with her body and mind that she is no longer coughing up blood from inhaling the dust, no longer refraining from tears to conserve water. No longer fading away beneath that blinding sun. The only thing Grace is capable of, in this moment, is panic.

The beeping of the monitor at her bedside has picked up, and the commotion of Grace waking and starting to spiral must've been enough to wake Crew, because before she can utter a single word, or cry, or whimper, he is there. Standing, pushing his hands into her hair, holding her cheeks between his warm palms and leaning down until he's staring her directly in the eye. It's reminiscent of the way he found her on that field, and again, he knows on some instinctive level that he has to get her to *see* him. To understand, without a shadow of a doubt, that he is here. He is real. He is with her. "Hey, hey, it's all right," he says, and the soothing lilt of his voice is an instant balm to the turmoil raging through her. He moves in slowly, carefully, giving her time to recognize what he's doing, and then presses his lips to her cheekbone. He lingers there, just a hint of contact, further reinforcing the notion that he is *here*.

Grace crumbles. The heat of the panic, the fear, the devastating resolve of a woman who had given up—it rushes out of her in a gust so heavy and thick that her body actually seems to deflate. She starts to cry, responding to his instincts with her own and leaning her face into his touch, craving more of it. All of it. Crew gets it—he always has. Within seconds, he's sitting at her side, pressing kisses against her cheeks, her nose, her eyelids. And in between each one, she can hear his reassuring words, spoken with a voice more wrecked than before but no less comforting. He kisses her brow.

"Grace. Sweetheart." The tip of her nose. "Breathe." The apple of one cheek. "You're all right." And then the other. "You're safe." The corner of her mouth. "I'm here." And finally, her lips. "I love you."

Grace's voice is raspy and slightly wheezing when she finally finds it. "Crew," she manages, and with her good hand, she reaches up to hold his face. His eyes flutter shut, and he leans into her touch before pressing a quick kiss to her palm. "You're here," she repeats, the statement laced with tears, but no longer of despair or panic. Now, there is awe; there is disbelief and joy and safety flowing in rivers down her cheeks. "You came."

A watery chuckle sounds in his throat. "I'm sorry it took me so long."

"Your parents—"

Crew shakes his head. "They're all right. They're gonna be fine."

Grace's face crumples. "I—" The sentence dies in her chest, stopped by an onslaught of relief so sharp it's painful. She breathes through it, then lets her eyes fall to his chest, the wrinkled denim button-up that looks criminally good on him, even after days of wear. "I didn't think I'd ever see any of you again." She rubs a thumb across his cheek. "I thought—"

"I know." The tips of his fingers are at her chin, gently pushing upward until she's looking at him again. He exhales deeply through his nose, then gives a single, firm shake of his head. Now that she knows what it looks like—what it physically manifests into—the disappointment he feels in himself is evident. "I made a mistake, Grace. You were honest with me, and I punished you for it. I should've listened. I should've seen how scared you were. I'm sorry I didn't. I'm sorry I walked away from you, and I'm sorry I ever made you doubt—even for a second—that I will *always* come for you."

Grace lets his words sink in deep, lets them overwhelm her senses. For a moment, she can't do anything but attempt to process it all—the hell of the past week, the satisfaction and sweet vindication of seeing her uncle hauled away by the FBI, and now, the man she loves sitting at her bedside making sweet promises that she *knows*, in her heart, he will keep. He's looking at her so intensely, his eyes full of reverence and regret and relief, and she suddenly can't possibly allow even one more second to pass without kissing him, without promising him the exact same thing, but with her lips. Crew's hand lowers to her throat, and he holds her steady as he returns the aching affection, and it's a flurry of tongues and chapped lips and unbound bliss. Grace smiles, then *laughs*, and Crew's arching brow is full of amusement, but he doesn't stop kissing her, and soon enough, she's grinning into his mouth, rejoicing at the present, at the fact that she is a woman kissing the man she loves.

Left undisturbed, they probably could've kept going until they were both breathless and squirming, but not long into their congress, a faint knock sounds from the doorway. Crew breaks from her mouth abruptly, and he's breathing heavily, his eyes screwed tightly shut. For a brief second, Grace ignores their visitor and simply stares at him, that bright, gleeful grin still stretched across her lips. "I love you," she whispers, just for him. He presses his forehead against hers in response, and when his eyes open, they are shiny and wet.

Another knock, and Crew growls. With a frustrated, impatient sigh, he gives Grace a look. "Should've known I wasn't going to be able to keep you to myself for long."

"To hell with that," a voice says from behind him, and the rusty, melodic pitch of it has her eyes widening and her body angling around Crew's giant form to confirm her suspicion. Her *hope*. She finds Forty in the doorway holding a brown paper sack full of wildflowers. His glasses are on top of his head, pushing his silver hair out of his face and revealing swollen eyes and splotchy red cheeks. "Hi, kiddo," he says to Grace, smiling wide. "You had us worried there for a minute." He opens his mouth to continue speaking, but then someone is barreling past him, and he cuts himself off with an *oof* at the collision. And not just one—throngs of men start to pile into Grace's room, all in varying states of dress—and *cleanliness*, it seems, by the mix of odors that follows them in. But as the ranch hands of Halcyon gather around her bed, hair sticking up in all directions, boots halfway on and clothes wrinkled and untucked, Grace is sure she's never seen them look more handsome.

"Hey, Grace," Mikey says, waving excitedly.

"Welcome back. They got you on the good shit, right?" Raymond asks from where he stands next to her IV bag, assessing with pursed lips.

"Grace, did that bastard really make you rock rake by *hand*?" Caleb asks as he pushes his way to the front of the group. He lands at the foot of Grace's bed, leaning his hands onto the metal frame. "They oughta let us all have a go at him before they stick him in a cell."

Grunts of agreement echo around the room.

"Did they have to fuse your finger bones back together?" Harrison asks, staring wide-eyed at her cast.

"Yeah, Grace, is your hand gonna be like, permanently—" Bryan starts, then contorts his hand into a weak imitation of a fist, holding it up for everyone to see.

His head falls forward as Pierce smacks him, then does the same to Harrison. They both grunt and reach back to rub at the spot, indignant and scowling. "Dumbasses. Don't ask shit like that," Pierce scolds. "She's been awake for, like, ten minutes."

A female voice rises above the noise, and a head of blond hair peeks out from behind the sea of unkempt boys. *"Gentlemen."* Grace perks up, looking around the bodies crowded near her bed to find the person attached to that lovely, familiar voice, and her heart squeezes as June makes her way forward. Every head in the room turns to look at her, but June keeps her eyes on Grace. With a sly smile—like a secret shared between just the two of them—she says, "Why don't we all take a step back and give our girl some room?"

Dutifully, the sweet ranch hands of Halcyon obey, each looking a shade sheepish as they all take a literal step back from Grace's bed. June's smile brightens then, and she walks over to the unoccupied side of the bed and sets her hands on her hips. She scans Grace's form, taking an extra second to stare at her cast, and then back up, where her eyes seem to study every inch of Grace's face. After a moment, she sighs loudly and dramatically. "Well, I'll tell you one thing for certain," June laments, popping out one of her hips. "You are in desperate need of a facial. Sun exposure, dust, blood—your skin doesn't know what to do with itself. Good thing I spend most of my paychecks on skin care. And I packed accordingly." June's eyes find Grace's and they soften, along with the hard set of her mouth. Something like sadness etches itself into her golden features. "Figured you weren't keeping up with your routine."

"Without you around to hound me about it?" Grace jokes, smiling weakly.

June huffs. "Typical." She starts to walk away, but not without throwing the last word over her shoulder. "A couple more days of dryness like that and I think your skin might've started falling off in chunks. You're lucky I got here when I did."

She doesn't wait around for Grace's reply, but Grace gives one anyway. She stares at June's back as she hurries out of the room, then scans the faces of all these men she's come to know and love, deep within her soul. They smile at her, and there's so much genuine joy in their eyes that it brings tears to Grace's own. She laughs, a watery, pitiful sound. "I am very lucky," she says, to June, to the guys, but mostly—to herself.

Visiting hours end shortly after the hands visit, and Grace is feeling pampered and loved by the time they walk out of her room, waving their goodbyes and promising their return the next day. A green, gel-like product—aloe and something else she can't remember—is spread evenly over her face, and it has a cooling, relaxing effect that seems to increase the longer she keeps it on. June had given Crew strict instructions on how to remove it once forty-five minutes had passed—a damp, clean washcloth, and slow, *light*, gentle motions. "Don't go reversing all my hard work by scrubbing her face and destroying her skin barrier," June had demanded, and Crew had agreed, then promised, then promised *again* at her behest, though he clearly had no idea what she was talking about.

He follows the directions when the timer on his phone goes off ten minutes later, arched over Grace's bed and balancing himself on one hand while wiping her face clean with the other. He works slowly, methodically, and the cloth's touch against her skin is featherlight. It's nice, calming and comforting, and Grace lets her eyes close as he works. He tilts her chin up to wipe her jawline and any remnants from behind her ears, and then she feels something besides the washcloth brush against her lips. Her eyes open to find Crew close, his lips drawn into a small, only slightly crooked smile. He looks more relaxed than he has since she woke up, and this warms her inside, sparking a flame of something other than joy for their reunion. Grace leans forward, closing the tiny gap between their mouths, and presses her lips to his.

The washcloth falls atop the papery white sheets as both of Crew's hands come up to her cheeks, and Grace can practically *hear* June's reprimand about putting dirty hands on clean skin, but she ignores it completely, caring little about the consequences of him touching her wherever he pleases. They both moan at the contact, and Grace sits up straighter, bringing them closer, and wraps her arms around his neck. She wants his body to be flush with her own, wants him as close as he can physically be. When he breaks away from her to trail hot, messy kisses over her jaw and neck, Grace keens. Practically, she knows it's not a good idea for them to fool around in her hospital bed. She knows it'd probably be ill-advised to engage in any physical activity, but she can't quiet this need. This desperate desire for him, to feel him buried in her again, deep and pulsing and thick. She wants to be painfully *full* of him.

Crew sucks at her earlobe and lets his lips linger at the space between her ear and neck—the spot he knows will make her hips start to involuntarily rock and her breath start to quicken. Deep in the moment, he spends a few long seconds there, drawing those reactions out of her, whimpering slightly when she starts to pant against his temple.

But then he stops abruptly, and his forehead falls to her shoulder. Grace doesn't even try to hold back the *whine* that bubbles up from her chest, and Crew chuckles deeply, picking up his head to look at her. His eyes are glazed over with arousal, and her hindbrain takes that in itself as an invitation to start back up again. She leans forward, but he stops her, smiling sweetly but holding her firmly in place. "Baby, we can't," he says plaintively.

"But—" Grace sputters, frowning. "I want to."

"I do, too," he says, then looks down at the slight bulge in his jeans as if to prove the statement. He gives her a wry smile when he looks back up. "Trust me. But not here. Not with this." He nods to the IV stuck in her inner elbow. "And that." He nudges his chin toward the heart monitor. "Plus," he says, then looks backward toward the half-open door to the room. For a contemplative beat, he just stares in its direction, then exhales. He looks at Grace and says, "My entire family is here." The corner of his mouth lifts up, and he adds, "And you can probably guess how little regard they have for visiting hours."

As if on cue—as if he carries some kind of brotherly homing beacon—the sound of heels clicking against tile starts to make its way to the room. Crew doesn't seem surprised by this coincidence, nor does he turn around when the door swings open and Caia walks in, backward, her arms full of various bags: a chic-looking leather tote; a pink, floral-patterned duffel bag; and a slew of large, overly full H-E-B bags. When Crew doesn't get up to help her, doesn't even *look* at the haul she's lugging into the room, Caia rolls her eyes. "Oh, no, don't worry. I've got it."

Crew hangs his head, then blows a dramatic raspberry before leaning forward to kiss Grace's cheek and then leaving her side to help his sister. He takes the H-E-B bags from Caia and stops on his way to deposit them on the little coffee table when she points at the one in his left hand. "Give Grace that one," she says, then turns to Grace and winks. "The boys helped with it."

Crew sets the others down, opens the one in question, and huffs a laugh. He walks over to Grace and sets it gently on her lap. "Don't go crazy," he says, pushing a strand of hair behind her ear.

Confused, Grace reaches for the bag, and upon seeing what's inside, her eyes go wide with delight. Little Debbie Zebra Cakes. Ho Hos. Every flavor of Skittles you can buy. And best of all, Reese's. Three bright orange king-size packs, and then about thirty of the small, individually wrapped bite-size ones.

"Oh my God," Grace gasps, digging her hand immediately into the sea of goodies. "Chocolate."

Caia off-loads the other bags onto the love seat. She gestures to the duffel bag and says, "I brought you some clothes and shoes." In the middle of tearing open one of the packs of Reese's, Grace pauses, her eyes drifting to the pink bag. It's practically bursting at the seams—all the clothes Grace owns couldn't stuff a bag that much. Probably wouldn't even take up half of it. She stares quizzically at it, then looks back to Caia. The question must be written all over her face, because Caia levels her with a look, and Grace is starting to recognize the expression as her *Here's the deal* look. And whatever follows that look seems to have a way of ending arguments, complaints, and general dissent.

"All right, I *bought* you some clothes. And shoes. And toiletries." She nods toward the remaining grocery bags. "Couldn't have you using that watered-down crap they have here, and God knows the bunkhouse only has two-in-one."

Crew smirks at that and does not deny the truth of it.

Grace's cheeks have begun to bloom with warmth. People buying things for her, things she didn't ask for but desperately needs, isn't something she has much experience with. Most of the generosity she's experienced in her adult life has been with the Caldwells, and it still baffles her how they can be so giving, so welcoming. So genuinely concerned for her well-being, as though it's an instinct rather than a task.

An evasive, rejecting response would be the natural way for Grace to respond, but she knows Caia will hear no protests, so she smiles and says, "That was so kind of you, Caia. Thank you." It rings true and feels right coming out of her mouth, but it's still a little wobbly, like a colt trying to find its footing.

"Not at all. It was fun," Caia volleys back with a wave of her hand, and the shine from her dark blue nail polish reflects beneath the hospital's fluorescent bulbs. "I'm always happy to facilitate a makeover. Although—" She stares at the large windowsill, big enough for multiple people to sit on, or, in this case, where Grace's new skin care products are, neatly organized and mostly unopened. "It does look like someone might have beaten me to the punch."

"June," Grace supplies, smiling down at the washcloth on the overbed table covered in mint-green goop. "She insisted I do something about the state of my . . ." Grace waves an encompassing hand around her face. "My skin, apparently, did not agree with the conditions at Braxton."

Caia barks out a laugh and says, "Yeah, it was a real fucking wellness spa, that place. Years of dust, giant piles of exotic animal shit, and greasy, unshowered delinquents. You're telling me you *didn't* feel pampered?"

"I'd probably give it a negative star on Yelp," Grace says, unwrapping a Reese's and shoving it whole into her mouth. "If that's even a thing," she murmurs around the chocolate. Her gaze seeks Crew like a well-honed reflex, as if her eyes have gone too long without looking at him. When she finds him sitting on one of the armrests of the love seat, he's smiling at her softly, his eyes sparkling with quiet affection. Even with her mouth stuffed full of candy and not a care in the world for whatever remnants of it might be on her lips, he looks at her like there's nothing he adores more in the world. Even in this baggy hospital gown, with her hair an oily mess and her skin still ravaged from days spent unprotected in the sun, she is still perfect, exactly as she is. Perfect to him—perfect *for* him.

Unaware of the loaded look being shared between the two of them, Caia claps her hands together and says, "I'm sorry you have to stay overnight. That bed looks like it's stuffed with packing peanuts. But I figured, if you want . . ." Caia smiles, and for a brief moment, she almost seems nervous. It's a strange but endearing look on her, one that has Grace leaning forward, interest piqued. "Maybe I can come back in the morning and help you pick out an outfit. Not that it really matters—I know you're just going home. But, you know." She shrugs, that Caldwell confidence already back in full swing. "Might as well look cute doing it."

Grace grins, touched by the sentiment and warmed by the idea of Caia wanting to help.

"Plus"—Caia throws her hands up—"if my mother sees you in those threadbare Levi's you came in with, she might disown me for not *properly* initiating you into the ranks of Caldwell women," she finishes matter-of-factly, a playfully fearful look in her eyes.

But Grace doesn't think it's funny—nor does she afford the proper attention to Caia calling her a *Caldwell woman*—she's too caught up in the casualness of the statement, like seeing Renata is something she's going to do as soon as the next morning. Her eyes dart to Crew, whose expression has turned slightly more serious.

Caia looks between them, her brow furrowing. "What?"

Tears well in Grace's eyes as she asks, "She's all right? She's—awake and talking?"

In a flash, Caia is standing at her brother's side and whacking him in the bicep with the back of her hand. "You haven't told her?"

"It's been a chaotic few hours," he says evenly, catching Caia's hand when she tries to hit his other arm. He shoves it until it is stiff at her side and says, "I was going to tell her once things had calmed down a bit."

Grace can't see Caia's face, but she knows the glare that Crew is receiving right now, especially considering the challenging look he gives in return. Eventually, Caia relents, scoffing and turning around to look at Grace. "She's okay, honey." She takes a few long strides toward Grace's bed, and when she's close enough, she reaches down to place her hand over Grace's. Her expression is sincere and kind, only the slightest hint of mischief in that ghost of a smile on her lips. "Who do you think sent me out on the shopping spree?"

CHAPTER 31

For the second time in her life, Grace nervously consents to being the subject of a makeover. June joins Caia in the endeavor, taking on the responsibility of Grace's morning skin care and makeup. "Nothing crazy," Grace says, sitting on the edge of the bed as June presses a pink sponge repeatedly into her cheeks. When June doesn't reply save for a quick roll of her eyes, Grace insists. "June."

The sponge stills, and June rises to her full height and places her hands on top of Grace's shoulders. "Relax," she says, not unkindly. "I'm just gonna wake up your face a little, and color-correct the sunburn."

While she works diligently on that task, Caia strategically lays out the clothes she bought, ranging from jewel-toned athletic wear to dresses short enough that Grace is sure they wouldn't cover her entire backside. A pair of jeans lies buried somewhere in the mix, and Grace eyes them multiple times as Caia taps her chin in contemplation, murmuring to herself as she mixes and matches. She shows Grace multiple combos as options, then finally concedes with a scoff when Grace's eyes keep drifting to the jeans. "Fine," she sighs. "But I'm picking the top." She points at Grace with a firm index finger. "No arguments."

Crew is off somewhere with Cooper; he'd been shooed out of the room as soon as the two women had arrived. Grace wonders what he's doing at this very moment—almost laughs at herself for how pathetic it is that she actually *misses* him, even though she was folded up snugly in his arms less than an hour ago. She thinks about the lingering kiss he'd given her before leaving the room, the heated stare they shared for a long moment before Caia insisted he get lost. The message had been clear even without a single word being uttered: *We'll continue this later.* She'd nodded and let him go with only a tiny pout, but frankly, Grace is wildly impatient to get to *later*. She's impatient to touch him, to get lost in his kiss without the worry of being interrupted. She's impatient to feel the weight of him pressing down onto her, to look up and not be able to see anything beyond his breadth. Her mountain of a man. Her beautiful, freckled sky.

It takes nearly an hour before Caia and June are satisfied with the work they've done. They're careful with her casted hand as they help her into her top, a black ribbed tank that hugs her body and somehow accentuates her nonexistent cleavage. They also help her into a pair of black Ariats, shiny and new and stiff as all hell, but *hers*. "There's more where these came from," Caia says as she grunts and shoves one until Grace's foot is settled within. "I figured you needed a new brown pair, too. But then the saleslady started bringing out all kinds of pretty colors and patterns and I just couldn't resist."

Grace winces as the back of the boot scrapes her heel, then sighs once both of her feet are secured. They're comfortable even in their newness, and she can't deny that they look good. They probably cost more than she's spent on boots in a decade, but Grace tries not to think about that, especially considering

Caia's implication that she purchased *multiple* pairs. She stands from the bed once the boots are fully on and looks down at her body, taking in the way the clothes fit, the paint on her chewed-down nails, the little touches of turquoise and silver from the necklace and bracelet Caia had picked out for her. "We'll ease you into the jewelry," she'd said as she strung the silver chain with a small turquoise pendant around Grace's neck.

At the fifty-eight-minute mark since they walked in and took over, someone knocks on the door. Caia, who had told Crew and Cooper to find something else to do for an hour, shakes her head as she opens it, knowing exactly who is waiting on the other side. She folds her arms over her chest and says to Crew, "You are ridiculous. Being in love makes you ridiculous."

Grace can't see them from where she stands in the room while June fusses with her hair one last time, but she can hear his rumbling "Move, please. I want to make sure you didn't make over my girlfriend the way you used to do with your Barbie dolls."

"Oh God," Cooper exclaims. "I forgot about those. You were demented. Didn't you dye one of them green with food coloring?"

"She was supposed to be an alien!" Caia shouts, then, a little quieter and calmer, "I told you an hour. We still have two minutes—"

Caia's squeal is loud, part holler and part laughter, and Grace's face splits into a grin as she watches Crew lift his sister up by her biceps and physically move her out of the doorway. He walks in once she's steady on her feet and muttering something about him being a total brute, and his determined steps bring him right toward Grace, but as soon as his eyes land on her, he stops in his tracks. "Oh," he blurts, his lips parting.

"Yeah, *oh*. And no green food coloring in sight," Caia says, throwing her hands up. "Now apologize."

Crew doesn't look away from Grace, but he clamps his lips together and lets out a long, shuddering breath through his nostrils. He takes a step closer, leans his face down until it's only an inch from hers, but then stops himself. "I'm sorry," he says, still looking her straight in the eye. "Leave now."

Something that sounds a lot like the words *lovesick puppy* comes from Caia and Cooper's general direction, but Grace stops paying attention to whatever is happening around them. Under the intensity of Crew's gaze, she can't think about anything else. Soon, they're alone, June having joined the vacating siblings, and the door has barely clicked shut when Crew is backing Grace up against the nearest wall and slotting his mouth over hers. Delicious, intoxicating heat unfurls deep in her belly as his tongue starts to caress her own. His urgency, his need—it's obvious in the way he's holding her, keeping her in place as he attacks her mouth, the little groans echoing from his throat with every swipe of his tongue against hers. He breaks away eventually when they're both desperate for air, and he's gasping as his forehead rests against hers. When his breathing has slowed to a seminormal pace, he blinks up at her. "I'm sorry—you just—you look so beautiful."

Grace chuckles. "It's just jeans and a tank top. And a little bit of makeup."

He shakes his head, a small, closed-lip but adorable smile on his lips. "No, it's more than that. You look—alive. Healthy." He kisses the apple of her cheek, letting his lips linger there. In a voice no louder than a whisper, he says, "Glowing."

Grace kisses him softly in thanks. "Your sister will be happy to hear your stellar review. I wasn't—" She feels momentarily self-conscious, her eyes falling downward as she finishes her thought. "I didn't quite understand why they were doing all of this. It seemed . . . odd. To put so much effort into how I look, after everything that's happened. I'm still not entirely sure."

"They love you," Crew replies. He brushes his hand over her face, letting it sweep into her hair. She's noticed that he does it often, even when there isn't hair to push out of her face. Something about the motion seems to relax him, and Grace leans into his palm, pushing into it like a needy house cat.

A little distracted by his touch, Grace murmurs, "That seems unlikely. June, *maybe*, but she'd never admit to it." Crew's blunt nails scratch her scalp and Grace's eyes close. Everything he does—every way he touches her—sets her skin aflame. At this point, he could shake her hand and she'd be revved up and ready for him within seconds. "But Caia . . . she's only met me twice."

Crew kisses her, and Grace moans into his mouth. It's short-lived, and she gives a slight pout when he pulls away, smirking. "Caia loves *me*," he says, "and I love you. So, yeah. Maybe she doesn't *know you* know you, but she knows enough. And she enjoys taking care of the people she loves."

"Runs in the family, I guess," Grace says, reaching up to hold his face with her good hand. His unshaven cheek scratches against her palm, and upon closer inspection, she notices little specks of gray sprinkled throughout the dark brown. The sight of it *does* something to her. Images of him with more gray than brown flash through her mind, a silver head of hair to match. The smile lines at his eyes and cheeks—the ones she so adores right now—growing deeper and more beautiful with every passing year. She's suddenly overwhelmed with the desire to be at Crew's side for all of it—to witness the progression of him going from raven black to gray, to see his eyes darkening with age, the golden-hued amber of his irises shifting into something even more depthless, more mesmerizing, somehow.

He must see something in her face, because he lets out a sharp exhale and takes a step away from her. "We need to get out of here," he proclaims, looking at her with the same intensity she must be giving to him. "I can't keep ravishing you in this hospital room." Hastily, he gathers her bags and slings them over his shoulder, reaching out his free hand to grab hers. He ignores his sister's under-breath comment about *taking his sweet time* and walks past them, leading Grace to the elevator, where they'll go up two floors to get to Renata's room.

If Grace thought her room was luxurious, it's nothing compared to the *suite* Renata's in. It looks more like a penthouse apartment than a hospital room. Bouquets of roses, sunflowers, hydrangeas, tulips, and lilies cover every flat surface, and there are *many* flat surfaces in the palatial space. The antiseptic, default hospital smell is completely covered by the sea of flowers; a stranger could take two steps into this room and know immediately that Renata is beloved. The sight of it all makes Grace's heart ache—not just for the loveliness, but for the guilt she feels for nearly robbing the world of such an extraordinary person.

The entire elevator ride and down the long stretch of hallway through the hospital wing, Grace had wrestled with the idea of facing Renata, of seeing her laid up in a hospital bed because of an evil man's machinations—and Grace's abetment. This generous, warmhearted woman who had been nothing but kind and open to Grace since she walked into Murphy's all those weeks ago—she didn't deserve this. She didn't deserve to be caught up in the chaos and corruption of Grace's past. Braxton may be taped off and shut down, Bellamy may be spending the rest of his life in prison, and Grace may have been de facto acquitted of the horrid act she'd committed as a teenager, but there is no absolution to be had for this—for not speaking up, for being a coward when it mattered most. If there's any sane, logical bone in Renata Caldwell's body, she should scorn Grace and send her packing, should demand she get as far away from her son, her family, and her ranch as she possibly can.

But that's not what happens.

Not even close.

Instead, the hospital bed comes into view—adorned in eggwhite silk sheets, definitely *not* the standard-issue papery ones—and Crew and Grace find Renata and Clint bent over a folded newspaper with pens in hand. Renata looks comfortable in the bed, her back cushioned by two giant, plush pillows—also covered in silk—and Clint's right next to her, one leg spread out and flush with hers, the other hanging off the bed to keep him steady. They're having a sort of sword fight with the pens, arguing over the accuracy of an answer for what looks like a crossword puzzle. From where Grace stands, she can see there are lines drawn through some of the words already printed on the page, with the seemingly *correct* word written above.

"If you don't stop shoving my hand away, I'm going to stab you with this pen. Paradigm has a *G* in it. It's eight letters, not nine. And look!" Renata taps the puzzle adamantly with the tip of her pen. "The first letter is an *A*. It's absolutely, one hundred percent *archetype*."

"You think because you read all those fancy books that you're so much smarter than me, don't you?" Clint says, bemusedly shaking his head. "I'll tell you what, though—I've got you beat when it comes to street smarts."

"I'll tell *you* the only thing you've got me beat with," she counters, then taps the pen against his temple lightly. "Delusion."

Clint's mouth drops open dramatically. "Exc—"

He doesn't get a chance to fully articulate his indignation, because Renata spots Grace and Crew, who have been silently observing the loving spat. Her face immediately lights up, and the smile that blooms on her lips is bright and wide and quick. She looks between the both of them quickly and says, "*There* you are. Good God, I was starting to wonder if you'd just completely forgotten about me."

"Not possible," Crew says, and gives Grace's hand a comforting squeeze. "How're you feeling this morning?"

Renata shrugs. "Fine. The same. Ready to be out of here, but this numbnuts"—she tilts her head in Clint's direction—"and my doctor have decided to team up and overrule me at any chance they get." She throws her hands up with a quick roll of her eyes, only slightly exasperated. "So, here we are."

"Tuesday will be here before you know it," Crew says evenly, knowing he can't show too much vehemence or support for his father, or his mother will accuse him of *also* siding with the enemy. "You look good. Even better than yesterday."

Grace has no frame of reference, but Renata *does* look good—she may possibly be the most glamorous person who has ever been in a hospital, with her hair tucked back with a long gold pin, a pink terry cloth robe, and light makeup that doesn't entirely cover up the bruising on her face but does mute it substantially, drawing the focus to her eyes, which are as vibrantly blue and expressive as ever. Upon closer inspection, Grace sees the cast on her left leg, spanning from her upper thigh to just above her foot. Her left arm is also in a sling that's partially covered by the robe, and by the way she shifts in the bed, with less swiftness and ease than usual, Grace figures there are probably many other healing injuries that she can't see. The thought of them all, this never-ending list of hurt, makes her feel sick to her stomach.

"You're a terrible liar, son," Renata says, waving a dismissive hand in his direction. Her gaze drifts to Grace, and her smile softens. "You, on the other hand, my darling." She looks her up and down, the smile growing into something knowing, slightly mischievous. "I understand my daughter bullied you into this, but I've got to say, Grace—you look lovely."

Maybe it's the words, so genuine and warm and honest, or the way Renata's looking at her like she's *proud* and happy to see her, or maybe it's the whirlwind of trauma and emotion that has coursed through Grace's body over the past week, but when Renata smiles at her with all the love in the world and tells her she looks lovely, Grace bursts into tears.

Crew immediately turns to face her, grabbing her by the shoulders to turn her to him, but Renata's voice cuts in, stopping him.

"Honey," she says gently, reaching out to touch Clint's arm. "Son." She looks to Crew, and there's no confusion on her face—the two men both look slightly terrified by the sudden turn of events, but Renata is unfazed. She looks as confident and clearheaded as she always does. Even while laid up in a hospital bed with two limbs cast in plaster, she's ready to launch into action in a split second. "Why don't y'all run down to the cafeteria and grab some coffee? And get me a muffin. Blueberry or chocolate chip—none of the bran crap."

The implication takes a moment to set in for Crew and his father, but once it does, Clint is standing and nodding, making his way to the door. Crew lingers for a moment, looking between Grace and Renata, still holding on to Grace's shoulders. His mother gives him a reassuring nod, and Crew relents, dropping a kiss to Grace's forehead before joining his father. The door clicks shut quietly, and the two women are left alone—hot, relentless tears still streaming down Grace's cheeks.

"Come," Renata says, scooting herself to one side of the bed—as much as she can with one leg immobile—and then patting the cleared space. "Sit with me for a minute."

Grace does, lowering herself carefully and slowly onto the bed, being mindful not to jostle anything. The material of her jeans is almost slippery against the sheets; she can feel herself starting to slide down until she digs her bootheels into the tile floor. Wiping her cheeks with the back of her hand, Grace chuckles, ever unsure and awkward in highly emotional moments like this. "I'm sorry," she says, glancing at Renata, who is even-keeled and patient, leaning into her giant, soft pillows.

Renata's tone is light when she asks, "What're you sorry for, Grace?"

The two women hold each other's eyes for a moment. In Renata's deep brown irises, Grace can see many things. Among them: an age-ripened, wide-open honesty, a wholehearted generosity, and a pure, soulful kindness. The combination is comforting in ways Grace has rarely experienced; Renata is the kind of person who, just by existing in someone's orbit, makes the burden of living seem lighter. She is restorative and warm—her very presence a balm to even the most pointed anxiety. And because of that, even with the guilt and fear and overwhelming sorrow festering in her gut, Grace feels a sense of ease sitting next to her. She knows what Renata's really asking, and she also knows that Renata deserves her truest answer. There is, perhaps, no one in the world who deserves it more.

"I'm sorry I wasn't honest with you when I should've been," Grace says, as evenly as she can manage. She maintains eye contact as she speaks, though it pains her not to let her eyes drift to the floor. Her instinct is deference, but she knows Renata wants her to face this with her chin high, not bowing in submission. "I'm sorry I didn't speak up. I was afraid of so many things. I've spent so much of my life afraid." The fingers of Grace's good hand begin to tremble, and she curls them into a stubborn fist. "Even after you offered me the job, I still had this voice in my head telling me it was all temporary. A very specific voice," Grace muses, nostrils flaring. "It was stupid, impulsive, *cowardly*—I thought telling you the truth would mean I'd have to leave Halcyon. So, I didn't, because I didn't want to leave. After everything that happened, I couldn't imagine anything worse. And I didn't think he'd actually . . ." She trails off, finally letting her eyes drop. Tears are welling in them once more, but this time, they aren't tears of sadness or guilt—they're tears of anger.

"It's ridiculous, isn't it?" Grace throws her hands up, edging closer to full-on hysteria. "I kept quiet because I didn't want to leave, and because I didn't think you or anyone would be in any real danger, and both of those things ended up happening anyway. I shouldn't have called his bluff. I should've known he would do whatever he could to get back at me for telling you about the scams." A sob wracks her body, and she hunches forward, resting her face in her palm. "Halcyon was like a dream to me. More than a ranch, more than a paycheck and place to stay." She shakes her head against her hand, voice watery and thick. "Crew, the hands, you and Clint and Cooper." She sits up, and she can feel the swelling beneath her eyes growing worse. She can barely see Renata through the haze of her tears, but she recognizes that look of patience, of acceptance. It makes her want to cry harder. "Halcyon—you all—felt like home. You felt like *mine*. I've never known that feeling before."

It's quiet between them for a beat, save for Grace's sniffles, and then she feels a hand cover hers and squeeze. She blinks away a few more tears, her vision clearing enough to see Renata opening her mouth to speak. "Grace, have I ever told you about the conversation I had with Maryann? I know when we first met, I told you she'd mentioned a horse trainer in need of a job. But have I ever actually told you what she said?"

Grace shakes her head.

Renata leans farther into her pillows, pulling Grace's hand into her lap, which brings her slightly farther down the bed, and brings them closer. At this distance, Grace can smell the subtle hints of cherry, rose, and sandalwood in Renata's perfume, masked slightly by the hundreds of flowers surrounding them, but still there. Familiar and warm and perfectly *her*. "You know, I hadn't talked to her in years. We had a little spat when she left Halcyon—I couldn't understand why she wanted to leave after almost a decade with us, but she was adamant. There was *something* she needed to tend to out in Everlake County, wherever the hell that was. Ronnie was distraught to lose her—she'd learned everything she knew from Maryann. Anyway, I learned a few years later that she'd taken a job at Braxton, and I was beside myself. *That* place? Over Halcyon? I couldn't believe it. I called her up that same day and gave her a piece of my mind—

I was a bit hot under the collar back then—and she just took it. Didn't argue with me, didn't deny anything. Once I was all red-faced and done with my rant, she very calmly and patiently told me the reason she left. And wouldn't you know it—it was for a *man*."

At this, Grace smiles. She tries to picture Renata and Maryann in their thirties, bickering in the Halcyon kitchen. It's difficult to turn back the clock and imagine them younger, softer, more impulsive; she's only ever known them as two formidable women who seem to have the answer to every question.

"Except it wasn't that simple. Nothing ever is," Renata continues, and then she leans forward slightly, squeezing Grace's hand again. "The man's name was Hal, and he was some kinda horse-training magician. I don't know the specifics, but they'd apparently had an ongoing thing, hot and heavy here and there, but nothing serious ever came of it. Cowboys and all that," Renata says, only slightly derisively. "But then, out of the blue, he called up Maryann and asked her to come to Braxton. When she told me that, I gave her a whole rash of shit for it. I couldn't *believe* she'd just uproot her entire life and go to live on that backwater ranch for some *guy* who was never going to commit to her. And that's when she said—after calling me an impatient, interrupting bitch—that Hal had told her about a teenage girl who'd started living at Braxton." The smile on Grace's face drops off in an instant, and her heart seizes in her chest. Renata lets the statement rest for a moment and then continues. "*A spindly little thing that life had chewed up and spit out* were his exact words, if I recall correctly. The niece of the proprietor, but that kind of family tie didn't mean much. Hal told Maryann he'd gotten Whitlock's permission to take the girl under his wing, but he didn't know his ass from his elbow when it came to teenage girls, and she was practically mute for the first two months. So, he asked if Maryann would come to Braxton. To be with him, for them to be together in the same place, and to help with the girl. *Grace*."

The knot that's formed in Grace's stomach while listening to the story tightens at the sound of her name. Shock, disbelief, awe—all of it courses through her like a tidal wave. That someone had been looking out for her back then, had been concerned enough to call on an old friend for help—Grace is helpless but to give in to the new batch of tears that fall down her cheeks. Hal, grumpy, intelligent, forgiving, cigar-stenched Hal. Her teacher, her savior.

"I didn't know," Grace says, though it's more of a blubber than a statement. "She—they never told me."

"I know they didn't. And the only reason I'm telling you now is because you need to understand something. You deserved to have people in your corner, Grace—back then, and right now. You deserve love, safety, and care. You deserve a place to call home, just as much as anyone else. *More*, really."

It still doesn't quite make sense, doesn't quite penetrate, even if Grace wants it to. Even if *all* she wants is to accept Renata's words as law, to go back to Halcyon and call it her own. It isn't as simple as flipping a switch and rewriting an entire lifetime of unease. She wishes it were—wishes she could close the book on that darkness once and for all.

Renata's hand leaves hers and reaches upward, landing gently on Grace's cheek. She leans in, and she must sense Grace's stubborn hesitation, because she waits for Grace to look her in the eye before she continues. Her tone at once firm and warm, inarguable and soft. "You've become so much lighter since I met you, and that kind of thing is infectious. You brought my son back to life with that light, and I'm thankful to you for that."

Grace notices a shine in Renata's eyes and leans her cheek lightly into her palm.

"Maybe this will be hard for you to hear, and even harder for you to accept, but I'm going to say it to you anyway: If it's forgiveness that you need to come home, you have it. A million times over. You've always had it. But more importantly, I need you to understand something," Renata says, and Grace simply listens, caught up in a whirlwind of unfathomable emotion.

"Halcyon *is* your home, Grace. Maybe you don't believe that right now, and you don't have to. But know that it's the truth. Halcyon is your home, and we are your family."

Without another word, Renata pulls Grace forward and wraps her tightly in her arms. Grace goes willingly, carefully, and lets Renata cradle her. She starts to cry once again—if she ever even stopped—and tries harder than she's ever tried in her life to let the words be true. To let her heart take them in, to let her brain believe them. It doesn't happen instantly, but there's an unexpected little give—a flicker of flexibility in those carefully crafted, steel-reinforced walls.

And while in this exact moment she can't fully accept the fact that she's found a place where she belongs, a person to share her life with, and a family that loves her, *wants* her, and will protect her—she knows now that one day, sooner rather than later, she finally will.

CHAPTER 32

Time is a fickle, funny thing. Minutes can stretch into eternities; days can pass in the blink of an eye. Time follows no rulebook. Its moods are arbitrary and unpredictable. For instance, the first time Grace sat in the passenger seat of this truck, the drive to Halcyon seemed to take days and not the four hours she knew it to be. The empty fields surrounding the two-lane highway had been like endless oceans of grass and wheat and dirt, and it seemed to matter little that the wheels were spinning and the engine was propelling them forward—she'd felt suspended in time, fated to never arrive at her destination. Now, as she sits in that very same spot, beside that very same man, the truck seems to devour the miles instead of nipping at them crumb by crumb.

And it's funny and fickle that Crew—who'd given her so little in their first encounter, who'd hardly smiled and spent more time picking sunflower seeds out of his teeth than he did talking to her—is now the furthest thing from a stranger. It doesn't make sense, and maybe it never will, but it feels like she's known Crew her entire life. Like even before they were physically in the same place, seeing each other for the very first time, some part of her always knew him. The way he made her body, her mind, her heart come alive—there was no other explanation for that kind of thing. Maybe they didn't know each other back then, but they were never truly strangers.

They pull in through the north entrance right after five, and though it's probably just her brain playing tricks on her, Grace swears everything looks brighter as they roll down the gravel road. The grassy fields are more vibrant, the wildflowers are oversaturated and taller than when she left. Crew's hand on her thigh squeezes gently, and she looks over to find him with a contented little half smile on his lips. Grace grins, covering his hand with her own. "What?"

"Your eyes are lighting up," he says, glancing at her. "The same way they did when I first drove you down this road."

She stares at him, and as soon as he's pulled the truck over to the right of the house to join the line of identical F-350s and put it in park, Grace unbuckles her seat belt and stretches over the center console to press a kiss to his cheek. Crew turns and catches her mouth, chuckling into her lips. "I love it here," Grace says in answer, stroking his coarse facial hair with her fingertips. "I always have."

They share a long, intense look, and then the sound of a door swinging open pulls their attention away from each other. Crew looks up into the rearview mirror and hums—the sound landing somewhere between annoyed and unsurprised—as he shuts off the engine. He looks back to Grace, then to the passenger window. "Incoming."

Grace turns just as Caia appears, mouth gaping in excitement. When Caia tries to yank open the passenger door and finds it locked, her expression tempers, and her eyes dart to her brother. "Unlock it," she says, voice muffled by the thick glass window. For the next twenty seconds, Crew decides to be a little shit and unlocks the door, only to quickly relock it as soon as Caia pulls on the handle. She pulls and sighs, pulls and sighs, and eventually smacks the truck with her hand. "You're such a dick," she huffs, then turns and walks away.

Grace looks over to Crew to find him with a shit-eating boyish grin, and she rolls her eyes before opening the door herself and climbing out of the cab.

Cooper sits on one of the rocking chairs that line the wraparound porch, and he waves excitedly when Grace comes into view. "You're home," he calls out, and Grace's heart clenches in her chest. How easy those two words seemed to be coming out of his mouth—she wonders if he has any idea, any inkling at all, that they mean everything to her.

The smell of garlic and tomato and basil hits Grace's nose as she approaches the house, Crew following close behind with their bags slung over his shoulders. She inhales deeply, already transfixed by whatever beautiful creation is being cooked up in the kitchen, and Cooper chuckles when he notices. "You're just in time for Ronnie's lasagna," he says, wiggling his eyebrows.

"It smells incredible," Grace says.

"It *is* incredible," Caia says, hoisting herself up onto the porch railing. Her legs swing back and forth as she surveys Grace, then gives an approving nod. With a wink to Grace, she says, "Glad to see you didn't mess up our masterpiece too much."

"Your mom might have helped me clean up some of the mascara that came off while I was crying," Grace says a little sheepishly.

Caia nods. "Of course she did."

Crew sets their bags down near the top of the stairs and stretches his arms out and up, then leans over to do the same for his back. He grunts as various joints in his body click when he moves, sounding very much like a man far older than thirty. When he's sufficiently stretched, he looks around, then at his sister, his eyes narrowing. "Where is—"

Like something out of a sitcom, the door swings open, and Crew looks over and nods in a *There you are* kind of gesture. A man Grace somewhat recognizes but has never met walks out of the house, hitting the wood slats of the porch like he's punching each one of them with his heavy bootheels. Grace's eyes trail downward to find black ostrich Luccheses, shiny enough to see her own reflection, and she knows that pair must've cost him a good ten grand, if not more, and that's just what's on his feet. The rest of him is equally sharply dressed—and by the looks of his sparkly clean nails, his effortlessly coiffed hair, and his precisely trimmed beard, he hasn't worked a day on this ranch or any other in years. Maybe ever.

The man walks right up to Grace and smiles, and it's undeniably a movie star kind of smile—blindingly white, perfectly straight teeth. Behind her, she hears Caia groan. He doesn't spare her a glance and instead keeps his eyes locked on Grace as he holds out a hand.

"You must be Grace," he says, and his shake is firm when Grace gives him her good hand in return. "Easton Beckett. It's a pleasure. I've heard a lot about you. It's not every day our little Crew-bear falls in love," he says with a wink.

Grace's lips part, and she can't help it—she turns to look at Crew over her shoulder, eyebrows hiking toward her hairline. "Crew-bear?"

The look Crew gives Easton in response is nothing less than scathing.

"You know," Easton continues. "Like Pooh Bear. His mom used to call him that because he'd run around the house without any pants on."

"All right, East," Crew warns, and while his intimidating foreman voice may work on most, it seems to be completely lost on Easton, whose smile remains wide and relentless, like he's just getting started.

"It's really great to meet you, Easton," Grace says, turning back to him. "I've heard a lot about you, too."

"Oh?" He straightens a little, putting a hand to his heart. "I hope only lovely, kind, *true* things."

Caia deadpans, "Well, that would be rather difficult, wouldn't it?" Then she hops off the rail and walks over to Grace. With Caia shoulder to shoulder with Easton, it occurs to Grace that they make a really, kind of ridiculously attractive couple. But from the face Caia's making, and the way said face seems to turn even *more* unpleasant the closer she gets to him, perhaps they're not . . . like that. If anything, they look like two equal forces that are actively *repelling* each other. Caia folds her arms firmly over her chest and looks at Grace, and only Grace, as she says, "You don't need to butter him up. His ego is already the biggest thing about him."

Easton barks out a laugh, then throws an arm around Caia's neck. *"Spitfire,"* he drawls, the word sounding well-worn and familiar on his tongue. He folds himself over slightly to catch her eye and says, "Don't talk about me like that when I'm standing right here. You're gonna make me blush."

Caia rolls her eyes and pushes him off, taking a large step to her left and leaving a wide gap between them. "Please," she hisses. The pure, unadulterated disgust on her face shifts into something much kinder and softer when she looks at Grace and says, "Grace, let's get away from all this testosterone and go wash up."

"Actually," Crew cuts in, and he's suddenly at Grace's side, and his strong, comforting hand finds the small of her back. "I want to show Grace something before dinner. Can y'all let Ronnie know we'll be a few minutes?"

Caia looks up at her brother, stares for a moment, and then a realization seems to kick in, because a smile folds into her lips and she starts nodding, more enthusiastic than Grace has ever seen her. "Right! Yes," she says, shooing them away with two hands. "Go. We'll keep Ronnie at bay."

Crew slips his hand into Grace's, their fingers interlocking. He looks down at her and smiles, nodding in the direction of the stables. "Come on."

Hand in hand, they walk under a sky that is cloudless and the most perfect shade of evening blue, stretching out over the ranch like a giant azure tent. The smell of freshly mowed grass mixes with the familiar scents of horses, and Grace feels tears welling in her eyes as they approach the stables. It doesn't seem real yet, that she's here, she's back. She's holding hands with Crew, and she's about to see the horses—and *her* horse—for the first time in what feels like years. She wonders if Waylon's missed her, if he's even noticed she's been gone, or if he's been spending all his time following Duke around like a lost puppy.

It seems the answer is a little bit of both, if the whicker Waylon lets out upon setting eyes on her is any indication. All the way at the opposite side of the ring, he stands—unsurprisingly—next to Duke, but as soon as he spots Grace, he's trotting over, vocalizing more and louder with each step. He seems to have a *lot* to say about her absence, and Grace laughs as he comes to stand right in front of her, a tear slipping down her cheek.

"I missed you, too," she says, petting his nose. "There must've been someone else around to give you carrots, though."

Waylon disagrees, or, at least, he must not think he's been given *enough* carrots, because he snorts and shakes his head.

"Dramatic," she says, then presses her forehead against his muzzle and closes her eyes. "I promise to make it up to you. A million carrots are in your future. Maybe some apples and bananas, too, if you're not difficult."

Another snuffle, a tentative agreement.

Crew chuckles from where he stands, watching them, and Grace keeps her face connected to Waylon as she turns to look at him. "Don't get me wrong," she says, "I love this horse more than I love most people. But I think we could've waited for this until after lasagna."

A slow, easy smile spreads on his lips, and he holds out his hand. "This—*He* wasn't what I wanted to show you."

Somehow, like the incorrigible animal that he is, Waylon seems to understand Crew's statement and lets out a grunt to tell them he does not appreciate it.

They both smile at him as Grace takes Crew's hand and he leads her to the other end of the pasture where the rest of the horses are grazing. She glances up at Crew as they walk, still unsure where he's leading her, but he keeps his eyes fixed ahead, that smile still present on his lips.

"What are you up to?" Grace asks affectionately.

He glances downward, and her belly swoops at the look he gives her. How one look can contain so much love, admiration, and devotion will never fail to amaze her. Grace bites her lip, entranced, and then she has to force her gaze away from Crew to keep from tearing up yet again, but any effort she's making to not cry goes completely to hell as they approach the back corner of the pasture.

Grace stops in her tracks, frozen. Every particle of air leaves her body in a stuttering exhale, and her legs instantly feel like they're made of Jell-O.

She looks up at Crew, not fully believing what she's seeing. The look on his face, that smile spreading into a grin—confirms it.

She looks back to the pasture as tears start to fall in earnest. Because standing at the back fence, eyes fixed on the western sky, is Vesta.

Grace is overcome. She can't move—can't go to her. She can only stare at Vesta's majesty, the beauty so uniquely hers that Grace had been sure she'd never again witness. Her stomach is tied up in a thousand knots as she utters, *"Crew."* It's hardly intelligible through the sobs that are building in her throat. "How?"

"I made some calls," he says, squeezing her hand. "My dad and Forty helped, too. Turns out she wasn't far away, and the ranch she was at wasn't a bad place, either. They were taking good care of her."

Grace cries then, lets a sob free in lieu of thanking him, but she knows he'll understand. He'll understand that she'll never be able to put into words how grateful she is not only to have Vesta here, safe, but to also know that she wasn't suffering or being mistreated in the place she'd ended up. A weight Grace hadn't realized had settled onto her shoulders lifts, and she is immediately lighter. She floats on air as she walks into Crew's arms, sobbing into the material of his shirt.

"But we had to go get her," he says, resting his lips against the top of her head. "She needed to come home."

Grace wraps her arms around him, gripping him as tightly as she can with the constraints of her cast. Vesta's sweet, familiar whinny sounds from behind her, and through her sobs, Grace laughs. A broken, watery sound made of pure, unencumbered happiness. She picks up her head, cranes her neck to look at Crew, and finds his eyes wet and his cheeks slightly splotchy.

For so long, Grace's life had been devoid of hope. She used to think about the future and feel only dread; she used to wonder if this was it for her, if despair was simply her lot in life, predestined and unchangeable.

But as she holds on tight to Crew and looks into his eyes, she sees all the love and reverence he carries for her. She listens to the sound of her horse's happy nicker in the distance, and she knows something else to be true. She digs her heels into Halcyon dirt and knows, deep in her soul, that she'd endure every heartbreak, every bruise, every hateful sneer in her direction all over again. Because all those terrible, hopeless roads were leading her in one direction.

Home.

ACKNOWLEDGMENTS

Writing this book, my first novel, has been such a beautiful and challenging process. There have been so many ups and downs, late nights, and early mornings. No one in my life was closer to me in all those moments—good, wonderful, horrible, tearful, joyful—than my mom. Mom, I dedicated this book to you for countless reasons, but particularly because you were by my side for every single step of this journey. Every email, every phone call, every chapter, every rambling brainstorming session where I needed to get out of a corner I'd written myself into—you were there. You're always my first phone call when something good or bad happens in my life; you're always the first person I want to make proud. I love you. Here's to a hundred more journeys just like this one.

My friends are the lifeblood of my existence. Over the past year, I've felt more support, love, and tenderness from them than I ever thought possible.

Christina Dunigan, I can't even begin to express how grateful I am to call you one of my best friends. I think a lot about everything you've done for this book and for me—every check-in, every read-through, every thoughtful question. You'd probably argue with me about this, but it's an inarguable fact that this story would not be what it is today without you. Everyone needs a Christina in their life, someone who listens deeply, challenges kindly, and raises the bar for what friendship should feel like. I am so unbelievably lucky you are the one in mine.

Caitlin Perkins, my angel girl, my vibe reader, my favorite new(ish) Swiftie—thank you for every two-hour phone call, for every draft you read, and for over a decade of beautiful friendship. You moved to another state years ago, but there's never been even a shred of distance between us. I love you to the moon.

Alex Mitchell, you've been my best friend since I was twelve years old, and you are still the most steadfast, supportive, wonderful person I know. You inspire me constantly, and watching you step into motherhood has been one of the most beautiful things I've witnessed. And Josh, thank you for your constant kindness and for always asking about the book. I'm lucky to have both of you in my life.

Callie Kmiec, my sister in everything but DNA. We've been through everything together—triumphs, heartbreaks, rewrites, and everything in between. I wouldn't trade any of them for the world. You've been beside me through so many chapters of my life—long before this book existed and, I'm sure, for a long time after. I love you.

Kelsey Scarborough Haggard, what a gift it's been to grow closer this past year. Your radiant, unfiltered support drowns out every insecure thought I've ever had. Your honesty lands like truth, never like criticism, and your humor is its own fire: Sometimes it burns, sometimes it glows, but it always keeps me warm.

Kyle Haggard, one of the greatest guys I've ever met. Earnest, encouraging, and empathetic. You, Kelsey, and Lucy are three of the biggest reasons Austin feels like home.

ACKNOWLEDGMENTS

Lacie Miller, one of my oldest and truest friends. We might not see each other much these days, but you're still one of the first people I want to call when something good happens—and one of the few who still cry when they're happy for me. You devoured this book in hours and then called me just to gush. I'll love you forever.

Caroline Duble, thank you for being a tremendous human all around, and even more for the best compliment anyone has ever given me about this book. You know the one.

Margaret Wiggins, my good-luck charm, my "before" and "after." September and December in New York, 2024—giggling in bed while watching compilation videos of our favorite guy, getting lavender matchas in the West Village, holding (squeezing?) hands during *Hold On to Me Darling*—will always be some of my favorite memories. Thank you for every spiraling text, every phone call, every bit of faith you had when I didn't. There was life before Margaret and life after, and I'm still pinching myself that I get to live in the after. I can't wait to cowrite a book together. 🩷

Garrett Czajkowski, thank you for being both a dear friend and a brilliant creative mind. You've helped me untangle more plot knots than I can count, and your insight has made me a sharper writer. I'm excited for the day your book is out in the world. It's not a matter of *if*; it's *when*.

Michelle and Ken Pujats—Mimi, my second mom, and Ken, the best chef I know. Mimi, I could listen to your voice for hours. You are the heartbeat of a family I'm so proud to call my own. Ken, being one of your only approved sous-chefs is the highest honor, and I hope we cook many meals together in the future.

Cameron Pujats, my go-to for medical accuracy and general

brilliance. You are a superhero, a fantastic mom, and one of the most loyal, bighearted people I know.

Marilyn "Nana" Wells, thank you for your stories, your care, and your kindness. The world is softer because you're in it.

To the whole Pujats-Thomas-Sinclair crew—Taylor, Jordan, Maddie, Andrew, and Shelby—thank you for wrapping me up as one of your own. You are joy and chaos and comfort all at once, and I'm so grateful for every laugh, every story, and every memory.

MaryAshley McGibbon, thank you for being my horse-world whisperer. Your feedback on early drafts was invaluable, and your warmth reminds me so much of those summer camp days when everything felt possible.

Erin Welker, thank you for capturing me at my most authentic in my author photos, and for nearly a decade of friendship.

Emily Barbin, thank you for your creative eye, your thoughtful brand work, and your kindness. You made me feel seen in a whole new way.

Kevin Gaylord, you're only in these because I rescheduled so many sessions while writing this book. But also because you make me laugh and have turned one of my least favorite things in the world into a place of joy and solace.

Milaci Ray, my talented friend who I'm thrilled to say now shares an editor with me, I'm so proud of you and will be your loudest cheerleader forever.

Michelle Harris, thank you for being there from the fanfic days to now, and for every late-night beta read and reality check along the way.

Joreen Beloclora, part of that unforgettable New York 2024

crew—thank you for your sweetness, your enthusiasm, and your friendship.

To my work family: Jenn, Alyssa, George, Max, Colter, RJ (big ups for the ranch expertise), Jordan, and Sean—thank you for supporting me day in and day out, for preordering, for asking questions, and for cheering me on even when I was delirious from edits.

Krystyn Flanagan, my hellei-dope, FTK, No Friends in the Wild™ work wife and one of the first people ever to read this book. Thank you for getting me on a molecular level, for encouraging me, for letting me vent to you about everything, for never telling me what I want to hear, and for always telling me what I need to hear. Thank you for sharing your prophet-like ability to predict my successes (and failures). Thank you for the laughter and the joy of Tuesdays and Thursdays in San Marcos. I wish I could articulate how grateful I am to have met you. I am honored to be your friend.

Hannah Yenofsky, you're an actual earth angel and one of the brightest lights I've ever known. You've only been in my life for a handful of months, but it feels like forever. Thank you for being the human embodiment of sunshine, the best hype woman alive, and a steady hand through every spiral of 2025.

Cole Wenzel, thank you for supporting me wholeheartedly through this journey, and also for inspiring me every single day to be a better, more thoughtful person and leader. You are truly incomparable. I'll never be able to fully express how grateful I am to work with you, to learn from you, and to witness your brilliance, grit, and kindness every single day.

Amelia Olivarez, thank you for putting up with me in the

workplace for nearly a decade, and for having the patience of a saint—especially during fall 2019, when I fell headfirst into my Adam Driver era and Slacked you nonstop about it like a complete psychopath.

Robert Sixsmith, there's no one like you. You keep us on our toes. You make me laugh without even trying. Our office—our company—feels like home because of the space you've created. Thank you for trusting me; thank you for getting me. Thank you for sharing your book with me. Maybe one day you'll come back around to the idea of us cowriting something.

To my incredible publishing team:

Cindy Hwang, my editor and fairy godmother—thank you for your faith, your guidance, and your unwavering belief in this story. And Elizabeth Vinson, Cindy's right hand.

Kim Lionetti, my agent—thank you for seeing something in me, for fighting for me, and for championing my words with both heart and humor.

Carmen Martinez, the brilliant artist behind my cover, thank you for bringing my world to life so beautifully.

Ali Hazelwood, the queen of the fan-fiction-to-trad-pub pipeline—thank you for paving the way and for your generosity in sharing your wisdom. You're the GOAT.

Emily Bewick, one of my first beta readers from the old Twitter days, thank you for believing in me then and now. I can't wait to see your name on a book spine soon.

To my teachers—Joseph Guyer, Amy Willeford, Richard Cox, and Allison Boerger (my fearless newspaper advisor)—thank you for encouraging my love of writing long before I knew where it would lead.

ACKNOWLEDGMENTS

To my family:

Grandmama, you left us in 2014 but are still in everything I do. You were also a writer, and I know you'd be so unbelievably proud.

Grandma, you are everything to me. You are fiercely loving and loyal, occasionally curmudgeonly, and completely iconic. I love you so madly.

Veronika Vasys, Alex's mom, whose love and light inspired the heart of this story—thank you for everything you brought into the world.

Dad, thank you for supporting me all the way from the Dominican Republic and always asking questions about the book. I miss you and hope I get to see you sooner rather than later.

And finally, to the readers. Thank you for taking a chance on me, for opening this book, and for giving my words a place to land.

Keep reading for a sneak peek of

BENEATH A NEON MOON

The next book by Taylor Esposito!

If there's one thing Caia Caldwell knows to be true about being the only daughter of a ranching dynasty, it's this: Everybody loves you until you stop sounding like your mother and start sounding like you have a mind of your own. There's a glass-shattering kind of dread that spreads over people's faces when they realize the benevolence of Renata Caldwell is not in fact hereditary. It's a familiar-looking disappointment—like they've discovered whatever the adult version is of Santa Claus not being real.

Among Sweetwater's finest at the annual rodeo benefit—the same benefit at which the Caldwell family donates millions of dollars in scholarships to agriculture students and young competitors alike—the look is a recurring sight.

It doesn't matter that Caia, as her mother's stand-in for the evening, is the one holding the keys to the vault of riches. It doesn't matter that if it were her mother standing here in this moment, there'd be a perpetual circle of admirers and sycophants ready to kiss the red dirt beneath her ostrich boots.

It would've been easy to opt out of coming in the first place. In fact, it's generous—no, it's downright *saintly*—that Caia even considered saying yes when her mother asked. "I just don't have the juice," Renata lamented. "All they'll want to talk about is the accident. A month later and they still haven't gotten their fill. Vultures." She looked uncharacteristically somber as she explained this to Caia, her reading glasses propped up on her nose, a hardcover book open on her lap. Since the crash, Renata has been spending more time around the house, particularly in silk pajama sets and cushy slippers—and she spends most of that time reading thick historical fiction novels about women in World War II. Caia, though she was probably the only person on God's green earth that could firmly deny Renata Caldwell anything, felt guilt flood her stomach just looking at her mother's tired face. She stayed quiet for a brief moment, contemplating. Then, without looking up, her mother sweetened the deal. "You can wear the Marquesa diamond."

And *oh*, how sweet it suddenly was. How brilliant and cunning her mother could be, knowing exactly how to instantly make this offer irrefusable. Caia made a monumental effort not to allow her eyes to light up. She did her best to sound nonchalant, but already, she was picturing her décolletage bedecked in that necklace—the same one she'd been eyeing since she could walk.

With a quick, measured clearing of her throat, Caia nodded. "Fine."

And even with Renata's chin dipped toward her chest and her eyes still scanning the page, Caia could see the twitch of a smirk on her lips. The subtle satisfaction of an easy victory.

But now, sitting at one of the twenty circular tables in the grand hall, half-drunk on sauvignon blanc, Caia realizes the allure of the Marquesa was not worth this.

It's heavier than it looks, and there's something about the

clasp that's making the back of her neck itch. Not to mention, the dress she borrowed from her mother is slightly too big, so the straps keep falling down, and the heels she also borrowed from her mother are slightly too small, so her toes are squished together and starting to go numb. It would be an unfortunate culmination of irritations on the best of nights. But on this night, rubbing elbows with Coca-Cola cowboys and smiling so wide for so long that her jaw is sore, it's a unique kind of hell.

One of the only mercies granted to Caia on this gem of an evening is that her brothers are here. Crew is across the banquet hall with Grace, and the two look picture-perfect beside each other—Crew in his nicest pearl snap, and Grace in one of the dozens of dresses Caia has bullied her into trying on over the past month. It's a dusty orange color and formfitting, clinging to Grace's lithe figure in a subtle, elegant way. If Caia wasn't holding a half-empty glass of wine in one hand and a fancy puff pastry pig in a blanket in the other, she would pat herself on the back for that particular choice of garment. Grace looks fantastic. Grace makes Caia's awkward, severe-featured brother look softer, warmer even, just by standing next to him.

Cooper is not as easily locatable. Last she saw him, maybe twenty or thirty minutes ago, he was leaning his elbows onto one of the bars and making a not-a-day-over-twenty-one-looking bartender blush. He'd been sipping whiskey neat the whole evening, progressively getting more and more flirty with every woman in a five-yard radius, and if Caia were a betting woman, she'd wager he's found one susceptible enough to sneak away with. She refrains from rolling her eyes at the thought and sends a quick prayer to the heavens that her little brother has the good sense to use protection.

With her mother and father notably absent from the event, there's been a slight buzz around all three of the Halcyon-born children. Too many eyes on them, too many lingering looks. Caia's generally inclined to like rodeo people—they're salt-of-the-earth kinds of folks, in her experience—but this fishbowl she's been begrudgingly plunged into is less like a rodeo and more like a petting zoo. She feels on display, too exposed—and maybe she needs to take a page out of her brother's book and work on the severity of her own features, because people are far too comfortable coming up to her and *touching* her. Her hair, her elbows, her wrists. They think that because she is an ancillary part of the benefactor list sponsoring this event, they have to connect with her. Personally. Professionally. *Physically*.

She finds her designated seat at a table near the front of the hall, though no one is paying much mind to seat assignments at this point in the evening. In fact, her table has been invaded by a group of middle-aged women dressed in mother-of-the-bride attire and adorned with some of the gaudiest brooches Caia's ever seen.

They don't exactly smile when Caia first approaches—they're more tentative, judgy quirks of the corners of their overlined lips. Until, of course, they do a collective double take and realize exactly who they're looking at—and whose table they've chosen to commandeer. Caia can hear her father's voice in her head as she lowers herself into a cushioned chair across the table, flashing them her most diplomatic grin. *Biddies*, Clint would call them. *Busybody biddies*.

"Well, don't you just look all grown-up," one of them says, saccharine sweet. Whoever this woman is, she's taken "the bigger the hair, the closer to God" to a frighteningly literal extent—

Caia can practically smell the Aqua Net wafting off her. "I haven't seen you since you were about this tall." The woman holds her hand out near her shoulder, measuring a bygone child no taller than three feet.

Caia regards her, giving herself a moment to actually *think* before she says something she regrets. She exhales through her nose and keeps her smile bright despite the shooting pains in her jaw. In a similarly sickly sweet voice, she says, "Children do often grow into adults, so I'm told."

The woman is not an idiot; she can tell there's venom laced in Caia's words, but like a good Southern woman ought to do, she simply smiles wider in response, readying her rebuttal like a knife on a whetstone. "Yes, they do, darlin'. They grow up and spread their wings, and sometimes they only find their way back when things get . . . urgent," she says. The two women on either side of her kink their eyebrows, bystanders witnessing a successful volley, an ace in the hole. They have the look of a group used to winning these kinds of sparring matches. The look of bullies dressed in satin and dripping in rare turquoise.

But Caia Caldwell isn't ten years old anymore. And she certainly didn't get to where she is in life—the youngest executive at her company, and it's not even close, thank you very much—by trading passive-aggressive remarks with rodeo wives who have too much time on their hands. "Well, I figured y'all needed something new to talk about. Lord knows your faces are turning blue from recycling the same Sweetwater gossip every day. So I suppose you should be thanking me." All three of the women stare at her, dumbfounded. The leader, the speaker, has let her mouth go agape, and Caia can see the mental gymnastics she's doing to try to make sense of how incredibly *bald* and exacting that barb was. No Southern subtlety—no beating around the mulberry bush. Sensing that she's struck a nerve, Caia homes in, twisting the knife of her worldly demeanor. "I know you're bored to tears by your husbands, and your kids are all grown and probably doing everything they can to get out of Sunday dinners. I've got to be the most entertaining thing that's happened to you three in the past decade."

Fury folds into the leader's face. "I beg your pard—"

Caia holds up a hand. "It's rude to interrupt. You should know that."

The woman's mouth snaps shut, but her eyes are wide, blazing.

"You're all the same, do you realize that?" Caia says, looking between the three of them. "You feed on other people's misery like vultures." She leans forward, gripping her glass of wine, giving each one of them a moment of pure, dead-on eye contact. "You're sinister women dressed in your Sunday best, hoping others will fail so you'll have something to talk about at bridge club."

The woman to the left of the leader puts a hand to her chest, fully scandalized. The leader is close-lipped, now nearly snarling. She is almost vibrating with tension, ready to pounce. Caia enjoys the sight even more than she enjoys the woman to the leader's right, who has donned a thousand-yard stare like Caia's hit a little too close to home with her observations. "It's pathetic, really—"

She's on the verge of the kill shot, ready to destroy whatever good nature remains between these women and her family without a single shred of regret or concern for the consequences. They could be three of the biggest donors in the room, and she wouldn't blink before eviscerating them. But then someone is gripping her shoulder, just tight enough to distract her, pulling her focus away from the matter at hand. Caia's head swings upward, and she's already annoyed at whoever it is interrupting; she's annoyed that these women are going to get off easily because of it. She's ready to redirect whatever vitriol was about to be spat at the women toward the interrupter, but when she lays eyes on them, the words die in her throat—and they go from tasting like acid and vinegar, tart and biting and unforgiving, to tasting like ash.

Easton. Here. Standing over her, sparing her one single glance of understanding before turning on his own million-watt smile and directing it at the women. "Ladies," he says, tipping his hat.

Instantaneously, the energy at the table shifts. The fire in the eyes of all three biddies takes on a different kind of heat entirely. Caia watches in awe as their body language changes, as they lean forward with dreamy, syrupy smiles. "Hello, Easton," the leader says, her voice reverting back to pleasant—though now with an undertone of desire that has Caia nearly grimacing.

"As much as I hate to interrupt such a riveting conversation," Easton says, squeezing Caia's shoulder, "I need to steal this one. Duty calls."

"Steal away, young man," the woman says. "As long as you promise to come back and sit with us for a spell."

Easton winks—all charm, no subtlety. "Count on it, ma'am." He looks down then, locking eyes with Caia. In the look there are a dozen questions asked without uttering a word. *Are you coming? Are you insane? Are you trying to get chewed out by your parents?*

Caia rolls her eyes and stands, offering not even a parting

glance to the women who have single-handedly reminded her why she moved over a thousand miles away from small-town Texas. Easton spins on his bootheel and makes for the opposite side of the room, and Caia follows, letting her perfectly poised smile slip from her face. When they reach a corner that is relatively clear of people—more vultures—he halts, turning once more to look at her. His face is soft, uncharacteristically earnest. It's slightly disarming, and it puts Caia immediately on the defensive. Easton Beckett can weave webs of charm and deceit with those unfamiliar with his MO, but Caia is not—never has been—one of them. She can see through the sparkling, gold-encrusted facade. "You didn't need to do that. I was fine," she spits.

Easton smiles, some of that boyish arrogance slipping back into his features. Good—Caia knows that well. She knows how to manage *that*. "Didn't seem like you were," he says. "Seemed like you were about two seconds from telling them to fuck off and die. In a more eloquent, evil, Caia-like way, obviously."

Caia's nostrils flare. "Just because I don't want to trade insults dressed up as compliments and *innocent* observations doesn't make me evil. It makes me a person with integrity. Which is more than I can say for most people in this room." The look she gives him then is pointed. Meant to sting.

Easton is undeterred. "Ah, yes. Ever the altruist. Want me to steal you one of those medals from the cabinet so you can wear it around your neck and show everyone how much better of a person you are than them?"

"What are you even doing here?" Caia bites out.

His brow furrows, but it isn't a genuine look of confusion.

He's toying with her; she can tell from the flare of mischief in his eyes. "This is a rodeo event. You'll recall that I am, in fact, a rodeo celebrity of sorts."

At this, her eyes nearly roll to the back of her head. They roll so hard she's sure they'll be permanently stuck. She throws her head back, blowing out a quick breath through her mouth. "God, spare me."

Easton chuckles. "I think I did, spitfire."

Caia swings her head up so quickly she feels the whiplash, but she steadies herself to say, with all of the malice she can muster, "Do not call me that."

Easton opens his mouth to argue, and that look is back in his eyes—that stupid, unwelcome earnestness. "Cai, I—"

"Don't call me *that*, either. In fact, don't call me anything. Don't talk to me at all. You need to be here because my parents want to show off their shiny toy to the donors and remind everyone they have 'famous' ties, fine. Whatever. But you can be here and not be anywhere near me."

Any light that existed in Easton's eyes, in his features, dulls. His head hangs low for a brief moment before he nods, and Caia can see his jaw flex with the motion.

Without another word, he walks past her, leaving her in the corner to relish her own solitude. She lets herself stand there with her back to the room for a while, only turning when she can *feel* eyes start to drift toward her. Lest she give the leeches anything more to talk about, she sucks in a deep, steadying breath and puts it back on: the smile. The Renata Caldwell special.

Caia takes a step toward the sea of strangers and tries not to think about the pang of homesickness in her belly. Not for the ranch, and not for her family. Certainly not for the man-child who destroyed her heart seven years ago.

But for her home in the city. Her fortress of independence. Her beautiful, wonderful escape into total anonymity.